MW00876373

CONSIDER MAN

Change the World

A J Merino

CONSIDER MAN
Change the World

Author: AJ Merino

ISBN: 979-8370010095

This is a work of fiction, although the general outline is based upon real events researched and supported by current accounts and news media articles. Included are the author's personal experiences, interactions with specific people, and events encountered. References to real people, events, establishments, organizations, or locales provide a sense of authenticity. All other characters, incidents and dialogue are drawn from the author's imagination. This story is completely true; except for the parts that are entirely made up.

For permission, please contact:
    AJ Merino
    ronmerino@hotmail.com

Cover design by: ebooklaunch.com

Book layout/design by David Larson

News media: source articles edited for length and clarity. [online access]

For
Laurel

We were there from first breath to the last
And blessed to share all the time in-between
Thanks for being that bright star in our life.

CONSIDER MAN

Change the World

A J Merino

Acknowledgments

Several research elements were vital to completing this work, including human sources of a wide variety, to the many individuals who assisted in the creative journey. I am thankful for them all.

To all the veterans from Vietnam to Afghanistan that served with distinction and honor, an overdue, Good On Ya! Jolly Green Giant pilot C. William Hoilman, William Petrie, CMSgt USAF ret, AC-119 Gunship Association, the AC-119 Copilot Richard F. Hay and crew members of the ill-fated Lemon 21, the 18th SOS, and the Veteranswritinggroup.org.

To the Beta proofreaders that improved and influenced this work's written word, a huge thank you I needed that: Heather Jacobs, Elinore Behanna, Carol Brown, Suzi Butler, Dr. Michal Hose, James Davis, Jan Prahl, and Brian Wages.

To those that provided meaningful, historical, professional, and personal insight, thanks for filling potholes along the literary path: David S. Larson, Neils Mohler, Frank Ritter, Robert Teisher, Jeffery Ward,

To Lynn Alloway Pappa, a debt of gratitude for her real-life experiences as an observant young child remembering the nature of a Cherokee Brave and Warrior that was her father. Those stories validated and substantiated the character of her father's life as a Cherokee Man duty bound as a proud native son and a US Air Force non-commission officer giving the ultimate.

Prologue

Time
Past, Present and Future
* * * *
Past

A Brief History of Time,
Copyright 1988, 1996 by Stephen Hawking

Forward
"The success of *A Brief History* indicates that there is widespread interest in the big-questions like: Where did we come from? And why is the universe the way it is?"

OUR PICTURE OF THE UNIVERSE
In an unchanging universe, a beginning in time is something that has to be imposed by some being outside the universe; there is no physical necessity for a beginning. One can imagine that God created the universe anytime in the past. On the other hand, if the universe is expanding, there may be physical reasons to be a beginning. One could still imagine that God created the universe at the instant of the big bang, or even afterward, in just such a way as to make it look as though there had been a big bang, but it would be meaningless to suppose that it was created before the Big Bang. An expanding universe does not preclude a creator, but it does place limits on when he might have carried out his job

Acts 17:26

"From one Man he made all the nations, that they should inhabit the whole Earth; and he marked out their appointed times in history and the boundaries of their lands."

The Bible, New International Version

Man - Humans

The term (from Proto-Germanic *mann* "person") and words derived from it can designate any or even all of the human race regardless of their sex or age. In traditional usage, *Man* (without an article) itself refers to the species or to humanity (mankind) as a whole.

Humans (*Homo sapiens*) are the most abundant and widespread species of primate, characterized by bipedalism and large, complex brains. This has enabled the development of advanced tools, culture, and language. Humans are highly social and tend to live in complex social structures composed of many cooperating and competing groups, from families and kinship networks to political states. Social interactions between humans have established a wide variety of values, social norms, and rituals, which bolster human society. Curiosity and the human desire to understand and influence the environment and to explain and manipulate phenomena have motivated humanity's development of science, philosophy, mythology, religion, and other fields of study.

* * * *

Present
Jon Voight on faith
984,878 youtube.com views
July 15, 2021
(partial transcript)

"I was in a lot of trouble at one point…I was really suffering for many reasons…I found myself on the floor saying it's so difficult, it's so difficult…I heard in my ear it's supposed to be difficult…can you imagine…a voice of wisdom, kindness, you know clarity. And I went boom, what! I got up and I knew…I am not alone, everything is known…I am known, that's what it meant to me…Whoa!.I felt this tremendous energy somebody was rooting for me. It's like don't give up there's purpose here. You got a ways to go son."

* * * *

Future
Rudyard Kipling
From Macdonough's Song

Whether the State can loose and bind
In Heaven as well as on Earth:
If it be wiser to kill mankind
Before or after the birth--
…Once there was The People--Terror gave it birth;
Once there was The People and it made a Hell of Earth.
Earth arose and crushed it. Listen, O ye slain!
Once there was The People--it shall never be again!

Introduction

A Tarantino-esque saga stretched over fifty years of competing plot lines. Borne out of a chronologically jumbled jigsaw puzzle of divergent circumstance. An Alien managed the petri dish Earth evolutionary process, genetic time manipulation and germ-line editing; dreams and detours. My story, a backtracked journey into my life and one night in 1970 off China Beach over the South China Sea, South Vietnam. The search for clarity started as a 2009 dinner table question. A simple question: "For one day, who would you bring back to life of the people you have known?" The choice was clear yet difficult. It has taken decades to tell the story. By screenplay, short story, a novel. It was all three; a journey rolled into a tale regarding an Alien, Others, and two men. A Man I didn't know, hadn't met, nor will meet in this life, but managed to talk to on his last day alive; he spoke his last words for me. It was more than a simple passing conversation between two strangers. He was desperate, exhausted, and drowning. I was trying to save him. Didn't.

Cherokee Native Son

"Talking to a dead Man drowning. *Pop flair! Is your strobe light on*? Holding on to him over the radio. A radio connection as tenuous as his efforts to stay above the surface of a calm dark South China Sea. I remember his last words 'I think I'm drowning.' Then there was nothing, no response. Those are my memories."

They took the whole Cherokee nation.
Put us on this reservation.
Took away our ways of life
The tomahawk and the bow and knife
Took away our native tongue

And taught their English to our young
And all the beads we made by hand.
Are nowadays made in Japan
Cherokee people, Cherokee tribe
So proud to live, so proud to die...
"Indian Reservation"
The Raiders
(The Lament of the Cherokee Reservation Indian)
written by John D. Loudermilk

Falcon Code
The Code encompasses meaningful descriptions that accurately captures the moment by associated radio voice communications that could not be transmitted openly, hence the numerical designation. Each prefaced or stated for example as, "That's a one-oh-one, meaning, You've got to be shitting me." The Code was found to be used in either combat or other less stressful operations. Brevity codes have been around since early warriors wanted to pass quick, encrypted messages. Falcon Code radio calls were developed to pass a brief comment or opinion about a particular state of affairs. It could be a dangerous environment: danger close, hostile fire, triple-A or an outrageous order by any number of those at a higher command level that fail to see, What The Fuck Over, is going on...can't say that on the radio waves but, that's a one-oh-four, 104 or WTFO is clear and understood by most. For instance in today's parlance, Let's Go Brandon is effective in the tradition of the Falcon Code, very close to a one-oh-eight, 108.

101   You've got to be shitting me
102   Get off my fucking back
103   Beats the shit out of me
104   What the fuck over (WTFO)
105   It's so fucking bad, I can't believe it
106   I hate this fucking place
107   This place sucks
108   Fuck you very much

MAN 1

The Year 2010
Dreamscape
April 14, 2010

Grant is in bed, dreaming again at two a.m. He's driving his blue 2004 Toyota Extra-cab Tacoma on I-5, heading South to San Diego. Grant's en route to his mother's to take her on a bi-monthly shopping trip.

Jackie, an old teenage friend, appears, standing on the running board. He swings open the door to ride shotgun, wearing 1958 junior high attire, the long, fingertip gray "cool dude" jacket he and Grant both wore. Jackie's hair is swept back and apparently not affected by riding in the running board wind.

Back in the day, Jackie, Grant, and their boy posse all wore Levi's, new Levi's that were never to be washed. Washing ruined the stiffened texture that allowed for the inside rolled tuck pant leg one half inch cuff. Dirt and grime added to the ambience, odor, and stiffness—and of course, the "look." Adding to the look were short sleeve button collared shirts straight off the rack at JC Penny or Sears. Collars were worn up back of the neck. The Levi's were belted and sinched just below the waist with leather loafers or cool brown tan suede tassel tied shoes. Grant's attire matched, with the exception of the shirt he made in the first ever home ed class for ninth-grade boys. Cool dudes all.

Grant's eyes widen. "Jesus, Jackie, couldn't you wait until I stopped?"

Jackie grins as always and puts on his seat belt. "It was cool on the running board, and you're not going to stop for like, thirty or forty miles. Going to your mom's?"

"Taking her grocery shopping."

"Wow, that doesn't sound like much fun, Grant." Jackie scrunches his faces. "How old is Katie these days?"

"Ninety in October."

"She in good health? She doing okay?"

"She's doing just fine, Jackie."

"Didn't she have a heart attack this time last year?"

Grant flips on his turn signal and switches lanes. "It really wasn't. She had chest pains, and they found prior heart damage."

"Heart damage? That doesn't sound good."

"She's on daily medication, when she remembers to take it."

"She's living alone?"

"She's been alone for six years, since my father died."

"Need to get her one of those monitors. You know, a medical alert service."

"She has one."

"That's good. Those can come in handy when you've fallen and can't get up."

"Yeah, they can, if you wear 'em."

"So, she doesn't wear hers?"

"No. Well, she's not very good about it. Says if she has a heart attack, she'll crawl over to the coat rack where it's hanging."

"Doesn't sound like that'll work too well."

"No, it doesn't."

Dwayne appears in the front seat, same 1958 junior high posse uniform, crammed next to Jackie" That sounds like Katie."

Grant swerves toward the guard rail, then corrects. "Holy shit!"

"Well, not exactly holy shit, but something close. Surprised ya?" Dwayne raises his bottle of Old Turkey

Grant, looking at Dwayne, "Shit!"

Dwayne laughs. "You better watch where you're going or you're going to get us all killed. Correction get you killed. We've already done that. Right, Jackie?"

"Well, damn, Dwayne, this is a surprise." Jackie's now outside riding on the truck's running board, looking in…dreams are funny that way.

Dwayne mocks Jackie "Well damn, Jackie. Why? We're both dead. It's just that you been dead a hell of a lot longer."

Grant struggles to stay on a dirt road in Proctor Valley, not on I-5 now. "Jesus, couldn't you both have waited until I stopped?"

Dwayne shakes his head. "Listen, flyboy, you can handle the pressure. You were an Air Force pilot, right?"

"I was, but I didn't like surprises then either, especially when I'm flying or driving."

Jackie pokes his head in the window with a cigar in his mouth. Yeah, you could've waited for a better time. We were having a conversation."

Dwayne is now behind the wheel, squeezes it in frustration. "Waited? Waited for what, Jackie? Your conversations, as I recall, were mostly bullshit, probably still are." Dwayne is not putting up with Jackie's BS.

"Yeah, wait until we're finished," Jackie says from the backseat, blowing perfect smoke rings linked like a chain.

"I didn't know I had to check your schedule first. Jackie, you were so full of shit. You were a bull shitter in life, and some things don't change. Even in death." Dwayne is on a tear.

Jackie, blows smoke over the front seat. "Hey, I was just like everybody else. We all threw the BS around. We all did it, Dwayne."

"Yeah, we did." Dwayne nods. "The difference was that for the most part we knew what was bullshit and what wasn't. Your bullshit move in Tijuana almost got us shot. I had a .38 stuck in my face after you tried to take the taxi without using the clutch. Talk about one dumb fuck move."

The three men are now in a Tijuana taxi at night, parked inside Hotel Nelson's bar with Cuba Libras in hand.

"Hey, I was close to getting us outta there." Jackie claims credit.

"Bullshit," Grant says, punching the dashboard. "You were close to getting us killed. That was a bullshit move."

Dwayne blows out a lung full of smoke. "Jackie, Grant agrees with me. It was a bullshit move."

"Come on guys, it wasn't that bad." Jackie clasps his hands in supplication.

Dwayne and Grant retort, in emphatic unison, "Bullshit!"

The trio is back on I-5, Grant's chuckles behind the wheel of his 2004 Toyota "You know, even after all the bullshit, we did have some good times."

Jackie nods emphatically. "See, I told you there were good times. Good times to remember."

"I remember you introduced me to underage drinking on ninth grade Friday nights, you stole a pint of Seagram 7 from Big Bear market."

"I knew the guy in the liquor department." Jackie boasts proudly.

"Anyway that's where I learned to really dislike whiskey sours, those were some awful drinks."

"I preferred Old Turkey shots." Dwayne sits shotgun.

Grant looks at Jackie in the rearview mirror, and says "You taught me my first dance moves or at least some of them."

"Dances at the gym." Jackie confirms. "We had some good times. The Tijuana trip wasn't that bad," Jackie insists with conviction.

"Bullshit!" Grant pushes back.

"It was the first time someone pulled a gun on me." Dwayne points out.

"And you both still owe me money for that, with interest. Got any celestial dollars on ya?"

"Sorry, we have no need for money." Jackie and Dwayne say in unison.

"We don't require much of anything." Dwayne now has a cigar.

"So, Dwayne, you were in the Mexico City airport, had a heart attack?" Grant holds court.

"Shit, yeah, I was heading home from Belize."

"Belize sounds like a party place." Jackie goes at Dwayne.

"Sounds like you partied too much, Dwayne."

"Well, fuck you, Jackie! I was construction supervisor on a new resort complex."

"I mean, you did like to drink, smoke a little dope, pop a few pills, party." He holds his cigar in the shot gun window wind stream trailing flame and spark filled ash.

"Maybe I did...liked to have a good time. But I took care of my family, left no debt and lived a lot longer than you, Jackie. By the way, why don't you tell Grant how you died? Let me see. Oh yeah, wasn't it somewhere in the East County? Weren't you out hunting? Guns involved, something like that?"

Grant had wondered over the years what had happened. "It was a hunting accident?"

Jackie now wears a black ball cap covering his eyes. "Hey, it wasn't my fault. And besides, it doesn't matter now." His cigar is out, he nearly bites it in half and flip it out the window.

Dwayne, "Jackie, it sounds like you may have partied too much, got in over your head. Your, bullshit caught up with you. You don't want to bullshit people on a hunting trip, Jackie."

"What were you hunting?" Still in the dark, Grant is waiting for an answer.

"This should be good," Dwayne says, holding a pint bottle of Old Turkey.

"It wasn't my fault. I didn't do anything. I don't want to talk about it." A door slams loud, Jackie is gone out the Toyota rear door and from Grant's dream...he didn't answer the question...what was Jackie hunting?

"Well, that went well." Dwayne is now smoking both his and Jackie's short bit off cigars, one in hand, one in his mouth, and driving.

"What happened with Jackie?" Grant see's he is gone. Where'd he go?

"Couldn't take the pressure, took off. Decided to walk." Dwayne says, now drinking Old Turkey from the bottle a cigar in each hand.

"What happened on the hunting trip? How did he die?"

"Jackie should be the one to tell you. He always liked to talk. He may turn out to be a god damn hero. You never know."

Grant is looking at Dwayne driving, wondering about Jackie's untimely death...how'd it happen?

Then he wakes up next to Becky. She looks at him through sleep-filled eyes, and she says, "Jeez, what was it about this time?" She doesn't wait for an answer, rolls over, pulling the blankets over her shoulder, and tries to sleep again.

Grant doesn't try to answer, but smiles thinking of TJ dreams and sorry he woke his wife and lover, Becky, again.

MAN 2

YEAR
2000

* * * *

Summary of Academic Research Paper 1992:
Alien Prototypes
Dr. Jacob Michaels
Associate Professor of History, San Diego State University

Noted history professor, Jacobs Michaels, is convinced extra-terrestrials, (ETs) are using Earth as a genetic lab for abductions, sperm and egg harvesting, and genetic manipulation. Dr. Michaels' thesis is that human existence has been influenced by alien intervention and prototypes. He theorized humans are being manipulated to become a hybrid species. Other human-like species were on Earth at different times in different regions around the globe. Denisovans hominids, Neanderthals, Homo floresiensis, Homo heildelberegensis, Homo erectus, all extinct. Homo naledi found in South Africa's Rising Star Cave ranged for two million years and became extinct 250,000 years ago. They all have different levels of evolvement, size, and intellect. Michaels contends that Darwin's theory does not work within the context of human evolution. There should be a slow and steady modification; it is not seen in these humanoids. Natural selection may not work; intelligent design is the alternative. He is convinced that ETs are making various versions of Man in an

Earth lab setting. They created several different humanoid models by DNA manipulation for thousands of years.

At the time, Dr. Michaels' paper employed less than accepted standards of evidentiary material and viewed as personal commentary. The Peer Review went nowhere; his paper presented the reader with an informed argument. However, some indicated backhandedly it was in orbit, not yet supported by then-current substantiated facts. Not ready for re-entry.

* * * *

8 June 2016
San Diego Union-Tribune article
New fossils Strengthen Case For 'Hobbit,' Species
By Carl Zimmer
Scientists digging in the Liang Bra Cave on the Indonesian island of Flores found a tiny human skull from a 3 1/2 feet tall, Homo floresiensis, known as the "hobbits," that died 60,000 to 100,000 years ago…prehistoric and stone tools going back 700,000 years, suggests that the ancestors of the Floresiensis arrived about a million years ago and evolved into their distinctive branch of the hominid tree…

Dr. Gert van den Bergh, one of the lead paleontologists, said it was unlikely that Homo erectus could have built boats that could have taken them to Flores. "Personally, I think it was some freak event like a tsunami."

The article leaves us with a question: We are left then with how did they get to the Flores Island? They were placed there and not by the freak of nature 1000-mile tsunami ride. Not likely.

CONSIDER MAN

* * * *

Fall semester
September 2000
Dr. Casey
San Diego State University
Catalog Course Description: Human Evolutionary Genetics
Anthropology 101. Introduction to Anthropology and World Prehistory Anthropology emphasizing the modern relevance of understanding the past, beginning six to seven million years ago in Africa, highlighting the physical and genetic evolution of our human lineage. Professor: Dr. Nicholas Casey, Professor of Evolutionary Anthropology San Diego State University.

Professor: Dr. Nicholas Casey
Eighty-year-old Nicholas Casey is a biological anthropologist specializing in evolutionary and dynamic approaches to human development. Believing that the evolutionary genetic model for human development has been manipulated, he has lectured and written articles asserting that at some point in the history of human development there had to have been interventional genetic manipulation in the evolutionary process. Placing the manipulated samples in geographic isolation, separated from the main population, would have led to dramatic evolutionary leaps. Casey further suggests Earth is an experimental lab of incubation sites, a place to create a hybrid human in the near future. These celestially designed humans are better suited to space travel, preparing Man for the future. And a return to the stars, where we came from as firmly believed by Dr. Casey.

* * * *

The Fermi Paradox
There is a well-known dilemma known as the Fermi Paradox, and it asks why we have not seen evidence of alien visitation or communications to date. The most likely resolution of the Fermi Paradox is the Aliens have indeed arrived, and we are they.

* * * *

Dr. Casey hasn't fully determined how the genetic mutation and manipulation took place, but he has some firm beliefs. He is perplexed and frustrated because he may never be able to prove his theories. A number of his colleagues, though, label him fanatical, obtuse, and significantly out of the mainstream. They suspect earlier studies he conducted involving the use of psychoactive drugs may have had a spillover effect, and that his current theories on evolution may have been concocted while he was under the influence of LSD, Peyote, or some other hallucinogen. Dr. Casey has an outlier reputation based on past lectures and class materials. He has been the subject of inner departmental criticism and, to some extent, censored regarding his out of the mainstream anthropological evolutionary theories. Many of his department colleagues tend to stay clear of Dr. Casey. Tenure is a beautiful thing.

Steve Fredericks is a former Casey student attending this September 2000 lecture via an online link. Seated in a worn EZ-boy, dark lit living room through newspapers and stacked book cluttered window. Late morning best, dressed in boxer shorts, a once white T-shirt and flip-flops...very old and well into a six-pack of beer, and tuned into the Casey lecture only out of curiosity; he overslept after a night out, causing trouble at the Navy's Admiral Kidd Club. He always went out of his way to insult as many "Navy Pukes" as possible...just before he buys a round for the bar. A lot of war stories and BS thrown about during these intriguing alcohol-laced sessions.

Despite the beer-drinking, Steve was always interested in Dr. Casey's human evolution theories. In 1992, the good professor gave Steve a research paper by Dr. Jacob Michaels on alien prototypes. Steve was subtly hooked, accepting the concept of evolutionary manipulation of the human genome on Earth.

Although Casey taught Steve close to twenty years ago, his lectures had a lasting impact and Steve recalls the material clearly during later discussions with his brother Grant.

Dr. Casey's interpretation of his research skirts the edge and possibility of time-travel evolution, a "time-repeat" process whereby, modified humans with genetic specific DNA profiles were analyzed incrementally over thousands of years. A specific number of breed stock Human subjects are placed around the Earth at various locations with sustainable environments that offer survival outcomes matched to their innate skills and capabilities. Dr. Casey's model includes Man, early Man, as the organism under extraterrestrial study on Earth for thousands of years. Future dimension time travel observation occurs almost immediately. The experiment managers travel into the future to observe milestone evolutionary DNA, genetic, social modifications that occur within the subject population over centuries. They observed multiple generations that are subject to systematic genetic evaluation. The time-repeat process of time travel to the future provides observable genetic outcome without a prolonged, or any, evolutionary time sequence. There is no time lost. Travel to any year or period of time is available once the subject participants, humans, are located within Earth's evolutionary environment. A living organism can be observed at any point in their life cycle. Genetic alterations observed, noted, analyzed and edited are manipulated, improved genetically in the next follow-on subjects: Man created by time-travel-evolution.

Lecture
September 18, 2000
Dr. Casey
ANTH 103. Human Origins
Lecture Title: Is it Possible? PETRI DISH EVOLUTION
In a lecture hall with about 200 first and second-year students, Dr. Casey stands at a podium reviewing his notes. He has been alerted by his department dean that this lecture series is causing some concern both in the department and outside in the community. Many religious groups say his lectures run counter to established spiritual teachings. Within the department, fellow professors and adjunct staff have questioned his research methodology and source material. There is a student gossip mill that refers to Casey, mockingly, as the "Messiah" of anthropology. His fellow department contemporaries are known

to use the terminology subtly. Regardless, Casey seems immune to this type of criticism and presses forward with his lecture series and his perspective. Casey relies on scientific research and is skeptical of his contemporaries and the dogma of widely accepted anthropological evolutionary theory they espouse.

Darwin's theory, Casey believes, doesn't provide adequate answers to the vast diversity of animal evolution, and human evolution specifically. The human genome from ancient Man forward is a picture of broad-ranged genetic components. Casey believes that the human genetic tapestry was woven by other means and scattered around the globe. The scattered genetic diversity of Man was not the result of accidental migratory encounters over land. And not the resultant of random drift of wind and sea currents over thousands of miles of open ocean. Darwin's theory opens the door to *how* evolution happens, but not *what* happened. Casey pushed students to visualize a more outside-the-box approach than "the standard and accepted" evolutionary theory. It just takes time. Students also come to believe Casey dressed as a 1960s San Francisco Haight-Ashbury homeless *bong gripper*. His department's contemporaries tended to agree as well.

* * * *

June 16, 2016
22 Surprising Facts About The Early Humans
tworeddots.com

Millions of years have passed with Man roaming the Earth. Archaeological and anthropological discoveries have led to many conclusions regarding Neanderthal, homo erectus and homosapien heritage. Homosapien ancestors of modern Man are believed to have originated in Africa. A theory suggests they migrated to Europe and Asia and began to replace another human species, homo erectus, approximately 80,000 years ago. It is also coincidentally believed that homo erectus followed the same route over 1 million years ago. The scientific community has discovered and believe that the genetic makeup found within these different human species are closely related. The assumption is that they all came from the same location in East Africa. It assumes that all human ancestors lived there. Maybe, not exactly that?

* * * *

Lecture commences: Dr. Casey

"Researchers once believed," Dr. Casey began folding his hands on the podium, "humans entered the new world from Asia as a single group crossing over the Bering Sea land bridge no earlier than 13,000 years ago. But that theory is at best faulty. A female skeleton named Eva, found in the Yucatán peninsula has been carbon dated at 13,500 years old." He begins pacing the stage, occasionally adjusting his ponytail. "The polar ice sheet started to melt 13,000 years ago and dramatically from 9,000 to 8,000, causing sea levels to rise and closing the Bering Sea Land Bridge. However, Eva was alive hundreds of years before the first accepted date of human settlement in the Americas. In other words, Eva's world was isolated by glacial ice sheets, and she was alive before there were supposed to be people in the Americas. Early humans were already in the Americas prior to travel via the Bering Sea Bridge, 800 years prior to the Clovis people found in New Mexico. In East Africa, DNA from a fossilized Man is much older, dated to 195,000 years ago by potassium dating argon of the soil. He is called OMO 1, a prehistoric Man, found in the Omo Valley of Ethiopia. The Homo Sapien human tree starts perhaps nearly seven millions years ago. The theory many accepted was that Man started in the Omo Valley and then spread to the rest of the world. The single source of Man from East Africa does not coincide to actual human development." Casey scans his audience for any sort of reaction; the young skulls full of mush are not engaged, he continued.

"There were, in fact, human 'hotspots' over several areas of Africa, Asia, Australia, the Americas, Europe, and each of these hotspots had different DNA traits. In actuality, they were ET operational *alien hotspots*, if you like, developing some Man in a petri dish of evolution."

At this startling assertion, Casey's audience was jolted into paying attention, student double-takes ricocheting around the lecture hall, giving rise to nervous smiles from some, stifled laughter from others. Having encountered this reaction before, Casey paused before continuing: "The current theory has that archaic, modern humans and Neanderthal interbred to create the genetic makeup of now modern Man, Homo sapiens, 'today's Man.' The DNA sequencing of Man today indicates 1 to 3 percent of Neanderthal DNA. Take, for example, the Australian aborigines, once a unique species, currently thought to have been isolated for tens of thousands of years since the last ice age 40,000 years ago. Australia's climate changed and limited the territorial survival of aborigines. The theory: they learned to adapt and interbred to survive. With whom? A big question. There were no Starbucks or community meeting facilities that provided interaction between different human species. So how did they interbreed? Think about it." The students open-mouthed, stunned by the direction of this lecture and unsure where Casey was heading. Note-taking had nearly stopped and diminished to doodling. Hearts, flowers, question marks.

Unfazed, Dr. Casey pushed on; moved to stage front in wrinkled, come-to-Jesus Haight-Ashbury khaki pants, sandals, an old Santana T-shirt, and a gray ponytail. He pauses momentarily, then proceeded. "Genetic researchers have found the Y chromosome in every Man today dating back over 150,000 to 300,000 years, from a single source male in western Cameroon. The Y-chromosome 'Adam' DNA, passed down exclusively from mother to offspring, is sourced back to a single female. She is estimated to have lived approximately 150,000-196,000 years ago from which all humans are descended maternally. In human genetics, 'Mitochondrial Eve' is the most recent common ancestor in a direct, unbroken maternal line of all currently living humans. This is the woman from whom all living humans today descend. An unbroken line on their mother's side, and through the mothers of those mothers, and so on, go back until all lines converge at one person." He pauses briefly to let his position settle.

"All mitochondrial DNA is passed from mother to offspring without recombination. All mitochondrial DNA in every living person is directly descended from hers by definition, differing only by the mutations that over generations have occurred in the germ cell DNA since the conception of the original Mitochondrial Eve." There were still no questions or any challenge to the lecture from the assorted mind-numbed students. There was much more to come.

Returning to the podium, Dr. Casey adjusted his ponytail and drinks from a water bottle while overlooking his captured attention deprived disinterested students. "According to some research paleontologists, there was a genetic bottleneck 50,000 to 100,000 years ago, where the human population sharply decreased to between 3,000 and 10,000. At the time of initial migration from Africa 60,000 to 70,000 years ago, the apparent human population was somewhere between 1,000 and 10,000 breeding pairs or a total of 20,000 for the entire Earth. Genetic analysis of the entire human genome has shown the effective human population 1.2 million years ago was less than 26,000. There had to have been periodic extinction events followed by replacement events for the human species; the petri dish required sterilization to start over. The genetic differences among humans today reflect changes within the last 70,000 years, not a gradual modification over hundreds of thousands of years."

* * * *

1999
Living Cosmos.Com/evolution

Evolution has never been fully understood. Few realize that there are not a series of graduated steps from one species to another, but rather the sudden appearance of new species... For more than a century we have contemplated the origin and extinction of species within the framework of evolution. Darwin claimed that evolution was the result of natural selection, known as "survival of the fittest." However, it merely plays a secondary role. The gene is the ultimate source of variability in living things, and it at this chromosomal level that the answers to evolution can be uncovered...

The very same gene sequence in a different location on the chromosome can alter the gene's action, leading genetic pathways into new functional alleys, and hence, new creatures...Genetic molecular manipulation, not natural selection, is the key to evolution. Changing the genetic coding sequence has caused sudden evolutionary transitions. However, the why and how it took place is an unknown.

* * * *

November 18, 2018
San Diego Union-Tribune [AP]
Farm Animals May Soon Get New Features Through Gene Editing

...A company wants to alter farm animals by adding and subtracting genetic traits in a lab...Last year a bull gene-edited by Recombinetics to have the dominant hornless trait sired several offspring. All were born hornless.

* * * *

Dr. Casey
[Continues]

"Extraterrestrials, ETs, used the Americas, Europe, Siberia, Southeast Asia, China, Australia as trigger points to develop hybrid humans," Dr. Casey continues. The introduction of ETs generates more double-takes throughout the lecture hall. Some students are thinking of leaving, mostly captured disinterested students. "The current scientific theory is archaic Man, ancestors of modern humans, intermixed and inner bred with Neanderthals to create the genetic makeup of modern Man, homo sapiens. The series of Man's supposed evolutionary changes resulted from the inner breeding of several modern men. The petri dish experiments of extraterrestrials created all the different subspecies of pre-homo sapiens. The process encompassed DNA and genetic switches, genome sequencing all monitored over time to observe and record predictive outcomes. The unknowns were how these 'human beings' react in terms of intelligence, health issues, resistance to disease, and environmental conditions. In other words, how do these newly minted species adapt?" Dr. Casey's enthusiasm and energy are peaking; he bounds about the stage. He is into his element; beads of sweat form on his brow. His Santana T-shirt shows signs of moisture showing through Carlos' guitar, though the air-conditioned lecture hall is at a comfortable temperature. Dr. Casey has become perceptively light on his feet; he thrusts his water bottle to emphasize a point and drinks repeatedly.

"Lab locations: Africa had five to six hotspots. Each would be monitored by a caretaker or monitor/researcher. ETs needed time to determine the outcome of DNA manipulation; however, once ETs were able to control the aging/evolutionary process, the results were readily available. The genesis of modern Man is the result of DNA manipulation by aliens in controlled experiments."

"Any questions?"

Stone-cold silence filled the lecture hall. Dr. Casey reviewed his notes. He was intent on convincing some in his audience of what he presents. He clearly understands that most will not accept his hypothesis. He can live with that.

* * * *

Lecture Continues
Dr. Casey's forecast event

"Consider Man, early Man, with an IQ of a preschool child or less. We know from experience that the child will mature intellectually and attain an IQ far and again beyond any associated with the many forms of early Man. Consider attempting to train a 4-year-old to build a fire with nothing more than a friction method or a flint spark. Fire is one of the most essential and critical elements of survival at any age. Once they master fire-making, continue their training with hunting-gathering techniques. Of course, after they master the ability to create stone tools, hunting, fishing, and weapons, they can be taught land and ocean distance navigation. Before those skills for basic survival, they need shelter, all types of shelter. Our 4-year-old, in order to populate and tame the entire world, should be able to build and outfit a watercraft that can travel thousands of oceans miles to an unknown location, find water and food sources along the way, and navigate by the stars. Our 4-year-olds." Dr. Casey pauses. "I wish them luck."

Now, most students are eagerly awaiting the hour's end. "There are charts showing ancient population groups around the globe. In reality, they are individual extraterrestrial lab locations. Nevertheless, both paleontology and evolutionary anthropology believe there are many dozens, or sets, of human species, tribes, people all over the world. It is difficult to imagine archaic and ancient human species containing the intellectual capacity to develop tools, make fire, and survive environmental conditions around the globe. Whether they have the mental capacity of 4-year-olds or 10-year-olds, they managed to survive by other means. Add to this the apparent wanderlust capability of these ancient humans, navigating thousands of miles across unknown and varied terrain to establish small sets of human habitats.

Additionally, these early human ancestors learned on their own to invent/discover the ability and expertise to build vessels capable of traveling many hundreds or thousands of miles to unknown landmasses. It is hard to comprehend, based upon the rudimentary intellectual capability of these early humans, that they became the Lewis and Clark's, the Spanish conquistadors, Columbus, and all the Vikings of their time more than 200,000 years ago. They had no navigation tools or implements such as the compass, nor maps and had no possible understanding of ocean distance navigation." Dr. Casey takes a breather, wipes some sweat from his brow, his Santana T-shirt now sticking to his body. He makes his way back to the podium for another bottle of water. He is surprised to see many of his students are back to taking notes. He feels a sense of encouragement but doesn't expect a breakthrough.

"Yet the scientific community of paleontologists and anthropologists pose a theory that these early human inhabitants were capable of traveling and navigating thousands of miles to destinations they knew nothing about or what awaited them there. They navigated across the open Indian and Pacific oceans to settle Polynesia, Micronesia, Australia, Hawaii, and all of the

West Indies, without navigational aids of any sort. It is hardly possible to consider that this early human ancient population could use a raft without sails to travel to Australia. Such a venture would require seaworthy vessel storage and freshwater. Also, how did they gather food, fish, or other wildlife to endure a very lengthy journey without navigational skills? What if this land and ocean navigation migration took place based upon the innate cognitive skills of these early human inhabitants? Then it is abundantly clear with that level of skill it should not have taken thousands of years for their descendants to discover more advanced methodology to both land and sea migration and enhanced survival skills.

Intellectually, it doesn't track that these early humanoid beings had the capability to populate nearly every continent over 200,000 years ago—and yet their advancement and evolution of tools, machinery, social skills did not advance with a significance beyond basic survival and rudimentary social tribal patterns."

Dr. Casey, a bit agitated, moves with exaggerated hand gestures. His voice, somewhat shrill and measurably louder, pushes his mission to drive home his salient points supporting his outlier theories of evolution. "Both Homo erectus and Homo neanderthalensis became extinct by the end of the Paleolithic period, having been replaced by a new wave of humans, the anatomically modern Homo sapiens, which emerged in eastern Africa 200,000 years BP. They left Africa around 50,000 years BP, and expanded throughout the planet. This argument is difficult to swallow, as pointed out, these early humans apparently had the capability of distance travel, land navigation as well as ocean navigation to repopulate the entire planet. Not buying it. They did expand throughout the planet—but not by their own devices: they were placed in different locations throughout the planet by an intelligent source." Silence again.

Wikipedia: Early Man

It is likely that multiple groups coexisted for some time in certain locations. Neanderthals were still found in parts of Eurasia 30,000 BP years, and engaged in a limited degree of interbreeding with modern humans. Hominid fossils not belonging either to Homo neanderthalensis or to Homo sapiens species, found in the Altai Mountains and Indonesia, were radiocarbon dated to 30,000 – 40,000 BP and 17,000 BP, respectively.

For the duration of the Paleolithic period, human populations remained low, especially outside the equatorial region. The entire population of Europe between 16,000 and 11,000 BP likely averaged some 30,000 individuals, and between 40,000 and 16,000 BP, it was even lower at 4,000– 6,000 individuals.

Dr. Casey
Lectures on

A front-row tank-top and knee-high shorts student raised her hand to ask a question. "You have a question?" Dr. Casey anticipates a controversial and perhaps an in-your-face rebuttal question to his somewhat outlandish lecture concepts. He moved from the podium, dripping sweat, marches front center stage and prepares to do battle and handle decisively any criticism leveled at his content or sources. Bring it on.

"Yes, what does BP mean?" front-row tank-top sheepishly asks.

Somewhat disappointed, Dr. Casey responds, *"Before Present.* It's a time scale used mainly in archaeology, geology, and other scientific disciplines to specify when events occurred in the past. It's the most commonly used convention in radiocarbon dating. 'Present' refers to the year 1950 AD, when the calibration curves were established. The term would be synonymous with AD, Anno Domino, years since the birth of Christ. Conversely, the term of BC would refer to the years prior to Christ's birth. Before Christ, BC."

"Thank you." The student sits back, never to ask another question in Dr. Casey's class. Her student neighbor, tie-dyed black and red t-shirt and black leather pants, touches her forearm, and they shrug together.

CONSIDER MAN

Silence again. He presses on. "By 50,000 to 40,000 years ago or BP," he says, realizing the front-row student clearly wishes to be invisible, "The first humans set foot in Australia 45,000 years ago. Humans lived at 61 degrees North latitude in Europe. By 30,000 years ago, Japan was reached, and 2,000-7,000 years ago, humans were present in Siberia, above the Arctic Circle. Some sources believe, at the end of the Upper Paleolithic period, humans crossed Beringia and quickly expanded throughout the Americas. It is nearly impossible to consider that this early human ancient population was able to use a raft without sails to travel to Australia. As I pointed out a number of times today, the impossibility of this venture would require skills, tools, and intelligence far beyond the innate capability of those early humans. They needed assistance with this journey."

Dr. Casey hesitates momentarily, takes a calming breath, then dives in and continues. "Alternatively, it can perhaps better be explained by the existence of evolutionary monitors and managers of the evolutionary process in the lab known as Earth. There are dozens of archaic records of the human species located throughout Africa, Europe, Asia, Australia, North America. They didn't walk thousands of miles or navigate there over vast oceans 'distances. They were located there by the lab managers to initiate a time-sequenced evolutionary experiment 50,000 to 1 million years ago or more. These pre-humans were incapable of accomplishing the elements of their rudimentary existence, relying solely upon their own archaic intellectual cognitive capability. With time travel evolution, the managers of the experiments could, and did, manipulate DNA genetic triggers. These early human species did provide insights concerning various environmental manipulations and cognitive understanding of different survival concepts. They were able to provide specific insights into tool creation and use.

I will leave you with a description of two competing theories in the archaeological world revolving around two separate models of how the Earth was populated by early Man. Researchers believe Homo erectus was a very successful species for over 1 million years in Africa, around 1.8 million BP through

300,000 BP. Accordingly, the studies point out they colonize much of the world. They supposedly shared portions of East Africa with other Homo types from 1.8 to 1.3 million years ago. One of the other species was Homo ergaster. Either in parallel or together, they may have been the first to use fire, and they developed a language form of communication.

However, the origin of Homo sapiens is still debated. There are fossils dated from 130,000 BP to 90,000 BP, both in East and South Africa to Israel. Neanderthals were most likely overcome by the dominant Homo sapiens and pushed to extinction between 45,000 and 30,000 BP. Their superior communication skills, it is believed, led to the development of a wide range of stone tools after 40,000 BP. They also had an impressive record of expansion across the Earth, reaching Australia and the Americas 55,000 and 13,000 BP." Dr. C, as his colleagues refer to him, takes a break and slows his presentation. He is nearing the lecture's end.

Dr. Casey moves on, "Two archaeological models exist representing the expansion out of Africa. The first indicates Homo sapiens left Africa two million years ago. That led to development of different Homo sapiens in Africa, Europe, Asia, and Australia. A major flaw with this model is the genetically identical DNA of the modern human ancestors and the impossibility of such because they were isolated for thousands of years. There were no pathways for genetic exchange or inner breeding." Dr. Casey takes a long swig from his water bottle. He and Santana are both soaked with sweat and getting wetter.

"The second model pushes the theory that Homo sapiens developed in Africa, Asia, and Europe and shared an exchange of genes with the indigenous Homo erectus populations. This model rests upon the assumption that the mobility of migration throughout the world is responsible for the shared traits of modern populations from ancestors who existed 500,000 years ago." Dr. Casey's rebuttal to the models mirrors his beliefs and research, spanning decades. He believes wholeheartedly that there was migration. His rebuttal encapsulates the source and method of transmigration, not whether migration took place.

"These models suggest early humans, on their own, learned distance travel, land and ocean navigation, to populate the entire Earth. They did expand, but not by their own devices. They were placed in different locations throughout the planet by an intelligent source: aliens, ETs. It is nearly impossible to consider that this early human ancient population had the capability to use a raft without sails to travel to Australia. I repeat. The impossibility of this venture would require vessels to keep freshwater, methods to gather food such as fish or other wildlife to endure a very lengthy journey without navigational skills.

Consider that both theories are flawed. Neither has considered the possibility of extraterrestrials having been involved in DNA manipulation in the lab Earth. The extended isolation and regional differences from continent to continent suggest something far beyond the capabilities of Homo erectus capabilities more than 500,000 years ago. The extended expansion to all four corners of the Earth by early Man clearly is impossible: he was not equipped for the trip. Consider, Man was transported to these isolated locations rather than migrating there."

Students are locked in place. They wait for another shoe (or genetically modified boot) to fall. It's on its way.

The lecture is over, not the presentation. Before dismissing the students, Dr. Casey announces details for anyone interested in participating in a "practice" grad research project. There are handouts with instructions at the lecture hall exits. He had no expectations that any of his students would accept his invitation. He was skeptical of student input and posed the practice research project as an irritant directed at his fellow professors. Two of his counterparts in the anthropology department challenged him to proceed on a dare of a $100 wager that not one student would take up his "Faux Grad Project." Dr. Casey even referred to the project as a faux research exercise; not much confidence anyone would bother. He was wrong. "Any student that wishes to contact me for further information or edification should call the department secretary and arrange an appointment. I am always available for inquiries and discussions regarding course material lecture topics." Dr. Casey hadn't had a meaningful student appointment for some time. Actually, for years.

Dr. Casey's
Faux Grad Project

As the students are poised to exit the lecture hall, Dr. Casey offers to sponsor his Faux Grad Project exercise for students interested in learning the nuts and bolts of research projects for their graduate degree. Each student must work under a faculty mentor, such as Dr. Casey. As one, he will provide a step-by-step guide to simplify the process and suggest timelines to complete a research project. He indicates that the first significant challenges in conducting research are consulting with your faculty advisor in an area of interest and seeking advice on researchable topics. Dr. Casey sells his research exercise as a preparatory step for students to develop a research project proposal at a later date. There are no grades, only access and practical experience associated with basic procedural research protocol that will benefit participants during their actual graduate projects.

In preparation for their research, Dr. Casey gives them a fictional research project topic to exercise their thought processes and challenge them at a higher level of research and thinking. Dr. Casey wants them to explore how an alien world could have used Earth as a research project. Topics within this research area would include considerations of the possibility of time travel, evolutionary manipulation, and genetic triggers.

This research project and topic's focus is twofold: get the graduate student thinking globally and accept a fictional premise for a fictional graduate research project. Secondly, Dr. Casey believes the research topic is not fictional. This exercise will subtly support his belief in his research on the subject of alien enhanced, controlled, and managed evolution. His students will be his research assistants as they derive supporting data from their research project. He doesn't expect much because he understands he and his students don't speak the same "research language" nor comprehend where his theoretical model is founded. Paradoxically, in the end, it turns out to be a French interpretation. Samantha French.

Dr. Casey provides a guide of assumptions on which grad students should base their faux research projects. He indicates subtly that his assumptions are not necessarily based on scientific or proven fact. The unvarnished truth is that he believes everything that he is presenting to his students. It was a subtle introduction of factors he wanted explored. Dr. Casey had researched the topic extensively, reached conclusions and assumptions, and believes he has an inside understanding of everything that is extraterrestrial evolution management on Earth. He was going to provide his students with an assumption of facts regarding their research project. The premises were the foundation of the practice research project—whether the students believe the hypothesis or not.

Dr. Casey's faux graduate research exercise assumes the evolutionary process among humans, gorillas, chimpanzees, and monkeys did not take place over millions of years. Instead, there was an indication that evolutionary DNA/Genome manipulation took place in an Earth lab setting managed by evolutionary manipulation. Dr. Casey's research and interpretation of his study includes the possibility of time travel evolution, via the time-repeat process whereby the subject material/DNA host is improved incrementally as the time sequence is repeated. The time-repeat method dramatically reduces the evolutionary time model by thousands of years. A living organism can be created, modified, and observed in its development on a foreshortened time pattern in a laboratory. Micro DNA sequencing and adjustment are made and observed within hours or days, not thousands of years. Ironically, time travel DNA evolution is the short answer to what happened on Earth: laboratory Earth is managed by an alien intelligent life form. Dr. Casey's understanding of it is, it could have and most likely did happen. When Steve Fredericks attended Dr. Casey's classes in 1992, he did buy into portions of the outlandish theories, perhaps influenced by his marijuana use and Dr. Casey's reputation of doing the same. Two nearly like-minded pot smokers had something in common. Nonetheless, Steve saw the possibility of some sort of evolutionary manipulation. The lectures had a lasting impact on him. Marijuana may have helped.

Fortunately, the period ended for the students, many of whom don't return to Dr. Casey's lecture series and drop his class. As students file out of the lecture hall, the front-row student that asked the BP question is animated, "Why did you let me ask a question?" she tells her desk mate. "He is so far out there that I thought he was going to jump off the stage. I wanted to die. Did you see how he was sweating? His Jerry Garcia T-shirt was soaked. All that stuff about aliens moving people. I think *he's* an alien. No way I'm doing his practice grad research whatever."

Samantha French sat next to the front row student. "It was Santana," she clarifies.

"What? The Santa Ana is over," the front-row student says, referencing the recently ended Santa Ana winds.

"It wasn't Jerry Garcia on the T-shirt," says Samantha, "It was Carlos Santana."

"I saw that guy on MTV, Jerry Garcia." Front-row again. Doesn't connect with Santa Ana winds, Santana or much else as they exit the lecture hall.

"It wasn't a live performance on MTV. He's been dead six years."

"Santana's dead?" Front-row can't believe it.

"Never mind." Says Samantha French who has decided to participate in Dr. Casey's practice research project.

Steve missed most of the last online hour sleeping it off in he classic E-Z Boy.

May 6, 2010
Office of Dr. Martha Denard, Psychologist
Pine Valley, California

Grant has been seeing Dr. Denard for several months; he felt a need to talk after playing his best with life's dealt cards, weary of all the losing hands. He has come to a point where he checks his bets rather than risk what will likely be another disappointing play. As a result, he has been considering folding out of the game altogether.

Dr. Denard's interview room is a cramped 15 x 20 office space, desk, chairs, a six-foot table stacked with journals and other publications, and a jar of assorted stale candy, cabinets, and drawers; overlooked by a three-window south wall and an artificial Japanese pink flowering tree. The remote Corte Madera Peak fills the window's distant horizon, about 4 miles beyond I-8. Grant sits facing the windowed wall on a leather-bound sofa. Dr. Denard sits in a leather-bound over, stuffed rocker-swivel chair. She has pen in hand and her notes on Grant.

She asks Grant about a comment he made in the last session. "Rather be in combat. I don't understand."

Grant replies, "There, you know the rules."

"Rules? What...was it that simple?" Dr. Denard searching for meaning.

"Those rules never changed." Grant speaks a simple combat truth.

Forty Years Ago
April 6, 1970
Da Nang Airbase, Republic of South Vietnam

The Da Nang Air Base had a north-south runway. U.S. Air Force assets were on the east side of the base. Aircraft included a wing of F-4 phantoms attack bombers, a squadron of Fairchild UC-123 Providers, aircraft that sprayed Agent Orange over a good portion of the South Vietnamese jungle. Assets also included forward air controller aircraft composed of OV-10s and Cessna O2 observation aircraft.

The South Vietnamese Air Force had a contingent of A-37 Dragonfly attack aircraft. Stationed there, as well, was a squadron of Jolly Green Giant Helicopters.

On the west side of the airstrip was a component of the 3rd Marine division. Their presence was for security purposes and other combat operations. The Marines took the brunt of rocket attacks.

The U.S. Air Force officers housing compound stood behind security fences. Their compound consisted of two-story barracks that the French built in the 1950s without air conditioning. The compound included the officers club, or O-club, that covered basics: dining room that seated perhaps 200, a small stage for the occasional B- to D-grade USO shows. And of course, there was a well-stocked bar. The food menu was stable, predictable, mundane, and limited. Fried egg sandwiches were always available, a regular substitute for almost anything.

Steaks, grilled outside, not a staple in Air Force kitchens, were obtained from Army, Navy, or Marine stocks through hard-nosed barter negotiations in exchange for alcohol, which the flyboys always had in abundance and the other services generally lacked. The compound included a mess hall for all grades of Air Force personnel. Its menu was limited, stable, and consistent, assuming one's standards were marginally low: always an abundance of SOS (Shit On a Shingle), chipped beef gravy on a slice of bread. For the evening fare, one could always count on an abundance of liver and onions, often accompanied some hours later by a case of the *Green-Apple-Quickstep,* and a rushed trip to the nearest men's room for a bowel cleanse—a combat zone dietary reminder of who was in charge.

The enlisted crew members have a duplicate NCO Club reported to have better service, food, and entertainment. It pays to know who runs and operates the supply chain.

Da Nang Officers Club, late that night
Three Jolly Green Pilots sit at the nondescript basic bare bones bar, one captain, two lieutenants. It is the end of the lieutenants' first day in the combat zone. They have had a few drinks each. None of the three have had time to change out of their combat attire: green flight suits, zippered pockets and a parachute switched blade knife pocketed on the left inside thigh for use cutting parachute lines…it could save your life. They wore survival vests while flying, that contained a survival radio and extra batteries, small first aid kits, pint of water, signal mirror, smoke flares, strobe light, hunting type eight-inch knife, a whistle and any item taken by individual choice. Some took candy,

snickers bars, gum, maybe a photo and their Air Force ID. A generally sterile package in case of capture or worse.

Their survival vests were turned in after each flight combat or training along with a 38- caliber revolver and ammunition.

The captain is holding court. "When you got orders to the Jollys, did they tell you some bullshit story about what a rewarding job it was?"

Lt. Tobin answers, "Yes, sir; saving lives."

"It is rewarding if you don't mind sitting in a hover while the NVA and all sorts of VC are trying to knock your asses out of the sky." The captain was stating a fact of combat reality.

"Yes, sir." Both lieutenants respond.

"Some of us may die trying to save others; some already have."

"Yes, sir." Both lieutenants wonder if the captain is speaking of current combat Jolly losses.

"You'll be lucky if your rescues are all feet wet (over water). Some say `feet wet or fuck 'em.' Not that easy; we take them all. Ninety percent are inland with heavy ground fire. Like they said, a very fucking rewarding job."

"Yes, sir."

"And you don't want to be taken prisoner."

"No, sir." In unison.

"Because they don't take prisoners where we fly. There was a pararescueman captured last year on a failed rescue mission. He was skinned alive before he died. So, if you go down, you need to be ready for a gunfight. The bad guys just want you dead…it's just the rules out there."

"Rules?" asks Lt Coder.

The captain replies, a bit lit from several rounds of alcoholic beverages, "Yeah, clear-cut rules: the bad guys are going to try to kill you and me. We are not going to let them. Simple."

"Yes, sir." In unison.

"You're here now, so, as part of your incoming briefing, there are few things you FNG's need to know and learn. One of the most important things to know is the Falcon Code. It will help sustain you in this combat environment. You FNG's heard of the Falcon Code?"

Somewhat dazed by drink, the lieutenants respond, "No, sir."

"You need to know that you will be considered FNG's until you know the code and are able to play bears around the ice hole effectively."

"Sir?" Lieutenant Coder responds. Both lieutenants are confused; it has been a very long first day.

"What is it, Coder?"

"Sir, what does FNG stand for?"

Annoyed, the captain replies, "Didn't the assholes at the newcomers briefing tell you, bring you up to speed?"

"No, sir. They didn't," Lt. Tobin says.

"Lieutenant Fucking Academy Grad Henning, admin officer extraordinaire. He didn't mention the code or bears around the ice hole?"

Coder is wide-awake now. "No, sir."

"You gotta be shitting me." He repeats the phrase: *You gotta be shitting me*—that's a 1-0-1 from the code. See how that works. Useless piece of shit. You two aren't Academy grads, are you? Just what we need around here, a few more ring knockers."

"Uh, no, sir. ROTC," the lieutenants confirm.

"Great. FNG stands for *fucking new guy*. You will find the code on the wall in the BOQ lounge. Learn it. And when you see Lt. Henning, give him a 1-0-8 from me. It's the code for *Fuck you very much*."

Lt. Tobin nods apprehensively, "Bears around the ice hole, sir?"

The captain takes a dice cup, shakes it, turns it over hard on the bar; the dice land in a tight pattern. After ordering another round, on the lieutenants, the captain says, "How many bears do you see around the ice hole? There are a lot of rules in this game. Remember them all. Go!"

Coder and Tobin stare uneasily at the five dice. It is going to be an even longer first day. Only one of many.

MAN 3

April 11, 2019
San Diego UnionTribune
A new human species discovered, AP reporting

NEW YORK (AP) — in April 2019, Fossil bones and teeth found in the Philippines have revealed a long-lost cousin of modern Man that evidently lived around the time early Man was leaving Africa to occupy the rest of the world... The exodus from Africa took place some 60,000 years ago.

Although Homo sapiens are the only surviving member of a branch of the evolutionary tree, it appears they weren't alone in that tree, there were others on existing branches for most of human existence... If this new species originated in Africa how were they carried out of that continent, the timeline doesn't fit. The Luzon find shows we still know very little about human evolution, particularly in Asia.

* * * *

Head-to-Head
Fall Semester 2000
Samantha French and Dr. Casey

Samantha made an unusual appointment with Dr. Casey to ask questions regarding the faux grad project. She is a Gothic adherent, dresses in black leather, make-up black, tattoos, and body piercings; however, she is extremely bright, focused, and driven. Sam's social skills are few, same as her friends. She doesn't seek advice from others, and prefers a solitary approach to any task. She is confident, self-assured, and finds input from others unwanted and irrelevant to her research process. Samantha French is an exceptional outlier and turns out perfect for Dr. Casey's graduate project. She was intrigued by the topic, particularly evolutionary manipulation managed by extraterrestrials in an Earth laboratory project setting. In her Gothic mindset, it was right up her alley.

She is waiting in the department secretary's cramped office, a little pressed for time. Her Gothic black outfit and lipstick and the half-shaved head are garnering some interesting visual observations from other grad students. Dr. Casey approaches wearing cut-off khakis, Birkenstocks. His gray hair is still in a ponytail; He looks to have traded the Santana T-shirt in for a Bob Dylan concert one. "Samantha?"

"Yes, Samantha French."

"Hope you haven't been waiting long. I don't get many student visits. Your appointment notice indicated you wanted to discuss the practice graduate project." Dr. Casey half-turns and leads the way to his office several doors down a cluttered hall. Anthropologists seem to accumulate various degrees of ancient clutter. Dr. Casey's office is small, with two windows behind his desk. There are bookshelves filled with multiple items. Books, folders, boxes stacked on the floor with no particular labeling to indicate contents or subjects. The floor has a worn tile installed decades ago. Dr. Casey's desktop sports a collection of various texts, papers, newspapers, magazines, and a very dirty ancient teacup or mug. It may contain mold; Samantha doesn't get that close. By comparison, despite her Gothic style, she maintains a meticulously neat and clean one-bedroom apartment. Her wardrobe choices are chiefly black and leather. She has a few of what would be considered standard piercings, nothing seemingly outrageous for the day. Not surprisingly there seems to be no guest or visitor chair in sight.

Dr. Casey takes a seat at the unkempt desk. "There's a chair behind the door, a folding chair." Dr. Casey points in the direction of the door. He expects this encounter to be relatively short and perhaps abrupt. He hasn't practiced being a welcoming host for many years.

Samantha retrieves the chair, takes a seat, extracts a notebook from her black backpack, and proceeds to her questions without reservation or intimidation; she did not look to Dr. Casey for an OK to proceed. "Researchers have found that chimpanzees share 99 percent of the same DNA with Man," she says, "making them our closest living relative. Humans have 23 pairs of chromosomes, while chimps, gorillas, and orangutans have 24. Human evolutionary genetics show that various early humans had genome differences from one to another. Your lecture material has provided insights into human evolution based upon empirical evidence beyond that of Darwin." Dr. Casey does not indicate affirmation or disagreement. Sam presses on, anyway.

"You have indicated in your research, writings, and lecture materials that Man's evolutionary tree has different branches that have been spliced, pruned, and cared for, in your terms, by outside 'arborist-managers' not of this planet. Do you believe that human existence and our evolution started in Africa with considerable oversight from extraterrestrial counterparts?" Sam makes confident eye contact with Dr. Casey.

"Yes." Dr. Casey is known for his short, direct answers coupled with a commanding presence and confidence. His hands have been folded in front of him on the desk as he pays close attention to Samantha. Beyond the "yes," he says nothing. He offers no indication regarding his acceptance other than his concise answer in the affirmative.

"Then," she continues, "can it be said that the divergence and difference within and among the various human genomes were created purposely by outside influences? The alien arborist created the divergent path of human development or evolutionary processes? In essence, different cell types possess different gene profiles from the same genome sequence?" Samantha is rock steady, well prepared for this meeting.

Dr. Casey has a stoic posture, hands folded, eyes fixed on his student, not sweating through his Bob Dylan T-shirt. "Yes to all."

"Is it your contention that, in your words, *alien monitors were able to manipulate DNA and forward the results through time travel sequencing?*" Samantha expects an answer. Given none, she continues. "In essence, aliens were experimenting with creating an animal design to include humans. They understood DNA genetic switching mechanisms and made adjustments over time as evidenced by a series of human prototypes?"

At last, Dr. Casey responds with more than a single word. "They would create a DNA formulation for a human predecessor and were able to observe the results through the time travel evolutionary model that they managed. The DNA manipulation dictated how, when, and where the different genes turn off and on." His answer is direct, confident, and professional with no equivocation as he begins to see promise in this young woman. There may be some measure of intelligent design under all the black garb. She is twenty-five.

Samantha asks what she feels is a critical question and subject. "If under your alien arborist model, the monitors were designing human forms for millions of time travel years, why is the divergence between Chimpanzees and modern Man, at two percent seemingly so close, and yet the resultant product is nowhere near similar? Is there a two percent difference in the categories of IQ, language, physique, social skills, tool use, and manufacture, etcetera, etcetera? What is contained within the missing two percent that seems beyond equity?" She calmly waits without expression behind her Gothic façade. Samantha is a confident woman, intent and focused on securing Dr. Casey's answers.

Dr. Casey is pleased with this question and line of inquiry. He senses an opening with a very interesting Samantha French. "As you know, DNA reflects an individual's unique identity and how closely related we are to one another. DNA consists of genes and molecular codes that shape how an organism grows as a unique entity. To support my conclusion, comparison studies of the entire genome indicate that segments of DNA have been deleted, duplicated, and or inserted from one part of the genome to another. Those genetic manipulations were done by outside sources."

"The two percent you refer to is actually a four to five percent distinction between humans and chimpanzees' genomes." Dr. Casey pauses for a reaction. None, but Samantha maintains constant eye contact. They are in agreement. He makes a final point: "The human evolutionary tree has been genetically grafted, watered, watched over, and pruned by an alien genetic arborist. And yes, human evolution began in Africa with a little help from cosmic friends."

He awaits a response.

* * * *

June 25, 2021
Researchers say 'dragon Man' skull found in China could be new human species
By Kaelan Deese, Breaking News Reporter,
Washington Examiner

Researchers believe a fossilized skull found in China and dubbed "dragon Man" could be the missing link between Neanderthals and Homo sapiens...it may be the long-sought evolutionary bridge between the two human species. They estimate that it is at least 140,000 years old...

* * * *

Samantha is locked in a visual embrace with the good Dr. Casey; she is not attempting to denigrate or challenge; she just wants complete information. "The percent seems far short of accurate by simple visualization. A chimp and a human counterpart look to be no more than a very, very distant cousin if that. We share a supposedly common genetic cousin six to eight million years ago." Dr. Casey moves near a window with a limited view. He stares through it as if there is one. "The genome contains DNA, genes, molecular coded proteins that represent the building blocks of Man. If you will, assume that these building blocks are actually an assembly of identical construction materials to build a habitable structure. Now employ several contractors to build separate structures with identical materials. Provide them with designs, then turn them loose to build. Inevitably, they will complete the project at different times, and the structures will not match. Something near 95 percent uniformity would be more than acceptable, only minor deviations." Dr. Casey moves from the window to near the front of the desk and Samantha. "Now, attempt to apply that same concept to evolutionary models that rely on DNA manipulation, genetic switches, and triggers. DNA switches control body shaping genes responsible for giving animals their unique appearance." He knows she is aware of these factors. "The alien monitors were able to manipulate DNA genetic switching mechanisms and those building blocks to dictate how, when, and where the different genes turn on and off. In essence, they were experimenting with creating animal designs to include humans; and a series of human form prototypes."

Samantha makes a few notations in a notebook then replies with a simple summary of Dr. Casey's point. "I considered the process from a different perspective—that of a potter's wheel. Throwing a clay pot to create a set of pots with, say, eight exact measured lumps of clay. Regardless of the eight operators' skill, no two pots would be identical. Ninety-five percent uniformity would be more than acceptable after throwing, firing, and glazing. Is it your contention that we, the chimps and Man, are the result of an evolutionary adjustment of the same DNA genetic materials and process manipulated by different alien arborists?"

"Yes, start with the same building materials, create different entities from your pottery kiln that turns out minutely different, by a few degrees, the end product." Dr. Casey is high, perhaps for the first time, without the assistance of an illegal drug smoked or injected. "Chimps and Man are mostly the same product, cooked at different degrees, by different chefs mixing the ingredients." He pauses. "Those very last two to five percent of DNA contain the capacity to alter the finished product dramatically by genetic adjustments. Call it fine-tuning. All the differences you reference are contained there: physical features, IQ, mental skill, cognitive ability."

Samantha responds. "So, from the last small percent of our non-shared DNA we evolved into modern Man, and the chimps came up far different? We, mankind, were participants in genetically managed experimentation." She pauses. "Then, the arborist must have applied the genetics by different methods or process."

* * * *

July 16, 2021
[see Extract listed by chapter]
Just 7% of our DNA is unique to modern humans, study shows
Christina Larsen, Associated press

WASHINGTON (AP) — What makes humans unique?...Just 7% of our genome is uniquely shared with other humans, and not shared by other early ancestors, according to...the journal Science Advances. The researchers also found that an even smaller fraction of our genome — just 1.5% — is both unique to our species and shared among all people alive today...that changes in the human genome are randomly distributed, rather than clustered around certain hotspots within the genome.

* * * *

Dr. Casey replies, "You are correct when you intimated different methods and processes. That is exactly how the last two to five percent of mankind's DNA was applied to create us."

"What was the process or method?" Samantha asks; she is puzzled.

"That is currently beyond our understanding; however, I have a theory that may allow us to accept a concept used by both alien arborist and Man. A paint palette."

Samantha is focused, both eyes and her mind. "Let's hear it, your theoretical paint palette."

Dr. Casey's Dylan T-shirt is wet at this point; he is still on a high as his conversation expands to a theoretical realm. "Take the two to five percent of our non-shared DNA from Man and chimp. Place both non-shared DNA equally on two genetic paint palettes. Give the palettes to two of our alien arborists. Let's assume that both arborists are extremely talented and gifted at adjusting genetic manipulation. The first takes his palette and creates and finishes a genetic model of Man. His finished product would be comparatively equivalent to Michelangelo's statue of David in the 1500s."

"Metaphorically, the arborist's genetic creation is a masterpiece like no other." Samantha relates calmly.

"That is exactly correct." Dr. Casey says. "Now, the second arborist is as talented as the first, and with his palette of chimpanzee non-shared DNA, he creates a genetic model. His finished product would be comparatively equivalent to the Picasso cubist painting of 'The Weeping Woman' in 1885. Very different end results." Dr. Casey's point is made.

"Again, a genetic creation like no other." Samantha responds. She knows of both classic artists and understands Dr. Casey's point. The 2 to 5 percent sample of non-shared modified genetic materials, one from Man, the other from the chimp, produces a different result. "The significances of a two to five percent genetic difference in a shared DNA structure encompasses the critical mass of the entire genome." She adds, "Metaphorically, the two-to-five precent is as the core of a nuclear reactor; without it, there is no power source. Without that minor-sized component, there is no delicately tuned, managed evolution process."

Samantha speaks with an elevated awareness. "Holy shit. You know, you just might be crucified for redirecting the creation of Man from God to an alien arborist. That is some heavyweight dogma changes you have discovered. Something to consider when considering Man." That is the closest Sam French has come to being excited. Her thoughts about evolution had matched up, to a great extent, with Dr. Casey's.

The religious aspect of Man's evolution has not been lost on Dr. Casey for some time, and now Samantha has opened that door. He asks, "Are you associated with a religious belief system?"

"I was baptized Catholic at a very young age, confirmation through the Lutheran Church. Drifted away from each over the past several years, began questioning the source of my existence and beliefs." She has a softer exterior for a goth girl.

"Your thoughts of religion, with your apparent interest in human evolution shepherded by a source beyond the confines of Earth. What place for God?" Dr. Casey is straightforward, interested in Samantha's answer. He realizes that she is like no other student, ever.

Without hesitation, she says, "Of all the major religions throughout time, there seems to be a consistent pattern of angelic revelation."

Dr. Casey is caught off guard. Is she venturing beyond his conceptual pattern of evolution alien arborists shaping the course of Man? Is she taking a diversionary path off the edge of his science research dogma? "Are you saying: angels?"

"I am saying the angelic revelations were the same multi-tasked arborist taking on a role as messengers." Samantha is tracking down a lane that Dr. Casey is unfamiliar with.

"Messengers of what, specifically?" A bead of sweat runs down his forehead.

"Messengers were providing guidance beyond manipulating DNA and genetic switches. In your lecture, you allude to early humans who were too deficient intellectually to create crafts and navigate long distances over land and oceans. They had to have a mentor or a messenger to fill an intellectual gap." Samantha is switching roles with Dr. Casey.

Dr. Casey is beginning to realize that his research and focus could have neglected to explore an avenue beyond Man's physical development. He returns to his desk, looks out his cluttered window to clear his mind. Bob Dylan is showing signs of sweating.

Samantha sees that Dr. Casey is deep in thought; she moves forward with clarification. "These visitations were initiations and inspirational starting points. Notwithstanding, religious and philosophical differences, the unifying factor of all reflect a visit from someone beyond an earthly being."

Dr. Casey returns from his reverie and sees something he hadn't seen before until now. "The Angel Gabriel visited Mary according to the Gospel of Luke. Mohammed likewise had an encounter with Gabriel and quoted him in the Quran in 610. The Angel Moroni, according to the book of Mormon, provided golden plates that established the Mormon religion. An angel or God spoke to Moses from a burning bush, and he received from God the 10 Commandments on Mount Sinai." He pauses in deep thought, "This reflects the Earth as an experimental laboratory for both human modifications in terms of physical attributes as well as socialization and development of civilizations with reflections of various moral and ethical codes and standards."

Samantha is ready to move on now that they have confirmed, sort of, cerebral conscious faith and a belief system based upon a supreme being, creator of all, including Man. "What of the extinction events for the past 250 million years and the Sixth one now?"

"Jesus, you don't slow down." Dr. Casey has a sweaty Bob Dylan T-shirt. He is on the blind side of his supposed expertise.

The last extinction terminated the dinosaurs to make a place for Man. There were nearly 20 or so extinction events over hundreds of millions of years. They repeated a DNA evolutionary cleansing of the Earth's paint palette bios system to set the stage for the next. Extinction events routinely eliminated up to 90 to 95 percent of all living species, and the recovery took as long as 30 million years. Both Samantha and Dr. Casey are well aware that volcanic events, floods, climate change, global warming and cooling, ocean oxygen depletion are leading candidates in the current extinction. The one factor unclear in the scientific community's repertoire of theories is ionizing gamma radiation.

* * * *

Wikipedia

Gamma rays are ionizing radiation and are thus hazardous to life. Due to their high penetration power, they can damage bone marrow and internal organs. Unlike alpha and beta rays, they easily pass through the body and thus pose a formidable radiation protection challenge, requiring shielding made from dense materials such as lead or concrete.

* * * *

Samantha opens with radiation. "In August 1971, a paleontological expedition in the Mongolian Gobi Desert uncovered two dinosaur fossilized skeletons, a Velociraptor, and Protoceratops. It is theorized that they died within seconds by something that overwhelmed them. They died locked in active mortal combat. High-intensity gamma radiation is the prime candidate that could kill that quickly."

Dr. Casey recalls his review of the Gobi discovery. "There is speculation that those fossilized dinosaurs could have been caught in an avalanche of mud or sand," he says.

Samantha has seen the fighting dinosaurs display at the American Museum of Natural History in New York City. "They are locked in combat, not struggling to avoid an avalanche; they're not covered with mud or sand until after their death 80 million years ago."

Dr. Casey recovers some ground. "Ionizing gamma radiation plays a part regarding the selective nature of extinctions. There is no known source of ionizing radiation in extinction events, yet there is geological evidence that it existed." He knows there were five mass extinction events or *Great Dyings*. The last was the dinosaur extinction 66 million years ago; it made a place for Man.

"We are the latest results living inside the experiment of Man." Samantha says, closing her notebook and shoving it into her backpack. "I don't have any other questions at this time." She folds the chair and returns it near the door as she leaves. Dr. Casey sits, somewhat dumbfounded. He needs a shower; his Dylan T-shirt needs a wash.

Late October 2000
The
Samantha French Connection
Faux Grad Project

Samantha French was an exceptional, out-of-sync, and atypical student. She returned a completed project paper within 30 days of its assignment. Coincidentally, as part of a different master's thesis project, she was researching genetic variation among human-linked structures of ancestral populations, principally in the Americas. She found the following: Native American populations showed a lower genetic diversity than populations from other continents. There is a decreasing genetic diversity as distance increases from the Bering Strait. However, there is a higher level of diversity and lower-level populations in South America. The pattern suggests the Americas were colonized by small numbers of individuals (effective size about 70), which grew by a factor of 10 in 800 to 1,000 years. Her initial research study indicated that small populations entered the Americas 11,000 to 20,000 years BP. All the ancient mitochondrial lineage detected in this study were absent from modern data sets, suggesting a high extinction rate of these population groups at some time. The data related genetic diversity from 12 genetic groups, according to tribal DNA from the Bering Straits to Southern South America. Reviewed by map, these genetic codes look reminiscently similar to a phone system distribution map of area codes. As in telephone area codes, only a minor change in numbers indicates a new area. These maps depict the exact visualization related to DNA variation and genetic DNA area code maps. The concluding summary of this study supported Dr. Casey's theory that genetic variation in these geographical locations was more associated with alien sites of DNA genetic lab experiments. It was not indigenous people's migration over thousands of years. Instead, the early humans were placed in varied locations for evolution experimentation.

Samantha's research suggested the Clovis-first model is outdated; they weren't the first humans in North America. She found archaeological evidence of human occupation in South America at same time as the Clovis settlement. In other words, people were living in the Americas before the Clovis people arrived. Take the Clovis-first model, as the population starting point in America's of less than 100 people, and it would have taken from 700 to 1,000 years for their descendants to reach the southern tip of South America. It is unlikely that the Clovis people could have migrated that distance in less than 200 years. They didn't populate South America. Others did.

The migration and evolution of the human population in North and South America is disputed. From the research articles and academic papers, there are many questions regarding the source and disposition of various human population centers and the evolution within North and South America. There is no clear-cut evidence showing where nor when human habitation of North and South America began. The Clovis habitation existed after and along with other human habitations, both in North and South America. The idea that Clovis migrated out of Asia along the Bering Sea bridge is, at best, skeptical. The Bering Sea bridge is an example of how the entire Earth habitat was populated by human clients/specimens in an environmental missionary management program instituted by an alien source.

In essence, the Americas were populated via alien evolutionary manipulation and were located there as evolutionary genetic experiments.

These experiments consisted of DNA manipulation and then sped forward via evolutionary time manipulation. This management system allowed for examining thousands of years of evolutionary modification without the necessity of waiting out the excessively lengthy experiment timing. In other words, move forward into the future rapidly by time travel to decide the success or failure of anticipated results and manipulation of the genome.

From the early 1930s, archaeologists believed that the first colonizers of the New World were the Clovis people who migrated from Siberia across the Bering Strait into the Americas from 13,200 to 12,800 BP. The model lost acceptance after at least 30 other pre-Clovis sites were discovered in North and South America. Accurate Accelerator Mass Spectrometry (AMS) and Radiocarbon dating of stone tools, implements, and other surviving artifacts, have put to rest the priority of the Clovis-first theory. The Clovis site is outdated by 20 to 30 pre-Clovis habitation discoveries by up to 4,000 years.

Wikipedia
Evidence of human habitation pre-Clovis
Genetic DNA area code map, human habitation pre-Clovis.

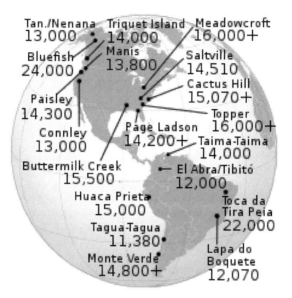

Listing of pre-Clovis sites and discovery date:
Archaeological sites that antedate Clovis:
Bluefish caves, Canada, 24,000 years BP 1977
Pedra Serata, Brazil,10,500 to 12,000 years BP 1973
Topper, South Carolina, 16,000 to 20,000 years BP 1980
Meadowcroft Rockshelter, Pennsylvania, 16,000 years BP 1950
Buttermilk Creek, Texas, 15,000 years BP 1998
Cactus Hill, Virginia, 15,070 years BP 2004
Monte Verde, Chile, 18,500 to 14,800 years BP 1975
Saltville, Virginia, 14,510 years BP 1978
Taima-Taima, Venezuela, 14,000 years BP 1964
Manis mastodon site, Washington, 13,800 years BP 1978
Connolly Caves, Oregon, 13,000 years BP 1994
Page-Ladson, Florida, 14,550 years BP 1983
Lapa do Boquete, Brazil, 12,070 years BP 1989
Paisley Caves, Oregon, 14,000 years BP 1930

CONSIDER MAN

Tanana Valley, Alaska 13,000 to 14,000 BP
El Abra, Columbia, 12,460 BP 1967
Nenana Valley, Alaska 12,000 years BP 1989
Tibito, Columbia 11,740 years BP
Tagua-Tagua, Chile, 11,380 years BP 1990
At least ten other sites are not listed.

* * * *

February 2013
The first Americans
Smithsonian,
The archaeology course book: an introduction to themes, sites,
methods and skills, Early Man
by Guy Gugliotta

At the Buttermilk Creek complex archaeological site north of Austin, Texas, in a layer of Earth beneath a known Clovis evacuation, researchers have found over 15,000 pre-Clovis artifacts–most of them toolmaking stone flakes. Researchers found that the oldest artifacts dated 15,500 years ago– Some 2000 years older than Clovis. The work confirms the emerging view that people occupied the Americas long before Clovis...

This new time frame requires the Siberian (Clovis) hunters to negotiate the ice-free corridor, settle two continents, put the megafauna on the road to extinction within 300 years, an incredible feat. Not possible. You have people in South America at the same time as Clovis, and the only way they could have gotten down there that fast is if they were transported like "Star Trek."

* * * *

Samantha French
Faux Grad Project
Conclusion:

Humankind shares a portion of Neanderthal's DNA in their genes; they are the closest extinct human relative. They lived in parts of Asia and Europe from 200,000 to 30,000 years ago. Genetic manipulation and management that coincide with time evolution easily explain Neanderthal's adaptation of tools and variations of social behavior, i.e., burying their dead, making tools, and certainly controlling fire. In the world of anthropology today, many of these topics are subject to speculation and conjecture; however, what if the experimenters were able to control the environmental evolutionary time sequence, i.e., speed up, and insert specific directives or instructions through evolutionary DNA triggers/management? Then, they could influence behavior and slowly achieve a particular pattern of behavior, i.e., toolmaking, fire, and other social interaction traits.

Nearly 80,000 years ago, there was a seismic reduction in the human population. Archeologists and others cannot determine the cause of the decline, but it wasn't random nor orderly; many died. In some scientific circles, they attribute extinction to a massive volcano eruption that pumped millions of micro-particles into the atmosphere blocking sunlight and heat. Freezing temperatures followed for years, severely affecting and reducing life on Earth with a decreased population survival.

In any laboratory where you are conducting experiments, the experimental subjects are likely destroyed after each investigation. This destruction is typical of standard laboratory protocol to sterilize, clean, and prepare the lab for the next experiment. Previous lab experiment results with DNA manipulation and time travel evolution are studied, analyzed, and then specific results are incorporated into the next subject of species experimentation. Then, the lab's management would undertake a cleansing and sterilization of the facility to eliminate cross-contamination of experiments that followed. Earth was the lab; a process to sterilize and eradicate prior experimental subject leftovers would occur [i.e., pre-human or previous human species.] The history of our Earth shows that there were several "Great Dyings." The exact process that eliminated the human species at different times is unclear. Some scientists say volcanic eruptions; others indicate gamma rays' presence to facilitate sterilization and eliminate the living matter. There are currently ancient layers of Earth's soil that have an unexplained presence of residual gamma radiation.

Human evolutionary progress from ape-like beings took an extended period. Man's inherited physical and behavioral traits evolved over thousands of years. The human species will continue to evolve as a response to a changing world: environmental, geographical, technological, and societal norms. For example, it is a standard dogma that humans 50,000 years ago navigated the world's oceans effectively. Some scholars believe there is evidence that these same homo sapiens traveled to Australia at that time without any navigation aids, sea training, or experience—an incredible feat.

Early humans came from the same location, and perhaps East Africa was used as a laboratory. The real reason for low genetic diversity is a DNA laboratory managed and operated by extraterrestrials involved in early Man's genetic and DNA manipulation, coupled with time travel evolution. In other words, lab operators synthetically developed and manipulated human DNA and fast-forwarded it through many generations via time travel. their observations or manipulations were based upon the results that they found. With these operating procedures, the lab managers and experimenters could observe their results almost instantaneously and then return to the lab to make adjustments within the experiment's subjects, i.e., early Man. Lab location Earth: greenhouse of human development, early Man then repotted in preselected environments. A combination of genetic evidence and fossil data has concluded that our species' first members evolved in eastern Africa 200,000 years ago. The same evidence appears in South Africa, Ethiopia, and elsewhere on the African continent, indicating no single region for human development. Effectively, these discoveries indicate there is no single Garden of Eden in Africa; in fact, the Garden of Eden would include the entire continent of Africa. It follows that the human species developed in isolation in different parts of Africa and elsewhere. However, aliens separated them into other regions without considering environmental conditions or their ability to independently establish diverse locations. These isolated human development locations were selected by an alien source to develop, monitor, and manage DNA environmental experimentation. Africa and other locations throughout the Earth were populated intentionally by an intelligent alien source managing the development and evolutionary transformation of the human race.

Samantha French
Legacy
2000-2022

With Dr. Casey's connection, she landed a graduate teaching position at San Diego State University while working on her Ph.D. After a short three-year tenure, she found no patience to interact with undergrad or grad students. In 2004 she left the academic culture to follow her search for evidence of alien evolutionary manipulation of mankind in her 2002 VW EuroVan. There were many established theories followed by little, if any, evidence. Samantha traveled over ten years to several early human sites in the Americas that she included in her Grad paper for Dr. Casey. She was fortunate her parents left a medium trust that allowed her to live outside of and off the grid in her EuroVan. The vehicle had, at the end of its' service life, over 800,000 miles when it died upon arrival at the New Mexico White Sands National Monument parking lot in 2014. She arrived there to study samples of fossilized animal footprints held within the museum collection. With her EuroVan dead, she called for roadside assistance from Triple-A; they were a day away. As it turned out, a day delay turned fortuitous and began a long-tenured adventure in the White Sands Desert. The monument's staff offered her EuroVan parking lot lodging for a night, and she stayed for years. That day and evening, both Sam and the monument staff shared their backgrounds and experiences. Sam had a long list of adventure-laden research travel and theories. Once the staff leadership found a world-traveled professional research doctorate of evolutionarily anthropology, with a master's degree in geology broken down in the parking lot, she was recruited on the spot. One call to the 95-year-old legend Dr. Casey sealed the position, which was vacant for a lack of applicants at a remote research site. Destiny for both parties. Samantha discovered a calling there and stayed on, first as a parking lot stranded visitor and soon after as an assistant research specialist. She literally followed ancient animal footprints that covered acres that were once a wetlands marsh thousands of years ago. The White Sands Dunes comprised predominantly of 275 square miles of gypsum crystals and thousands of fossilized footprints thousands of years old.

After years of research, Samantha French continued to believe that the diversions and differences within and among various human genomes were created purposely by outside influences. The alien arborist created the divergent path of human development or evolutionary processes in different habitats worldwide. In the September 2000 meeting with Dr. Casey, she expressed the opinion that coincided with his. The essence indicated aliens were experimenting with creating an animal that included humans. Aliens understood DNA genetics switching mechanisms and adjustments made over time, evidenced by a series of human prototypes worldwide. From her notes, she remembers commenting and responding to Dr. Casey that the human evolutionarily tree has been genetically grafted, water, watched over, and pruned by an alien genetic arborist. The alien nursery for the human evolutionarily saplings was Africa. Re-potting, grafting, and nurturing the human saplings took place both in and outside Africa throughout the's environments. She kept looking in the White Sands Desert Dunes for fossil footprints to prove it.

MAN 4
Heritage

Grant and Steve Fredericks were of mixed German-Mexican heritage dating back to when their German relatives settled in Texas under Spanish rule and began inter-marrying with the indigenous population. This goes back to the 1800s when their German relatives settled in Texas under Spanish rule. The first permanent settlement of Germans was in Austin County, established by a cousin, Ernst Fredericks, in the early 1830s. Ernst wrote a letter to a friend in his native Oldenburg. His description of Texas was influential in attracting more Germans to that area. Texas territory was a project of foreign colonization promoted during the Second Mexican Empire and Emperor Maximillian I of Mexico. The majority of these people were farmers and craftsmen: wheelwrights, shoemakers, cabinet makers.

Many Germans, especially Roman Catholics, left Texas for present-day Mexico after the U.S. defeated Mexico in the Mexican American War in 1848. Many gradually settled in Veracruz. Steve's and Grant's grandfather was born there in 1885. He moved to Mexicali in 1910, married, and had five children; the youngest was father to Grant and Steve.

Youth Years: Grant Fredericks
Grant Fredericks and siblings five boys and two sisters, grew up in the small town of Chula Vista, California. His childhood consisted of a free-range existence with vast untethered experiences, including boat building, dodging police, a mixture

of firearm encounters, and underage drinking. Grant was the third born son.

Those are the numbers, but the conditions of the family were far from sanguine. Grant's Mom, Katie, had a high school education. She was book-smart more so than her husband, Carlos. He chose not to recognize her as such. He was old-school Hispanic and thought a woman's place was in the home. That view set her on a path to rely on and abuse alcohol. Katie became an alcoholic long before her children left home. She drank not necessarily because she enjoyed it, but because her aspirations were stifled at every turn. Nearly any outward initiative she had was belittled; she lived for years in quiet desperation. She drank to even the score and almost died trying, surviving two drinking-related car crashes; one solo, another with Grant's very young sisters along … a time before seatbelts. She never drove again after the second one.

The kids were casualties of the marital conflict, abused by drunk and sober indifference. All of Grant's siblings left home at an early age. As an empty nester in her 50s, Katie managed to break out and train as a nurse's aide. She was good at it. Carlos came to rely on her income as his restaurant-bar wasn't profitable enough to support the household finances. She opened bank and savings accounts, but kept on drinking. Some things didn't change. Katie quit cold turkey the day after her husband died. It took 65 years in coming to be free of the alcohol escape, unfortunately her liver didn't.

For Grant, those formative years set the stage for his moral strength and character. From time to time, his experience as a youth faced with near-death situations molded his approach to life. At some point, he gave in to not controlling his life's direction with an affirmation that something else was the controlling feature of his destiny. In other words, Grant came to believe that something kept him out of harm's way throughout his life, though many times he came within a hair's breadth of fatal disasters.

Grant was always drawn to challenges, never knew exactly why. He was relatively fearless in approaching life in general.

Many children typically have fears about one thing or another—boogey-man-type concerns—but not Grant. He always had a cool, calm exterior for the most part; he listened before taking action. He would get angry from time to time; in recent years, it was mostly about his relationship with his wife and his children and their lack of direction. In essence, Grant tended to remain calm in stress-related situations, including being shot at while engaged in combat rescue operations.

Close encounters of several kinds

In the ninth grade, Grant began expanding and exploring his social network to include boys he met at school who didn't live in his neighborhood. Grant's home life was such that he wanted to escape his alcoholic mother and dysfunctional family. There was not much love and affection among Grant's four brothers, and though Grant had established a bond with his two infant sisters, he was their senior by 13 and 14 years. As Grant spread his wings beyond his family and neighborhood, he became close to a boy named Jackie.

Jackie perceived himself as a tough guy and ladies' man, even in the ninth grade. As it turned out, Jackie had an alcohol supply connection from a local Big Bear grocery store. He didn't buy the pints of Seagram's Seven. Instead, he shoplifted them from behind the counter while the clerk was distracted getting a cold Coke for Jackie from the back cooler. Jackie simply leaned over the counter and took the pint of Seagram's Seven, a heist that typically happened on Friday nights. Jackie, Grant, and several other boys would meet at somebody's house whose parents were gone. And then the boys, who weighed an average of 110 pounds each, would proceed to get lit on whiskey sours. That was Grant's introduction to alcohol abuse. He was 14.

As it turned out, Jackie never got over the party phase and graduated to other drugs. Fourteen years later, he was shot and killed by a navy sailor who dealt drugs. The crime had sexual overtones. Jackie made an aggressive move on the sailor's woman. He was twenty-eight.

In hindsight, Grant had some excellent times with Jackie. Others were crazy, fraught with danger, and close calls. Jackie's father carpooled to work and left the keys to his '56 Ford four-door sedan at home. Jackie would drive the car, again at age fourteen or fifteen, pick up Grant, and then drive around on back county dirt roads. Proctor Valley Road was close and easy to get to. One time, Jackie lost control and went sideways, nearly into a ditch. They managed to get the car clear of the ditch and returned it to Jackie's home, washed and cleaned it; his father never knew.

Grant's longtime occasional juvenile delinquent high school pals, Dwayne, Leo and Paul, including Jackie, would go to Tijuana and meet at the Hotel Nelson bar. The high school posse's attire clothing choices changed from cool dudes to college prep-like, khaki pants, low cut tennis and tighter fitting short sleeve shirts. The hotel bar was a regular stop on trips to TJ: small, dark, no music, no crowds, or hassle. House special was their drink of choice, rum and Coke. On one particular TJ trip Jackie, Paul, and Dwayne decided to take a taxi to a backcountry whorehouse. Grant and Leo were opposed, "I don't think that is a great idea," Grant protests. "Where is this place? I don't want to go." He had no interest in the carnal nature of the trip.

"Man, come on guys let's stay here." Leo had no interest at all. He and Grant were trying to short-circuit the trip with logic, a losing battle.

"Come on. It will be cool. Come with us," says Dwayne, the lead horn-dog pushing Paul and Jackie for backing. "You don't have to do anything. Just wait for us, then we'll make for the border."

Jackie adds, "It'll be OK. Just come with us. You don't have to do...you know?"

Paul doesn't say much, but throws in with Dwayne and Jackie. "Let's go do this; I'm ready for a little lady time," Paul says.

Grant still objects; he had no interest in the ladies of the night. He and Leo, outnumbered, relent. They didn't want to stay behind alone at Hotel Nelson. That view changed once the group arrived via taxi on a potholed dirt road at an out-of-town back-lot, poorly lit, rundown house of pleasure. The interior combination lobby and bar offered no amenities. There were no chairs or tables, only wooden benches along two walls, where scantily dressed women sat. There was a stained plywood floor. When the five boys entered, the women rose from the benches and approached, doing their very best to impress. Paul, Dwayne, and Jackie negotiated briefly and were led down two halls to individual parlor rooms. Leo and Grant used their limited Spanish language skills and turned down all offers. Both thought the worst was over.

The brothel visit went off without incident. Their teenage sex drive met, the three participants returned to the rundown lobby, where Leo and Grant had spent an unpleasant 30 minutes on a wooden lobby bench fighting off unsolicited offers by scantily dressed pleasure emporium staffers. It was after they left in the taxi, things turned to shit. Turns out, five teens, a bit drunk, in the cab wasn't a show of strength. They were only a couple of miles from downtown TJ but, without any sense of direction or location.

No one of this five-person brain trust knew how to get back to Hotel Nelson. At this point, the taxi driver decided to stop in the middle of nowhere and demand more money for the trip back to town. But, of course, nobody had any money. They had spent it at the brothel. The cab driver got out, stepped away, left his door open with Jackie riding shotgun. As the driver turned away from the door, Jackie harkened back to his car theft experience with his father's '56 Ford. Why not…engine running…open road ahead…no clue where we are…go for it! He reached for the column gearshift and attempted to put the taxi in gear…without using the clutch.

Grant and his fellow passengers were dumbfounded. In panicked whispers and hand motions, Grant says, "Jackie what the hell are you doing. Don't, don't!" It didn't discourage Jackie from attempting a solo taxi heist from the shotgun position. So, with the grinding of gears, the taxi driver understood that someone was trying to steal his taxi. He smartly kicks Jackie in the face with his right foot. Some words were exchanged, and the next thing Grant and crew knew, there is another individual, perhaps another taxi driver at the right rear passenger door holding a 38-caliber revolver to the head of Dwayne. There was a collective "Fuck" from the rear seat quartet. That kind of put a damper on the whole evening and instantly killed the alcohol buzz. The pissed-off taxi driver, whose name was Arturo, reiterated his request for an additional fee. He had found a convincing argument and additional leverage. Another subdued "Fuck" was a subtle response.

Grant, who had spent no money on prostitutes, had 20 bucks, a considerable sum in 1960 TJ, which he gave to Arturo, who drove them back to Hotel Nelson. Jackie sat still for the remainder of the trip. The back seat quartet, though thoroughly pissed at Jackie, was glad to have escaped with their lives. Jackie would not be riding shotgun anymore. Dumb shit move! Hopefully, Jackie would learn from this encounter and avoid situations that may involve firearms...time would tell.

Baja Cliff Jumping

Another trip south of the border, this time off road camping. Car sleeping and skin diving. Night arrival at an unknown location south of Tijuana on the coast after a stop off at Hotel Nelson. Someone knew some of the directions and location of the off-road site. No state park, just moonless night, pitch blackness illumination only by the car headlights.

Grant rides shotgun as one of his buddies drive the dirt road relatively fast for the blackout conditions. As the car's, load of alcohol-laced teens, heads toward a black cliff abyss, someone yells, "Stop!" Just in time.

Out of the car, and walking forward in the car's headlights for about 15 or 20 yards. As luck would have it, someone had a flashlight, and during the last several feet, the group saw a severe drop-off. It turns out had they not stopped and proceeded another 20 yards; they would have flown off a 130-foot cliff and ended up on the rocks at the shoreline. A near death leap; another bullet avoided...near miss.

* * * *

June 21, 2019
San Diego Union-Tribune
From the Archives
1969: Evel Knievel jumps at the Carlsbad Raceway
By Johnny McDonald
Evel Knievel, whose motorcycle jumping feats (and falls) had attracted world-wide attention, made his only San Diego County jumps in June of 1969...IT TAKES A LOT OF STEEL Cycle Act Cracks Him Up By Johnny McDonald. Handsome, limping and hurting Robert Craig Knievel is a Man of steel.

* * * *

GUNS

Grant and his brothers had access to firearms. The initial introduction was by Grant's father, Carlos, one Christmas in the late 1956. He gave Grant's two older brothers pump action 22 Remingtons. A real nice Christmas present. Grant never gets one. Anyway, that was the first introduction to firearms ownership and not necessarily firearm safety. The two Remington rifles were mounted in the boys' bedroom on a gun rack his oldest brother made in high school wood-shop; it actually was well-done. Back then, there were no requirements for locks, ammunition was available, and anyone could reach out and bring one down. Within a year or two after rifles were introduced into the household, one of Grant's best friends and neighbor was handling and cycling the pump-action, pulling the trigger, and on about the third or fourth time, the gun discharged into the roof. Grant and his friend weren't scared but were curious whether the round pierced the roof. So, the inquisitive teenagers scrambled to the roof over the bedroom and searched in vain for a .22-bullet hole. They found none. That whole scenario could have ended with the different trajectory of that 22 round and changed or ended Grant's or his friend's life. Good thing it wasn't a 12-gauge shotgun. Grant didn't know someone or something was looking out for this; some would say, ignorant teenager.

A few years later, Grant acquired a 7mm Mauser bolt action rifle. He and his friends were out in the East County of Chula Vista, shooting at random targets, including the exposed zinc-coated inner tank of a discarded water heater. Grant took aim from ten feet and fired; there was not enough power for the bullet to penetrate the metal tank, and it ricocheted off in some undetermined direction. A guiding hand apparently was involved in Grant's aim. Had it been a few degrees lower, the discharged round would have more than likely returned from whence it came, i.e., Grant. He once again avoided an inadvertent, accidental, dumb-shit shooting incident that could've ended his life or that of anyone near him.

Truck'n 'Roll

Wayne Gregg was a risk-taker in high school in a somewhat similar sense as Jackie. The difference was Jackie was arrogant and needed to prove himself to his friends. Wayne wasn't arrogant but self-confident; no need to prove anything. They pushed the envelope concerning obedience to authority and following the rules. When Wayne was in junior high school, his father died, and it seemed he was searching for something. In any case, he was laid-back, confident, and self-assured. It was the confidence and self-assuredness that almost got several of his friends killed, including Grant.

Wayne had a '56 hardtop convertible Chevy and access to other vehicles, and money wasn't a problem. One early summer evening, Wayne had six friends packed into his mother's work pickup truck. After her husband's death, she stepped up and ran the family roofing business. In the truck's bed were Grant, Robbie, Bob, and Wayne; Paul, and Mike were in the cab. Wayne, of course, was driving fast. The unusual part was that he was going fast on a recently cleared right away for electrical power lines. The terrain was up-and-down rolling hills. The texture of the Earth was nearly like sand with not a lot of traction. On this terrain, Wayne had the truck wound up to at least 50 mph.

Just after the crest of one of the hills, the terrain dropped down hill at about a 40-degree angle. So, it seemed. At that point,

Grant, from the truck bed, looked over the right side and realized they were in deep trouble because there was a significant change in terrain at the bottom of the hill. From a downslope to almost an immediate reverse upslope at the same angle. There was no gentle flat transition. Grant immediately knew this was going to be an *oh-shit* situation. Robbie was seated on the truck bed, arms extended with his back against the back of the cab. He had no idea what was about to happen. No clue. Bobby was on the left side of the truck bed, sitting on the wheel well. As the truck crested the hill and started down the other side, it was clear that slowing down was not possible. It only had the effect of causing the truck to begin swerving out of control. First left and then right. Wayne let off the gas, which had little or no effect on the downhill speed. Grant prepared himself for the collision with the uphill bank by holding on to one side of the truck bed railing and just behind the cabin window and flexing his knees to absorb any G forces during the change of direction at the bottom of the slope.

As the truck crossed from downslope to up, the front bumper dug into the opposite hill and threw dust, dirt, and debris 30 feet in the air. At impact, Robbie was thrown four feet into the air and came down flat on his back on the truck's bed. A number of his vertebrae cracked; he had to wear a walking cast for six months. Bob went airborne from his left wheel well position and found himself balanced precariously with his shins riding the top edge of the tailgate. Grant's cat-like positioning absorbed the shock of the impact. He was not hurt but covered with dirt. In the cab, no one was injured. Just covered with dirt and thankful that they didn't roll over and kill everyone. Another bullet avoided.

Hilltop

When Grant and his group were juniors in high school, Friday night alcohol events were still popular; however, several of the boys gathered in the parking lot of Hilltop High School on one particular Thursday night. Hilltop and Chula Vista High were playing a basketball game. The group in the parking lot included

Leo, Dwayne, Paul, Grant, and, of course, Wayne and some others who had been drinking.

For some reason, Jackie wasn't there. Since it wasn't a Friday night, the group was short of their alcohol supplier. The Friday night drinking club members who had alcohol sources were Dwayne, Paul, and Wayne. The trio had made short work of two twelve-packs of Olympia beer, one of the favorite brands back in the day. The Friday night drinking club had a reliable, shady, clearly breaking the law connection to an alcohol source in neighboring National City. "La Tienda" was a back street and reliable source of underage alcohol sales; no ID age checks. Cash sales were the accepted transaction language norm. The group used La Tienda as a backup source when they had transportation and money available. They had Wayne and his 1956 Chevy hardtop convertible. Dwayne and Paul, along with the wild one, Wayne driving, made the Tienda run earlier. All met in the Hilltop parking lot. Cigars and beer.

Grant and Leo, waiting for the others to arrive in Leo's father's work pickup truck. "There they are," Grant saw Wayne's car pull into the lot. They parked three spaces down beyond other vehicles next to the truck. Cigar smoke is rolling out the windows. Dwayne, riding shotgun, yells out the window. "Hey, Two-Can we have beer,"

Leo hears Dwayne, says to Grant, "Fuck me, They've been drinking," Leo earned the name 'Two-Can 'from his capacity to drink only two cans of beer before he was out of it. He claimed otherwise. However, the proof was in the drinking; Two-Can stuck.

"Where did they get beer?" Grant sees there may be an issue trying to get into the game. "Not cool," The arriving trio made their way to Leo's truck. "Where have you guys been?" Grant asked.

"We hit La Tienda and spent some time at Dwayne's," Paul explains.

Dwayne lived in a converted detached garage at his parents; it was a great meeting and drinking place. All the group spent time there over the last couple of years.

Wayne jumped into the bed of Leo's truck, cigar and beer in hand. Then, avoiding the Naugahyde cover, rolled back about two feet. He sat with his back to the tailgate. "Cool truck, Two-Can."

"We're going to have trouble getting Wayne into the game," Grant laments.

"Shit, let's go back to my place, there's beer there." Dwayne invites all.

"That sounds like a plan," Two-Can says. But unfortunately, timing is everything.

As it turns out, a Chula Vista police car entered the parking lot heading directly toward them: the contingent of cigar smoking, loud, cool dudes. Seeing the police car approaching, Two-can and Grant, the sober ones, had Wayne, clearly wasted, lie down underneath the pickup truck bed cover. "Wayne, slide under and be quiet."

The Naugahyde cover stretched taught, and they hoped Wayne would not be discovered; After several minutes of interrogation by Chula Vista PD, it looked as though the group would be dismissed and head for the game. The group's yes sir, no sir, polite as could be, seemed to have worked. So close. One of the more than thorough Chula Vista PD officers, as an afterthought, decided he should look under the pickup truck's bed cover. As he rolled the Naugahyde cover back a foot or two, he looked down and met the eyes of a cigar-smoking teenager that responded by saying, "Don't bug me, cop." Game over!

Soon after, all of the boys were placed in the back of two of Chula Vista's finest police cars. Dwayne, Grant, Paul, and, of course, Wayne were in one car with his still-lit cigar. Police search procedures were very different back then.

The three boys in the back seat with Wayne all thought they were in a bit of hot water. Wayne stoked the flames. During the short ride to the Chula Vista Police Department, Wayne asked the officer driving, "How much money would it take to stop and let us out?" There was no response, except all back seat heads turned toward Wayne. "Geez, Wayne; cool it," Paul said, not looking forward to facing his parents. Things went downhill from there.

Grant was the only one sober. While trying to act sober, the other boys attempted to keep Wayne quiet and not make things worse. Wayne, not having made any progress with the attempted bribe, decided to heat things up. He took a couple drags on his cigar, built a large ash, then purposely raked it across the metal wire cage partition. All dudes were open-mouth-stunned and couldn't speak. The burning ashes fell immediately behind and adjacent to the officer driving. He immediately pulled over, made a rapid exit, and brushed out any remaining ashes. The cool dudes had a very different opinion of Wayne from that night on. In hindsight, it was a comical situation unless you were in the backseat heading for the police department and a night of incarceration. In the end, parents took the juvenile delinquents home and appropriately dealt with them to varying degrees.

The next school day, Leo and Grant were summoned to Vice Principal Geyer's office. Lumping them in with their counterparts, Geyer said they had been drinking in the school parking lot and tried to cover it up with breath mints. Ironically that was the one night they weren't drinking. Their undeserved, punishment: season-long banishment from the track team.

Being booted from the track team in his junior year had an impact on Grant. As his senior season came about, Grant was more focused than ever to recapture what was lost the prior year. Grant worked hard on conditioning well before the season started. He focused on the high and low hurdles. Won most of his races during that year, and in the league finals, he won both hurdle races and the triple jump. The half mile relay team he ran for came in third. Stone-cold sober.

Blackie

Blackie. It must've been around 1957. Grant's family lived within walking distance to the San Diego Bay via a tidelands slough. One summer, Grant, Mike, and Jimmy his teenage neighbors, came up with the idea of building a boat to navigate the waterway outing to the south end of San Diego Bay. Grant and three neighbor boys drew up rough plans.

They gathered material from Grant's father's collection of lumber leftover from his twenty-year family home remodeling project. The boat was flat bottom rectangular shaped, 10ft by about 45 inches wide; the gunnels were about 18 inches, and three bench seats, middle, aft, and bow spread across it. It took them three and a half days to build a boat from scratch. They sealed the wood planks with cans of tar and twine and made quite a mess on the concrete patio. Grant's Dad made him clean it up with paint thinner, and gasoline.

It was painted black, oil-based paint, with "Blackie" in red on both sides. Mike had scrounged up a four-horsepower gas outboard motor and a single shot 22. He was prepared to take on any unsuspecting duck engagements. The three teens made the initial voyage via the slough to the south end of San Diego Bay. Unfortunately, the boat was not remarkably stable, and if they had run into any winds or waves of any significance, they probably would have been swamped. As luck would have it, Blackie's encounter with a slight wave sent Mike, off-balance, firing a .22 round into the front seat between Grant and his best friend, Jimmy. That was the last time they took the .22 on Blackie.

In any case, it was quite an accomplishment for three teenagers at the time. They had to haul the boat a quarter mile to the water and stored it underneath a road overpass adjacent to the slough. The slough, at high tide, was only about fifteen to twenty feet wide and maybe two or three feet deep, and it ran about a quarter-mile to the entrance of the bay. A very barren landscape bordered it, low shrub chaparral bushes not much to look at, and few trees. Their great boat-building achievement, though, didn't last two weeks. They found that somebody had destroyed the boat, kicked out the sides, and dropped large boulders through the bottom within a few days. The boat builders always suspected one of the neighbor kids. Don't know if anybody asked him if he did it, but the evidence seemed to point toward this individual. He was a bit of an outsider and had some strange habits. His habits included taking women's clothing, specifically underwear, off outside clotheslines, breaking and entering businesses and homes. Turns out later in life, this neighborhood acquaintance, i.e., a friend, ended up being convicted of serial murders along highway 5 and 99 in the Central Valley. He picked up prostitutes and the occasional unsuspecting individual female, knocked them unconscious in his vehicle with a short iron pipe, sexually assaulted and strangled them, cut off their clothes, and dumped the bodies like highway litter. Grant had no idea who he was growing up with. He found out this neighbor from three doors down was an eight-time serial killer while watching a criminal documentary many years later. There on the screen was his one-time teenage neighbor sitting at the defense table in a courtroom. Grant recognized a nervous twitch his neighbor had even as a boy...touching his face with his three fingers. He knew him immediately. His one-time teenage neighbor negotiated a plea bargain to avoid a death sentence; eventually, his sentence, life without parole, seven times for eight murders. Died there in 2021. Neighbor kid third house down the street.

Criminal Friends

Joe Harris was a junior high friend. Joe was just one of the guys, not very big, and could be funny at times. Grant's group would have classified him as a "cool dude," they all were "cool dudes" in the ninth grade. Grant didn't know much about Joe, except what he knew about him at school. They interacted in the school environment with the same group of guys. He was not a bully, just a cool dude. So, it was a shock to the rest of the cool dudes when they came to school one day and found out that Joe had murdered his invalid sister and mother. Beat them both to death with a bat. Not cool, Dude. Joe ended up on death row and, at some point during his incarceration, murdered his cellmate, Joe, a real "cool dude."

One family at Grant's family's Lutheran Church had a father figure that seemed rather strict. The Dad didn't smile much and seemed to be in a foul mood most of the time from Grant's observation. Yet, it came as a surprise to Grant and the whole congregation when the eldest son bludgeoned to death his entire family. Grant never did figure out what went wrong or why the eldest son killed his family. So, the tally of criminals in Grant's background includes: a neighbor who would turn serial rapist-murderer, a member of his church who terminated his entire family, and an unassuming cool dude from junior high killing his invalid sister and mother.

Teenage Impact

The night at beach cliffs in Mexico, the Tijuana taxi incident, boating on San Diego Bay, riding in the back of a pickup truck, had a subtle impact on Grant not to try so hard to control his life direction. He believed that a force beyond him controlled and directed his life journey, be it God or some other unexplained source. Grant grew up with different sources of tragedy around. He had a hard-nosed sense of survival within his family, growing up without a lot of love or compassion. His older brothers didn't care for him. He was the only athlete in the family and was successful at it. None of his siblings were so gifted. His adolescent home life allowed and forced him to develop an independent strategy for social development and character building. He forged a survival strategy separate and beyond one encased within the mold of quiet desperation. He was forced to develop a survival strategy independent of any semblance of a close-knit family unit. Though he was not close with his older brothers, he wanted to be. He was closer with his younger brother Steve, who looked up to him, and Grant gave him recognition.

All of his youthful experiences had made him accustomed to remaining calm in the presence of the unknown and, in some cases, dangerous circumstances. It came from a sense of a destiny controlled by some other force. He had looked for inner peace without knowing precisely the direction of his life. Others controlled life events while Grant was a participant in the script, but not the scriptwriter.

MAN 5

Grant, Steve, and Becky

Grant and Becky met in the seventh grade. They married two years out of high school. Becky worked as an administrative assistant at a local community college, and Grant was looking to teach at the high school level. He was working on a degree in finance and enrolled in the teaching credential program during the Spring semester of 1965 at San Diego State College.

It seemed to be going well until he student taught 9th-grade geography for two weeks. Grant determined he had made a career error...he didn't hate the kids exactly but wanted nothing to do with them. In addition, he realized that the teaching environment was not what he had envisioned. The 9th graders weren't much interested in the learning process and couldn't care less about the geopolitical climate of Eastern Europe. Nevertheless, they did well at lunch. Alternatively, Grant took his degree and found employment at a local aerospace firm until the Spring of 1966.

Becky and Grant had discussed the military since he being draft-eligible once graduating from college and could be drafted at any time. Grant thought going into the Air Force was a better option than the Army or Marine Corps and a one-way ticket to Vietnam carrying a rifle.

Soon after graduating from college, Grant looked to the Air Force and perhaps officer training school and pilot training. He and a classmate while in high school tested for the Air Force Academy. Grant didn't make the cut; his friend did. Becky wasn't on board. She had a vision of the future that had them staying in Chula Vista, raising a family. She had an extensive close-knit family in Chula Vista. On her mother's side, she had aunts, uncles, and cousins. They all grew up together. Becky's vision didn't include leaving the hometown for an unknown future as an air force wife. Becky knew Grant was testing for the commissioning program through the Air Force recruiting service. If selected for Air Force Officer Training, they then had to choose: accept the offer or roll the dice on the military draft. Grant said he was going to select the Air Force to fulfill his military obligation.

Becky was unhappy and threatened to leave Grant over the issue and move back home with her parents. She was leaving that night, was throwing clothes into a suitcase; then remembered she had to go to work the next day. She unpacked.

He was accepted to USAF Officer Training School, Becky didn't leave him, and the day after he left for San Antonio, his draft notice arrived in the mail. Grant by then was in the Air Force. He and his brother, Steve, both ended up serving in Vietnam simultaneously, 1969 through 1970. Steve flew combat operations for the US Army as a Cobra gunship pilot, call sign Banshee 21. Grant flew combat rescue for the Air Force in Jolly Green Giant helicopters. Both brothers were shot at when they flew.

1987

Grant Fredericks retired as an Air Force officer, while his brother, Steve, was retired Army. Both brothers served over 20 years and are troubled men. After Grant retired from the Air Force, he was led into the mortgage business by his prosperous mortgage broker neighbor. Since he didn't have any pre-planned post-retirement work plans, he opted to try the mortgage lending agent route. Turns out, he was moderately successful at it, yet he had a real distaste for working with real estate agents. He was often confronted and challenged by prospective homebuyers' dreadful credit scores and their real estate agent's insistence that the loan be approved to close the deal.

Their military background and mindset conflicted with the private business world for both Grant and his brother, Steve.

They were both combat veterans and understood that "your word was more than your bond." It could mean life or death for them and, more importantly, for others. In the civilian environment, they found that an individual's word meant far less. Both Fredericks' brothers didn't cotton to civilian business ethics. Thus, although they kept their word, those they encountered out of the military constantly challenged their patience.

Grant and Becky's daughter, Deana, has pushed Grant to the edge of what he considered sanity due to her meth addiction and incarceration for human trafficking. As a child through her teens she was an excellent student and exhibited exceptional skills both athletically and academic. It was in college where she was introduced to methamphetamine as a recreational outlet. The meth took over her life. She turned away from family, friends and after repeated treatment interventions she chose drugs over everyone. Grant and Becky have a difficult time comprehending how their one daughter would sacrifice everything for drugs and being involved indirectly with human trafficking. She is in her 40s; they see no way out for her. Her condition and addiction have led them into an existence of quiet desperation... Grant sees no way out for the both of them. Becky and Grant are damaged emotional goods. Grant left mortgage banking due to the stress of Deana's activities and the typical concentration required in that financial arena. He made errors, significant ones. He lost the touch for the business and confidence. Deana's addiction sidetracked his focus to personal objectives, seemingly out of reach.

Steve Fredericks trained as a diesel mechanic after his army retirement. It was his way of avoiding business dealings with the folks he didn't care for. Steve had leverage as a mechanic. In that line of work, he quite frankly didn't give a shit what anyone thought. He married three times, got prostate cancer, received an Agent Orange category 100% disability and nearly $40,000 a year tax-free from the VA. Your classic good news, bad news, and you're going to die. Flying helicopters was bad on Grant's back and hearing. He had a 40% disability and a small tax-free deduction. Agent Orange kills you slowly but pays much better.

They both had problems. Steve was cantankerous all the time, and he understood he had bought and paid for the ticket to the show. He was Grant's younger brother by five years. No family lived nearby besides Grant's; he enjoyed mountain biking and, like Grant, was very opinionated. Over the years, he had a drinking problem and dabbled with marijuana and other controlled substances. Actually, he had a number of LSD acid trip experiences. He stopped cold turkey several years ago when a bad trip scared him sober. Does talk about it, other than comments that tripping and especially bad tripping could kill you. He knew trippers that died confident that they could handle acid trip travel conditions. Big mistake on their part, actually a deadly mistake.

He had few friends, none very close. He had a distant relationship with his only son. Nevertheless, he accepted his fate and position, unafraid of any challenge. His third wife is a Korean national and lives in South Korea. A different kind of arrangement.

Grant was unsettled, trying to find answers to his life's drama and a clearer understanding of where it was all going. Of the two brothers, only Grant was seeking any psychological assistance. He was seeing a clinical psychologist for little more than a year to sort through the occasional depressive episodes brought on by his desperate concern for Deana and a man he left stranded, drowning, during a Vietnam night rescue mission; the man died.

He has always felt an inadequacy in his professional and personal life. He had made a decent income over the years, but for some reason, it doesn't seem to satisfy some need he had. His wife, Becky, who didn't bother to hide her feelings, something was missing in their relationship. In addition, their two children were up and gone, out of the home for some years.

Both went to college to complete some sort of nondescript degree. One made it. Deana didn't. She majored in addiction. Their son, Fred a long-haul truck driver they see a couple of times a year; has no lasting significant relationship and no prospects that Becky and Grant know of. They remain in contact with him through long-distance phone conversations a couple of times per month. There are no grandchildren and not many prospects for any.

From Grant's perspective, it seemed he was going through the motions of a quality marriage when in fact, it was a comfortable routine relationship. Their modest home was in East San Diego County in the city of Santee. Santee offered nearby access to mountain biking, which Grant and Steve took up several years ago. Mountain biking for Grant provided solitude away from the stress of business, family, and regrets. On most occasions, he would typically ride alone or sometimes with his brother Steve. Grant usually wore a Go-pro on his helmet to record his mountain biking exploits.

Fall 2010
Elfin Forest Dream

Grant is solo hiking coming up a bike path. He is without his mountain bike and doesn't know why. Just hiking gear, has trekking poles, a broad brim hat, a small backpack; listening to an iPod. He comes upon a teenage girl, dressed in odd attire, sitting on a bench that he doesn't remember being there ever. He is puzzled, curious, and disappointed. He thought he was near the end of the trek, not just starting. Now a girl out of place.

The girl says, "Was your walk enjoyable this morning?"

Grant struggles to remove his earphones. "I'm sorry. I didn't hear what you said."

The girl says, "I said how was your walk this morning, did you enjoy it?"

Grant looks quizzically at how she was dressed: a long skirt, saddle oxford shoes, a scarf covering her hair. Not exactly what you would find hiking trails these days. "It wasn't bad. Great day for a hike out here." Grant was the only one on the trail.

"I didn't meet anybody else on the trail either. You'd think more people would be out here on such a nice day."

Grant wonders how she could have come that far dressed that way, very strange. "Did you come up the Way Up Trail? It was difficult in a few spots with the rockslide from the rain last week." That trail was miles away from where they were.

Composed and fresh after a 4.5-mile trek. "It wasn't that difficult for me to get here. I tend to travel light and fast." The girl says.

Grant is puzzled, "Well you are certainly traveling light. When did you start out?"

"I started a little bit before you, guess you didn't see me."

Grant, still puzzled, "There were no other cars in the lot." The parking lot was empty.

"I don't drive. Are you doing the rest of the trail?" She replies.

Grant, perplexed and still wondering. "Yes, then back down to the trail head."

"Mind if I walk along with you?"

He's not wanting company, likes being alone, but his plans are changing. "No, that would be...that would be great. By the way, what is your name? Mine's Grant."

"I am called JD."

"Have you hiked this trail before? You look really familiar to me."

"No, this is the first time I've been here, but I find it peaceful and quiet."

Grant says, "Yes, it is that. Expected more people out today. I have to say the way you're dressed seems out of place for hiking."

"It may be a bit dated, but I like it."

She seems young, around sixteen or seventeen. "So tell me JD what is it that you do? Are you a student?"

"Well, I do make it a habit of studying things, people in particular."

She's so young. "Oh, I see, study people's cultures and ethnicity?"

"Well not exactly. I'm more focused on individuals."

They are now, suddenly, on a much rougher trail covered with rocks. Grant has to use his trekking polls while JD glides effortlessly through the same trail conditions. "So you study individuals. What is it that you are hoping to learn or find out from these people?"

"You could say I do observations, monitor people in their relationships."

"Monitor people in their relationships? You sound like a private investigator."

"I am more of a guide than investigator," She says.

Slowly Grant responds, "I get it, then, you're a counselor of some sort?"

"Well, I would say more like a trail guide."

"Who are the people that you observe? Guide? Do you work for a company or some organization?"

"The people that I work with have a diverse background. They generally have a need. I get them to a solution in most cases."

"So tell me how long have you been doing it?" Grant does not believe her. "Is it working with people with drugs or alcohol issues?"

JD is very matter-of-fact. "I've been around for sometime. No...no drugs...no alcohol."

"Around for a long time? You look like you're no older than sixteen or seventeen."

"I am much more experienced than you would think."

The trail now abruptly is uphill. Grant, short of breath, struggles to catch his breath and speak at the same time. JD has no problem with either. "What is your background training? Where did you go to school?"

"Schooling is really not important for what I do."

"Don't you have to have some sort of license to practice your trade, your guidance counseling, or whatever it is?"

"No, I really don't require a license."

"No schooling? No license? And yet you look like you're not even out of high school."

JD sets the hook. "Well, I am long out of a high school."

Grant takes the bait, "Where did you go to high school, at least where was that?"

Expecting a reaction, JD says, "It was here fairly local, Hilltop High."

"Hilltop High in Chula Vista?" Grant asks.

"Yes."

Grant is now very interested. He knew a lot of people from Hilltop High. "When did you graduate?"

"I didn't graduate."

"Where did you finish high school?"

"I didn't finish anywhere."

"You didn't finish?" Grant is curious now.

JD moves ahead of Grant. "I was involved in an automobile accident. There were two of us in the car stopped at an intersection. She started, my friend, started across the street, pulled out and didn't see the other car approaching."

"How bad was it? You seem OK now?"

"Sandra wasn't hurt at all. I suffered some injuries and didn't return to school. Everything is OK now."

"When did the accident happen? I mean, were you freshmen or sophomores?"

"It was October of our senior year."

They are now at the trailhead parking lot. Other people in the lot are gathered around listening to a group playing "Boot Scoot Boogie," it's Brooks and Dunn. Grant often listens to them while biking or hiking.

"By the way, what does JD stand for? And what year would you have graduated?"

"Judy Dupree, but JD seems to work just as well. The year was 1961."

"Do you mean 1991?"

"No, it was the '61 graduation I missed. Sandra was there but not me."

They are now over a shallow stream on a small concrete bridge. JD is at the railing, looking down at the water. Grant approaches her. There are a few hikers beyond the bridge heading up the trail. JD does not look at him. Grant looks around at the scene and the other people with the Brooks and Dunn background music. Grant is visibly angry he knew Judy Dupree; they went to high school together. He went to her memorial service in October 1961 after her tragic T-bone intersection collision killing her instantly. "All right, JD, or whoever you are, who put you up to this? Judy Dupree? Yeah, this is a really strange joke. Someone has gone to a lot of trouble to make you look like her and go through all of this. Where are they?"

"No one. Only you and I are here." Grant turns around the parking lot is now empty. "Remember on the trail I said I was somewhat of a guide. I know you have a hard time understanding it. There are some things I need to show you. Look over the rail down at the water."

Grant is next to JD, reluctantly looks over the railing down toward the water. The water is very slow-moving. There is a clear reflection of Grant. There's no reflection of JD. Impatiently, he looks again, "All right. What was I supposed to have seen? The water is clear, but wouldn't drink it, so what?"

"You need to look again. It's right there on the surface."

"There's nothing on the surface, no leaves nothing. It's smooth as glass and my reflection."

"Then you saw it? Our reflection?" JD asks.

"Yes, our reflection so what?"

"Our reflection. Did you see it?" She asks again.

Grant looks down at the water again. Then back and forth several times between JD and the water below. "Of course, you're right next to me. Shit! Shit! How are you doing that? Shit!" He looks at JD with a strange and perplexed face of astonishment; he turns and looks around for her accomplices.

"I told you: I travel light and fast."

"It's a trick, I don't know how you're doing it, but it's a trick. It's got to be."

JD walks further into the sunlight on the bridge. "No tricks. Look at my shadow. Do you see my shadow?"

In the empty parking lot, Rascal Flatts music has taken over from Brooks & Dunn. "No." From up the trail comes the sounds of mountain bikes traveling downhill. In rapid succession, the three bikers pass over the bridge and through the spot where JD is standing. Grant couldn't move to help her. He seems to be in a sluggish state, almost like a dream.

JD, untouched by the mountain bikers, says, "It's no trick. This is who I am."

He thinks this must be a dream. It couldn't be real. Grant is openly perplexed, mildly convinced, but unable to fully understand. "So why are you here?"

"As I said earlier, I am a guide. In many cases, I facilitate the resolution process to solve unanswered issues. You came to my attention a few weeks back. There seems to be an issue you have that could use my guidance."

Grant takes a step forward and looks directly into JD's brown eyes. He recalls they were one of her many favorable features, beautiful and captivating, coupled with a determined, forceful personality uncommon in the 1960s. Grant has his breath taken away. He realizes she is the very girl he remembers. She confronts him now. And Grant responds, "Issue? What Issue?" He is grabbing at straws, "OK, so I've been unemployed for two years and my painting career has gone nowhere is that where this is going? That what this is about? Becky send you? Oh this is nuts! I don't believe this."

"No I don't do employment screening, but there must be something going on, or I wouldn't be here. You came to my attention after a dinner at your brother-in-law's last Thanksgiving. There was a question asked that evening."

"The question about who you would want to spend the day with? Someone that had passed away, bring them back for a day? That question?" Grant clearly recalls the night when it was asked. He didn't have an answer then or, more correctly, wondered why anyone would want to re-enter this world when he was looking to leave it.

"Yes, what was your answer?"

Loudly, "I don't think I had one." He backs away from JD, hands extended in frustration. Looks for an exit point now from the Four Corners trailhead parking lot. There is no music.

I assume you still don't have an answer or anyone in mind." She said, "Why is that?"

74

"I don't...I don't...I couldn't think of anyone. I know a lot of people that aren't around anymore." Then, very loudly, "I don't know. Why would anyone want to return to this? Any of this? I wouldn't!"

JD comes on with an equal response. "No one stood out? family? friends? Vietnam?"

"They all stood out in one way or another. This is why you are here? An answer to a parlor game question? Aren't there more important things that could use your assistance? Why me?"

"It isn't a game. Some things are better not left undone, unfinished. You are involved in the process."

"And this is one of the something undone?" Grant is feeling the pressure. "You do this often?"

Matter-of-factly, JD responds. "Yes, this is some unfinished business, and it's not done often. Only when needed."

"Needed?" Dumbfounded, he says, "Holy shit. I don't need this now."

After waiting a bit, JD asks, "Who would you choose if you have to?"

"Choose only one?"

"Only one," she says, "How would you do it?" JD is following Grant around the empty lot as if he is searching for an answer or escape route.

"How do I know? There's got to be a couple dozen I could choose from." Then, still waving his arms in frustration, avoiding JD's eyes.

"I have confidence you'll make the right choice." JD stops next to Grant as he is chucking rocks over the empty bandstand.

It is the same question from last Thanksgiving. Steve asked Grant recently if he had anyone in mind for the return visit. He didn't answer it then, and he's struggling with it now. "How are you supposed to make that judgment? They're all different."

"Yes, they are all different, but you have experience with all of them."

"Some of these people I haven't seen in over 30 or 40 years."

"That's true. You'll have to refresh your memory."

"Just how am I supposed to do that? Google them on dead people I used to know?"

JD's eyes widened excitedly. Then, she says, "How about treat it like auditions. Tryouts, interviews? That could work."

"Great," Grant throws his hands up in the air, "Casting call for the dead. American Idol the post mortem version. If you're dead you're in."

"I'm glad to see you're on board with this! I'm sure this will work."

"And just how will this work?" Grant is more than skeptical and wonders why the music stopped. He sees two people sitting in lawn chairs on the bandstand, Willie Nelson and his son, Lukas, wearing a Belly Up t-shirt. They're not singing. There is no audience.

"Simple. You'll interact with them. You will judge for yourself."

Bob Marley and The Wailers are now featured playing "Exodus" on the parking lot bandstand. "Where? Will anyone else know about this? What am I supposed to ask?"

"Won't be a specific meeting place if that's what you're getting at. No one else will know about this unless you tell them. The questions you ask are up to you."

"How many people are we talking about?" Grant is searching for an answer.

"I don't know. It's up to you." JD fixes her hair into a ponytail.

"Really?! And when is the parade of the dead supposed to start?"

"Soon."

"Today?"

"Maybe."

"I don't know, I just don't know if I've can do this. I got to be hallucinating." Grant gets the sense that JD is about to leave.

"Well, you're not hallucinating this is real. I think I'm about done here for today."

Grant is nearly in a panic, moves closer to JD. Doesn't want her to leave and be alone. "I'm not ready for this. You can't leave,

I have questions. How long will this take? What if no one shows?"

"Trust me they'll show." She is serious. Stone-cold sober. "It'll last until it's done."

"How...How do I explain this to...Anyone? I..."

"Good question, let me know what you come up with. When you wake up."

JD turns to walk away. Her image begins to fade. Grant starts after her. But then he falls out of bed. He's alone on the floor with puzzled thoughts, unsure of what just happened. It was so real. JD, the hike, the heat, the music...he can still hear it.

"Are you OK?" This is not the first time Becky has asked that question. "What were you dreaming of this time? Who is JD?"

Fumbling for an answer. Grant says, "Just hiked a trail and fell" He didn't add he was accompanied by a classmate that died some fifty years prior, no older than seventeen, her age when she died.

"Well, you were yelling some foul language in your sleep. Your dreaming episodes seem to be an issue to take up with Dr. Denard." Grant climbs back in bed with a Marley tune playing in his head

Grant and Becky Fredericks

Grant and Becky move into their living room, relaxing after a barbecue steak dinner and finishing kitchen chores they share. The barbecue meal still fills the air as they sit in twin lazy-boy leather recliner rockers. They settle into a routine of watching news reporting, turmoil in Mexico with drug cartel repression going on. Hundreds of people were killed involved with drug trafficking. Becky is playing Words-With-Friends on her iPhone.

"Who was the first person that died that you knew?" Grant asks.

"What do you mean?"

"Well, when you were growing up did anybody you know die?"

"I don't remember anybody dying when I was young. Who do you remember?"

"My uncle, Dad's brother, he died. I was about 10. There was a boy from our church that accidentally shot himself. He was about 13, I think. Our best Man, Dwayne, had a heart attack at the Mexico City airport...not a kid though."

"I don't remember any when I was younger, Dwayne was our age...not healthy at all." Becky says, still focused on Words-With-Friends.

"Your grandmother," Grant remembers.

"My grandfather died before her. She was 96."

"That's right."

"Why are you asking?" Becky is mildly interested.

"I was curious. Been thinking about it some...and the question last Thanksgiving about bringing someone back who died. Spend the day with them." Although he is perplexed with the question that has lingered with him for some time, he can't determine a definitive answer or why.

Becky is not listening. "Ha, ha, I just got seventy-two points on Train Wreck." Nodding and laughing, she adds, "So sad, so sad."

"That's Jolene, right?" Grant asks, "You didn't know anyone that died while you were in school?" Grant asks again.

"No, I really don't remember any."

"Judy Dupree died when we were seniors. Car accident." Judy retold the story in a dream sequence just the other night, Grant thinks.

"I didn't know her. Did she go to Hilltop?"

"She went there after our sophomore year." In his dream, she hadn't changed at all over the years. "We really had different friends." Grant had been wondering about his JD dream and its forecast. Where is it taking him?

"Your friends were the weird ones," says Becky, pointing her iPhone at Grant.

"What do you mean, weird? Who?"

"Your neighbor. Didn't he become a serial killer?" Becky now caught his attention.

"Well, yeah, the I-5 Strangler, but he wasn't my friend. We just grew up on the same block. He graduated two years before us. He was strange. He broke into places, showed us how to smudge fingerprints—really helpful hints for the criminal-minded."

"How many people did he kill? Six or seven?" Becky is back to her iPhone.

"I don't know. I didn't know he was even in prison until I saw him on "Unsolved Mysteries" or something like that. I guess it all fit. Strange guy."

"So you grew up on the same block with a future serial killer?"

"I guess, Grant says, then exclaims, "Now I remember! In junior high. Do you remember Joe Harris?"

"No, I don't."

"Don't you remember? He killed his mother and invalid sister when we were in the ninth grade? He was sentenced to life. What were we, 14 or 15 then? Then he killed another prisoner, his cellmate. He was a little guy. Quiet. Got along with all of us. It was a total surprise when we heard about it."

"See, your friends *were* weird." Becky doesn't bother to look up from Words-With-Friends.

"There was a kid from our church that killed his family. That was strange. I didn't know him. Only saw him at church."

"As I recall, you were happy to date me back then."

"I didn't know what I was getting into. Then it was too late. There were no background checks then." She drops her head in mock disappointment.

Grant, almost hurt, says, "That is really cold. Do you remember Jackie Turner? He's the one in junior high that would get us guys liquor on Friday nights."

"I remember Jackie." Becky didn't know Jackie or his relationship with Grant in junior high. "He seemed like a nice guy."

Grant says, "I did a lot of things with Jackie. He thought he was like a cowboy lover."

"I remember he didn't make our ten-year reunion. I think he died," Becky says.

"That's right, I remember now. Leo said he was shot by a jealous husband running out the back door and jumping over a fence. Something like that."

"Well, I don't know if that's true."

"I wonder. How you'd find out?"

"Find out what? If he was shot?" Becky asks, wondering why.

"Yeah, where would you look?"

"I don't know. What does it matter anyway?"

"I'm curious how it all went down," Grant says. In an earlier dream, Jackie and Dwayne made an appearance. But it didn't provide an answer of how Jackie died.

"Sounds like a jealous husband caught up with him."

Grant still wondering, "Maybe...Leo really didn't have any details."

Becky gets up and gathers her things: knitting bag, purse, keys, and heads for the door. "Well, whatever. I'm going to Knit-Wits tonight. There are leftovers in the fridge."

"Great. Are the brownies for the Knit-Wits?"

"Yes. I'll leave you a couple. You need to eat something besides brownies. Are you going biking in the morning? Back to that mountain, Corte whatever, with Steve? Becky is not a fan of their mountain biking trips.

"Planning on it. If he shows up."

Isn't that Corte place near Pine Valley where there was an earthquake two days ago?"

Grant follows up confidently, "It is. It was only a 5.8, not much to worry about. Could have blocked a trail. We're riding mountain bikes. Can handle rough trails. At worst, we turn around. Nothing to be concerned about."

Grant didn't know it yet, but Steve isn't going to show, and Grant is in store for a life-altering adventure.

MAN 6

20:30 hours
June 6, 1970
AIR FORCE OPERATIONS CENTER
Da Nang Air Force Base, Republic of South Vietnam

The operation center was co-located inside a large aircraft hangar, with the 37th Aerospace Rescue and Recovery Squadron, 37th ARRS. The squadron helicopters consisted of HH-3E and HH-53 helicopters. The 53s were the latest upgraded version with more power, speed, and armor. The operations center itself consisted of about 2,000 square feet. There was a cramped briefing room for preflight mission planning equipped with maps, chalkboards, tables, and chairs. The critical components of the operations center, in space about the size of a walk-in closet, were behind an eight-foot-long, chest-high counter. Mounted on the walls were clear back-lit grease boards, maps, several radios, and phones. It was a compact radio communications center that allowed the duty staff and non-flying crews to follow rescue and combat operation via several radio frequencies, UHF, VHF, HF. The radio transmission were piped in throughout the squadron facilities both operations and maintenance offices. The duty officers monitored operational conditions and notices of impending rescue requirements. In addition, they maintained constant radio contact with all Jolly crews while executing any airborne operations.

Any rescue requests were funneled through the duty officers' communication network. They gathered as much information as possible before and after the rescue crews were notified of a mission request. Once the operational rescue request was verified and authorized, the duty officers would notify the Jolly Green crews that were on alert. The individual alert crews consisted of two pilots, a flight engineer, and one or two pararescuemen. There were typically four helicopters ready and "cocked" for an immediate or scrambled takeoff. The Jolly Green crews could be airborne within minutes when the scramble takeoff alert claxton was set off by the duty officers. Before any launch, the Jolly crews would receive an operational briefing from the duty officer. The briefing could be very short, however succinct. Often the crews would launch and receive additional operations guidance or conditions while en-route.

The counter was usually vacant, except during rescue operations when it became a crowded gathering place for all Jolly Green personnel to monitor, over external speakers, active Jolly combat radio transmissions.

Behind the operations counter, an Air Force Captain is the night duty officer. He is briefing four Air Force pilots and crews about a night rescue mission they are about to fly. The duty officer says, "You are being scrambled for a 119-gunship crew who bailed out thirty to forty minutes ago. There are ten of them; they may be all in the water."

Captain Hoilman, one of the pilots, asks, "Where did they bail out?"

"They were basically overhead between here and Marble Mountain, off China Beach and Monkey Mountain. They were heading almost due east. Runaway prop, I'm told."

"Why didn't they just land here? Why bail out?"

"Beats the shit out of me. You can ask 'em when you pick 'em up."

The copilot asks, "What is their bailout call sign?" A bailout call sign for aircrew members is typically designated with the aircraft call sign. For a two-seat aircraft call sign, the pilot would be alpha and the copilot bravo. The AC-119 gunship call sign was Lemon 2-1; it had a crew of ten, a numeric system rather than an alphabetic one was used.

"Their call signs are Lemon 0-1 for the pilot, Lemon 0-2 for the copilot, through Lemon 1-0 for the rest of the crew." The duty officer was very efficient.

"Really should be close if they bailed out off Marble Mountain. Shouldn't be any ground fire tonight. Feet wet or fuck 'em." The flight engineer of the Jolly crew's spoke out, an attempt at dark humor. Poor attempt.

The Duty Officer responds, "Vice Squad is On-Scene Commander and dropping flares." Vice Squad was an Airborne Battlefield Command and Control Center (ABCCC) based on a basic C-130E fixed-wing aircraft platform. It provided tactical airborne command post capabilities to air commanders and ground commanders in low air threat environments. "They have radio contact with a number of the crew in the water. They are one to two miles off China Beach. Maybe some landed on Monkey Mountain. Haven't heard. Call sign Lemon 2-1. One reported being tangled in his chute. The Marines have a few choppers out looking, so keep your heads up for other traffic. You and Jolly 6-4 are primary tonight. Go get 'em."

The crew exits a door leading to the flight line where the Jolly Green Giant aircraft 2-7 and 6-4 are waiting, all cocked for rapid starts. and liftoff.

June 4, 2010
Dr. Denard's Office
Pine Valley, California

Grant asks a question. "Have you solved the riddle, rhyme whatever?"

Dr. Denard re-reads the riddle, "Where is Touchstone 101 CD? It is located at the entrance of Hotel Crazy. Touchstone 101 CD is not a what. It is a where. *Make a choice, live there.* I have no idea what it means. Your thoughts, state of mind?"

"My thoughts. Not sure. 101 CD let a little light in."

"I'm in the dark as to its meaning. It's not a Highway 101 destination? Hotel?" Dr. Denard is lost as to where this is heading.

Grant's reply. "It isn't numbers." Surprises Dr. Denard.

"What isn't?" Looking perplexed toward Grant.

Grant explains, "101 CD is all letters. No numbers. 101 are the letters I – O – I. 101 CD stands for If Only I Could Die. My touchstone 101 CD. If only I could die, things would change."

"Wow, "Dr. Denard says, clearly surprised. "What would change? You would be gone. That wouldn't help."

"That is the dilemma of contradictions. I only want a new life menu to order from."

"You want change. A new touchstone."

"If only I could die. There would be peace, serenity and all the bullshit in my life would be gone." Struggling with it, Grant says, "But don't...don't think I can."

"You can't because it would be wrong?" Not a statement, but a question.

Stoically, Grant says, "No, maybe. Too many people depend...depend on me."

"You make it sound like your importance is a chore. An unpleasant chore."

"Exactly. It's my own fault. I did it."

"What is it you did? Or think you did?" Denard needs to know.

"Too good at being a good guy. Responsible. Dependable. I am the rock, as my mom would say."

"You care about people in your life." Denard states what should be obvious.

"Guilty. Too much."

"Too much of a good thing?"

"Yeah, if only I were a bit more irresponsible, shiftless, and selfish."

"Can you do that?"

"Haven't been able to." Grant shrugs. "The Boy Scout curse."

"You're there to save the day?"

"Yes. Need to end it. I'm so weary of the responsibility. A replacement would be nice. Send in the second string."

"Who would that be?" Denard again searches for an answer.

"There isn't one," Grant replies, being completely honest in his belief.

CONSIDER MAN

June 6, 2010
Early Morning
Santee, California

Grant is standing on Corte Madera Mountain overlooking a drop of 200 feet and a panoramic view of miles of San Diego County backcountry. He takes a revolver from his backpack; it looks light, almost weightless. He walks farther out on a potato chip-shaped granite slab and sits on the nearly paper-thin rock outcropping. He is in deep thought. Suicide thoughts. There is something behind him. He turns but it's only a dragonfly sitting on a willow leaf.

Grant wakes from this dream and gets quietly out of bed, careful not to wake Becky. Still dark, sunrise an hour away. He goes to his walk-in closet and dresses in biking clothes. Cargo pocketed biking pants cut above the knee, a tight-fitting poly-made jersey depicting the flag, red, white, and blue, 'We the People' front and back, zip-up with pockets along the back waist, and half-ankle socks. The rest of his biking gear is in the garage with his mountain bike, shoes, and small combination hydration backpack.

Once dressed, he moves to the kitchen, retrieves a smoothie prepared the night before, then goes into his home studio and stands at a high worktable. He is preparing to take a ride from which he may not return. He opens a file cabinet drawer, takes out a revolver; opens the cylinder and loads one round, closes the cylinder, and places the pistol in his biking backpack. From the drawer, he takes a white envelope addressed to his wife. He holds the letter envelope in front of him, clearly considering what will happen later this day. He is planning to leave the note in his SUV at the trailhead parking lot. It all depends if Steve shows up to the mountain biking trailhead they have ridden often. Corte Madera peak is about 30 miles east of Grant's home. It's about 60 minutes east on Interstate 8 and five miles of dirt road to the Four Corners trailhead staging area, a seldom-used dirt lot. They usually don't see other bikers. That is the trail's appeal for them.

The Ride

Despite all the baggage, Grant is a likable guy. He downsized out of the mortgage business a few years back and did project consulting work for a few years until that dried up. He's 67 and unemployed. He taught himself oil painting. Got to be good at it, but not enough to sell much of anything. He is currently working on a surf-related mural project on the side of a commercial building. He and Becky have a good relationship, except for unemployment and his painting a mural for free. But that's the type of guy Grant is; he tends to be a giving sort. Maybe too giving, according to Becky.

Steve doesn't show at the Corte Madera trailhead, sent a brief text cancelling out. So, Grant is riding solo a few days after a 5.8 earthquake. After an hour of hard climbing to 4,000 feet, he stops near the highest point of the remote trail. Grant gets off his bike for a drink of water, and to answer nature's call. As he relieves himself, he sees a slight movement along a granite face down the bike trail. He can't quite make out what it was, probably loose rocks and soil from the earthquake. He saw little slide evidence of the quake on the way up. Finishing his break, he gets back on his bike--nothing of concern.

Rounding a familiar rock face, he sees a small man or boy, seemingly trapped under a flat granite rock weighing 300 pounds or more. The person looks as though they had been there for some time. Grant thinks of the earthquake days earlier that could have caused the granite to break loose, trapping its victim, who looked very odd, unlike anyone Grant had seen before. He first thought the person had no clothes; it looked like he had none. And very featureless dull skin. Opaque. But that didn't make sense. Who would be out here without clothing? He appeared to have stunted facial features. His skin was smooth and looked to be supple without flaws. He had no hair and large eyes; almost no nose or ears, except for openings in that specific location. His exposed arm was not muscular, with the same skin texture at his wrist and hand. The hand had three unusually long fingers and thumb, and fingernails showed. Grant noted that the exposed skin had no sign of age, no wrinkles. Newborn-like. Very odd.

CONSIDER MAN

Grant approaches and asks, "Hello. Are you okay? Can you move...can you move at all?" No response.

The person was unresponsive: he looked to be sleeping. Still breathing. Not dead. Grant noticed the individual's left arm just beyond the edge of the granite slab had a bracelet-type device attached. Grant thought it might be some form of GPS device or cell phone. However, it looked nothing like any device or cell phone he was familiar with.

As Grant drew closer, he saw that the man's left arm and shoulder were trapped under the granite rock. It looked as though the individual had tried to reach this device with his right hand, but it was several inches out of reach and immobile. Grant attempts to rouse the individual again. "How long have you been here? What is your name? I'm Grant."

Because Corte Madera Peak is close to the Mexican border, the guy may be an illegal immigrant, not wanting to be helped, Grant realizes. He tries a little Spanish. "Como se llama?" Nothing. Grant moves closer. It seems the individual is unconscious or sleeping. It is weird.

Nothing seems to be working. He can't wake this guy up. Grant looks for possessions. He finds nothing. No backpack, no water, no trekking poles, no trail shoes. And apparently no clothes. Well, no shit? Grant struggles with what to do. "Come on, fella, help me out here. Wake up."

The individual opened his large light blue eyes and stared at Grant momentarily while trying to reach his right arm or wrist with his left hand. At this point, he makes some sounds that are the result of his struggles, not an attempt at speaking. Grant then assumes that the guy is a deaf-mute without the ability to speak. He is really curious as to how and why this individual got out here in these conditions. The guy doesn't talk and is unequipped for this remote environment.

Grant moves closer, places his hand on the right shoulder. "Take it easy. I'm here to help." This only agitates the person, who further attempts to reach the device on his left arm. At the same time, Grant is hit with what feels like a migraine. Somehow, he knows that the trapped person is the cause. "Holy shit. Now what?" Rubbing his temples, he says, "Now look, you're going from a pain in the ass to a pain in...in my head. Jesus, I'm just trying to help. Please calm down."

The more the little man moves and struggles, the more intense Grant's migraine becomes. Finally, Grant stumbles blindly and backs away from the ongoing futile physical effort at the granite rock.

"Take it easy. I'm trying to help. What's your name? God damn, would you speak?!"

The farther Grant steps away, the more his headache subsides. "Holy shit. Please calm down. I'm trying to help you if you let me. How long have you been here?" Nothing is clear.

Grant backs off further in a state of confusion, trying to determine the next step, if any, in helping this Man, boy, whatever he is. In Grant's mind, the individual is in shock and confused. So is Grant. Plus, he realizes the closer he gets to the granite rock, the pain in his head intensifies. He backs away even more, the pain lessens. How did this guy get here and so strange looking? Grant is starting to wonder not so much *who* is trapped under the Granite, but *what* is. There seems to be a clear relationship between his struggle and Grant's head pain. He thinks about walking further away and saying, screw whatever it is under the Granite...let him figure it out. If he doesn't want my help, I'll get my bike and ride the hell outta of here. But he stays.

It's his rescue experience, still ingrained. Grant was involved in nearly 40 life-saving rescue operations in the Air Force.

His head pain now is nothing in comparison to the shit-scary combat operations where every bad guy on the ground wanted you dead. They threw every anti-aircraft artillery shell at your slow-moving, underpowered helicopter. Grant came close to buying it a couple of times, but other squadron members were the real heroes, some of whom didn't come back. So instead of leaving the intense pressure environment, he chooses to face it. He can't do anything less.

Grant sits down fifty feet away on a rock and tries to gather his thoughts on how to help. He realizes the granite rock has to come off the left arm and shoulder but can't figure out how to get close enough or move the 300-pound slab without his head exploding.

The individual is calmer now that Grant has backed away. Grant takes a drink from his camelback water hydration tube and sprays water on his face. Upon seeing this, the pinned non-cooperative individual reacts as though he is thirsty and needs water. His lips and mouth are dry. Grant recognizes this and takes a hesitating step or two forward with the water tube extended. This only adds to the individual's agitation, his fear; however, this time Grant's head pain seems to diminish. Grant goes through a series of gestures while manipulating the hydration pack and tube water valve. It is a basic military demonstration performance routine. Watch and learn how something works, then do it yourself. He then indicates that he would give him water if he would allow him to approach. Grant takes off the water carrying backpack and comes slowly, arms extended, and places the pack near the individual. Grant backs off, his headache nearly gone. After a few moments, the trapped person with his right hand reaches for the hydration tube picks it up, and is able to manipulate the water valve. He only takes a minimal amount, just to wet his lips, but not drink. All this seems very strange for a person who has been without water for hours and most likely at least a day. It's hot, about 85 in the shade. This guy is making it hard to assist, much less rescue, him from under a large granite rock.

Running through Grant's mind is to move the rock, but how? It is far too heavy for Grant to lift, and if he tried, the rock would be hard to control. It could drop on the little man and cause more injuries. Additional rescue resources were hours away. The little guy under the rock isn't and hasn't been much or any help at all. This was a solo bike ride, thanks to Steve not showing up, and, now, it looks to be a solo rescue.

After the individual takes the hydration pack and wets his lips, he seems to be calming down, or at least he's not as agitated. Grant needs to do something even though it would just be him. He remembers several downed oak trees and large broken branches that he and Steve had to clear from the trail several months before. They were heavy deadwood branches that were three or four inches in diameter and several feet long. This starts Grant thinking about how to use these resources on his first solo rescue. He walked among the deadwood and formulated a possible plan. It just might work.

Grant figures the only way he's going to convince this individual of his intention to help is to show him what he wants to do. It's showtime again. Grant decides to demonstrate how he would remove the rock that has trapped the odd stranger's right arm and shoulder. First, Grant finds and gathers a few small stones and sticks and goes about via sign language, pointing, and using a miniature lever fulcrum set up to demonstrate lifting a small flat rock. The trapped audience of one watches passively. Then somehow, Grant senses an agreement with the individual, not spoken but sensed as if it just came to him. The same sense married couples or twins often have as they completely understand one another without speaking.

With this apparent sense of understanding, Grant, without further head pain, searches for a length of deadwood to use as a lever. There are rocks galore to use as the fulcrum. He carefully sets up the lever and fulcrum near the trapped right arm. He determines there is just enough clearance to move the deadwood lever four to six inches under the edge of the granite rock. Grant plans to use the lever fulcrum device to lift the rock enough to free the left arm and shoulder. There is an understood non-verbal agreement between the two as the process moves on in silence. Next, Grant struggles with placing a granite boulder with a reasonably flat top side, about fifteen inches in diameter, positioned to be the fulcrum. He carefully moves the deadwood lever over the fulcrum and inserts it just under the edge of the granite rock near the left shoulder.

Grant rechecks his setup. When ready, he says, "Here goes nothin'."

Grant gradually applies his weight on the nine-foot lever. The granite rises a slow few inches. Then, finally, the traipee is sprung free and what edges out from under the 300-pound granite slab is a pint-sized, two-legged something Grant hasn't ever seen before. So small, he or she, Grant is not sure which sex at this point, couldn't have budged the Granite at all. Most likely, it would have died right where Grant had come upon him or her.

Once freed, the pint-sized stranger cradles its left arm in its lap and makes adjustments to the bracelet device. Grant sits across from the odd new acquaintance and realizes that this person is not like him at all. Short in stature, less than five feet, wearing a onesie covering its features, neck down, including its feet, and leaving no revealing evidence of being male or female visible. Once he had a good look, Grant now thinks he is male for no reason other than some intuitive conclusion based upon looks and stereotype reasoning. Only a male could have gotten himself trapped in such a set of circumstances. Grant also figures a female counterpart would be dressed differently. Stereotypical reason rises to the surface once again. Not sexist, just simpler to think that this new acquaintance is male at this point in their relationship. It could change.

It was easy to see why Grant thought his victim had no clothes. His one-piece clothing apparel showed no visible features: no pockets, no seams, no buttons, no zippers, no Velcro. The suit, skin-tight, only exposes the individual's head and hands. The onesie material matches the tone and coloration of the individual's skin. Grant thought he would've had to have been poured into it the way it fits and conforms to his body.

Grant is perplexed but not frightened. He has always been fearless for no clear-cut reason. The sight of this strange person would typically upset the average man but not Grant. He knows this about himself and has never been able to understand it clearly. Some would say he just doesn't give a shit about a lot.

As the rescued granite rock slide victim works the device on his arm, Grant senses movement in the granite face across from them. He is startled by a subtle, rumbled low pitch vibration and assumes it is an earthquake aftershock. He needs to move and fast. Grant has no intention of becoming an earthquake rock slide victim, nor does he want his newly rescued someone to join him. Grant reaches for his rescued onesie-clad stranger as he tries to form an exit strategy.

Meanwhile, the massive granite rock wall in front of them opens and exposes an enormous void. Their escape route is gone. Grant anticipates a fatal fall.

Grant experiences a calm, coming over him. It is a sense of assurance that there is nothing to fear. No need to move. His rescued victim just communicated without speaking. Grant, for the first time during this encounter, realizes something extraordinary is happening. "Jesus, who the hell is this guy and what now?"

He sees it is not an earthquake-caused shifting of rock but an opening that wasn't there before. Grant jokingly says, "Holy shit! you're an ET."

At this point, the newly named ET indicates that he needs to get up and enter the rock face via his nonverbal communication. Grant again senses, almost hears it, an understanding that his assistance is required to help the ET or whoever enter the opening. Puzzled by his sense of calm and lack of fear, Grant helps his new extraterrestrial acquaintance to his feet; there is no adverse reflex response or head pain thankfully. Grant holds the one uninjured arm that reminds him of a young child's. There is a softness and yet a measure of strength that is not child like. The onesie material is smooth without seams and has a life like feel and appears to be a true one piece. He notices his elongated fingers again. As they approach, his attention quickly shifts to the opening in the massive granite pinnacle of Corte Madera. It is difficult to comprehend how a massive pinnacle that he has known for years seems to contain a chamber of some type. The chamber doesn't have a door but a translucent, almost fluid-looking membrane. Grant holds his breath involuntarily as they step into the suspended fluid substance. Once inside the chamber space, he has to remember to resume his regular breathing pattern. The entrance membrane looked wet, but it wasn't. Instead, it had a pleasant coolness to it. His heart rate is still elevated, and his mind races to try to comprehend the reality of just what happened. He just rescued an injured extraterrestrial being from under a granite slab and walked with it arm-in-arm through a solid granite wall. Not something he anticipated at the beginning of his bike ride. Strange, very strange but not foreboding for some unexplained reason. The chamber has no structures: no furniture, no chairs, no benches, no tables, no lamps, no doors. The floor is a light-colored, polished substance that glows with subdued light. There are no angular walls. Right angles do not exist within this structure. The chamber dome-like, over an apparently free-floating disc floor structure with holographic outer images of the star filled cosmos. A 360 degrees surround above and below the disc. And yet a sense of stability.

Once inside, Grant and the onesie-clad ET continue to communicate on a nonverbal level. Grant is puzzled by the empty space. He was anticipating, at the minimum, something or someone who could assist the injured ET. There is nothing, no one. He is unable to assist with any first aid treatment for the ET. They are in an empty chamber alone. Then he senses a calming reassurance from the ET.

Grant provides an arm to lean on as his new alien friend approaches a small glowing outlined circular section of the larger oval floor. As the ET stepped onto the space, it illuminated and supported his weight and stabilized his balance. Grant could also see that ET was near-weightless while still on his tiny alien feet. He concludes that the small glowing circular area must be some sort of life-support device. A Star Trek like Tri-Corder ET designed.

At this juncture, Grant becomes much more aware of the utterly foreign environment which he has entered with his new friend. From where he stands, he can look through the visual opening in the solid granite structure of Corte Madera. It is a solid, massive granite pinnacle only reachable by foot or mountain bike trails, seldom used. Yet, that is the reason Grant and his brother came here: The solitude. The passageway was translucent, puzzling, almost liquid in texture. Grant was overcome by a sense of well-being, intense curiosity and experienced a higher level of kaleidoscopic consciousness. He knows that somehow ET is responsible for the new level of consciousness he is experiencing. The granite wall passageway was a threshold, not only to a physical chamber but an entry point into a new and unexplored dimension for Grant. He was safe, the ET was recovering, and a whole new world was about to begin for both of them.

Over the next several months, Grant returns to the dome chambered Lab. They communicate. Grant speaks, the ET doesn't; he listens and responds without speaking. Grant hears clearly without any audible sound from his extraterrestrial counterpart. No spoken words, none. Replaced with a clear, concise communicating language. Not verbal, though transmitted, articulated, and received. But they understand one another. They are an odd couple. The ET is clearly beyond Grant in intellectual capacity. They have a chance rescue in common, apparently nothing more. Sometime later, Grant realizes that the ET can erode all memory of their Corte Madera encounter. He could have sent Grant off finishing his bike ride that day, yet he chose to remain in a portion of Grant's life. He chose not only to stay but to enhance it.

MAN 7

Understanding Our Existence

It was Grant's calm even non-panic approach that made the encounter with the ET work. Much like the original "ET" movie, the young boy Elliott thought it was cool to have a pet alien in his bedroom. Grant didn't view his ET as a pet as Elliott did; rather, he was intrigued by the possibility of interacting with an alien that needed assistance. Grant borrowed Elliott's ET's name for his "ET." It was a process of discovery and enlightenment for Grant. The arrangement tended to fill a knowledge vacuum related to his world, the alien world and, later on, how evolution fit in and brought it altogether.

Grant wasn't necessarily a religious person; however, he always felt that there was some power, some higher power out there that fit within his concept of his reality. For him, there had to be a more scientific explanation for mankind and evolution. He didn't necessarily feel there wasn't a God, but if there was, he had to have one hell of a scientific background to create Earth and the entire Universe. Even Stephen Hawking, the astrophysicist, didn't necessarily question the existence of a God that created everything. Rather, Hawking wanted God to explain how he did it. The answer could be that God chose the initial configuration of the universe for reasons that we cannot hope to understand. His creation certainly would have been within the power of an omnipotent being, but if he had started it off in such an incomprehensible way, why did he choose to let it evolve according to laws that we could understand?

* * * *

A Brief History of Time
Stephen Hawking
A Bantam Books
Copyright 1988, 1996

Ever since the dawn of civilization, people have not been content to see events as unconnected and inexplicable. They have craved an understanding of the underlying order in the world. Hawking's point: In the end, mankind still yearns to know why we are here and where we came from.

* * * *

To answer those questions, Grant is crossing his Rubicon with a mentor and guide not of this world. In 49 BC, when Julius Caesar led a roman legion across the Rubicon River he committed to an irrevocable course of action; a fateful and final decision. For Caesar to do so was treason. The tiny stream, Rubicon, would reveal Caesar's intentions and mark the point of no return thereby starting a victorious war that changed history.

This journey affects everything that is Grant. His entire being and reality. His sanity or lack of it. It is as exciting as it is perplexing. Unknown to him, rather than expanding Grant's concept of being, it works to do the exact opposite. The insignificance of mankind is on display holographically in front of Grant. Perhaps Man is nothing more than a lab experiment.

In Grant's case, it was a concentrated immersion, composed of a compressed learning regimen coupled with time acceleration and a bit of mind manipulation; his IQ went up a few notches in the process. At the end of each session, he had a very painful short duration migraine; drinking water tended to relieve the issue. This process in real time was short, very short. Grant figured at a later time, that ET had used time patches that ran many days together, and yet it was only a number of hours in Grant's "real time."

The real time posed a scheduling management issue. His "training" was compressed yet there was actual time expended. Grant's time now encompassed a supposed addiction to mountain biking two to three times a week, much to Becky's chagrin. He was unemployed and on a biking binge.

Traveling and biking to Corte Madera took real time, one hour drive to the trail head, plus an hour bike ride to the lab. Longer if towing a wheeled travois carrying other essentials: coolers, ice, beer, drinks, and TP etc. But time spent in training was reduced to a matter of hours by time acceleration fore and aft. However, there were unforeseen issues. His vehicle could be ticketed for overnight parking at the Four Corners staging lot. He could be gone for days. This was avoided after the first two training sessions by "returning" within posted time parking limits. He and ET could be involved in multiple days long training sequences as long as they return to near current time. County Ranger parking enforcement cares little about any excuses, even extraterrestrial ones. Becky was also one that wasn't pleased with missing meals or arriving consistently late. Grant worked out and managed the timing pattern that avoided unnecessary complications. He managed adequately most everything with the exception of the traffic on Interstate-8. Even ET couldn't solve that dilemma.

He can't help but feel he is the subject of an alien study, a high-tech lab rat. Grant for the life of him could not figure out why ET was providing him all the knowledge he gained, although he knew it was limited by the vast difference between the two of them.

He is intrigued by all that he sees and attempts to learn and understand, yet he's light-years away from comprehending it all. ET used time manipulation to streamline and concentrate Grant's learning process. His comprehension was built step by step over seemingly months, when in actual time it was a day or two repeated over and over.

When Grant later on answered Steve's question as to how he learned so much about the alien operation he referred to the movie *Groundhog's Day*, doing February 2nd repeatedly. It was like Bill Murray's repeated piano lessons in one day, over and over. And his attempts to pick up the girl in the bar every night until he found the right combination of dialog that she could relate to. Grant, with ET's oversight, is able to manipulate ET's lab workshop to discover the pass key to time travel. Just ask and in most cases, it is done.

MAN 8

Thanksgiving 2009
Family gathering
Encinitas, California

A family gathering around a large dining table. An assembly of various relatives, brothers-in-law, sisters-in-law, Steve, and Grant. Bob first introduced the question at this family gathering. The family consists of three brothers and Becky, the one sister. James was a retired commercial insurance executive; his wife is Gerry. Divorced and remarried, Cole has been in healthcare for his entire career. Bob is a blue-collar union, educated firefighter, which is to say he's always looking for a deal; he's married to Toni, a successful sales manager for a Toyota dealership.

Bob always has something to share, "I have a hypothetical only question for everybody. If you could, what person would you bring back to life to spend one day with?"

It wasn't a loaded question, and, in most cases, people responded with a loved one, parent, or some historical figure. On the other hand, Grant was somewhat stymied and couldn't come up with a precise selection from his list of deceased individuals. He had several.

Jolly 27
June 6, 1970 – near 2100 hours
Air Force Helicopter Cockpit
Offshore South China Sea
China Beach, South Vietnam

A night rescue mission over water. The cockpit instruments glow in red to save the night vision of Jolly 2-7's pilots. The noise from the engines and rotors deafens those aboard. Through the windscreen, parachute flares are illuminating the night over water with a dull yellowish glow. There are competing radio transmissions of the many aircraft involved; a very chaotic evening with radio traffic cutting off and blocking each other. The copilot handles most of the radio calls while the pilot focuses on flying and keeping clear of other aircraft and flares.

The copilot says, "What a cluster fuck. Ten bailed out, how many in the water?"

His Pilot answers, "Don't really know. We need to keep our heads out of the cockpit. Keep your eyes out for other aircraft."

Copilot adds, "And keep your heads up, looking for those parachute flares. Want to avoid them."

"Vice Squad relayed that Lemon 1-0 was tangled in his chute and needed immediate assistance, no one has a position for him." The pilot tells his crew.

Copilot suggests to the pilot, "Maybe we should gain some altitude try to locate him by DF." Radio Direction Finding wasn't always reliable.

"Let's give it a try, going to 2000."

Arriving at 2000 feet, the crew of Jolly 2-7 finds radio transmissions difficult to hear due to competing radio traffic and static.

Copilot, "Lemon 1-0, Jolly 2-7 do you read? Lemon 1-0, I am Jolly 2-7, do you read?

"Jolly 2-7, Lemon 0-7," A crew member from AC 119 Gunship, Lemon 2-1.

"It's one of the other crew members." The pilot says.

"Lemon 0-7, Jolly 2-7 say your position?" Copilot response.

"Jolly 2-7, Lemon 1-0." Radio call from another Lemon 2-1 crew member.

"Lemon 1-0, Jolly 2-7 say your position over." The copilot responds to most radio calls.

Copilot, "Fuck…. I hope they're close together. They've been in the water for about an hour."

A very weak radio transmission, "Jolly 2-7, Lemon 0-7, position south...Monkey Mountain."

Pilot, "Lemon 0-7, Jolly 2-7 say again your position. Do you read?"

"Lemon 0-7 is on the south side of Monkey Mountain. I'm sure that's what he said." The copilot clarifies.

"Okay, okay let's get over there." The pilot directs the crew, "Keep your eyes out for either flare or a strobe."

The copilot repeats a call, "Lemon 0-7, Jolly 2-7 do you read? Lemon 0-7, Jolly 2-7 do you read?"

"I read you Jolly 2-7. I'm about a half mile south of Monkey Mountain." Lemon 0-7 return call.

"Roger that Lemon 0-7, we're on our way." The copilot points toward a point past Monkey Mountain.

Pilot, "Okay, keep your eyes out there we just cleared Monkey Mountain to the North." It took Jolly 2-7 three minutes to arrive at the current location.

"Jolly 2-7, Jolly 2-7, Lemon 1-0." Broken radio transmission goes unanswered by Jolly 2-7. Heavy radio static. Lemon 1-0 caught in his sinking chute.

The Flight Engineer interjects, "It is darker than shit out here."

Copilot calls, "Lemon 1-0, Jolly 2-7 say your position, over."

Pilot, "Anyone see anything? We're just outside the parachute flares. Jesus. The radio chatter is bad. Too many aircraft."

Pararescueman (PJ), "I have a Tally-Ho on a strobe at two o'clock, three quarters of a mile."

Pilot, "Roger that, coming around to the right."

2009
Thanksgiving
[continued]

Later that Thanksgiving evening, Steve and Grant are alone on the backyard deck, which offers a panoramic view of the ocean along Coast Highway 101. They are finishing drinks. Steve's determined to find out the name of the individual Grant would to hypothetically return for a day. He presses harder for an answer.

Grant is used to his brother's occasional drunken behavior and tends to ignore the questioning. In the end, Grant relents with the hope the inquisition will end. "The question about who you would want to spend a day with. Someone that had passed away, bring 'em back for a day? That hypothetical question?" Grant does not like being pushed.

Steve, "What's your answer?"

Grant, "I don't think I had one. No one came to mind."

"I assume you still don't have an answer or anyone in mind? Why is that?" Steve steadies his balance with a patio stool resting against the outdoor bar.

Grant pensive and dealing with a bit of alcohol himself, "I don't...I don't. I couldn't put my finger on anyone in particular. I've known a lot of people who aren't around anymore. Picking just one struck me would take some time, uh, consideration. I don't know!"

Steve, emphatic. "No one stood out, family, friends; it's all hypothetical, Vietnam?"

Grant shows a pained expression. "They all stood out in one way or another, but how to choose, which one gets the time...which choice is more meaningful? Why are we talking about this anyway? It was a simple dinner game question; it doesn't change anything. They're gone and we move on, right? Aren't there more important things that we need to figure out?"

Steve, "It isn't a game. I know whatever your hesitation is, it has bothered you for years. It may just be a significant event you need to deal with."

Grant, a bit hyper. "And this is one of them hypothetically? Are you telling me that?"

Steve, a matter of fact. "Exactly hypothetically, how would you choose if you had to?"

Grant, exasperated. "Choose only one?"

Steve, "Only one, how would you do it?"

Grant, "How do I know which is the correct choice? What if my choice is wrong, should have chosen someone else? There's got to be a couple dozen people I could choose from?"

Steve says, "I have confidence you'll make the right choice."

Grant is shaking, tense, and searching for his voice. "How do I rank them? Line them up and choose just one? I knew them and they died...I wasn't there." Grant is trying to clear his mind's choice and direction. Where is an answer? "They were people that I cared about, had common experiences, unfinished connections...cut short. What could I say? We had some great times, sad times...you lived your life and here you are. Family gone in the course of living, Dwayne drank too much, Jackie screwed around with drugs and got shot. How do I deal with those circumstances? I wasn't there. Life happens, shit happens!" Struggling, finally, Grant asks, "How do I make that judgment? How do I evaluate them all? They're all different."

Steve, "Yes, they are all different but you have a common experience with all of them. However, you have a very incomplete experience with one individual during a rescue operation off the coast of Da Nang. Do you remember the night rescue, feet wet? You have told that story partially, many times, and I know you would like to change the outcome or at least find closure. It is an unfinished connection, cut short, as you just said."

Grant, remembering clearly, "Sergeant Alloway! Son of a bitch, that poor bastard drowned while I was talking to him on his survival radio." Grant knows he should have changed the outcome many years back, and he didn't. He thinks he could have.

Steve says, "What happened? What's the full story?"

Grant hesitant, a bit shook, "I had a short conversation with Sergeant Alloway over 40 years ago. I kept asking him his location and he kept telling me he was tired, tangled in his parachute. Thinks he's drowning. I was talking as he struggled to stay above the surface. He died that night, caught in his parachute chords and canopy."

"What does that mean for you?"

Grant feels intense, "I was looking for him but not listening. He was struggling to stay alive. I should have told him to take his knife and cut himself free and then call us. I was the last person that he spoke to before he died. Talking to a dead man...drowning."

"Good time to deal with that now?" Steve shrugs.

"Sergeant Alloway and I have an intimate connection. I could have made a difference but didn't."

"Are you saying you didn't do your best that night?"

"No. That's the trouble. We did our best. Our, my best wasn't good enough."

Emphatic Steve, "You and the other Jollys saved four of the ten people, rescued nine lives total. That sounds like success to me."

"90% doesn't cut it when you're trying to save lives. When a simple instruction may have saved him!"

"That is something we will never know. What you could have said may not have changed the outcome. You did your best. You tried. So now what?" Steve continues, "There were a lot of people you had connections with, now gone." He adds.

"I knew who they were. We spent a lot of time together growing up, raising kids, work and just living life. We shared good times and bad, and when they were gone, I had those to hold onto."

"And the memories of Sergeant Alloway? What do they consist of?"

"Blank pages. Talking to a drowning man. *Pop flair! Is your strobe light on?* Holding on to him over the radio. A radio connection as tenuous as his efforts to stay above the surface. I remember his last words 'I think I'm drowning.' Then there was nothing, no response. Those are my memories."

"Is that enough?"

"We have a shared moment in time that brought us as close as one man can get to another, his dying last words and breath."

"Can you live with that?"

"Don't know I can."

CONSIDER MAN

Jolly 27
June 6, 1970 – 2120 hours
Offshore South China Sea
China Beach, South Vietnam

The copilot pointing through the windscreen; talking on the radio and intercom. "I have a Tally-Ho on a strobe 12 o'clock 300 yards. Lemon 0-7 we're south of your position near Monkey Mountain."

The pilot responds, "I got him." Slowing Jolly 2-7 from 100 knots to 40, closing fast on Lemon 0-7. "OK, we're going into a hover, get ready to deploy PJ." The PJ is wearing a wetsuit, swim fins, life preserver and will be exiting the helicopter at about 10 feet above the water. He is standing at the door alongside the flight engineer.

Copilot, "Pre-pick up checklist complete." At this point, the copilot's duties, while in a hover over water, monitor engine instrumentation and respond to radio calls.

"Lemon 0-7, Jolly 2-7, I have a tally on your lights." The pilot is in visual contact with Lemon 0-7 and adjusting his approach to establish a hover above him.

"Roger that, Lemon 0-7."

"Going hot on mic." The Flight Engineer switches to an open microphone to free his hands to manipulate the cable hoist system and assist the PJ and direct the pilot in recovering PJ and Lemon 0-7.

Pilot. "Roger that, hot mic."

Flight engineer, "Survivor two o'clock 200 yards." Rapidly closing the survivor, slow forward speed.

Pilot, "Roger that."

"100 feet 40 knots." Copilot calling out altitude above water and airspeed. There is virtually no wind; the indicated airspeed is the same as ground speed. The radio chatter from a dozen other aircraft is a constant distraction. The pilots have to filter it out and focus on their rescue process. Parachute flares are dropping randomly near their location, offering a yellowish dull flickering light.

Flight engineer, "Survivor 12 o'clock 100 yards, slow forward. PJ in the door ready to deploy...forward 50 yards." The flight engineer is estimating the closing distance and speed to the survivor. "Forward 30 yards. Ready to deploy PJ."

Copilot, "20 Knots 30 feet." Jolly 2-7's landing lights illuminate the incoming greenish South China Sea swells 3 feet in depth. Jolly 2-7 makes a water landing pick-up.... too dark, no reference light for a hover. The Flight engineer is leaning out the cargo door secured by a floor attached cargo web belt, "Survivor 12 o'clock 10 yards, slow forward, slow forward."

Copilot, "15 feet." The copilot assists the pilot's altitude positioning.

Flight engineer, "PJ ready to deploy, forward five."

"Deploy PJ." The pilot clears the PJ to depart the doorway. He jumps with a thumbs-up signal by the flight engineer.

"PJ away...PJ in the water, PJ swimming toward Lemon 0-7 10 yards." He will determine the condition of Lemon 0-7 in the water and prepare him for the water landing recovery process.

"Roger that." The pilot will hold Jolly 2-7 in position until directed by the flight engineers as necessary.

Flight engineer, "Drifting right, come left, stop left, hold your position, PJ is at survivor."

"Roger that."

"Clear down fifteen feet." Flight engineer directs Jolly 2-7 to a water landing for survivor and PJ pick up. Jolly 2-7 has a boat hull and will float on its own for several hours without difficulty. The pilot maintains position by looking out the right-side windows and direction by the flight engineer. The copilot's duties on the water landing are to watch the helicopter's left side and adjust the collective flight controls as waves or swells build. The copilot will increase power as necessary to maintain a stable position in relation to growing swells or waves. Both pilots work in coordination to maintaining a stable platform in an unstable shifting water environment.

"Roger that down fifteen."

"Down five," Jolly 2-7 will sit lightly on the water surface...half hover, half floating.

"Stop down at water. PJ moving survivor to door. 15 feet...I have the survivor's back to the door...bringing him aboard." The flight engineer pulls Lemon 0-7 several feet from the door to a cargo seat. The PJ is assisted aboard next. "Survivor and PJ aboard."

"Roger that."

Forty-five seconds pass. "Both survivor and PJ secured cleared for takeoff."

"OK, let's go look for another one." Pilot turning Jolly 2-7 south.

Copilot, "Lemon 1-0, Jolly 2-7 do you read? Lemon 1-0, Jolly 2-7 do you read?

MAN 9

Grant Frederick's
Alien Accelerated Knowledge Transfer, a Journey

ET didn't *befriend* Grant; such a concept was not part of his alien consciousness. Instead, their interaction is an unconscious connection and acceptance within a cognitive bubble of two diverse questioning minds and travel companions, Grant and ET, from different worlds, separated by millennia of time and evolution. Both companions were searching to learn from and about each other. ET is perplexed for the first time in his existence, and Grant is searching to understand his. From Grant's perspective, ET has taken the role of a tutor, a cosmic proctor. ET provides Grant with access to an incredible historic database through a transfer of compressed, accelerated knowledge comprehension and retention.

Additionally, Grant gains an incomplete glimpse of ET's presence and purpose on Earth. Grant's brain knowledge, storage, and processing capability are expanded and accessed with a *mind-enhancing* drug delivered by aerosol. The process mimics downloading from the mainframe to a thumb drive, e.g., Grant. A data transfer using enhanced brain capacity processes is coupled with time acceleration. Essentially, the method unlocks the human brain potential at the cellular synapse level.

The time acceleration compresses and stores immense conceptual data within a highly advanced and unconsciously accessible memory. Memory is the key: it is the faculty of the brain through which data formation is encoded, stored, and retrieved when needed. It is the retention of information over time to influence future action. If Man could not remember past events, it would be impossible for language, relationships, or personal identity to develop. Memory is neural synapse pathways activated in a brain. With an increase of these neural pathways, IQ, learning, and memory storage increase significantly. The mind enhancing aerosol, is a neurotropic drug introduced by ET. It increases cognitive brain function, abilities, and capacities. Neurotransmitters and receptors increase across the synapse gap, expanding memory and learning potential, mainly executive function, memory, and creativity.

Neurotropic Road Trip

Like Spring football training camp, the first day's session was the worst. The positive thing about a Spring training was understanding what to expect and the schedule for several days or weeks. Concerning an alien time-compressed holographic brain IQ boosting base camp, the participant, Grant, had no clue of any reasonable expectations. There were only three similarities between Spring football and ET's camp: Start and stop time, exhaustion, and hunger. ET's camp started whenever Grant arrived back at the Corte Madera ET lab and dosed with the aerosol. Stop time could take days. Holographic time travel allowed an individual to venture nearly anywhere in the future or the past. ET exposed Grant to endless historic significant scenes, events, and complicated concepts. Grant was, by and large, able to absorb much of what he saw. The drug aerosol had a definite purpose. The time-compressed knowledge absorbing holographic events could and would encompass days. In some cases, the number of days, or weeks, were compressed within ET's process; the actual Earth time that passed would be a matter of minutes, sometimes hours. The physical effects on Grant were dramatic.

He was gone in a time travel dimension compression only for hours. However, his body felt as though he had been gone a day or more. Hunger, thirst, exhaustion, and headache were intense upon return and an urgent need of a bathroom break. There are no chairs in ET's training camp; Grant stood the entire time. The neurotropic aerosol worked and staved off the physical symptoms until a return to current time. Grant realized after the first couple of time-compressed training sessions, and he had to make some adjustments. Grant got smarter.

The ET aerosol opens and stimulates human brain capacity to 90 to 100 percent, versus a typical human's use of 20 to 30% brain capacity—providing an individual with unlimited cognitive skills coupled with a comprehensive encyclopedic database accessible by high-speed memory. During this doping effect, Grant is beyond most any others; Einstein, da Vinci could be classmates of Grant when he is in this enhanced mode. Grant later discovers that Einstein, da Vinci, and Nostradamus were subjects of other ETs not Grant's, using a subtle accelerated learning protocol. Those three gentlemen had an IQ much higher than Grant to start with, and their end level topped out beyond Grant's; however, the three had a disadvantage based upon the current technical and scientific environment in their time. Einstein was an exception; he had more than 500 years of established scientific achievement, beyond da Vinci and Nostradamus. By and large, their technical vocabulary and exposure were, unfortunately, at times, inadequate to encompass and comprehend future-based technology. For da Vinci and Nostradamus, the lead pencil and the printing press were newly invented items in the 15th-century. A computer monitor, cell phone, and laser pointer were incomprehensible and beyond the grasp of that scientific community. There were no vocabulary terms that they could use to explain such inventions. Einstein came close at times.

The drug effects on Grant, however, were not permanent and had a limited active time. There is a residual and gradual long-term effect that does boost mental cognitive skills and IQ. Along with the "drug" process administered by an aerosol component, ET uses time acceleration both fore and aft. For Grant to learn the volume of foreign conceptual data far beyond average human intelligence, time is required. Grant's learning routine included days and weeks of concentrated study due to the vast number of new concepts and data, but Grant completed each phase in a compressed timeframe through time acceleration. The time acceleration does not affect a human body with suspended aging. Grant grows younger age-wise while in the time acceleration process. The time on any separation process allows Grant to spend significant hours/days learning and acquiring "new knowledge." When he returns to the original time start point, there is no time lost or gained. The only visual indication that is noticeable is Grant's beard growth, which continues during the sequence. Effectively the learning process took days or weeks of Grant's time metabolically, hence the beard growth.

He found the effects of aerosol drugs not permanent but they significantly enhanced his perception of data. He understood much of the accelerated process. While in the learning zone, there was a logic pattern he understood. While outside the zone and off the neurotropics his understanding of prior learning concepts exceeded his cognitive abilities. He knew what data he had absorbed but could not wholly apply it outside the time-accelerated environment. Although he understood the concept as a man, items were just out of touch but could not adequately use or enlighten anyone about what he had learned. At times it came down to the confidence of understanding. He was at the edge but unable to step into the subject matter with mastery. Grant called it "tip of the tongue data." It was similar to watching the game show "Jeopardy'" and trying to compete with the contestants. Once they disclosed the answer (in the form of a question), it would be clear that the answer was just out of reach.

In other words, he knew enough of the concept but not enough to master navigating through it. He was exposed to repeated accelerated knowledge dumps or downloads, increasing his intellectual capacity three or four-fold. It has an addictive ability without withdrawal, accelerated knowledge capacity, and accompanied comprehension. Grant is no Einstein, but could easily carry on a theoretical debate with Albert when in the learning zone.

Grant's brain activity before the aerosol neurotropic application is similar to an electric grid infrastructure of a small town with one house lit up in one neighborhood. After, his "grid" lights up the whole village.

Jolly 27
Cockpit
June 6, 1970
[continued]

Jolly 2-7 finished picking up Lemon 0-7 and PJ from the night water rescue off China Beach and Monkey Mountain, South Vietnam. They were sitting lightly on the water's surface, awaiting a status check from the flight engineer. The two pilots now focused on the next course of action and a continued search for Lemon 1-0. He is somewhere struggling nearby, caught, entangled in his parachute.

"Vice Squad is still trying to contact Lemon 1-0," copilot recalls. "Maybe we should gain some altitude, try to locate him by DF again." There is an urgency in his voice and request.

The pilot is trying to decide where they should search next. "There may be a survivor on the south side of Monkey Mountain. Jolly 6-4 just picked up Lemon 0-2. Were there any transmissions from that area?" Pilot asks.

The copilot is sensing an increasing measure of frustration. "Don't know, Lemon 1-0 didn't know his location. He didn't say anything about seeing parachute flares, aircraft or city lights." This search is becoming more difficult by the minute. Jolly 2-7 finds radio transmissions difficult; too many aircraft trying to find one of the ten members of AC-119 Gunship, Lemon 2-1. Radio traffic is full of noise and static.

The copilot has handled most radio transmissions, searching for information and clues on Lemon 1-0's location. "I heard intermittent calls from Lemon 1-0 while we were in a hover over Lemon 0-7."

"Keep trying." The pilot knows they are running out of time, as does the whole crew.

Copilot calls on the radio, "Lemon 1-0, Jolly 2-7, do you read? Lemon 1-0, Jolly 2-7, do you read?

Flight engineer reports on the intercom, "Captain. Hoilman we have the PJ and survivor on board and secure. The survivor is OK, but cold and wet."

Copilot is to find more "Feet-Wet" survivors, "We're having a good night. Let's go see if we can find Lemon 1-0."

"Roger that. Have you heard any other transmissions?" The pilot relies on the copilot and crew, and so far, the night has gone well. They need to find one more.

"I'm getting broken transmissions from Lemon 1-0. Sounds like he is struggling to stay above the surface," the copilot says, encouraged by positive contact with Lemon 1-0.

The pilot is encouraged, too. "You have his location?"

"No, with all the radio traffic, it's hard for an accurate fix. Lemon 1-0, Lemon 1-0, Jolly 2-7. What is your location from Monkey Mountain?"

Lemon 1-0, exhausted voice, "I am...not sure."

"Lemon 1-0, Jolly 2-7 can you see the lights on Monkey Mountain or Da Nang Harbor? Can you see our aircraft lights?"

Very weak, "No...not sure." Lemon 1-0 is fading. He has struggled for nearly two hours with an entangled parachute.

"Bill, I can't get any visual reference from this guy," the copilot says. "I can tell he is in trouble. Exhausted, he maybe caught in his chute."

"Keep trying," orders the Pilot.

"Lemon 1-0, Jolly 2-7 can you pop a flare? Do you have your strobe on?"

Feeble halting reply, "No...I think...I'm drowning...can't get out of my chute. It's pulling...me...under." He is exhausted.

Jolly 6-4 comes over the radio intermittently, talking to another crew member in the water. "Lemon 0-3, Jolly 6-4 we have you in sight."

Copilot implores, "Lemon 1-0, pop a flare, and we'll find you. Can you see our search lights? Can you see the parachute flares?"

Increasing weakness, a sense of futility...an acceptance. "No...I'm caught...It's...can't get out." Then nothing. An absolute reality.

"Lemon 1-0, Jolly 2-7 do you read?" The copilot is asking Lemon 1-0, do you hear me? They can't locate him without radio contact. "Pop a flare," asking him to light up the world with one of his 15000 candle power 60-second flares. "Lemon 1-0, turn on your strobe." Copilot is almost demanding. Turn on your flashing 20-lumen strobe light. "Lemon 1-0, Jolly 2-7, Lemon 1-0, Jolly 2-7," desperately waiting for a reply, "Lemon 1-0, Jolly 2-7, do you read?" Copilot asking, "do you hear me...talk to me...we are listening...waiting. Shit." copilot's final word to pilot and crew of Jolly 2-7. Almost.

Epilogue
Last call. Lemon 2-1's aircraft commander, Lemon 0-1, contacts Jolly 2-7 in the final moments after losing contact with Lemon 1-0. "Jolly 2-7 Lemon 0-1." With the aid of his strobe light, Jolly 2-7 makes another water landing picking up Lemon 0-1 from his life raft. The last rescue of the night. Nothing more. Jolly 2-7 returns to Da Nang Air Base with Lemon 0-7 and 0-1. Nine crew members, rescued that night. The AC-119 Gunship, Lemon 2-1, took off with ten.

Skywriting
Corte Madera Trailhead
Grant stopped along the fence line at the Four Corners staging area base of Corte Madera. He has been riding his bike for what seems to be hours and is not in his biking gear, wrong shoes, and shirt; no helmet. He is watching four young men radio controlling model airplanes. One is seated on a bench. He gets up and walks toward Grant while maintaining control of his model, leans on the fence near him. "Some of these guys are really good with their model aircraft, don't you think?"

"Very Good." Grant is sitting in a lawn chair now, watching the aerial display.

"Yeah, really docs take a little time to learn the technique."

Grant asks, "Which one is yours?"

"Oh, the powder blue one." It is going through several advanced maneuvers; sky writing strange multi-colored symbols rather than letters. Odd.

"You're pretty good at that."

"Well, it does take a little time to learn to control them."

"How long have you been flying models?" Grant asks.

"Just today."

"Today? Today is the first day to ever fly these?"

He turns to face Grant, his back to the model, which continues its intricate maneuvers. "Grant, from my side, it is really easy to do."

Grant is surprised. "How, how are you controlling it? How do you know my name?"

"Grant, I've known your name for a long time. We go back a long way".

"We do?"

"Come on, Grant, try to remember. Ninth grade, Friday nights at the Vogue Theatre. Whiskey sours. You gotta remember that."

Open mouth, wide-eyed, look of surprise. "Jackie?" He was shot and killed at age 28.

"You got it. Now you remember."

"I understand you get to pick someone to spend the day with. I'm available. It would be great talking about old times."

"I don't know yet; you are among the first I've seen. I'm new to this. I don't know who else will show up." Hopefully, no more. Grant is struggling to comprehend.

"Don't sweat it; we can do this. Pick me. You won't have to see anybody else."

Grant drifting in thought. "I guess. I just don't know what to do, meeting dead folks."

Jackie is excited. His model airplane landed on his shoulder. "Do you remember in junior high, we wore the same jacket? We were so cool back then."

"I remember we thought we were."

"We really had some great times. Our group of guys pretty much ran the school. Dwayne was president of the student body, Becky was secretary."

"We couldn't drive. But didn't you take your dad's car a couple of times?"

"That's right." Jackie is 15 now. "That was a blast driving. Proctor Valley Road, all dirt."

"You almost rolled it in a ditch."

"It really wasn't that close."

We were lucky to have survived those years, and that was just junior high." Grant remembers more.

"High school was really great." Jackie relates

"We did have some interesting times."

"Interesting? We had great times. That's what I mean. Grant. Man, I'm available, we can talk about all those times. It'll be great just make your pick; we can get started."

"I don't think I'm ready yet. I am having a hard time getting my mind around this. It's all so freaking strange. I just don't know what I'm supposed to do." Grant is uncertain.

"Grant, you're supposed to pick me." Jackie demands. "You'll come around. I'll be a real expert flying the next time you see me." His model takes off overhead, trailing red, white, and blue smoke.

"I just, don't, know, I have to think about it. I got to go; I can't do this." Grant grabs his bike, throws his leg over the seat, and falls out of bed onto the floor again. Becky doesn't move this time around.

MAN 10

POST ET RESCUE

Grant was headed home after his Falcon Code 1-0-1, migraine-inducing initial ET encounter; it was not routine. Grant's mind pored over the events of his cosmic day. A curiosity of discovery beyond which he had never known or envisioned encompassed Grant's newfound reality. He could have run, but escape was never a solution, ever. He stayed and faced tense environments to a conclusion. He didn't know where the interactions with an ET would lead. He only knew that he was along for the ride. Grant had to bike back to his car; his focus was elsewhere. He left ET with no goodbye ceremony; it was an understood, unspoken communication, a manuscript of shared enlightenment that the two were just starting to unroll. The cosmic version.

Grant, very tired, struggled with focus and concentration while navigating the trail to his vehicle. He managed to make it down the very familiar trail, only crashing three times, once in a ditch, ate a lot of dirt, and ended up in a growth of manzanilla bushes. Grant had some difficulty following the dirt road off Corte Madera back to I-8. He finally came to his senses after driving about 25 miles going in the wrong direction on his way to Yuma. He reversed course, drove back west, pulled into a rest stop just east of Pine Valley, facing Corte Madera. He parked looking for answers somewhere on the peak above him. His mind was going in several directions, all at the same time wondering whether or not he could believe what he had just experienced.

117

Was the whole encounter a hallucination? He wasn't sure and questioned his sanity. It couldn't be real, he thought to himself. It wasn't the end, though; it was just the beginning.

After about 20 minutes of staring at the mountain peak, he remembered the Go-Pro camera attached to his helmet. Typically, it was on whenever he rode his mountain bike. He reached for it on the passenger seat; the recording light was still on, blinking red. Grant realized that he recorded his encounter with an ET. "Holy shit!" he says aloud, fumbling to rewind and play the footage. The recording captured his ride up until it abruptly stopped just after he approached the rockslide area. The screen turned to static images as if there were some sort of electronic interference. Grant is shocked; that has never happened before. However, the last visible images captured what appeared to be someone or something wedged under a rather large granite slab. It seemed to be the exposed arm and hand of ET. Grant paused the image. He focused on the image for some time until he stopped questioning his sanity, realizing his recollections were reality. The extraterrestrial experience happened; Grant's mind filled with questions. Everything about his existence transposed him into a new reality. Part of him wanted to turn away and never return to this bike trail. His encounter with ET had sowed an extraterrestrial experience seed of curiosity in the fertile field of doubt surrounding Grant's new reality. That curiosity forced him to make a decision: should he return to Corte Madera or ride away from it? He looked at his torn biking shorts; his legs scraped and bleeding, as are his arms and elbows. He had a fat lip. His biking jersey, also torn, was sprinkled with blood. An entirely new reality followed him home.

Grant had seen challenges before. He had been challenged his entire life, from physical skills to academics and career. He always accepted the challenges and made every attempt to succeed beyond expectations. Grant, with dogged determination and a focused attitude, grew when others expected him to fall short. He honed those skills and applied them throughout his life. Grant was a college athlete and an exceptional Air Force officer who flourished in leadership positions. He orchestrated the life-saving rescues of 40 individuals. Unarmed, he diffused a hostage situation, convinced the armed individual to hand over his 357-magnum handgun, and then drove him to military confinement. That was a challenge no one else was willing to accept, except the military SWAT team. Grant was at his best when challenged, and he knew it.

In recent years, he had been living in quiet desperation in the shadow of issues not of his choosing. Today, he had considered checking out. Then he met someone, an ET, and everything changed. This was the most significant, challenging moment in his life. He embraced it, for some reason, stepping willingly into a life-altering cosmic reality. There was no turning back. He chose to march forward; besides, no one was shooting at him; it wasn't like combat. He would make that bike trek several more times, and the challenges would mount.

BEARD DILEMMA

Grant found his beard would continue to grow while training with ET, and was surprised to find the five-day growth after his first time learning zone training session, which lasted in his real time only a matter of hours, at ET's for days. Grant realized that time travel didn't include how bodily functions continued even though you returned to the exact time you left. Aliens designed the Time Travel function and process for the recharging of ETs, which amounted to a glowing Oval on the floor and had absolutely nothing for Grant, other than a bit of dull floor lighting. There was no consideration for other time-traveling passengers or crew. Hence, they didn't include human bodily functions.

Grant's beard caused him some concern on his way home and stopping off at the 7-Eleven for a drink and something to eat. He saw himself in a mirror clearly with a five-day growth of beard. He hardly recognized himself and initially mistook the mirror image as someone else in line. The clerk asked him, "Will that be all?" *Not really,* Grant thought; he needed to shave before returning home.

The 7-Eleven stop and revelation spared Grant from having to explain to his wife, Becky, how his facial hair had grown in one afternoon. Grant became a fan of 7-Elevens. Turned out to be more of a godsend, saved his bacon, and came with a bathroom where he could trim his unexpected beard. Time travel doesn't slow down the aging process or metabolism. One can travel through the millennium and more—but only in one lifetime. That means a time traveler's bucket list could include thousands of items, people, places to see or visit, but only a lifespan to fill it.

Grant arrives at his home after his encounter on Corte Madera and 7-Eleven. He parks and enters the converted garage and his workshop studio that takes up half the garage floor. Designed as a creative workspace, Grant has wall-mounted easels for his painting projects, mostly surf and snowboarding action scenes. There are stacks of large blank canvases against one wall and even larger ones mounted by ropes to the ceiling. A lighted workbench and shelving unit, cluttered with various tools, built by Grant's father, backed up to the garage door. At the other end of the garage is shelving stacked with a library of his mother's books he promised to read after her death seven years ago. He is working on it. Grant built a tall two-shelved work table for storing paint supplies, framing, and canvas stretching with a carpeted top. Only one car can park in the garage, Becky's.

Grant walks into his dimly lit Man cave, hit by the out-of-place smell of cleaning fluid. Becky is cleaning a few plates and other leftover food items on his worktable. He doesn't notice. He's still thinking about the ET encounter and how to process it. He needs to find out more about ET and why he was chosen.

Becky asks, "How was your ride; wasn't it hot?" She is not looking at him, doesn't see his scrapes, cuts, bruises, and torn clothing.

"What?" Grant tries to catch up and clear his mind.

"Wasn't it hot? I don't see how you can bike; too hot."

"Oh, it wasn't too bad once you get moving."

Becky looks up from her cleaning and notices how banged up he was. "Are you all right?" She asks, concerned. "How many times did you fall? You look drained. Did you drink enough?" She steps back to assess Grant's condition.

Grant places his backpack, gloves, and bottles on the worktable. "I fell a couple of times wasn't paying attention as I should have. Just went a couple extra miles today." *And saved an extraterrestrial life form from a granite rockslide. I entered his laboratory contained within the solid granite peak of Corte Madera. It communicated with me without speaking. He is my newest and best friend from outer space. By the way, he wears a Star Trek Tri-Corder if you're interested, and it works rather well. So that was my day, how was yours?* "Nothing unusual" is what he says, though.

Becky picks up an empty plate. "You didn't have brownies for breakfast did you? Not the best food for going on a bike ride."

Not entirely with it, he shrugs, "Maybe a few. I forgot to make my smoothie last night, and the brownies were quick and easy. I took some bars with me, and a banana."

"You've done that before," Beck says with mild irritation. Brownies are not a breakfast food group."

"Well, they should be: milk, eggs, nuts, wheat, sugar, chocolate chips, and frosting."

"You're not a kid. You're going to get cramps again."

"I didn't get cramps, besides there were other, uh, people on the trail today," he lies, sort of.

"See anybody I know? Pete and Fred show up?"

Grant wonders if he should tell her, decides against it, can't tell her, can't believe it himself. "No, no, I...I didn't see any of those guys."

"Anyway, finally great news. White Cap called. They got approval for your mural project. Said they would put up the scaffolding. It's been years waiting for the approval."

"No kidding?" Grant is still not all there.

"They said they sent you an e-mail today confirming it."

"Then they got the OK from the owners. Finally. I thought it was dead. I'd given up any hope of that happening, ever." Grant shakes his head, "This is a strange day."

"Said they got the forms signed a couple days ago. I'm concerned about taggers or some kid falling off, breaking a leg, and we get sued."

Still not quite focused, Grant reassures her, "The scaffolding company has a release of liability and insurance for that. I still can't believe it. What a day, what a day."

"I hope the mural is worth it for all the time you put into it. For no pay!? You need to talk to them about that again. They're getting a lot of attention for their building for nothing." She tosses in a few of Grant's paint-stained rags into a trash bin.

"Yeah, that's only if the mural gets attention."

"Well, we'll see. Oh, Dr. Denard's office called. You have an appointment Wednesday at ten? I thought you were done with her?"

Grant feels uneasy. "I...I thought so, too."

"Well, figure it out. Don't want to pay for it, if it's not needed,"

"I'll handle it." Grant runs his hands through his hair.

"I have to go to Costco and pick up Freda and Daisy at the vet's. Anything you want from Costco?" Becky is done cleaning.

"Beer?"

"Beer? There's half a case right by the small fridge. You need to spend some time cleaning this place up. It's a mess."

"Oh, OK. I'll put some in the fridge. Beer sounds good about now."

Becky ignores his comments and walks out of the room, calling over her shoulder. "I'll be back with the dogs." She takes the cleaning solution, dishes, leaving assorted trash scattered on the worktable. Grant is alone, stares at his backpack on the worktable for a prolonged moment. He opens it and removes the handgun then sets it on the table. He turns to his mother's bookcase and picks out Stephen Hawking's *A Brief History of Time*. He thumbs through the pages he highlighted when he read it. He stares blankly at nothing. "I think I'm going nuts," he says outward. "What a day." He walks to the refrigerator, takes out a beer, opens it, takes a long swig, and then comes back to Hawking's book.

122

CONSIDER MAN

July 8, 2010
10 AM Wednesday
Dr. Denard's Office

Grant wasn't planning on seeing Dr. Denard again, but recent events drew him back. He is not sure what he can say, if anything, without seeming to be ready for a commitment to a mental institution of her choice.

"Hey, Doc," Grant says as he takes a seat on the leather sofa. Dr. Denard sits across from him, pen in hand, note pad in her lap.

"Grant, I'm glad you came today. Can we talk about your riddle? Touchstone 101 CD? Not much there to work with. I don't understand." She says with a dismissive hand.

"101 CD? it's not much of a riddle or rhyme or story."

"You said it was a dilemma of contradictions."

"It was." Grant pauses. "I guess it still is."

"If that is the case, will it solve anything?"

"I never said it would." Grant pushes back into the leather sofa.

"But you did say the riddle or whatever it is would offer clarity to your state of mind."

"Clarity? I said that? Jeez." His mind feels muddled since his encounter with ET.

"I think it may be more than that." Dr. Denard suggests.

"I'm not sure. Not today, anyway."

"What's different about today?"

"Spoke to other...eh, people." But, of course, Grant can't disclose any of it. He has problems processing it, understanding it.

"So you found somebody to talk with?"

"Yeah, I guess." *Don't really talk with ET but communicated. How do you explain that?*

Dr. Denard asks. "Friends?"

Maybe ET could be, or will be, a friend? "Yeah, people I've known for a long time," he lies. He's known an ET part of a day, anyway.

"Well, that's good."

"I suppose." Grant wonders how good it could be.

"Is it helping?"

"I'm not sure. Just started talking with them." He thinks he's just about done with these sessions. He is anxious to explore new worlds.

"Do they know about your daughter, Deana?"

"Haven't spoken about it." Grant doesn't know how Deana's drug addiction and incarceration would end up being an ET concern, as it is his. He can't imagine a drug problem within an ET world.

"Are you going to?" Dr. Denard asks.

"I think they know." The ET knows everything about Grant, even though he hasn't communicated anything about Deana. Grant can't keep secrets from the mind reader, time traveler, teacher.

"They found out?" Dr. Denard's curiosity is peaking.

"Not much they don't know." ET knows all.

"You're still searching for a solution?" Deana is only one issue he is dealing with, and she may no longer be the primary one.

"Always searching for a magic bullet," Grant says. It's a prophetic statement because Grant and Steve had dodged bullets in Vietnam combat.

"There may not be one." Dr. Denard suggests.

Grant made eye contact with the doctor. "I know. No fixing it, ever." At least in this time, he thinks.

"What she did can't be fixed. Fixed by you," Dr. Denard says. She puts down her pen.

"I know that; it's still there." Grant reflects, no changing it?

"Deana doesn't fit the image you have for her. Can't fix it to meet your expectations. And she'll be released someday."

Grant thinking, *She is serving five to fifteen for drug and human trafficking.* "Welcome to my nightmare. No fixing it ever." *There may be a chance...an ET?*

MAN 11

December 15, 2010
The Brothers Ride
Morning
Grant and Becky's Home
Santee

Steve knocks once and enters through the garage kitchen door without being invited in. He is wearing mountain biking cargo shorts, zippered biking shirt, and sandals. His worn outfit is tight-fitting on his overweight frame. Grant has similar clothing, also sandals. They have a practiced routine when they arrive at the trailhead. Both will change to socks and biking shoes; they carry small hydration backpacks including granola bars, essential tire repair, and first aid items. Grant and Becky are sitting at the kitchen table with coffee in hand. An excellent view from the sliding glass door overlooking a deck, the backcountry mountains east of Santee, and the neighbor's backyard fence. Becky keeps the space very organized without clutter, compared to Grant's workspace studio in the garage.

"Hey, are you ready for this ride? "Steve says. "I didn't see your bike out. Is it ready?"

"It's in the garage," replies Grant

He notices Becky, "How's it going, Becky?" Steve asks, walking over to a bowl of fruit and a plate of brownies. He chooses a brownie. Steve and Becky are not on the best terms; she prefers Grant to spend time with his brother away from her presence. She disapproves of his rough edges personality and manly vocabulary. However, she made accommodations do to his active prostate cancer condition. Steve had a checkered past concerning his three wives. His first wife, Nancy, without notice, sold his Austin Healey while he was in Vietnam. He loved that car. Deal breaker, the marriage dissolved very soon after his return; no children. His second wife, Roxy, had issues with Steve's fatherly/parent instincts and car fetish, a 1968 Pontiac 389 cubic inch V8 GTO convertible; he loved that car too. They had his one son; as a teenager, he lived with his mother after the divorce. There wasn't a great deal of father-son interaction due to his army posting to Germany and Korea; not sure they even like each other. Steve made a point of sending his teenage son a lump of coal for a Christmas present in 1989. Great relationship. It didn't seem to help the relation much. Becky wasn't a fan of Steve's marital and parental track record. She thought that Steve deserved the lump of coal. Steve's son had a career in law enforcement as a probation officer. He liked cars also.

"Doing okay, Steve." Becky responds, wearing a bathrobe and slippers, not looking up from her Words with Friends App. She has become hooked on the word game and is good at it.

Steve's attention is drawn toward the small television next to the microwave. There's a news alert about a woman found brutally beaten in a Pine Valley home.

* * * *

KFMB 8 TV News

"Welcome to the 7 o'clock morning news. We start off this morning's newscast with the report of a death of a Pine Valley resident. Andrea Alvarez is on scene outside a resident home in Pine Valley. Andrea, what have you found this morning?"

"Good morning, Tim and Kimberly. I am standing in front of the home of Paul and Julia Serrano. This is where, late yesterday afternoon, Pine Valley Sheriff deputies were responding to a 911 call from Mr. Serrano's sister, reporting her sister-in-law's death, an apparent murder victim. After the deputies entered the home, they found a body inside. At this time the indications are that it was Mrs. Serrano, apparently deceased for a number of days. The sheriff's spokesman also indicated it appears Mrs. Serrano was a victim of a homicide and perhaps a home invasion. The time and nature of death were not disclosed by the sheriff spokesman. It is noted that Paul Serrano is missing and hasn't been seen for days. The sheriff's department is considering him a 'person of interest' and indicates he hasn't been at work for a number of days."

From the studio, Tim asks, "Andrea, I understand Paul Serrano's parents live out-of-state and called the Sheriff since they hadn't heard from their son and his wife for several days?"

"That's correct. Paul's parents apparently couldn't get them to respond to phone calls or any of the emails they sent. They called the sheriff's office and asked their daughter to check on their son and his wife. I understand from the sheriff spokesman that they were very concerned about their son's welfare in light of what happened here."

Tim asks Andrea, "The Serrano's have a young daughter in intensive care at Rady Children's Hospital?"

Andrea reports, "That's correct, from what I understand, she is quite ill with an undisclosed ailment. The sheriff is asking for assistance in locating Paul Serrano. Back to you in the studio."

"Thanks, Andrea. We hope the sheriff has success in finding Paul Serrano and catching the perpetrators of this home invasion and homicide."

Tim on camera, "Anyone with information regarding this apparent murder should call the San Diego Sheriff's Office in Pine Valley at the number on the bottom of the screen.

* * * *

"I can't believe some son–of–a–bitch would do that to his wife and leave his sick kid in the hospital," observes Steve. He is munching on the brownie and has a mug of coffee he poured himself.

"There are screwed-up people all over," relates Becky, "Can't imagine that the husband did it. Need to wait and see." She starts washing dishes and baking pans in the sink.

"Well, I hope they find him and hang him by the balls." Steve doesn't conceal his thoughts.

"Calm down, Steve," Becky says. "At this point they don't know who did it, could've been anybody."

"They'll find him and then we'll find out what happened," says Grant.

Steve grabs an orange to take on their ride. "What trail are we going to hit today? Noble Canyon?"

"How about we go Corte Madera Mountain? That's a short ride compared to Noble Canyon. It's got great views all the way to Mexico and not many people are on that trail."

"Okay, we don't have enough time to do Noble Canyon anyway," Steve relents and waves to Becky. "Let's get going. See you later Becky."

A half-hearted wave, Becky is not pleased with Grant's seemly recent addiction to mountain biking.

From her perspective, he has gone off to that godawful mountain far more often than he ever did while working. In the past few months, it seems he's constantly mountain biking on Corte Madera. Grant has made a habit of missing meals or at least being late for them. Becky has given him a pass because she thinks he is struggling with his unemployment issues. He has had several dream episodes that have taken him out of bed, finding him on the floor and not remembering why. Becky realizes that it got worse after his return from Corte Madera two months back. She doesn't know why.

Mountain biking is Grant's cover story for returning to the ET's laboratory for more accelerated training.

He and Steve load their gear and bikes into Steve's truck. It will take them about an hour to get to the Corte Madera trailhead. Steve is unaware of Grant's reason to push the Corte Madera trail. Grant plans to introduce Steve to his alien friend as "ET" like in the movie "ET." And knowingly not having answers for all the questions that will be asked. The ET, newly named ET, will be at center stage front.

In his many years of managing DNA-altering projects on Earth, the extraterrestrial, ET, had never encountered directly and consciously any humans. The apparent coincidental and

128

accidental circumstances resulting from a minor earthquake that resulted in his injury and entrapment led to an "Alien Encounter" with a human subject, i.e., Grant. As a result of his entrapment, he could not initiate routine countermeasures designed to prevent "face-to-face interaction" with human subjects. Uniquely, Grant was instrumental in saving an alien life form, ET.

ET initiated a first-of-its-kind relationship with Grant in the rescue aftermath. That this occurred came with odds greater than winning the Powerball lottery. ET easily could have marginalized or eliminated most of Grant's recollection of his rescue efforts and the encounter. ET chose not to, initiating other options. The drug aerosol and process introduced by ET wouldn't make a person a genius, but it does enhance focus, memory, motivation, attention, mental clarity, and cognitive skills. It accesses and stimulates portions of the human brain that are typically not active.

The drug and accelerated learning process opens access to an individual's mental and intellectual capacity and builds upon it. The systematic approach via time travel can take an individual's mental acuity to a highly elevated intelligence boundary layer. Some individuals would not achieve the same intellectual and IQ capacity. ET's system is a reflection of an individual's innate intelligence capacity. Not all human subjects could be brought to the same level. The end product is based upon enhancing the foundation there to build upon. The result of this process compresses knowledge and intellectual acquisition to brief periods. Virtually years of study and retention of subject materials is reduced to a matter of minutes or hours. The only dilemma associated with this advanced accelerated learning process was Grant's beard and hair.

After his first 7-Eleven stop over shave, he had to remember to bring and use his electric shaver before returning home. He had one awkward experience when he inadvertently returned home with a growth of beard and saw a neighbor. Fortunately, this particular neighbor wasn't someone Grant saw on a routine basis. Nevertheless, it was a wake-up call for Grant. He was doubly fortunate that he didn't have to explain to Becky his beard because she wasn't home when he returned. He was able to shower and rectify the situation before she returned from her knitting group. After this experience, Grant left his shaver on the driver's seat as an uncomfortable reminder. The Alpine 7-Eleven knew him by name.

As usual, Steve is speeding; I-8 was clear, no traffic, and they know where the CHP hangs out. It was an easy transition from Grant's Santee home. It took about five minutes to be on a very familiar route heading East on I-8. From Grant's perspective, the trip to Corte Madera trailhead is going agonizingly slow, yet his mind is in overdrive. They couldn't have asked for better conditions to trail bike: bright sun, light wind, and 72 degrees. Steve's talking, but Grant doesn't hear him. On this trip to Corte Madera and ET's introduction, Grant had a marginally tentative plan to unpack his relation with an alien, a real alien. An ever-shifting plan to tackle the complicated cosmic subject matter of his relationship and discovery of ET. After all, it's not often that you introduce a relative to an extraterrestrial (ET) alien life form that you have been working with for months. What could go wrong with that scenario.

Steve, sort of complaining, trying to bring Grant out of a perceived funk, "You must enjoy this Corte Madera trail" Grant is focused, gazing out his window. "You spend a lot of time up there by yourself." Steve punches Grant's shoulder forcefully.

The punch brings Grant back to reality, he responds, rubbing his shoulder. "Well, it has more to offer than you think. May run into someone up there today." Grant smiles apprehensively and adds, "I think you're going to be surprised what you find on that trail. You've only been up there once or twice."

"Well, it's much more remote than Noble Canyon and there are not many people that ride it. I haven't been there in several months." Clearly, cares less about meeting anyone.

"Who knows, you may find you want to come back here more often, you never can tell." As it approaches, Grant wonders about Steve's uncertain reaction.

At the top of the switchback climb from interstate 8, they approach the Four Corners Staging area, where mountain bikers typically leave their trucks and vehicles while out riding the trails. There are no bands playing today, as they did when Grant was dream-hiking with JD. They find only one other vehicle and a couple of dirt motorcycles on a trailer when they arrive. There's a black Cadillac Escalade with the lift-back open, and four men gathered around looking at what appears to be a drone. The men give Grant and his brother the "stink eye." None of the men are dressed for motorcycle off-road biking, short coats, Levi's, and fancy cowboy boots; not gear for the terrain. Grant thinks this highly unusual. Two of the four men apparently will ride the dirt cycles: helmets, gloves, and boots. Grant has never seen them before but doesn't give it much thought. *Stranger things have happened on this trail,* he thinks.

As Grant and Steve gear up and unload their bikes, Grant says, "Looks like we have company today. I very seldom see dirt bike riders here, and I've never seen riders so unprepared for this terrain. Is the trail even open to motorcycles?"

"Don't know about that. Those cycles look new." Steve says. "This sure ain't the place to test them out."

"And what's up with the drone? I don't know if they know what they're doing, experimenting with a drone up here. If that thing loses power, they're going to have a hard time finding it and may never recover it in this terrain."

Steve says somewhat sarcastically, "Maybe I'll go ask them what they're looking for with that drone. They may be with a commercial company. Land survey or something?"

"Shit, no, look at those guys—they're not with any company, and it's clear they are not very happy to be here, and they're not happy to see us."

"Yeah, let's hit it and get out of here."

Grant and his brother take the mountain bikes off the truck and set out on one of the four dirt trails leading away from the staging area. They hope they've seen the last of the drone and dirt bike crew. The bike trail is primarily uphill switchbacks, a bit of a struggle for Steve. Finally, after about 45 minutes, they approached the Corte Madera peak turn-off.

They proceed on the route nearing Corte Madera. Grant is so familiar with the trail that he notices something out of place. There's a flash of bright red color shrouded in and among several oak trees to the left and somewhat downhill. Grant comes to a stop. Steve follows shortly.

Steve somewhat out of breath. "Thanks for stopping. It's been a while since I climbed that hill; not in great shape, I guess."

"Look off down there." Grant points downhill. "Do you see that red material in the trees? I've never noticed it before." Over the past two months, Grant has ridden this trail dozens of times and knows it exceptionally well, and the red seems out of place.

Steve looks, not seeing what Grant was referring to at first. "Yeah, there's some red; looks metallic red. Wonder how long it's been there?"

"It hasn't been there very long. I've been riding this trail consistently for a couple of months, and that's something new."

Steve takes a drink from his water bottle. "Looks like it could be one of those party balloons people turn loose, watching them drift on the wind. They end up as litter cluttering the back country, tangled on power lines."

"Looks out of place and a bit large for a party balloon. I'm going to go check it out, just a little too bright for balloons." Grant leaves his mountain bike against some brush and starts making his way toward the colored object downhill.

Steve doesn't follow. "Let me know, but I still think it's a balloon. Too hot for me to go bushwhacking in this heat."

As Grant makes his way toward the object, it becomes evident that it isn't a party balloon. It's a colored canvas-like material caught in the trees. The closer he gets, he sees a black tubular structure and what looks like a lawnmower engine near the tree's base. The engine, a wooden propeller, and a series of black bags, duffel bags, or canvas bundles are in front of those.

Grant yells up to Steve, "Steve, you need to get down here now! I think this is airplane wreckage."

Disbelieving, Steve responds, "That's a good one, Grant. Now, if you're done screwing around with the party balloon, let's get back on the trail and finish this ride."

"Steve, I am not shitting you, and it looks like the pilot is still in his seat, so get your ass down here now! I don't think he made it, from the looks of it."

Realizing that his brother was dead serious, Steve makes his way down to Grant's side, falling twice into Manzanita bushes. What they find yards off the trail is the wreckage of an ultralight aircraft. Approaching the badly broken aircraft, they see that there is a person in the tangled wreckage. Upon moving closer, looking for signs of life, it is clear that the pilot has been killed. Grant recognizes it as a two-seat tandem Silverwing Ultralight aircraft, and it had to have crashed one or two days earlier; Grant is sure he would have seen it when he was here three days ago.

They double-check to see if the pilot is alive. He is not. Both have had more than enough first-hand experience with the deadly results of aircraft crashes. Regardless of the frequency of such incidents, it is always a solemn occasion. Flies are covering exposed skin and wounds that stopped bleeding long ago. The pilot is armed with a chest-mounted antique silver forty-five caliber 1911 semi-auto pistol.

The brothers are Vietnam veterans who have experienced combat injuries and death up close. Steve, as a Cobra gunship pilot, had significant combat action. Grant flew combat rescue. Neither of them misunderstood the realities of this scene. After the unexpected discovery, they made an initial assessment of the situation and what sort of response they needed to make. Clearly, the pilot was killed in the crash. He had evidence of significant blunt force trauma to his head and torso. He was still strapped in his seat; it was clear he did not attempt to unbuckle himself. A collision with a tree at any speed while in an ultralight aircraft is not survivable. The pilot is wearing jeans, a Hells Angels T-shirt, a black leather jacket, and a camouflage helmet. They found the aircraft equipped with a radio, and his helmet had a microphone attached, which indicated he was most likely in radio contact with someone.

One of the two black duffel bags is torn and exposing its contents, bundles of $100 bills. They open the other bag and find it also contains bundles of cash. Grant and Steve are perplexed, wondering why someone would be flying over this remote region carrying duffel bags of money. After the initial shock of finding the aircraft wreckage, a dead pilot, and a lot of cash, their situation escalates intensively. A remote-controlled drone like the one seen at the staging area is directly above them. It is 30 feet overhead camera-equipped monitoring the crash site. Not good. Then, from a mile across the valley, Steve and Grant see and hear the same two dirt motorcycles from the Four Corners staging area.

"Holy shit—this is drug money on a border drug running ultralight. We need to get the fuck out of here!" Steve says. They now know the drone, and the motorcycles are from a Mexican cartel searching for the cargo of drug money going south to Mexico. The duffels were supposed to have been delivered a few days ago; the cartel wants it back, all of it.

"They are not going to be happy we found their money." Grant says.

"They should give us a reward. There's got to be a couple million in those bags." Steve says jokingly as they both race uphill to their bikes. He always joked when in a tight combat fight. Not really funny, but pressure-releasing. No one was laughing.

With their newfound wealth fleeting, they both ran up the hill much faster than when going down. They try to put as much distance between them and the crash site cash as possible on their mountain bikes. Both were hoping that the motorcycle riders would be more interested in the money and not follow them. They, unfortunately, realize that the drone and camera are following them, and, of course, their position is known, with nowhere evident to ride and hide.

Their dilemma focused on drug cartel soldiers that were now pursuing them along the mountain bike trail. They couldn't reach Steve's truck since the cartel's soldiers had seen them before entering the trail system. So instead, the chase funneled them uphill to the massive granite rock pinnacle that is Corte Madera. No other trail to consider. Only one trail and no forks in the road. They can't outrun the motorcycles and are almost out of options.

Grant realizes the only place to hide from the cartel dirt motorcycle riders is at the ET lab. "I know a place we can hide," he shouts, peddling wildly," We need to get to the lab!"

"What the fuck are you talking about?" Steve is struggling to keep up with the rapid uphill pace. "Lab, what lab? Where the hell are we going?" Steve yells because he is familiar with the trail that ends in less than 200 yards. He feels there's no way to escape the cartel dirt bike riders unless they jump off a hundred-foot sheer rock face.

Grant impatiently implores Steve, "Get your ass in gear." He has a place, a safe place if they can get there in time. The cartel dirt bike riders are hauling ass and getting instructions from the drone operator. From Steve's perspective, they are in a world of hurt. There are no other trail options. They're boxed in.

Grant leads the way to the lab and ET. They move quickly on their mountain bikes, needing time. Unfortunately, the much faster cartel dirt motorcycle riders reach them just short of the granite wall that looks to lead nowhere. They are cornered. Shit out of luck; off their bikes, Grant and Steve turn to face the cartel bikers as they prepare to open fire with semi-automatic Tek 9 handguns. Steve is a pace or two in front of Grant; by reflex, they raise their hands in a futile attempt to shield themselves from certain, violent death. Steve is struck with an apparent fatal shot. At this point, time came to a halt.

ET is controlling the time stopped scene. He had been monitoring the entire cartel encounter from the lab's holographic imaging database. A time-travel monitoring view into what would occur with Grant, Steve, and the cartel gunmen from their initial contact at Four Corners. ET calmly took over to prevent damage to his human subjects.

The chaotic scene is replaced by total silence. No gunfire was heard. The cartel gunmen, their guns firing bullets, all frozen in space and time. Steve, who had taken a bullet or two in the chest, had fallen backward. Initially, Grant is suspended same as the others but ET selectively removes him from the scenario, unharmed and able to move. Grant views this scene as if someone had hit the pause button on a television remote.

There is no sound. There is no movement except for Grant, his heavy breathing and rapid heartbeat. He sees the stationary gun muzzle flame and smoke of the cartel men's weapons. He views the rigid features of his brother and the cartel members. Yet while he moves forward, he sees bullets hovering stationary between the guns that fired them and the direction they were traveling, toward him and his brother. The muzzle flashes are not moving. The ejected casings lie in a motionless tumbling arc trailing to the ground. There is only silence. His anger and sorrow are building. He struggles to comprehend the enormity and significance of what just took place, all for drug money. Somewhat dumbfounded by what he saw and panicked by his brother's wounds, he instinctively notices ET's wrist device glowing with an amber light that seems to encompass everything within view. He pulls back from Steve, beginning to absorb the totality of his brother's loss. He is devastated. He stumbles back, turning to face the gunmen with anger building. He realizes he, his brother, and the cartel gunmen are all in a 'Pushback' time sequence, like a freeze-frame photo. Over the past two months, Grant named the procedure.

ET communicates with Grant, "Recalibrate sequence," which will allow Grant to use the Pushback opportunity to recover Steve. Grant repeats the phrase, "Recalibrate sequence."

Grant had learned from ET the effect of recalibrating sequence or Pushback in other time settings, a basic time reset or a do-over. Pushback allowed a rollback of time in seconds, minutes, or more. It wasn't complicated as long as the bracelet time setting device, on ET's wrist was activated. To roll back time in a calibrated sequence required an actual physical push to reverse time. For Pushback to work, a movable object in the time sequence is needed. You can't Pushback a fixed object; to work, it has to have movement. Since the bullets, now suspended in space, were moving, Grant was able to hand push them back in time. He slowly starts pushing a stationary bullet by hand back toward its original location in the muzzle of the Tek9 mm semi-automatic weapon with his palm. Grant feels unsure if his Pushback efforts would reverse the massive wounds in his brother's chest. While he moves from Steve, Grant sees that time stopped bullets and their casings are changing course. They are returning to the Tek9s and into the barrel and cartridge ejection port.

He stands there briefly, perplexed, trying to understand what is happening in front of him. Then it all comes to him in a moment of clarity. With the palm of his hand, he continues to push the bullet back toward the cartel guns. The muzzle flashes are becoming smaller, all contracting; everything is moving in reverse order.

Knowing now what is happening, without panic, Grant turns and looks at his brother and his wounds while pushing a suspended bullet back toward the gunmen. As he slowly proceeds, Steve's body moves from its prone position to standing upright. Blood starts to flow back into his brother's wounds, and the bloodstains on his shirt shrink, retracting around the bullet hole. Grant keeps the process going until the penetrating bullets exit his brother's chest. From all indications, his brother should be without injury and safe. Steve is still stopped in time, but without his wounds; his expression still shows the sheer terror of being shot. Hands extended out in front in a defensive posture, useless against 9mm lead slugs. Once Steve comes out of the Pushback, Grant will introduce his brother to ET, a unique event, circumstance notwithstanding.

At this point, ET manipulates Steve out of the time Pushback scenario. However, the two cartel motorcycle riders are still time-stopped as well as the drone following them. Before this intervening cartel shootout, Grant had planned on a more controlled, calm, and reasonable introduction that would most likely challenge his credibility in his brother's eyes. He had expected that Steve would be highly skeptical of his explanation regarding his association and ongoing relationship with an actual extraterrestrial.

Being the recent focal point of a Mexican cartel money retrieval hit team, intent on ending his life had altered the landscape of Grant's hesitation regarding his brother's reaction to ET. A near-death experience in a shootout tends to change one's perspective and focus one's attention. Both brothers have avoided a sure-death shooting. They are alive thanks to ET and a Pushback event. Grant understands it; Steve will eventually. He is going to have a reality check beyond belief, plus video playback. A real unfucking-believable-you-gotta-be-shitting-me, discussion. A 1-0-4, WTFO!

Steve regains some sense of reality. "Okay someone want to tell me what the fuck is going on? What just happened and who is the bald guy with the skin tight suit?" So much for controlled, calm, orchestrated, and reasonable. He was dead just a minute or two ago, and he doesn't know it yet. He will.

Steve is pointing at ET, "Holy shit. You said we might meet somebody. Is this the guy? Would someone start talking or wake me up from this cluster fuck?" ET stands without any indication of expression or visual cues. His eyes move slightly between Steve and Grant. He is observing and recording the encounter.

"Let me start. You're going to have a hard time believing all this and what I'm going to tell you," Grant begins.

"No shit," Steve grunts. He moves closer to ET while re-examining his chest for bullet holes.

"Shut up and listen," Grant says, knowing this is a complicated story to relate to and a hard sell. "The bald guy is the person I told you about that I rescued a couple months ago from a rockslide after the last earthquake. It was very near here where the incident occurred. If you remember, I told you I came upon another mountain biker trapped in the rockslide? Well, that wasn't the complete truth. He really isn't a mountain biker, although he hangs out here at Corte Madera. This is the guy."

Steve grunts again, still watching ET. "And the two guys." He points to the cartel gunmen. "Toting the Tek9s. Why aren't they moving? Weren't they just shooting at us?" "Shit, they *were* shooting at us!" Steve's eyes open wide, and his jaw drops—he remembers. He strokes his chest again, searching for a bullet wound. "Jesus." He stops and just stares at ET, then at Grant." What the shit is going on?" Steve does have a memory of the shootout and being hit twice. He doesn't know what followed in Pushback. He keeps up his litany of profanity and wants someone to explain what just happened. The babble and profanity pour out in a constant stream. He continues spouting and searching for bullet holes and blood. There are none.

Grant is irritated, "If you will shut the fuck up, I will get you all the details you can handle and more!" Steve finally stifles his tirade as Grant begins to explain, "The bodysuit bald guy is an alien, He's not from here."

"Well, no shit. I already figured that one out. So, where is he from? He looks like nobody I have ever seen before: the body suit, no shoes. I don't get it. Where do people dress like that? He looks straight out of a Star Trek scene. A hairless albino on top of it all, with the Tri-Corder on his left arm. Star Trek. He needs sun."

"Jesus, when I say he's not from here, I mean he's not from Earth." Grant is stressed. ET, standing alone, is not. He chooses to observe intensely, following the conversation between the two brothers. It is a first. He is the subject of dialog between two humans; they exhibit emotional reactions to his presence and existence. He experiences a touch of alien curious enlightenment. An aha moment for ET, if there was such an experience in his alien world. There isn't.

"Not from Earth? so he's a Martian?" Steve is not taking this as seriously as he should.

"I honestly don't know exactly where he came from. We've never discussed that."

ET is standing still, watching and observing Grant and Steve.

"Well, let's ask him, what's his name?" Steve gestures toward ET.

"He doesn't talk, or, rather, he doesn't speak and has no name."

"Doesn't speak or won't speak?"

"He corresponds without speaking." Grant turns his hand's palms up, "He doesn't need to."

"Okay, how does he correspond?" Steve is genuinely puzzled and still pissed about being shot at. "Sign language? What's up with those funky hands? He is missing a finger on each." "I'm not sure how to explain it, but he is able to communicate without verbalization. You will know when he communicates with you." Grant expects ET will jump into the conversation at some point. He stands very still, observing.

"Okay, how will you know? Is he using Spock's Vulcan mind-meld method?" Steve turns toward ET and asks. "Tell me your name? No, better yet, send me your name?"

"He doesn't have a name. I refer to him as ET as in extraterrestrial. Using that name was initially a verbal crutch for me. I found it awkward to attempt a conversation without a name. Hence, I borrowed the term ET, from the 1982 film ET."

"I know the fucking movie, but ET? Really? You got to be shitting me. Not very original." He is pacing looking puzzled among the cartel men still pointing their guns, Grant and ET.

"He truly is an extraterrestrial and he doesn't speak, doesn't vocalize, doesn't need to. I find that I have one-way vocalizations with ET. That works well for me and him. He is able to respond to you with a clear mental image. It is basically corresponding with visualization without vocalization. You don't have to hear to understand without words."

"So, it's mind-reading? You communicate by reading each other's mind, is that it?" Steve walks over to ET and bends down, looking at him closely, almost inspecting as he did with army recruits. ET backs up a bit but maintains eye contact. Steve is nearly 18 inches taller.

"It's not mind-reading. It would be more appropriate to call it mind-tending, a mind visualization, or more clearly communicating on a level without the need to speak." Grant gives Steve an example of a shepherd tending to his flock of sheep. "The shepherd and his flock know their routine without speaking; they communicate effectively without an abundance of vocalizations. The tending, goes both ways. Both sheep and shepherd communicate on a nonverbal level."

"Okay, okay, is he mind-talking-tending to you? I don't hear it in my mind, up here." Tapping a forefinger to his head. "Anything he, ET, is saying to you without speaking? Is he mind-talking-tending now?" Steve moves away from ET.

"It doesn't work quite like that. Take, for example, identical twins. In many cases, they're able to finish each other's sentences. They are on the same page and able to speak in place of one another."

Suddenly, Steve stops speaking and looks startled. He is nearly locked in place once again. He moves his hands to his forehead, turns left then right as if someone had tapped him on the shoulder. He looks at his brother, and they both stare at ET. "He just sort of told me to shut up and listen," Steve says. "Holy shit! That's mind-tending? Acid tripping without the acid."

Grant nods, "Did you hear it?"

"I didn't hear it. I think I saw it. It was up here in front of me, in my fucking head all around me. He asked me to walk to those bullets and casings suspended in midair. How is he doing that? What's keeping them suspended in air? Jesus, what's going on?" Pushback and time manipulation seem more like a Las Vegas magician's stage act. This has to be a trick.

"Well, what are you waiting for? Looks like you two are having a mind-talking or tending conversation right now, or maybe a planet Vulcan mind-meld with ET! Either works." Grant smiles.

This initial communication with ET has Steve back on his heels. Within the last several minutes, Steve has been initiated into a new and very different reality. He was not prepared for any of the events that took place within the last hour. He could deal with the earthly affairs, running from the Mexican cartel, finding the ultralight crash and cash, to the shootout. He had been shot at before, knew how to deal with it. Then the suspension of his reality and waking up in a new one blew his mind. He tries to get his bearings and wrap his mind around everything. His reality is changed forever.

Grant points at the suspended bulletin cartridges and says, "Well, get going."

Steve looks at his brother, then at ET.

Steve approaches the suspended bullets and, apparently at ET's direction, nudges them back toward the 9mm weapons from which they were fired. As he accomplishes this, the bullets suspended from his chest wound and casings start to return as the weapons' muzzle flashes, smoke, and flame diminish slowly back into the guns. In slow, staggered motion, he notices the Mexican gunman absorb the recoil of each bullet fired. Their eyes blink in slow motion and remain focused on their human targets, he and Grant. They have no recognition of the circumstance of their time-paused condition. Steve, curiously, with an open palm, pushes the last bullet into the barrel of the extended gun to determine the effect on the gunman. He keeps constant pressure, and slowly the gunmen start to back up toward their dirt bikes. He continues walking the gunmen backward. They are reversing the path they took when they hopped off their motorcycles.

Steve notices their eyes are intense and focused on shooting and killing both him and his brother. He stops and asks ET. "Could we back their actions all the way to the Four Corners staging area?" ET answers, mind-tending that he could back those gunmen back for days. However, he did indicate that the more individuals encountered during the Pushback becomes much more problematic because the impact can have unforeseen consequences.

Steve had limited memory of what went on with the two motorcycles riders; however, he helped develop a scenario to push them back down the narrow trail. ET "replayed holographically" the Pushback for Grant and Steve to view the whole chase to its time-frozen conclusion. Grant came up with a plan for the gunmen.

Grant knew from experience with Pushback that he had to disarm the cartel gunmen. Since Pushback only delays the actual sequence of events, the cartel gunmen would exit Pushback firing their weapons at both Steve and Grant. Or at least they would be firing in the direction where they were last standing. Grant realized an adjustment needed to be made to disarm the gunman temporarily. He needed time to devise a permanent nonviolent solution. It involved an extended Pushback that moved the cartel soldiers nearly on hundred feet back from when they first discharged their weapons. During ET's playback of the shooting, Grant noticed that the initial weapons discharge took place approximately twenty feet before a second burst struck his brother. Once determining this initial firing location, Grant was confident that he could manipulate each Tek9 magazine release button and remove them, leaving one round left in each chamber. He knew those rounds had missed his brother, and once fired, the Tek9s would be empty due to the missing cartridge-filled magazines. Grant would be able to accomplish two goals with this maneuver. First, when he releases the cartel gunman back to real-time at the 100-foot point in the pursuit, they would fire their weapons at 20 feet, missing both him and his brother. At that point, the gunman would realize their guns were empty or malfunctioning, forcing them to pause to reload or switch to backup weapons. This distraction would only last a matter of seconds, but it was enough time for his brother to join him on the other side of the Pushback event, removing both of them from the scene and danger. It was an elaborate, time-consuming plan. Ultimately, ET short-circuited Grant's strategy. He managed to manipulate the gunmen's short-term memory over the last fifteen minutes. It is at this point, Steve and Grant displayed for ET a somewhat human characteristic of revenge. They communicated with ET that they wanted to provide the motorcycle cartel members that had just tried to kill them with water. ET indicated that physical contact needs to be avoided to reduce the compromise of the Pushback event sequence. The brothers state that there would be no physical contact, just water left for the two bike riders. Grant suggested that ET time pause the Pushback to the point that the cartel bikers had stopped and been still sitting on their motorcycles, just as they were ready to get off and start shooting. Once they were in that position, time froze. Steve and Grant took two water bottles and entered the scene. Steve, in particular, wanted to bash both riders in the face, but he held back and provided them both with water. After all, it was a hot day. They approached the two riders sitting stationary on their bikes and proceeded to dump water on the seats. They were soaking their seats and crotch.

Steve and Grant exited this scene, and it was clear that ET, perhaps for the first time, was confounded and baffled. When the time pause was released, he was further puzzled by both the reaction of the cartel bike riders in addition to Steve's and Grant's. The brothers laughed almost hysterically, watching the bike riders trying to grab for their weapons, at the same time holding their crotches. The Pushback worked to the relief of Grant and Steve. Sweet revenge. Their only regret was that they wished they had Mickey D's coffee instead of cold water. Grant laughed while reciting from the Falcon code, "That's a 1-0-9."

Steve disagrees, "I think a 1-0-8 is a better fit for those two dirtbags.

"You just might be right, Steve. What do you think, ET? Have you ever seen the shit-heal-stomp?" ET is strangely silent while watching his two human subject's reactions.

ET took control of the cartel's actions by Pushback to a position where Grant and Steve do not come upon the crash, the cash, the dead pilot, nor the dirt bike cartel soldiers. They are no longer involved or seen, avoiding the shootout by taking an alternate route away from the crash site and the lab.

In essence, none of the cartel personnel know of Grant and Steve on mountain bikes near the crash site. When ET ended the edited Pushback, Grant and his brother were no longer there. They were able to observe the confounded, confused and bewildered cartel gunman searching in vain for a memory that vanished in front of them. They did take the duffel bags of money from the wreckage and returned to the Four Corners marshaling area and the drone operators. Likewise, ET adjusted the cartel members' short-term memory operating the drone and altered the drone's camera recorded images to show Grant and Steve taking another trail well away from the crash and cash. Under these conditions, the cartel members had no evidence or memories of Grant and Steve being near the crash site. They were concerned that they managed to recover their drug money without incident or witnesses, with just a bit of déjà vu and water cool down. From

ET's perspective, it was an exercise for Grant and Steve. They observed and found that merely manipulating short-term cartel memory attained the desired outcome without gunfire.

Steve looks around, searching for where ET came from. "When we were running from those guys you said you know a place, the lab. I didn't understand what you were saying then, and I don't see 'the lab' you were talking about. I don't see anything around here. Where's the lab? Nothing here but the bike trail and lots of granite." Hands out palms up, turning around facing a granite wall.

"That's exactly where ET came from when he stopped those guys with the Pushback."

"All I see is granite. Giant granite walls. He was standing in front of a 40-foot granite slab when the shooting started. Where's the door, portal, Gateway, whatever?"

"He was standing at the lab entrance. It's right behind him." Grant says, pointing to the granite wall behind ET.

"Okay, I got it. He's able to walk through solid granite walls." Steve walks to the granite wall, puts his hands on it, and is not sold. "This wall? He is able to move through this?"

Grant interrupts, "Just watch. ET, it's time for show and tell."

"Jesus, he just said, 'watch closely' mind talked or tended it." Steve is still amazed.

ET manipulated his wrist band device, and, in doing so, the granite structure behind him turned translucent. He turns and enters. He communicates to Steve and Grant to follow suit. Steve feels a bit skeptical, not wholly understanding the transformation of solid granite into a seemingly transparent membrane. Grant gestures for his brother to pass through the entrance. Steve, holding his breath, cautiously steps into and through the entry port to the lab. Once inside, he finds himself standing on an Oval disc about 40 feet in diameter surrounded by what seems to be vast open space. At ET's mind-tended invitation, Steve turns around slowly and then begins to walk toward the edge of the Oval. As he approaches the edge, he notices the open space is outer space. In his mind, he visualizes it as a planetarium.

Looking over the edge, he realizes the Oval is not only surrounded by outer space; it is suspended there. They are standing on an Oval disc like platform that is without supporting features. He looks for a foundation structurally holding it in place. Steve walks the entire circumference, searching to understand his current environment. He finds there are, in fact, no supporting structures visible. He is genuinely confounded and amazed at his total lack of understanding. It is one of the most humbling experiences he has ever encountered in his life.

ET communicates with Steve, "The platform that you're standing on is free-floating. I believe those are terms you can understand. The depictions surrounding the platform is your solar system. In your terms, it is a holographic creation much like a screen saver associated with your computers. The screensaver here, you will learn, can be replaced with historic depictions chosen for recording and observation."

ET moves the depiction surrounding the platform. The surroundings give Steve vertigo, as it seems the disc is turning 90° downward. The perceived movement forces Steve to his knees. On all fours, he clutches for support to prevent him from falling from the disc. Grant walks to him, encourages him to stand up, holds his arm, and ushers him toward a lawn chair.

"You're really going to need to get used to this. Try sitting in my lawn chair."

"I never get vertigo. I have over 3000 hours of helicopter time. Only occasionally was I hit with spatial disorientation. But nothing like this. Never had and acid trip like this."

"Believe me, it'll get better."

"Lawn chair! You got to be shitting me. I'm sitting on a lawn chair on an alien frisbee. So much for the high-tech encounter." Steve is having a hard time focusing. A lawn chair in an alien craft is beyond comprehension.

Grant attempts to clarify, "As you will notice, this is a very spartan environment, but high-tech beyond our human capabilities. There are no chairs, sofas, recliners, or other sitting or sleeping platforms. ET and his alien counterparts stand, never sit. Everything he does, he does standing up. By the way, they don't eat, they don't drink, don't consume food and liquid as we do. ET doesn't sleep as we know it; he has a hibernation sequence, I call it, still standing up."

"Standing up? Hibernation like a bear...really?"

"Yes, somewhat. ET receives some sort of supplement during that period that sustains him. The best way to explain or try to comprehend it is he is in a recharging sequence, getting his tank filled, so to speak. He is absorbing the sustenance and liquid required by his body systems. During his short periods of hibernation, he can fulfill the need for food, liquid, or sleep. And, apparently, there's no need for any sort of bathroom facility, hence no indoor plumbing required. ET has an internal consumption, digestive system that is 100 percent efficient. Hence, no waste."

"Well, no shit? I mean, literally, no shit. You eliminate the need for food and drink and consequently no need for a latrine break. That would change the whole human equation and eliminates how we humans survive. It fucking changes everything." Steve removes his biking helmet, slapping his leg a couple of times. "So, when, where does he hibernate standing up?" Steve looks around the lab.

Grant points to the small, dimly lit Oval disc on the floor." He will be standing on that oval section on the floor, very still stationary and out of the way. No eye movement, very shallow breathing, head down, and not responding or communicating."

Steve asks, "How long does he take for his hibernation break for recharging or whatever? Is it minutes? Hours? What?"

"It is dependent on how long since the last recharging. No more than one or two hours." ET communicates. He has been observing the interaction between Steve and Grant. He is fully aware of the total lab environment, every detail, and nuance.

Steve, dumbfounded, looks in Grant's direction.

"So yes, I have a lawn chair and brown bag in here. And for bathroom breaks, I make my way out of here to the surrounding environment and take care of business. You'll notice a small spade, hand sanitizer, and TP in the small backpack on the side of the lawn chair. Not so high-tech, but it works. I've come to believe that we could accomplish so much more if we didn't have to eat and use a bathroom, but of course, we would die. Something in the future perhaps. I can't stand standing for very long."

"I'm going to need a lawn chair," Steve replies.

"It will take some time to get familiar with the operations within the lab. There are a lot of new concepts to learn and embrace. ET will explain via his 'mind-meld,' as you put it."

"This is way beyond acid tripping." Steve struggled to comprehend.

Steve volunteered to undergo time travel accelerated learning. ET did provide it, although not as extensively as his brother's learning curricula. Steve, however, was an avid, eager student and absorbed the advanced learning like a sponge. In some regards, Steve was equal to his brother, especially in his inquisitive questioning nature. In actuality, this whole concept of reality came into question. Yet, he was convinced he wanted to be part of it, knowing that he could never fully understand everything this new reality brought.

Steve became an ET disciple after the encounter with the Mexican cartel in which ET engineered a Pushback of time and saved the brothers from being shot to death. Steve's Army training mirrored ET's demonstration-performance method: show it, do it, know it. He was a relatively easy sell when he observed the apparent simplicity of reversing fired bullets back to their origin. However, he came away with an attitude that he needed to learn much more about ET and his relationship with Grant.

Grant explained in as much detail as possible the circumstance that brought himself and ET together. Two months ago, his solo mountain biking trip on the Corte Madera trail days after the East County earthquake led him to discover ET trapped in a rockslide. He explained how he recovered ET and assisted him back to his lab. ET's lab. Once they were back in the lab, ET could manage his own recovery. Grant's physical assistance no longer needed It was during that time that Grant and ET came to an understanding regarding their future relationships. Grant explained that ET is interested in a relationship with him outside the scope of his purpose on Earth for some reason. It may be the intriguing nature of the rock slide assistance, compassion without judgment, and legitimate concern for another being.

MAN 12

Brutal Reality

After the Mexican cartel bikers retrieved their money, Steve and Grant returned to the ultralight crash site. They weren't sure what they would find or do. Maybe identify the pilot. Approaching the wreckage, they saw that the pilot was in a state of decomposition, indicating he'd been there for some days.

The pilot's severe head trauma was caused by a six-inch oak branch that collapsed the aluminum frame of the ultralight. The wreckage was partially suspended in a long-dead oak tree; the branches were extremely dry, hard, and brittle. Death had to have come rapidly. Grant noticed a cell phone in the breast pocket of the pilot's leather flight jacket, which seemed undamaged. The gunmen overlooked or ignored it in their damp-crotch confused haste to retrieve the drug money. Grant let Steve know, " Got his cell."

"How about his wallet or ID?" Steve replies.

Grant stretched for the other pocket, trying to holding his breath. "Jeez, flies are all over him." He retrieved the wallet and pilot's license, handed them to Steve.

Looking through wallet and license Steve remarks. "His name is Paul Serrano. An ultralight instructor pilot. From the money we found, he apparently was also an air courier for cartel smuggling to Mexico." Steve recognizes the name. His wife was found murdered a couple of days ago in Pine Valley."

Grant chimed in, "He is a person of interest in his wife's murder, he has been missing for several days." They both recall the news story. There was speculation that he was a primary suspect, and it is known that they had money trouble, upwards of a million dollars associated with their daughter's leukemia treatment. The sheriff reported that Paul's cell phone had no tracking capability; however, there was no record of its use in several days.

"Holy shit," Steve is pissed. "This is the guy I said they should hang by his balls if they ever caught him. I was certain he killed his wife."

"I know you were on the warpath and ready to join the vigilante lynch mob committee."

"Those sons of bitches on the cycles and drone took the money. They did it. They killed her. I'm sure of it." Steve puts the ID's back into Paul's wallet.

"You don't know that, at least not yet." Grant presses the screen of Paul's phone. It comes to life. His phone is not locked; there are several missed calls and videos. Grant starts to scroll through them.

There are two days of missed calls from his wife and harrowing videos of the woman tied to a chair and systematically tortured. A man off-screen indicates that Paul had better return the money, or things would get much worse for his wife. And things did get much worse, graphic and brutal to watch.

MAN 13

**Pine Valley
December 12, 2010
Three days prior
Serrano's Home**

Pine Valley Sheriff's officers respond to a hysterical 911 call from Paul Serrano's sister. She was calling from the Serrano's home where she was doing a welfare check since her sister-in-law, Julia Serrano hadn't been at work for three days, nor had she answered her phone. Paul's sister found her body and, in hysterics, called the sheriff's office.

Two sheriff deputies enter the unlocked house to find the body of Mrs. Serrano tied to a chair. She is nude from the waist up, and apparently was beaten, burned, and cut; her mouth was stuffed with a cloth and taped shut. A large "Z" was carved into her chest. One deputy runs from the house and vomits on the lawn. The home was ransacked, indicating the intruders were looking for something. The husband, Paul Serrano, is missing. The sheriff's deputies need to talk to him.

Paul, Julia, and Tam

Paul Serrano has been an electrical contractor for 22 years. He also had an ultralight instructor pilot's license and instructs in a dual tandem ultralight. For Julia's 25th birthday, her family and friends gave her a lesson on an ultralight. Paul was her instructor. They hit it off and were married two years later, fifteen years ago.

They have one daughter, Tam, short for Tammy. She is 5, with several life-threatening conditions: leukemia and mucormycosis a fungal infection. The condition can affect the gastrointestinal tract and cause thrombosis and tissue necrosis. She required a complicated operation that removed portions of her colon, spleen, and kidney. The medical bills $1.25 million. The Serranos' insurance would cover some of the costs, but the Serranos need to find $250,000 to begin treatment. Tam's projected survival rate is fifty-seven percent.

Paul is familiar with the drug cartels 'cash transfer operation. Flying cartel cash over the border to Mexico has been common knowledge among the ultralight community. He had been approached in the past to provide a similar service. At the time, he had no interest in participating in illegal and dangerous operations. Paul, reluctant to work for the Mexican cartel, chooses to take the risk with the advent of his daughter's illness and the requirement for significant medical treatment and costs. He was desperate and had exhausted all other funding sources to help with his daughter's critical life-threatening health condition. He needed the money so that she could live; he let the word circulate of his change of attitude. Within a short time, contact was made by a representative of the Sinaloa Cartel.

Mexican drug cartel personnel aren't recruited because of their warm personalities; they are coldhearted killers. The brutality of their cartel environment is routine; compliance with their bosses comes without question or hesitation. Orders are followed implicitly. Their lives depend upon their total loyalty, and no shortcomings are tolerated. Mistakes, actual or perceived, lead directly to termination, not only for the cartel soldiers, but their families pay the price for errors in judgment. Not many retire gracefully or at all. Paul has second-guessed his involvement, but his daughter's life is his only focus.

At no time was the cargo discussed. It was only a contract to fly first-time orientation training flights. Paul and the cartel agent understood the full meaning of the flight. Fly a cargo across the border, land, unload and return to the original takeoff location. It was a high-risk illegal operation for Paul, but it was also lucrative and a method to raise the necessary funds for his daughter's treatment. Paul hoped to deliver cartel cash for only a short time, then get out of the business. However, you generally don't quit the cartel and live to talk about it. He was desperate and willing to face all the risks involved.

Paul expected to be paid $20,000—a fraction of what he needs—for his first drug run. Ten to fifteen trips might do it. Paul can transport $6 million in cash strapped to the second seat of his Silverwing ultralight. He meets his cartel employer at the base of the Corte Madera Mountain on a dry lakebed five miles south of Pine Valley.

Paul has the key code for the gate and access to the private field. He assures his partners that the few high-end vacation homes on the shoreline nestled among pine trees are unoccupied that time of year. They don't care; his job is to deliver the cash as told! Four men in a black Cadillac SUV arrived at the gate. Paul recognizes only one: the man he has dealt with, Quintero James. There are no greetings. Paul activated the access panel, drove his truck towing his ultralight trailer, followed by the Cadillacs. The gate closes after 30 seconds. They travel a short distance to the dry lakebed. Paul unloaded and assembled his ultralight without asking or wanting assistance. Three men armed with automatic weapons watch the surrounding vacant homes and tree line. Quintero monitors Paul until he indicates he is ready for the cash cargo. Two black canvas bags are strapped in the rear seat of the tandem ultralight. There is no conversation.

It will be a very late afternoon takeoff, with light diminishing an hour or so before sunset. The weather for his flight includes clear skies with some wind turbulence over the Corte Madera Peak; he is very familiar with this area. He is to fly the money directly south across the border and land on a small dirt strip west of Tecate. After the delivery, he will collect $20,000 and return to the Corte Madera valley dry lake field, disassemble and load his ultralight on his trailer, head home. He will be contacted by text and given the next scheduled cash run. There will be several deliveries within the next two weeks; just the beginning.

CONSIDER MAN

All goes well until after he's airborne on the first delivery run south. The takeoff was routine; the elevation is approximately 4,400 feet, with a takeoff run of about 300 feet. Once airborne, Paul climbed to near 500 feet, which put him about 200 feet above the rising mountainous terrain. Crossing directly over Corte Madera Peak, Paul's ultralight encountered engine and turbulence problems. Paul didn't know exactly what the issue was and tried desperately to regain engine power. He lost altitude in short order, a nose-down dive; there was virtually nowhere to put the ultralight. He crashes on the south side of Corte Madera Peak at 50 knots into a stand of dead oaks. He is killed immediately on impact. The ultralight does not burn; no smoke or fire. This is problematic for the Mexican cartel for they have no idea where their money went.

The cartel soldiers in the valley didn't see Paul crash because he had passed the mountain's crest. Radio communication died with Paul. It was some hours later before they knew he was missing. Cartel members in Mexico say Paul never arrived. They stationed members at each site throughout the coming night. The local leadership makes frantic phone calls within their network, notifying other members to be on the lookout for Paul's ultralight and the money. They have no reports or ideas where Paul and the $6 million were located. They had their men watching for Paul at his home, his ultralight storage facility, and the dry lake bed takeoff strip. Early the next morning there is no evidence that he is anywhere near either location. As a result, they decide to go to his house, searching for information regarding his disappearance. They send a black SUV and three individual members to Paul's home office. Someone is there, perhaps his wife?

The Serrano home and workshop are located down a 50-yard driveway on about two and a half acres. There is a four-vehicle detached garage storage structure. The entire site is nestled neatly among old-growth oak and pine trees. It is semi-secluded, with the nearest neighbor down the road about 150 yards. The SUV is somewhat obscured from the driveway entrance. As they pull up near the house, they see that a woman opens the door and steps on the porch. They don't know the woman; Paul's wife, Julia, looks concerned. They walked to her door, and one member introduced himself as Quintero James. He guesses the woman's identity. "Good morning, Mrs. Serrano. Is your husband, Paul, here?" Quintero speaks without a hint of an accent.

"No, he's not here. She took a migraine sleep aid last night; zonked out early. I think he got up early for a client meeting." Julia looks over all three men; she has never seen them before. All three men are dressed in black with Mexican type boots and short leather jackets. Julia doesn't know Paul's flying clients. She takes a hesitating step back toward the open screen door. She has an uncomfortable feeling about them.

Quintero seems to have a legitimate interest himself regarding Paul's whereabouts. He replies, "I am also concerned. We had a meeting yesterday evening, and he didn't arrive as scheduled. Has he called you or contacted you in any way?"

Julia didn't know of his night flight. She is in the dark. "No, he hasn't answered his cell phone and hasn't called or texted. Haven't heard from him since yesterday, late afternoon." Julia is not recognizing this person asking the questions. "How do you know my husband?"

"We have a business relationship, a contractual relationship, actually. Perhaps we should go inside and wait to hear from your husband."

Julia's ready for them to leave. "I'm sorry. I have to go to work this morning. I'm sure he will be along later today, and I will have him contact you. Would you like to leave your contact information and I will see that he gets it?"

"Are you sure he is not here? I think we need to look for ourselves to be sure he is not." The three men forcefully push their way into the Serrano home. Julia is caught off guard. She is quickly subdued, struck in the face, gagged, and tied to a kitchen table chair.

The men search the house and outlying buildings for Paul and black cash canvas bags. He and duffels are not there. Quintero asks where Paul is, Julia is no help. He has instructions to stay and wait for further developments and seek information from Julia. She needs to contact Paul. "You will call your work and report you are ill, can't work today." Quintero demands. Her gag is removed.

"I can't. I have clients who expect me to be there." says Julia, struggling tied and bound; she can't move.

Quintero nods at one of his men, who backhands Julia across her face. She is stunned and nearly rolls the chair over. "You will call now."

After two more forceful backhands, she is compelled to call in sick with an apparent case of food poisoning accompanied by diarrhea. She may be out for a couple of days. "Please cancel any appointments or reschedule for next week." She advises her coworker stylists; they understand.

Julia is a devoted wife, and mother and has no knowledge of Paul's dealing with these men. Consequently, when the Cartel members interrogate her, she has no idea where her husband is and certainly knows nothing about his flying money to Mexico. She is asked repeatedly where Paul has gone with their money. Their questions dumbfound her. She is grateful that Tam is at the Rady Children's Hospital and not subject to this horrific scene. The Cartel men don't believe her and don't care. They just want information on Paul's location and their money. They step up the intensity of the questioning. Quintero instructs the other two to cut away Julia's blouse and bra. They are now off-camera videotaping with her cell phone, bare-breasted, mouth taped over, Julia tied to a chair. They are transmitting a live video to Paul's cell phone.

"Paul, you need to contact us," a voice accompanying the video says. "Your wife, as you can see, requires your attention. If you don't call and return the money, your wife will look very different." At this point, a hand reaches into the video and caresses her breast. In the other hand, with a knife, Julia's breast is cut, not deep but long and painful. Her muffled screams can be heard clearly as the blood flows down her chest to her waist.

"Paul, this is just the beginning; you must contact us. The longer you wait, the more difficult time Julia will have. She is an attractive woman, and my men may need to play rough with her as they get bored waiting."

As time goes on and no call or contact from Paul, the games with Julia turn brutal. They continue to use her cell phone to send Paul graphic video images of his wife bare-breasted, gagged, cut, burned with cigarettes, and molested. She's repeatedly cut about her breasts, slapped, punched, and questioned over and over with no meaningful information revealed. Paul never sees the images. Julia dies with her throat cut.

Paul won't be found for two more days by Grant and Steve, two mountain biking brothers. The cartel has no idea where their money or Paul went. He took the money and ran. He was now a dead man in their eyes. The two days later, the cartel motorcyclist recover two cash duffels from the ultralight crash site on Corte Madera; a few dead bodies, Paul and Julia, were incidental to their operation. The cost of doing business. They don't recall encountering two mountain bikers near the crash site or how their motorcycle seats got wet.

Only after Steve and Grant recovered Paul's cell phone with the video of his wife's torture did they understand that he had nothing to do with his wife's suffering and death.

"Boy, did I get that wrong." Steve remarks, "He was dead the whole time."

"She didn't know shit; she was in the fucking dark and died in the dark." Grant nearly explodes." It was also the event that focused their efforts on a cartel payback of some sort.

Grant continues, "We need to stay in the lab and finish this conversation. I know it's getting late but we need to make some decisions with regard to the direction we're going from here on. We can use Pushback to give us the time and we can still leave before it gets dark. Pushback gave them time, none lost."

From time to time in a person's life, significant events alter an individual's direction and outcomes. For many, an important emotional event will generate a dramatic change in direction. For Steve and Grant, Julie Serrano's torture and murder was a powerful emotional, life-changing event. Likewise, Grant's and Steve's encounter and relation with an extraterrestrial alien was the first of two life-altering events.

The first is a relationship that encompasses a vast cosmic, seemingly unlimited source of knowledge that questions nearly everything they understood of their world.

"You know our lives have changed forever," Steve spoke as they made their way to the Lab. "Everything we have known is based upon faulty assumptions." ET has been aware of their conversation well before they re-enter the Lab.

"I don't know if I would go that far, I think what we are looking at is a clarification of everything we have experienced," Grant replied.

"It seems pretty clear to me, we are objects in an earthbound lab controlled by an ET." Steve says.

Grant had expanded his consciousness and IQ, undergoing all his advanced time-altered training. "I think there is a need for greater clarity of that data. Assumptions are typically derived from best data available."

"Best available data? I question our very existence. Are we masters of our destiny? From what I have seen just today tells me not even close." Steve was dealing with a reality check he wasn't prepared for.

Grant tried to bring his brother off the ledge. "We are experiencing nothing that anyone, recently has experienced. However, we are not the first."

Steve looked perplexed and puzzled. "Not the first, you had somebody else up here before you towed me up to this godforsaken rock?"

"No, not here specifically, but on Earth."

That got Steve's undivided attention. "Is it anybody I would know?"

"Not in your lifetime. But da Vinci, Fibonacci, Nostradamus, and Einstein are a few predecessors to our experience that you would know." That is what he knows of who came first. Grant is confident.

"You're shitting me? When were those guys here or wherever?" Steve knows the names and their significance. They were beyond their time intellectuals and consummate influencers of all mankind. Science and the arts from da Vinci. Fibonacci math, Time relativity, and nuclear science Einstein. Prognostication and future prediction visions Nostradamus.

"Hundreds of years ago, except for Einstein," Grant states with knowing confidence.

Steve is thinking, then asked, "Were those guys who were involved in an extraterrestrial-like rescue mission like this one, your's? Was ET involved?"

"None experienced," ET responded, mind-tending.

Grant noted both ET and Steve and proceeded, "It was completely different for da Vinci and Nostradamus they did not have a physical conscious interaction with an ET. If you can believe it, the technology was different 500 years ago. They were covertly influenced over various periods and then returned without explanation." Both Nostradamus and da Vinci have unexplained absences historically recorded, amounting to some years.

"How could they get away with that disappearing for a couple of years and nobody noticing?" Steve, with his hands on top of his head, is wondering out loud.

ET mind-tending, "The communication system 500 years ago was quite ancient."

Grant adds, "Communications were written, delivered by messenger, and in many cases, it took years to arrive. It was not uncommon to not hear from someone for extended periods. No printing press, telephone, telegraph, nothing. People died without relatives knowing of it for years."

They are at the entrance of the Lab. "Okay," Steve says. "What about Einstein? He wasn't in the dark ages; there was the telegraph and telephone. He gave us quantum mechanics, the theory of relativity, and paved the way for nuclear weapon development, the Manhattan Project. He didn't disappear for years?"

"He was administered tailored advancement protocol," ET mind-tended. "He was a critical component to future life on Earth."

"Einstein couldn't be taken for any significant time," Grants adds. "He was subconsciously indoctrinated by ET with advanced scientific theory, principles, and a boost of IQ. His was a unique management model for a human subject."

ET mind-tended, "His compressed training was foreshortened due to his genius, to begin. The soil of his knowledge was fertile. Made minimal adjustments around edges, items and concepts sowed there, grew abundantly well, thrived." Grant and ET are in concert-mind-tending mode.

Steve is bewildered. "Holy crap! Where do you get all that from? I just asked a simple question: didn't he disappear for years?" Steve is intrigued by Grant's remarks; he didn't use to be that smart.

"Short answer: times changed." Grant is moving on.

The brothers 'other life-altering event was their run-in with the ruthless Mexican cartel. Grant and Steve vowed to pay them back for their butchery of Julia Serrano using resources made available by their new best friend from outer space.

Steve was still absorbing the alien encounter, and being shot, but he was hellbent on extracting justice for the Serranos. Grant agreed: they would make payback very costly for the cartels.

MAN 14

Commence
Payback

* * * *

December 16, 2010
San Diego Union-Tribune East County edition
Ultralight Plane Crash
San Diego Sheriff officials found an ultralight crash site Friday, just South of Pine Valley. The wreckage was spotted from the air at about 9 AM by a sheriff-operated helicopter. The aircraft crashed into what looks to be a dead-looking tree. The site was determined to be located at about 4000 feet, not far from Corte Madera Peak. The body of the pilot, an Alpine ultralight enthusiast who had been missing for several days, was found in the wreckage. His truck and ultralight trailer were found in a private gated community below Corte Madera, 1 mile from the crash site. The pilot had been wanted for questioning regarding the death of his wife several days before. Officials said the ultralight might have been used to transport contraband across the border to or from Mexico. The wreckage was located based on information phoned into the Pine Valley station from an anonymous source. The investigation continues as to cause.

* * * *

Cash Flow
During their lengthy lab discussion regarding Einstein, da Vinci, Fibonacci, and Nostradamus, Grant and Steve determined they had two courses to pursue: change the Serrano's life course and

disrupt the Mexican cartel's operations. Specifically, the money flow back to Mexico. They find unexpected obstacles regarding both. Their discussion grew longer and required them to focus on a workable ET lab-like solution.

We need to find a way to help reverse what happened to both Serranos," Steve says. "It is just so fucked up they both died and didn't need to. Those cartel bastards killed that woman in a brutal way."

"I don't know that we can," Grant explains. "We can make adjustments as we did in Pushback, but I don't know if we can change what happened to them. Paul was killed because of some mechanical or weather problem with the ultralight. It was an accident. The cartel gunman didn't kill him."

"What about their daughter?" Steve says. "Wasn't Paul transporting drug cash to raise money for her medical bills? From the size of those duffels, he was transporting millions for the cartel." It was exactly $6 million.

"They probably weren't paying him near enough to cover his daughter's medical bills. They had their hooks in him. Wonder how many more flights he needed to raise the money?"

"He would have had to fly at any time the cartel said." Steve kicked the lawn chair, stepped out of the lab opening, and said back through the open entrance membrane, "They had him by the shorthairs along with his family; there was not a thing he could do about it. If he refused, they take all of them out. I don't know if he knew who he was screwing with." Steve is pissed. "He was screwed in that arrangement, he was never going to ever be able to quit period! They had him by the balls. Fly our money to Mexico or we kill your wife and your kid. Then they would kill him. You don't get to quit on the cartels. They call the shots. They tell you when you can quit with a bullet in your head. Paul Serrano was screwed from the moment he made his first flight with drug money. In fact, this may have been both his first and last flight."

"We don't know that," Grant suggests.

"Well, it was sure as shit his fucking last one." Steve kicks over his bike, spills hydration bottles, and his helmet. Looking for something else to take his rage out on, kicked his open backpack, scattering loose tissues, empty snack containers, which were swept up by the mountain winds. He did not attempt to chase any items; he just watched it all scatter downwind. Turning back, he grabbed his head with both hands and ranted, "We need to time travel back, Pushback, to Paul Serrano's home." His thoughts ran free, "Convince Serrano not to take the flight, rescue his wife from the cartel."

Grant and ET just look at Steve and say nothing. They both could read his mind. Steve thought his scenario required a Pushback, including Paul Serrano not flying at all. Grant can't see a scenario in which Serrano survives.

"You can't change either of their outcomes," ET mind-tends.

"ET, we have to do something," Steve replies. "This is just so much bullshit!"

ET replies, "The Holographic System platform was designed for observation recording. Manipulating time sequenced events; change one sequence for another, not structured for such an event outcome. Consequence doing manipulation will impact far beyond specific events or outcomes. Your time manipulation would initiate unforeseen consequences, create time-motion error for future events. Once in motion, chaos would follow unrepairable damage."

"A time-motion fucking error; are you shitting me?" Steve spews.

"The condition for the Serranos is unfortunate," ET tells them. "It can't be changed."

"Shit!" Steve and Grant respond in unison.

They attempted to brainstorm a correction of Paul Serrano's flight scenario where he is not killed. They can't find one.

They are limited by the amount of time-compressed by a specific Pushback. Longer lengths of time necessarily incorporate time patterns that consequently include other sequential time patterns. Short duration and focused Pushback have a significantly limited effect on associated time patterns involving additional individuals. The longer the Pushback, the more significant the impact of non-targeted individual's time patterns. A few individuals can effectively be controlled within Pushback limits. However, even with a very small group, there is a risk that those associated time patterns could be more than marginally affected. The longer the time pattern and increased numbers of individuals causes a tangential effect expanding geometrically. ET compares the possible impact to the human Chaos Theory. A seemingly small and inconsequential event can create significant future time-altering results of unintended consequences. Longer Pushbacks and the more significant numbers of people involved, most assuredly, need to be avoided. The Pushback they envision for Paul covered weeks and for Julia several days. ET was able to provide a holographic preview depiction of Paul and Julia's lengthy-time pattern Pushback. Their's expanded geometrically and resembled a viral ever-expanding network of unintended consequences affecting hundreds of people. It *was* chaos.

Grant and Steve choose another course of action. First, they had to accept that the Serranos were both killed, and there was no changing that. Their second option was finding a way to disrupt the cartel's operations. More lab work is needed.

Regardless, the brutality of the Mexican cartel had a far-reaching irreversible impact on both Steve and Grant. They focused their efforts on disrupting the Mexican cartel operations to the greatest extent possible. They wanted to interfere with the cartels' operational capabilities and, if possible, have them go to war with each other. Their plan of making drug money disappear from secure locations would create distrust in cartel leadership from within and outside of their organizations. They finally left the lab after their time was reset out of pushback... No time lost.

They determined earlier that one of the most effective ways of interfering was to disrupt cartel cash flow. It was common knowledge that cash was the lifeblood of all cartel organizations and continued operations. Turning off or, in some measure degrading the effectiveness of cash transfer delivery distribution was critical. Grant and Steve came to understand basic facts regarding drug cartel cash flow; most of what they found was public records courtesy of internet data culled by ET's computer system's access to worldwide data systems. They also were able to track cash as it flowed south to the cartels. They were often overwhelmed with abundant information.

Wikipedia was beneficial in their research efforts: The Sinaloa cartel buys a kilo of cocaine produced in Colombia or Peru for $2,000, the first step upon its way to market. In Mexico, that kilo reaches a value of more than $10,000. Across the border in the United States, it sells wholesale near $30,000. Broken down by dealers into grams for distribution, it goes for upwards of $100,000. That's just cocaine. Among Mexican cartels, Sinaloa produces and exports marijuana, heroin, and methamphetamine as well. The cartel has annual revenues of over $3 billion.

Their research resulted in the following. The cartel business model revolved around inordinate amounts of cash. Cash flow for cartels has two functions: first, the cash in their routine business operations. The other is the actual delivery of cash from their drug dealer network. The cartels weren't interested in public relations. Customer acquisition costs were nonexistent. Customer satisfaction, they could care less. Repeat customers and repeat orders were solid, consistent, and growing. They had no advertising costs. Product production cost compared to product sales margin is insanely low to nearly nonexistent. There were no customer or employee complaints. No employee strikes. No employee benefits program other than cash and a one-way retirement system. They lose millions in law-enforcement drug confiscations, but the net effect is insignificant. The cartel distribution network has an army, navy, and airborne component filled by eager money-seeking volunteers. The payoffs can be rewarding, profitable, and deadly. The life of cartel employees can be brutally short and violent.

Grant and Steve concluded that if you could disrupt the delivery of funds from drug dealers to the cartels in Mexico, it would have a significant and dramatic effect on the operations of the entire cartel. Interrupting the cash delivery system in away that pointed blame at a rival cartel, would result in rivalry chaos. Drug wars would undoubtedly follow.

Their plans included the holographic system platform to implement their cash disruption-confiscation plans. Both Steve and Grant needed to establish an aircrew-like discipline. They needed, working as a team, "flying lessons."

Under ET's accelerated tutelage, Steve learns that the lab's holographic system is mobile and can maneuver and navigate through time. It has a navigation system capable of traveling to specific locations on Earth within a matter of seconds, encompassing particular time parameters. Grant initially, and then Steve, discover it is like a GPS map app only on steroids, with time travel forward and back. Once they learned the system was routed through the computer system program manager, they could request a specific time, date, location, travel there and observe the holographic images. It is a virtual live view of a scene in time as if the observer is part of the environment.

The computer system became a gatekeeper and mentor-monitor for the two novice operators. ET, Steve, and Grant realized that achieving a holographic virtual live view in time required an upgraded system. ET made a significant modification of the computer data manager program. It needed a dumbing down for the two human neophytes, more than simple computer system directions. It was reprogrammed to recognize voice commands in literally any language. The voice-activated program manager would provide them with an overabundance of data and time sequences that required their culling through the time data if they weren't thorough with their instructions.

Steve and Grant soon realized that achieving the holographic virtual live view of the scene required more than simple directions for the computer program manager. To overcome their inadequacies, they realized they needed to learn to walk in time first before moving effectively through it. They decided to backtrack and start from simple and less complicated points in time. They observed specific past events for both Steve and Grant because they knew the exact time and dates. Weddings, birthdays, and other dated events revisited offered a training platform and increased their time travel proficiency. As their competency level grew, they expanded time point visits to well-known events: Custer and the Battle of The Little Big Horn. It was bloody, and it was clear the Indians were focused and determined. It was nothing that either of them expected based upon their combat experience. The weapons and tactics were different; the dying was the same. Both of them had visited the Gettysburg National Monument and wondered just how that battle played out. They went back to the actual battle of Gettysburg. During this observation visit, they realized that not only could they see and hear, but they could also sense the battlefield, taste the intensity, and smoke.

ET observes and records these outings, not so much the events, but the impact and reaction on his two humans. He has no data or experience interacting so closely with human subjects. He is learning from them as well.

These battlefield observations had a dramatic impact on both Steve and Grant. They weren't just visiting Gettysburg or Little Big Horn, they were in it, experiencing the carnage of the lives lost and the anguish of battlefield savagery. It wasn't clean. There was discipline and chaos coupled with a tragic, brutal reality in blood-soaked mud. The Vietnam veterans served and fought at a different time with better equipment and resources, but the outcomes were the same: some lived, some didn't.

Steve soon became familiar with the operations capabilities of mobile holographic time travel. A scout ship was not its name but its function. Steve named the lab Dragonfly, and Grant concurred. They both were intrigued by actual dragonflies. While in college, Steve took a couple classes in etymology. He was impressed with the Dragonfly then and thought it was an appropriate name for ET's laboratory. Unfortunately, mobile-holographic-time-travel-sequencing-observing-recording-device was just too long, and the acronym, MHTTSORD, was hopeless.

Steve recalled his long-ago college biology field trips and dragonfly facts. They have existed on Earth for millions of years and adapted to all the changes of Earth's environments. They have survived everything, including Man. They lived through the great dyings of millions of years ago with minor modifications in their size; they are much smaller than their ancient ancestors. Dragonflies are powerful and agile flyers capable of migrating across oceans, moving and changing direction suddenly. In-flight, a dragonfly can propel itself in six directions: up, down, forward, back, left, and right. To Steve, Dragonfly seems to characterize how he and his brother used the holographic virtual lab vehicle. Their Dragonfly could travel fore and aft over time, hover, and observe the time sequences they were searching. Steve also liked the fact that dragonflies were predators.

Their dragonfly vehicle allowed them to observe and act as predators. Dragonfly, the holographic time travel vehicle, allowed them to enter any environment and hold time motionless while they moved within it. The characters in the time sequence, such as the drug cartel soldiers, would be halted in place. During this manipulation, one of the Fredericks brothers would enter the scene and physically adjust people or objects, altering outcomes or the sequence of events. The brothers found that the cartel members' confusion generated by such manipulations was a bonus and a fitting, minor payback on behalf of the Serranos.

Additionally, they could manipulate outcomes by observing and reviewing printed, written, or electronic communications that would allow them to determine the next destination and strategy. They required a computer system to assist in the translation of foreign language documents. Once at the designated location, the Dragonfly would allow observation before entering a particular time sequence. In other words, they were able to navigate fore and aft through the time location window selected, like sitting unnoticed on a park bench watching passersby. It was an observation and reconnaissance of the location to determine the presence of the targeted people, their situational environment, reactions, and interactions.

ET demonstrates, and Grant learns the technique of "hovering in time," this gives them the ability to observe in actual time as the event takes place while not being seen or heard. It is a windowpane in a specific time through which one can observe but not necessarily interfere. By this technique, ET or any other observer can simply manipulate the scene forward and back. They became adept in the practice of hovering in time, occasionally with some unforeseen risk. A learning experience for both. After a time, Steve, in particular, began to believe that they were the real "Time Bandits."

* * * *

Time Bandits
1981 British fantasy film starring
Sean Connery and John Cleese

Plot: Eleven-year-old history buff Kevin can scarcely believe it when six dwarfs emerge from his closet one night. They were once employed by the Supreme Being to repair holes in the spacetime map fabric, but instead, they realized the potential to use the map to steal riches. They've purloined, stole, the map charting all of the holes in the fabric of time and are using it to steal treasures from different historical eras. Taking Kevin with them, they variously drop in on Napoleon, Robin Hood, and King Agamemnon before the Supreme Being catches up with them

* * * *

Wikipedia:

In physics, spacetime is any mathematical model that fuses the three dimensions of space and the one dimension of time into a single four-dimensional continuum.

* * * *

Time Travel Limerick

There was a young lady named Bright,
Whose speed was much faster than light;
She started one day
 in a relative way,
And returned on the previous night.
    A. H. Reginald Buller in *Punch* (19 December 1923): 591.

* * * *

The Fredericks brothers' military flying experience helped with their ability to operate Dragonfly. One challenge was the verbal commands. In their military tradition, both gave and received orders while on active duty. Their flying experience was hands-on, stick and rudder, physical manipulation of the flight controls. They both had to transition to dependence on verbal commands with Dragonfly's computer system.

An inner active computer system operates Dragonfly. It is artificial intelligence [AI] based, literally light-years beyond anything on Earth. The holographic database system incorporates voice commands and directions in conjunction with manipulation by hand gestures. ET doesn't require voice recognition. He operates all Dragonfly systems without speaking. Voice command recognition of the Fredericks brothers is a feature ET added. Grant's advanced training with ET before Steve's involvement provides him with a greater understanding of the systems and database.

The Dragonfly computer system responds to voice commands from both Fredericks brothers. Typically, any voice commands are responded to with a monotone-voiced "compliance." The requested information, destination, or data is immediately available via holographic images. Each time a travel request is initiated by the command "destination." At that point, the computer acknowledges the order. It awaits a specific time, date, location, and personnel data with the initial command. The holographic system display defaults to a representation of Earth about the size of a basketball. As the time, date, location, or personnel are included, the holographic image expands, rotates, and encompasses the lab's entire interior. The more detailed the information, the more rapidly the image focuses on a specific location. Visually, it is as if the lab is zooming in from a telephoto lens. There is a sense of speed and movement that both Steve and Grant learned to overcome. Initially, during the zoom-in moments, they both reached for something to hold onto. They found nothing other than the lawn chairs, but they finally got used to it.

Depending on the computer system's data, Steve and Grant could find themselves a matter of feet away from their intended subject or target. Conversely, with lesser detailed data, they could find themselves visually suspended above a street scene attempting to locate their destination or the individual they targeted. They found they could use hand and arm motions to sort through the holographic depictions, much like culling through photos on an iPhone with your thumb. They could display the holographic time depictions in miniature or full size; it depended on the search parameters. Once Steve or Grant found the target's location, it required full size for them to enter the scene.

The voice-activated Dragonfly system is devoid of personality. It does not; as a rule, question commands received. Instead, it acts upon them. The system will implement command directions as received. The system was designed for alien operators, such as ET, so there isn't a readily discernible judgment component. ET and his alien counterparts don't make errors or misjudgments associated with operating the Dragonfly computer. The system, under ET's guidance and direction, works flawlessly and instantaneously. The upgraded data system, later named SAM, an descriptive acronym provided by Steve, was reprogrammed to recognize human error and fault recognition. The system had a database that encompassed all known languages. In theory, Steve and Grant could give commands in any language, and the computer would comply. Compliance would follow without question and without any semblance of personality or emotion. Only rapid and efficient compliance would fulfill the command request unless SAM questioned an error or compliance parameters.

Steve has a difficult time working with an impersonal, vacant voice. There is just enough doubt, in Steve's requests, to expect feedback and or discussion. Steve is accustomed to openly discussing his suggestions and or direction. His leadership style encompassed input from various members of his military unit. He has in the past seriously questioned a superior officer's decisions. Grant, on the other hand, does not share his brother's concerns. From his perspective, the Dragonfly computer system has an impersonal detached source of information, a data management tool, and an essential partner. His concern, Steve seeks a personality from an artificial intelligence source.

Their internet research provided a wealth of knowledge regarding the organizational structure of the cartels. Additionally, they found news articles about law enforcement, DEA, and treasury department raids and money confiscation operations. Many of the articles pinpointed locations where cartels stored millions of dollars of cash in Mexico. They also highlighted cartel money centers around the US before funneling it into Mexico.

With the Dragonfly scout ship's assistance, Grant and Steve could time travel to those specific locations and time hover to observe. Additionally, the navigation system would allow them to meticulously track the cash movement to its destination in Mexico. The Dragonfly system would track vehicles, airplanes, boats, and individuals. Once identified, Grant and Steve move forward in time to where cartel personnel delivered the cash. At that point, the Fredericks brothers have access to the cash storage facility from the Oval. They would be in the time-hover mode after determining a safe time to enter the holographic scene. Initially, this process was trial and error. First, they required an entry command. SAM would provide a stable narrow platform extended off the Oval; they called it "Gateway"—a holographic image that could be walked on yet seen through to the vast open space below. They likened it to walking the plank off a pirate ship. Walking the Gateway gave Steve some vertigo, a feeling like he would fall into the void of space. He complained that there were no handrails. The Gateway wasn't needed if they were just to observe and record the scene. They stayed on the Oval monitoring a holographic visit, standing or siting in lawn chairs. There was a learning curve for both.

During one of their early operations to retrieve cartel cash, Steve was left in a storage facility when cartel personnel returned unexpectedly. They weren't suspended in time due to a rookie operator error by Grant: he had inadvertently allowed the time scene to progress in real-time, a live feed rather than a stationary one set in a Pushback mode. Grant nearly fell out of his lawn chair and off the edge of the Oval when a cartel member walked partially through the facility door. As he fell, Grant yelped, "SAM, Pushback, Pushback." SAM complied. Everything stopped. The brothers were shocked, especially Steve who could've been shot holding several $10,000 bundles of bills.

Steve did not notice Grant's mistake was because he was in a storage room without any visual references to the passage of time. There were no clocks, no television programs playing, and nothing that showed evidence of time movement. Consequently, Steve thought he was free to move about and transfer bundles of cash to Dragonfly as they had done many times. The transfer was amazingly simple. Grant and Steve, learned that any item that fell, was kicked or thrown from the Oval into open space, was immediately returned to the Oval and stacked neatly near the lawn chairs. Any item from a holographic scene, cash, pushed or thrown through the Gateway entry port, likewise would end up placed neatly on the Oval. Stacked cash. ET's alien telekinetic programming at work.

When the drug soldier opened the storage room door, he realized he had forgotten a cash inventory ledger and turned to retrieve it. Otherwise, he would've come face-to-face with Steve, who stands dumbfounded in mountain biking shorts, shirt, shoes and stares at the door, "Grant, what the fuck was that? Who was that guy? You got this room on hover?" Steve is dropping bales of money, looking for someplace to hide.

Steve exits quickly. "Jesus!" Grant says. "Hang on! Let me get you out of there. Shit." Grant reopens the portal from the storage facility to Dragonfly, and Steve manages to leave the scene just before the men return.

The men notice several bales of cash are out of place. One of them asks, "Who else was in here?" SAM translates from Spanish to English as the other man replies, "You and I are the only ones; no one else is here." Only Grant and Steve can hear SAM.

Both cartel men are confused, so they recount the money. All is well, and they're relieved: but an error in inventory can be deadly.

"Jeez, what just happened?" Steve asks and decides to wear other clothes and shoes for their future cash heists.

Grant explains what happened. "I had the time sequence wrong," Grant says sheepishly. "The hover system works."

"Christ, hovering was something you did all the time in the Air Force." Steve makes his case to SAM. "SAM, maybe the flyboy needs training wheels."

"Training wheels. Not clear on concept" SAM communicates.

Steve isn't mollified. "Look, I've been shot once by these SOBs, not looking for a repeat. Let's get back in there and get the money. Maybe I'll set fire to the place when I leave." Dealing with the cartels always angers Steve.

After this experience, ET took time away from other elements of research projects on going on Earth. He provided hands-on training for them, and they soloed before time traveling completely on their own. He was acutely aware of his total Earth operational environment. He made sure Steve and Grant were reacting within system guidelines by programming a certain measure of failsafe parameters for the human operators. A failsafe system was not required when ET or SAM operated Dragonfly. They didn't make mistakes. ET understood the frailties that human operators brought into any environment. A failsafe mode was deemed essential.

Grant and Steve managed to work out the time hover procedure sequence and avoided future miscalculations involving the cartels. They now could collect vast amounts of drug money. However, they soon became aware that there were issues donating any large amounts of cash to nonprofit charitable organizations like hospitals. First, the cash had to be cleansed of any drug residue; any residue detected would void the donation. ET made available use of a Dragonfly scanning process that cleansed any drug evidence. A high-tech cash laundering operation. However, their cleansed-cash-laundry was still dirty, untouchable to nonprofit organizations.

The first money drop, a milestone event, was aimed at the expensive care of the Serranos orphaned and still gravely ill daughter, Tam. Even so the brothers couldn't walk into San Diego Rady Children's Hospital and drop $250,000 in cash on the reception counter in Tam Serrano's name. They had to employ Dragonfly for surveillance to determine a time envelope of less than two minutes to place the cash on the counter unobserved. It worked. The cash seemed to appear from nowhere. Security cameras showed an instantaneous arrival of a cash package on the receptionist counter. Security personnel couldn't explain or determine where the package came from, nor how it was delivered. Not wholly satisfactory as donation method go, but the only viable option, the brothers thought. The hospital's donation reporting system led to the cash being turned over to the FBI. There had to be an improved method to access and move the readily available cartel cash.

With Dragonfly it became routine for the Fredericks brothers to locate cartel drug money storage facilities. They had access to millions upon millions of dollars, distribution was a major impediment. The only non-profit they were able to donate considerable cash was the Salvation Army kettles during Christmas season. A one-gallon kettle would only accommodate six $10,000 cash bundles of non-sequenced $100 bills. A very labor-intensive use of Pushback, and Dragonfly time travel; additionally the two Christmas Frederick brother elves were overworked and had a mountain of cash to distribute. The giving was simple, the time and effort exhausting. The FBI and IRS were flummoxed; they couldn't solve where or how the kettles were filled, or where the cash originated from. Some good use of the cash followed. They also generously left cartel cash via donation boxes, tip jars and random cash fundraising events by anonymous donors.

The work effort they realized was not impacting the drug cartel's operations system as they had intended. The influx of money into the cartels was overwhelming, Grant and Steve would need a fleet of "FedEx-like Dragonfly" deliveries to make any significant impact. They were, however, able to create distrust and suspicion among some cartels. The brothers often would remove personal items—such as a cell phone—as they hovered and grabbed the ill-gotten cash. One gang suspected a competing source of such thefts and some cartel members died as a result. It may have been unjustified by some but, the brothers figured, so what; they were drug traffickers dealing a slow death to their addicted clients and tearing apart communities.

The FedEx Dragonfly deliveries provided a measure of personal satisfaction for the brothers and a revenge factor for the Serranos and Tam. Their involvement became overwhelming, yet it was a small-ball effort by every meaningful measure. The scope and the cartel organizations 'width were vast and required a tremendous amount of time and planning from the brothers Fredericks. From a management perspective, they were not effective in moving cash from storage facilities to deserving entities. From a time management perspective, there wasn't enough time. Logistically money and storage locations exceeded their physical capabilities to locate, access, and transfer cash. There were only two of them. It was a physical strain; they were moving tons of cash. Typically, only one of them would enter the holograph time hovered scene, manhandle the bales of cash or distribute at a select location. It was physically hard work, and they wanted to move as much cash as possible. It was not only a physically demanding scenario. The mental, psychological component began to strain the working relationship. They were tired, although they were both driven and focused on continuing to impact the drug cartel's operations.

"We can't keep this up. There is more money stored than we have the capability to find, move, and deliver. I'm physically drained," Grant complained.

"Beginning to hate the sight of bundled $100 bills." Steve says, sitting in his lawn chair.

"Not too long ago we were captivated by being surrounded by millions of dollars," Grant agrees. "Ours for the taking."

"I suppose, to a great extent we found ourselves in a position of strength," Steve says, head back, eyes closed.

"Now I feel we are captive. The thrill is gone. We need to find an alternative to what we're doing. We can't keep this up." Grant is sagging his head down in his lawn chair. Both are indifferent to the bundles of cash available to them. They really would need the capacity of a fleet of eighteen-wheelers for the amount of cash they were planning to move. Logistically, they couldn't accomplish the impact they were hoping to achieve.

So, Grant and Steve looked for other ways to bring down the cartels. It was a reasonably simple solution: burn the money. It sounded direct and straightforward, but this proved to be short-lived. Setting fire to slow-burning tightly packed cash bundles takes hours to destroy millions; not possible under cartel cash storage surveillance. The brothers only burnt small amounts of cartel cash, the amount wasn't significant in disrupting cartel operations on a wide scale. The Fredericks brothers went searching for an alternate solution. They found more than one.

Grant asked ET, "You are aware of our dilemma in donating recovered cartel cash to legal entities in this country?"

"You have a legal barrier preventing such transaction within your financial system."

"Yes, we require an alternative to access cartel cash sources accepted as legal currency within that system." Grant needs ET's insight.

"You are referring to Laundered money. Money laundering is the process of concealing the origin of money, often obtained from illicit activities such as drug trafficking, corruption, embezzlement, or gambling, by converting it into a legitimate source. It is a crime in many jurisdictions with varying definitions. It is usually a key operation of organized crime." ET provided a Wikipedia definition.

"Well thank you for that definitive definition of money laundering." Steve goes on, "we know the money is laundered; what we need is a method to access it after it is laundered."

"How are we able to donate such cash to charitable or other organizations without determining the money is laundered cartel cash?" Grant asked.

ET responds mechanically, "Drug cartels of which you inquire, have a history of bulk cash smuggling to another jurisdiction depositing it in a financial institution, such as an offshore bank, that offers greater bank security or less rigorous money laundering enforcement."

Steve replies, "Can we," via SAM, "access those bank systems without their knowledge?"

"It can be done." ET responded.

"Great, let's hack into their accounts and donate to the Rady hospital for Tam Serrano. She'll need about $250,000 initially."

"Steve's term Hack is not accurate. The request for the donation is technically legal and will cause no undue interest by the financial system, nor cartel." ET confirms.

Grant adds, "An electronic transaction without a traceable footprint?"

"Correct." ET. "An inquiry would not be a favorable option for cartels activity."

"I could use this system myself." Steve laments.

"Need only your financial institution to facilitate." SAM replies.

"Shit Hot SAM."

Grant shutting Steve down. "Steve we're not doing that, stay focused."

They stayed focused and redistributed million of cartel offshore banked illicit drug cash proceeded to dozens of charitable organization worldwide.

Houston, Texas, is a hub for distribution of drug money, which is transported to Houston by various means, and it is trans-shipped into Mexico by multiple concealed transportation methods. The brothers discovered the U.S. Drug Enforcement Administration, DEA has a "revenue denial" program designed to bankrupt Drug Trafficking Organizations, DTOs. The DEA's financial enforcement strategy is focused on the flow of money back to international sources of illegal drugs. The Fredericks brothers decided to approach the cash flow operations from a white-collar crime campaign. Their cash hauling response was labor-intensive and went beyond their capabilities. The new campaign would utilize the DEA's financial investigation resources and associated muscle.

From the DEA's perspective, drug proceeds are used to pay the supply sources, support infrastructure, and acquire personal assets for the DTOs. To assist the DEA and other federal and international financial law-enforcement agencies, Steve and Grant opted to become "snitches" or unofficial confidential informants, CIs.

All drug trafficking enforcement agencies were principally interested in identifying the movement of Mexican-bound cash. The Fredericks boys simply provided that information in a time-sensitive pinpoint accurate detail. They found tracking the cash flow sources, transportation routes, storage facilities, quantities, dates, and time via the Dragonfly scout ship hover operations was far more straightforward.

First, they had to infiltrate the DEA investigative facilities and observe their supposedly secure operation and phone system in a Dragonfly hover and Pushback stationary mode. Passing actionable information into the DEA network by burner phones was, at first, questioned since the information was from an anonymous source. It took several such burner calls and highly accurate drug money transfer information for the DEA to accept the validity of their new burner phone CI source. But it didn't take long. The data were pinpoint accurate. The feds tried to track the source of information, but they never were able to, burner phones are not traceable. After a while, the DEA didn't care where the data was coming from; they were just glad to have it.

Steve and Grant also provided names, addresses, and phone numbers of significant members of the drug cartels operating within the U.S. That turned out to be a nightmare for a large number of drug traffickers. The information provided to the DEA resulted in $345 million in interagency currency seizures within the first three months. Additionally, the tips allowed the dismantling of a half dozen national organizations involved in transporting bulk drug currency from various points in the U.S. to Mexico. The investigations led to the arrest of nearly 500 drug traffickers and the confiscation of $25 million in assets, sixty-seven metric tons of marijuana, 10.3 metric tons of cocaine, significant amounts of methamphetamine and heroin, 305 vehicles, and 965 semi-automatic weapons. In addition, Mexican authorities were able to increase their seizure activities from the information shared by the DEA.

The brothers also disrupted the operations of the Juarez, Sinaloa, Los Zetas, and Gulf cartels by passing along seemingly reliable yet false information regarding conspiracies, alleged alliances, and territorial disputes. With SAM's computer system expertise, the brothers hacked into secured Twitter and email accounts and fueled hostilities among rival cartels. SAM seemed at some measure of AI satisfaction, maybe a micro degree warmer, regarding the Dragonfly operationally tethered human amateurs.

The success of their disruption for the Mexican cartels cash transfer operation reflected a negative impact for Grant's married life. Becky tended to be an understanding spouse, yet there were limits. She was aware of Grant's apparent focus on mountain biking as an avenue to release or deal with his internal struggles. She believed they were related to Deana in particularly, and Fred as a distant second. No real close relation with either. Steve seems to be a substitute stand-in for better or worse. Worse from her perspective, and mountain biking addiction. However, Grant's White Cap mural project approval lessened the focus on Corte Madera for a short reprieve. They had something of interest for both to discuss. Didn't last long.

Next on Grant's and Steve's agenda: starting a shooting war among cartels for control of the critically important trafficking routes into the U.S. The brothers built on the distrust that already existed among cartels and intensified it, which resulted in staggering operational setbacks for the cartels. It was white-collar bombs for the cartels. The white-collar interference campaign turned out to be very successful and expanded dramatically.

Grant and Steve realized white-collar interference required less effort. Yet, with success came a realization that they were at a limit set by the capacity to endure beyond a two-person team filtering information to the DEA. The targeted recovery amounted to a relatively minor obstruction to narco trafficking long term. They needed additional resource strategies to impact the cash flow generated by drug sales. The brothers were in a drama of covert accommodations consisting of critical assets: ET, Dragonfly, and SAM. Regardless of their cosmic partners, they were limited in ability to impact drug trafficking cash flow. A broader all-encompassing approach was needed to include a governmental aspect and currency policy directly addressing the issues of illegal covert cash flow transfer to Mexican cartels.

Their solution: A future devaluation mechanism to reach stored U.S. currency in Mexico or worldwide. The brothers Fredericks concluded that there was no need to handle tons of illicit drug cash when devaluing it was straightforward, more effective, and scheduled years in advance. So, the only heavy lifting shifted to the Mexican cartels.

Devalue cartel cash where it is stored; a new US government policy, in addition to DEA actions. Their concept requires a presidential executive order that directs the US Federal Reserve to implement a US currency devaluation program. When implemented, all future legal US currency would have, when printed, an expiration or exchange date some years into the future. Actual existing US cash would be, in essence, recalled back to the US Treasury Federal Reserve Bank exchange system for the newly issued and dated replacement currency.

The devaluation strategy would include all US currency regardless of its source, location, legal or illegal. The holder of any physical US currency within a financial structure system, business organizations, both public or private, would be subject to the devaluation process on a scheduled recurring basis. In essence, all current US currency would, on dates specific, lose value on a sliding scale.

Once the future currency system is established, any newly printed currency would include an expiration date-certain in the future within one or more years. All US currency would have to be redeemed with updated cash as that date approached.

CONSIDER MAN

The US Expiration and Redemption Program (USERP) when formed within the US Fed, would include five redemption milestones dates. All cash redeemed on the first date would be at a rate of 100 percent exchange into the new dated currency. On the second redemption milestone date, 70%, 40% on the third, 20% on the fourth, and 10% on the last date. All redemption transactions would require associated documentation of origination source of funds, ensuring legal entities foreign and domestic, private, public businesses, institutions, individuals, profit, non-profit, and any facility or entity possessing milestone dated currency. All cash exchanged must meet the exact documentation requirements; failing to do so renders such cash ineligible for exchange. As a result, billions of drug or crime-associated generated U.S. cash would recurrently and effectively become worthless on a specific date. Zero redemption value.

The hard part. Grant pushed Steve with a hard sell in the beginning brain-storm-sessions. He dragged Steve aboard, as a reluctant partner. The headaches begin, "Grant you understand that the USERP requires a presidential executive order to institute such a future agency program by the US Federal Reserve." Steve is skeptical of expectations establishing such a program. "We both know that all this devaluation talk is farfetched and not likely to happen."

"I do understand that it will be difficult." Nevertheless, Grant has some optimism and hope for a bit of cosmic extraterrestrial assistance. "ET, what can you offer to assist these efforts? Can we Pushback, event-marker and influence policymakers?"

"Event-marker difficulty associated with semi-conscious influence circumstance targeting government members. A vast and varied set of unintended consequences to obtainable desired resultant."

Grant still wants to move forward. "It would take just one Senator to start the ball rolling."

Steve adds. "Has to be an event-marker and Yogi to work if it all, a detour."

"What the shit is a Yogi? Another movie reference from your reading list?" Grant asking.

"A fork in the road...a Yogi, a detour?" Steve adds, "When you come to a fork in the road...take it. Yogi Berra. New York Yankees. a classic Yog-ism."

"That quote, his quote was never called a Yogi...you just made it up?"

"It just came to me. It fits our cash problem." Steve boasting somewhat.

Grant makes a connection, ET doesn't, "Shit, that's it, gotta turn one way or another. The redemption program is your fork in the road. Detoured routing a Yogi as you say."

"Correct, favorable devaluation program support incurs extreme prejudice response." ET mind-tending gets it now.

"Are you saying the USERP puts some in jeopardy...by the Cartels?" Grant can't believe it.

"Not only senators." ET relates.

Steve has a legitimate concern. "The cartels are not going to sit still, they will respond...could be brutal."

Grant follows up, "You already know the future of this policy and candidates." He knows ET and SAM know the future routinely without Grant's knowledge.

"Correct, time travel forward set in place currency devaluation program." ET mind-tended

"What happened?" Steve and Grant both ask.

ET. "Devaluation unsettled, consequences, political inertia, varied opinions and chaos." ET continues without expression. He clarifies that the currency devaluation program has a significant chance of approval in the 2024 or beyond Congressional elections.

"Hell, we may come up short but not by lack of effort ET." Steve is up looking out over the cosmic vista from the Oval. "We tend to do our best work when challenged and we are sure as hell challenged in spades. Bring it on."

"Spades associated with card." ET doesn't get it.

"Exactly, get out of the way we're dealing ourselves in...all in.

Steve relates, "The future Chaos encompasses one, or more likely both, of these storied truths, The Peter Principle or if you can't dazzle them with brilliance...baffle them with bull shit. ET is somewhat lost on the meaning though it seems to fit.

Steve still curious about changing past events. Working with SAM and Dragonfly, he has a measure of confidence that the past can be changed and has been trying to determine an appropriate event or individual to target and test his theory. He has begrudgingly learned from working with SAM the concept of event-markers and detours of and to alternate time patterns that assisted with the Serranos.

An event-marker is a point in time. Some of those points consist of much more significant features than others. Life and death are two such event-markers. Birth is a start, and death an end. However, if manipulated via a Pushback, the event-marker becomes a detour, a detour to a parallel life pattern diverted from the original. Life continues on the other side of the event-markered detour. The event-marker detour redirected the Serranos into a parallel life, leaving their counterparts in the original deadly scenario life pattern. Not wholly satisfactory, but the only viable option. Pushback has its limitations.

Steve and Grant both are somewhat perplexed with what to do with the Dragonfly and time travel. Can they make a meaningful difference somehow?

Fall 2010
Starbucks
Dream
Santee California

Grant sits at a table alone outside a local Starbucks with a hot tea, reading a newspaper. Not many customers. Quiet. A man in what seems to be an Air Force flight suit approaches.

"Do you mind if I sit here?" He sits without pulling a chair out. His flight suit is clearly out of date, looks damp, almost wet.

"No, no. Go ahead; have a seat." Grant takes a long look around; almost all the other tables are empty.

"Seems like it's going to be a nice day...clear sky, lot of sun," the flight-suited stranger says.

Grant, puzzled look on his face, replies, "Yeah." So, what is this guy up to? He recognizes the uniform, but no name or insignia visible. And yet, it doesn't seem odd to him; he feels comfortable in the stranger's presence.

"I guess you are sort of used to this by now," the guest says.

I'm sorry...used to what? Grant drops his paper on the table, looking for an answer, Loud music is now playing. "I Put a Spell on You" by Creedence Clearwater Revival.

The stranger ignores Grant's question. "Trying to figure out who to spend the day with? Someone who died?"

Caught off guard, looking around, Grant replies, "Well, not completely."

"I'm not either; this is the first time."

Grant is perplexed, "I don't think I know you."

"We sort of met a long time ago...in Vietnam." He is now wearing a survival vest like the one that Grant wore in Vietnam, like all Air Force aircrews wore.

Grant tries to make sense of time and place. "Were you on one of the Jolly crews that got shot down?" Major Bell and his crew were shot down by a North Vietnam Mig 21. They were near the DMZ.

"No, I was on a gunship."

"Air Force gunship?"

"AC-119 Stinger Gunship stationed at Da Nang." He is padding his chest with his hands as if trying to locate something on his vest. CCR is blaring over the speakers with "Bad Moon Rising."

"When?" A ham and egg sandwich is delivered by a female Vietnamese waiter; his cup of tea and newspaper are gone.

Tablemate says, "69 - 70." He is now wearing leather flight glows; they are soaking wet; he just dropped his survival radio and looks nearly panicked.

Starting to understand, "I was stationed there with the Jolly Green Squadron." Grant says.

"Yeah I know, that's what I understand." He is dripping wet.

"So, what happened to you?" Grant asks.

"Runaway prop at night overwater."

"Was your aircraft call sign Lemon 2-1?" Grant is now holding the survival knife from the vest he is wearing.

"It was. My call sign was Lemon 1-0," his name, "Sergeant Alloway."

"We spoke that night."

Alloway says, "I was number nine bailing out. It seemed like forever before I hit the water. I landed OK, but the parachute came down on top of me; I got caught in the parachute lines. That was it. I drowned."

"Were you able to release your risers?" Grant asks.

"I think I did, but the parachute still came down on top of me. I was struggling with the parachute lines from then on."

"Did you inflate your LPU?

"Yeah, I had it inflated, but the parachute was everywhere." He looks puzzled.

"How far offshore were you?"

"I don't think it was that far out. I could see the lights from the city and China Beach." Now the men are sitting on China Beach; there are flares in the air offshore. It is nighttime.

"How long were you in the water before you saw or heard any sign of rescue?"

"It seemed like forever. Then the parachute flares started falling. That helped some, I thought I was going to be picked up then."

"Both Jolly crews were thinking the same thing. Easy night rescue. We were airborne in about 30 minutes after the initial scramble launch alert. When did you hear any radio com about rescue?"

"Took out the radio right away. The chute lines were everywhere. When I got to the radio, everyone talking at once; hard to pick anything out."

"I was in Jolly 2-7. We made two pickups before we were able to talk to you. The radio traffic was the worst I had encountered the whole time over there. There must have been a dozen aircraft all talking at once, trying to locate you and your crew. We were lucky with the first two, but couldn't determine your position before you fell off the radio."

"I didn't fall off. I was having a hell of a time with the chute, and talking on the radio was difficult. I got tired in a hurry."

"I remember you were having a hard time with your chute; 'Tangled' is what you said, and 'Getting tired." Grant is still holding his survival knife; his vest is gone.

"I was. That was one of the hardest things I ever encountered talking on the radio in one hand, trying to stay afloat and get clear of the lines. The chute sank and was pulling me down. I was drowning"

"The last thing I heard you say. I think I'm drowning."

"It may be just before the end. I was so exhausted, watching the flares floating over the water with their eerie dull light."

"We couldn't figure out where you were; you must have been south of Monkey Mountain if you were next to last to bail out."

"I don't know where I landed."

"The radio traffic was bad." Grant says.

"All that chatter didn't help things." Sgt. Alloway is watching out over the water.

"You know the rest of your crew was picked up made it back?"

"I figured that since I was the only one who moved on."

"Did you take your survival knife from your vest? That has always been something that bothered me about that night. Something I think may have changed things." Grant had second-guessed the knife issue for years.

"What's that?"

"Your survival knife? Did you have it out, in your hand?" Grant is still holding his.

"I don't recall that I did."

"Damn, I should have told you to put down the radio and get your knife out and cut yourself free of the chute. I was so caught up in finding your location that I didn't think to tell you the obvious. Cut yourself free then we can work on finding you!!" Grant points his knife for emphasis.

"I don't know if there was time for that. I was so tangled in the chute, don't know what would have helped."

"All the same, that is the one thing that if I had a chance to do over again I would tell you to take out your knife, cut yourself free and swim away from the chute."

"Don't know that would have helped. I was a really poor swimmer, never learned. I hated flying overwater."

"How did you manage to get on that crew without being able to swim?" China Beach setting has returned into the Starbucks in Alpine; the tables are full. Grant is in a flight suit, Sgt. Alloway is now wearing a white T-shirt and jeans. Both have cups of tea.

"Our missions were typically over the Ho Chi Minh Trail. The only time we were over water was for takeoff and landing."

"Talk about bad fucking luck."

"Tell me about it. We flew 99 percent of the time over land. Our concern was triple A and missiles. If we went down over the trail, our concern then was avoiding capture. We knew the VC and North Vietnamese didn't take prisoners along the trail. They would cut you up first and let you die slowly. Never thought we would go down over water."

"Did you know one of your navigators swam to shore? Apparently, he swam about a mile and walked out of the water on China Beach. The way he told it he came walking out of the water, and there were two Marines sitting in lawn chairs, drinking beer and watching the aerial show. He said the first thing they offered him was a beer. He swam one to two miles to shore and got a beer, He was in good hands. You couldn't swim and drowned."

"I think that was Captain Chamberlain. He swam at China Beach a couple times a week. I guess his swimming practice paid off."

"He was a navigator; he knew where he was."

"I have a question for you. What is the purpose of all of this? What are you doing?"

"What I'm doing?? I didn't start this." Grant is holding his tea.

"You're having conversations with people who have passed away. You're talking to the dead," The late Sergeant Alloway calmly states, teacup in hand.

"Yeah, so then it began." Grant scratching his head with a fork.

"What's the point? What're you searching for?" The drowning victim is dead serious.

"This wasn't my doing. It was just a dumb family question about bringing one dead person back into your life for one day. I couldn't pick one." Grant is frustrated and struggling. "It was like something left undone. I didn't have an answer for things that had been left unfinished in need of resolution.

"Have you determined what was left undone?"

"No, I haven't. Most of the time I've talked to the dead, there doesn't seem to be a need. They don't seem needy. With this clarity on your side, there seems to be peace, tranquility, and fulfillment. How much could the dead want?"

"I can't answer that, but for me the clarity does provide a view of things past. I suppose I've found understanding and acceptance without regret."

"Are you shitting me? Without regret? You drowned because we couldn't find you in time. Wouldn't it have been better if we were able to get to you before the chute dragged you under?"

"I have no regrets, and the view from this side is clearer than from yours; I can't change it. I left a wife, a son, and a daughter. Their lives were deeply affected after I was gone. They had no husband, no father, no parent or partner to share their lives with but they did and do have the memories of a loving caring person in their lives. Surviving that night would have changed everything for them and me. I can't bring that back to life: it is done, and here we are."

"Are memories enough?" Grant holding his hands together as if in prayer. But he's not.

"Memories are the only things that survive us. Each is unique in the eye of the beholder. They are moments in time shared by two people, hopefully, more good than bad. Isn't it memories you have shared with those friends and others who have returned for your auditions? What other things did you talk about when they all came calling?

"Memories. Shared times. Good, bad, and sad," Grant speaks out loud.

"There you go."

"Grant, wake up," Becky says. "What memories?" Becky handles his face roughly, wakening him from a deep sleep. "I need to get some sleep. Go to the spare bedroom if you want to have a sleepy-time conversation."

Grant jolted awake by Becky sat up in bed in a cold sweat. Realization hits. He was the last one to speak to Lemon 1-0 before he drowned. He heard his last gasping efforts to stay above the water's surface. "Holy shit."

"You need to go talk to Dr. Denard, apparently. Were you dreaming again? Bad language." Becky says.

"I was at Starbuck having a ham and egg sandwich with a stranger." This revelation inspires Becky to roll over and back to sleep. Grant stays awake. Wide awake.

MAN 15

DISCOVERY
Find a Way

Steve and Grant realized that to perhaps alter the way Sergeant Alloway died; they would have to travel back to the night of the bailout.

Steve navigated Dragonfly to June 1970 and the airspace just west of Da Nang, South Vietnam. They were able to intercept Sergeant Alloway's gunship, Lemon 2-1, an unfortunately appropriate callsign, at takeoff. With Dragonfly, they could "fly along" with the aircraft until the crew bailed out. They were observers and could move back and forth literally through the aircraft holograph, observing what all crew members were doing. They could hear everything said among the crew because the noise of the four engines was canceled out by SAM. Steve and Grant were living and observing these conditions along with Lemon 2-1's crew. There were the aircraft aromas: fuel, oil, exhaust, humidity, an accurate reminder of as it was in 1970. The holograph brought to life the cramped cargo compartment and the marginally small unused floor space. The cargo hold was packed tight with flare canister racks, hundreds of pounds of ammunition cans, shelves of electronic components, and barely any room for the crew to maneuver. Each crew member wore a survival vest packed with essential survival gear: radio and batteries, knife and handgun, flares, water, and maps.

CONSIDER MAN

Lemon 21
Bailout 1970

The 18th Special Operations Squadron stationed at Da Nang Air Base flew a third-generation, side-firing gunship called Stinger. It flew mostly at night, hunting enemy trucks along the Ho Chi Min trail. The aircraft itself had a rather unsavory reputation among the crews. It was okay in the air, you could shoot it full of holes, and it would still get you home. But anywhere near the ground, it was flat-out dangerous and prone to mechanical failures. "The Flying Crowd Killer" was one of its nicknames.

Steve and Grant were able to watch the events of June 6, 1970, Sergeant Alloway's last mission. The Stinger gunship was a 1950's era modified C-119 cargo aircraft that carried four 7.62 caliber mini-guns and two 20mm Gatling guns. The AC-119 gunship had a reputation for engine failures, runaway props, and typically flying grossly overweight. It was also underpowered.

In its modified form, it had state-of-the-art systems on board, many of which were top-secret at the time. The aircraft was so heavy with all the gear, ammunition, guns and crew that two small jet engines had to be added to the wings so it could take off and wallow into the sky. A huge gas turbine auxiliary power generator was permanently bolted to the cargo compartment floor because the four-engine driven generators could not come close to supplying electricity to operate all the electronics.

They flew all their missions at night. That's when the Vietcong and North Vietnamese trucks were moving on the Ho Chi Minh Trail. After a long takeoff roll from Da Nang Air Base at approximately 8:30 p.m., the pilots slowly climbed the aircraft to 10,000 feet while turning west toward the Ho Chi Minh Trail.

The Lemon 2-1 gunship carried a crew of ten: pilot; copilot; flight engineer; three navigators, one of whom operated the forward-looking infrared radar; the other operated the night observations system; three gunners loading, maintaining, and calibrating four mini-guns and two Vulcan cannons; and the I/O, or illuminator operator, which was Sergeant Alloway. As a senior noncommissioned officer, (NCO), Alloway supervised the cargo compartment, including the gunners. He also was the Jump

Master in case of a bailout and ran the illuminator that could light the area below in either visible light or invisible infrared. More importantly, he was responsible for the industrial freezer-sized flare launcher rack mounted in the open door with dozens of parachute flares to light up the combat zone for troops below. He was one of four scanners tasked with reporting anti-aircraft-artillery, (AAA) and surface-to-air-missiles, (SAMs). The gunners also scanned, two men on each side of the aircraft, their helmeted heads out in 100-knot slipstream wind looking down, calling out triple-A or missile sightings.

"Jeez, this is worse than I thought, Steve says. "There is no room to move in this accident-waiting-to-happen; it just barely cleared the end of the runway. What a dog. It climbs for crap." Grant and Steve watched from the lab Oval; they observed only on this night. They need to find out what happened to aircraft and crew.

Lemon 2-1 was fifteen to twenty minutes into their flight when the left engine propeller went uncontrollable, a runaway prop.

* * * *

A "runaway prop" is caused by a failure of the pitch control mechanism of a constant speed propeller. Feathering turns the prop blade as close to 90 degrees to the wind as possible, minimizing the effects of the airstream. This obviously reduces drag and is used when an engine is shut down.

"I knew that was gonna happen, but not this soon." Grant says. "They won't be able to feather it. Things are going to get worse."

All attempts fail to feather the propeller and stop it from turning. The airplane itself was suffering extreme vibrations and was barely controllable. In the midst of all this, the prop went supersonic, generating a high-pitched, loud screeching sound. This condition drives the engine's RPM to exceed structural limits. The engine starts to fail internally.

"SAM, turn that down!" Grant says as both he and Steve cover their ears with both hands; the sound is a devastating screech. "Shit, we need ear protection on this flight." Steve yells out, while covering his ears. SAM complies; the sound is muted.

In short order, the engine appeared to be on fire and was emitting a 50-foot trail of flaming sparks and failed engine parts. The pilots declared a Mayday over the radio while turning back toward Da Nang and the coast. They were hoping for a friendly over-water bailout before airframe failure. Bailout before that put them over the Viet Cong and North Vietnamese troops and most likely execution if captured. They were running to the coast.

"It's getting hot in here." Grant says as Lemon 2-1's pilots roll out on a heading back to Da Nang and the coast. They are losing altitude and airspeed.

"Remind me what the emergency procedure is for a runaway prop?" yelled Steve; he doesn't seem to remember.

"Bailout. The other option is airframe failure and certain death." Caught up in the moment, Grant yells over his shoulder to Steve; he didn't need to. It is quiet in Dragonfly. He has stood up from his lawn chair and starts to pace, anticipating what is coming.

Grant is right; there were no other options. A runaway prop inevitably would lead to a catastrophic engine and airframe failure followed by an uncontrolled high-G dive into the jungle below. The crew would be pinned to the airframe by G forces and couldn't bail out; they'd be killed on impact. The aircraft was barely controllable. The cargo floor was vibrating so powerfully that it made movement by the crew extremely difficult.

"The floor vibration, I can feel it here," as Steve picks up his alternating feet.

The aircraft and its failed engine had already exceeded the aircraft's flight manual's predicted time of failure by more than five minutes. The radial engine cylinders were being consumed by intense internal heat and were twisting structural wing supports. The other engines were redlined at maximum power as Lemon 2-1 continued to lose altitude.

The entire crew of Lemon 2-1 knew bailout was the only emergency procedure for a runaway prop. The aircraft commander gave the signal to prepare for bailout. At this point,

Sergeant Alloway went into action. What Grant found at the back of the cabin was also entirely unexpected. The crew used the left cargo troop door in cases of a bailout; first, the flare launcher had to be jettisoned to clear the doorway.

Sergeant Alloway over the intercom, called the Aircraft Commander (AC) and asked if he should jettison the flare launcher containing nearly 5,000 pounds of highly explosive and flammable magnesium flares, smoke markers, in a 4x5x6 ft reinforced aluminum frame. Jettison is accomplished by a pneumatic system that ejects the whole flare package out of the aircraft through a side troop door. The AC's response was "Standby," but Alloway in the high-pitched din heard an OK to jettison and sent the launcher out at about 8,000 feet. Unfortunately, they were right over Marine Corp Air Base Marble Mountain.

"That flare package impact, explosion and fire caused quite a reaction at Marble Mountain. The Marines thought they were under a VC sapper rocket attack. Those flares burnt for hours, hard to put out. Saw it on the way back after we stopped looking for Alloway," Grant recalled sadly.

Grant and Steve knew what was next. From the cockpit came six short rings, three long rings, and an oral "Bailout. Bailout, Bailout" from the aircraft commander.

They heard the AC say, "Get the fuck out of here!" to the copilot once over water. The copilot didn't need a second invite; he unbuckled his seat belt, and was out the troop door in less than five seconds.

Grant, by closely watching Sergeant Alloway during this sequence, made it clear there was some confusion during this traumatic event. It seemed that he knew his responsibilities and acted appropriately. Once the flare launcher was jettisoned, the troop door was clear. The first one out was the navigator, followed by six other crew members. Alloway, as jump-master, was at the door each time.

At this time, about 9:15 p.m., Lemon 2-1 was a mile off the Da Nang coast and at about 5000 feet. The night was clear, and visibility was unrestricted. All the crew members ended up a mile or two offshore.

Last, aboard Lemon 2-1, the aircraft commander and Sergeant Alloway were alone next to the troop door. The AC tapped Sergeant Alloway on the shoulder, directing him to jump. Alloway did, and the aircraft commander followed; both stepped into the black night over the dark South China Sea.

Sergeant Alloway didn't survive the over water bailout once again 40 years later. To change Alloway's fatal outcome, Grant planned to enter his life and send him in a different event-marker alternate life pattern direction. Grant had to learn more about this man and know him better. With SAM's assistance, they learned Alloway was half Cherokee, born on a reservation in Oklahoma. Grant developed a detailed dossier for the Alloway family from Clyde Alloway's birth to the sergeant's death.

MAN 16

Steve Fredericks

Steve gets a thrill out of taking cartel money and stretching the limits of his time travel visits to the source of the drug money. His new non-mountain biking attire includes a small fanny-pack with pen and paper. It was his idea to leave notes suggesting other Mexican cartels took the missing funds, creating animosity among the cartels. His sense of humor nearly gets them caught in a drug cash vault more than once. He would rearrange furniture so that the cartel soldiers would stumble over them after he and Grant left with stacks of cash. Has few friends, none really very close. He was a movie and fiction novel buff, hence his reference to Time Bandits, once he and Grant start taking drug money to serve other purposes.

Initially, Grant and Steve have a disagreement over how the drug funds should be spent. They find options restricted. First of all, they have access to literally tons of US currency stored by the Mexican cartels. They don't have a desire or capacity to keep any of the currency. They want to redistribute or destroy it. Grant knows that significant amounts of cash can't be used without undue interest by the treasury department when $10,000 is deposited or transacted. They can't deposit funds in legitimate financial institutions; hence they buy everything for cash. It's' a lot of $100 bills, and they don't pass easy. Their dilemma is access to hundreds of millions in US currency and no natural capacity to use it legally.

They choose to donate. Early on in their charitable donations scheme, Grant and Steve inadvertently took cash while time traveled several years into the future. However the donated cash was not yet printed when they donated it to some current worthy cause. The Secret Service is still trying to figure that one out. Perfect counterfeits with a future printing date. Their alternate source of funds, betting on horse races, sporting events, and blackjack in some cases. They figured out time travel and Pushback. They were sure winners at Indian casinos.

Time-elapsed Training

Grant returns from a time-elapsed training episode with ET; he enters through a holographic entry port to the laboratory platform. ET moves to his recharging Oval and enters a trance-like state. Grant approaches his brother, sitting in one of the lawn chairs added to the interior decor. Grant takes a seat, rubbing his two-day-plus beard. From Steve's perspective and reality, Grant has only been gone several hours and has returned with a two-day stubble. He still wears biking clothes, except for shoes, he does a lot of standing while training with ET.

"What exactly is going on when you're gone with the ET on these so-called overnight trips? You say it is time progression advanced learning, compressed learning, but what exactly does that mean?"

"It can be complicated to explain." Grant was tired and thirsty, and takes a long draw from an electrolyte drink.

Steve presses further. "From my perspective, you've been gone three hours—yet you have a two or three-day beard growth. Just how does that happen?" He takes a drink of beer and stares intently at Grant.

Grant makes an attempt to explain the accelerated learning sessions and beard growth. "When ET and I leave this laboratory through that holographic port gateway, two things happen on the other side. I am administered an aerosol drug that enables me to absorb and comprehend complex concepts, facts and advanced materials beyond current scientific achievement as we know it."

Steve is puzzled, yet not surprised. He has opened another beer. The subjects taught to Grant might take perhaps decades to comprehend. He has been introduced to nearly incomprehensible scientific technological advancements beyond anything Man could imagine.

"You said there were two things that happened on the other side?" Steve says. "Sounds like you've been getting a high dose of the aerosol or something like it. So, you're able to learn and understand more than, let's say, me? That's still only one thing. What else happens?"

"Actually, it is probably three or more."

"Okay, I'll bite. I am all ears."

"Coupled with the capacity to learn and understand complex factors that I would never be able to understand without the aerosol is an enhanced super-charged-turbo-blown, memory capacity." Grant presses his lips tightly, looks to his left, and wipes a hand to his forehead. "Plus, constipation, sort of."

"What, you're constipated? Are you telling me that your accelerated learning sessions bind you up? You got to be shitting me." Steve laughs at his joke, drinks more of his beer. "You're not shitting me?" He laughs louder.

"It happens just about every time for some reason." Grant's digestive system seems to slow down dramatically; no desire for food or drink. "Like we talked about, with no need to eat, drink or sleep, a person could accomplish a great deal and be significantly efficient and productive. Takes a couple hours getting back to get things working again: eating, drinking and relieving." Shortly Grant will be using the portable honey bucket (a toilet that does not use water and empties manually) commonly recognized as a 5-gallon white plastic paint type bucket lined with a trash bag. Seat not included.

"Now that you mention it, after your training sessions; you pick up the honey bucket, TP and spade." "You leave for a half an hour. I guess holding it for a couple of days can really be annoying." Steve is half-serious.

"Man is not built or designed for that." Grant smiles and laughs. "I find it annoying and uncomfortable after each session. Well, I guess I'm not sorry, I haven't gone on any ET excursions. It is amazing he doesn't need indoor, or any plumbing. We provide our very own five-gallon bucket toilet. Then we dump and bury it in the woods. Cosmic waste treatment facility. Burningman has better toilet facilities than ET." Steve then chug-a-lugs his current can of beer, throws it off the Oval, it returns immediately, and lines up with three other empty cans. "No littering in the lab either." Steve laughs. "So, your memory is better than mine. I don't see what memory has to do with your advanced tech fore-shortened learning episodes." Steve is developing an attitude.

Grant's Wikipedia-like memory kicks in with clarifying accuracy and a stunningly blunt response. "Memory is the faculty of the brain by which data or information is encoded, stored, and retrieved when needed. It is the retention of information over time for the purpose of influencing future action. If past events could not be remembered, it would be impossible for language, relationships, or personal identity to develop."

"Okay, clear." Steve's on the edge of not following Grant's new-found logic pattern and technical data source material.

"There's more that would be helpful in your understanding of human memory and the accelerated learning processes." Wikipedia-Grant dictates on. "The hippocampus is a major component of the human brain. It is part of the limbic system and consolidates information from short-term and long-term memory, and in spatial memory that enables navigation. The hippocampus is essential for learning new information, consolidating information from short-term to long-term."

"Is this leading into anywhere near where I can understand?" Steve says.

"The delivery system is by holographic images, images of reality." Grant says.

"The compressed learning, the accelerated learning is like a, binge session watching Battlestar Galactica or Deadwood every season on a continuous loop. All five seasons until you know the dialogue for every episode, word for word. *Star Trek* is fiction and not reality. The images I encounter are not video fiction, it's time-captured reality displayed in holographic form."

"It sounds like you're talking about a video library of some sort, online courses, correspondence courses." Steve says.

"Yes, it is like a video library, however the subject matter is actual reality."

Steve bites. "I get it, it's like *Cops*, filmed live coverage of ongoing current events."

"Well, it's not exactly filmed live coverage. It is, in fact, *"life coverage."*

"I'm not sure what the differences are between live and life coverage." Steve near the Oval edge.

"Live coverage is captured in the current moment with a second or two delay to a satellite and then back down to a television broadcast studio. Sports events, local news, game shows, would be considered live coverage and recorded. Dragonfly life coverage is completely different. With it we are able to see a holographic view of actual life patterns throughout history, including future events. The holographs are historic life pattern events designated by date, time and location. They are actual visuals of reality of past, present and future events."

Steve asks, "Time travel, Dimensional travel? Is that what you're talking about?"

Wikipedia-Grant responds from his unconscious memory database. "Time travel is the concept of movement between certain points in time analogous to movement between different points in space by an object or a person, typically with the use of a hypothetical device known as a Time Machine. Dimensional travel is the process of leaving the space of our universe and entering that of another one, accomplished by physical or technological means."

Steve is on the feathered edge of not knowing what he's asking. "When you and ET depart on your learning exercise, is it via time travel or dimensional travel?"

"Time travel is moving between points in time within a particular universe. Dimensional travel is between parallel universes, such as a parallel version of Earth."

Leaning forward in his lawn chair, Steve is holding his head down in both hands, looking at the neatly arranged row of empty beer cans. "I think I'm gonna need a dose of the aerosol to comprehend all of this." Steve is clearly out of his element, and he knows it. "Go slow and explain it to me, I am clearly not on your level."

Grant continues, "For the most part, accelerated learning is visuals of life patterns. Life patterns are what we as individuals are or how we exist. That is coupled with population life patterns that are typically associated with different cultures around the Earth that have existed for millions of years. In simplistic terms, think of every moment of every day accessible as a video recording. Every moment is recorded. Each of these recorded moments can be retrieved, viewed, and in some circumstances, visited. In some cases, the visited life pattern can be altered. We both experienced that with ET's manipulation of the Mexican cartel gunman—the gunman who put two bullets into your chest. That altered life pattern reversed the gunshot condition—you're alive because of it."

"I got that part very clearly," Steve says, searching for a drink.

"I don't know how it's done. Don't have a clear understanding of the concept; however, I accept it because I have seen it. We both have seen it. Up close and personal. My rudimentary understanding of the concept is so basic that I don't have the qualifications to question it. I accept it as a vehicle to a greater understanding and significance of who we are as mankind."

"Any small insight would be helpful," Steve says.

"I'll give it a try. Let's assume you're on a train, a passenger train. You are sitting next to a window watching the scenery rapidly pass by. The speed varies and the visual of the scenery extends from fractions of a second to minutes, or a stationary view if the train stops moving."

"Great, I haven't been on a train in years." Steve adds.

"The train is actually transporting you through time. A different dimension, perhaps a parallel universe. The visual that is seen through the window is actually life patterns at some designated point in time, past, present or future. The slower the train goes, the slower the time and scenery passes. If the train stops, the characters in the scenery or the visual stop; they are stopped in time, if you will. The motion is reversed as the train backs up the track. Remember how ET backed the bullets out of your chest and back into their weapons? Backed them up on their motorcycles and down another trail head?"

Steve is still wondering where this conversation is headed. "Yeah, I got that part. I remember seeing the visual and their wet crotches." Steve smiled at the memory.

"That is basically the concept involved in the foundation for accelerated learning. It really is accelerated exposure to life patterns, in some cases, over thousands of years." ET uses the system to observe and record the effects of evolution on Earth.

"Compressed learning, accelerated learning--are they the same? Not sure I understand the difference if there is one." He looks in this cooler again. Still no beer.

"The accelerated learning is exposure to time element realities repeatedly until committed to memory as acquired knowledge. The compressed learning is accomplished by returning to the initial start time for repeated sequences. For example, a holographic reality session starts at a specific time and runs for several days or hours; at the end of the session, the time is reset back to the initial start time. In essence, a three- or four-day lesson would be completed at the same time that it was initiated. No time expanded; no time lost."

"What are time element realities?" Steve asks.

"Life patterns consist of elements that compose reality that exist within a time continuum. In its simplest form, life is a stage. Everything in a scene moves along a time-driven dialogue, everything on stage is a time element reality. Accelerated learning views these elements in fast forward or back and stop point. Retention in implicit memory is the key."

Steve asks about the drug aerosol, "What's its role, purpose?"

"It's like the flux you use when soldering two wires together. As you know, without flux, the soldered wires unravel. Likewise, without drug aerosol compressed knowledge is short-termed, diminished, or lost. With it, a strong bond is formed in long-term memory, retained and usable."

"Okay, I got the flux fix. What about your beard? It grew three days in three hours?" Steve asks.

204

Grant answers. "The human beard appears not to be affected by this time-sequenced alteration. The beard grows in time acceleration in what seems to be incredibly short periods of time. The human body ages without effect during time travel acceleration and return."

Steve has a beginning of understanding that the rules of reality have changed him forever. He realizes Grant has moved on intellectually. "How much more of this? Where does this journey end? I don't see any light at the end of the tunnel."

Grant is pleased. "How very interesting that you mentioned lights. How familiar are you with electrical grids? They produce electric power that distribute electrical voltage from source generation to end users or customers."

"I am familiar with the term and understand the distribution system for the electrical power grids in this country. What does the power grid have to do with your advanced learning, your, uh, advanced compressed learning?" From Steve's perspective, Grant is drifting off point.

"Have you ever seen satellite views of the United States at night?" SAM displays a holographic U.S. nighttime electric grid image. "Thank you, SAM." Grant points to the image. ET is recharging at this time.

"Of course, the country is lit from coast to coast, north and south. It is a visual light image of the electrical grid system of this country. The lights are on nearly everywhere with the exceptions of sparsely populated areas." Steve gets it.

"Stay with me, what about North Korea?" Says Grant.

"Where are we going now, North Korea?" Steve still in his lawn chair.

"North Korea at night. What is the visual there? What is the evidence of the electrical grid in North Korea at night?" SAM shows North Korea at night.

"There are no lights at night except a small pinpoint source in the capital of Pyongyang. The rest of the country is basically blacked out. I'm not planning to go there."

"So, would it be safe to say that their electric grid infrastructure is limited in capacity or at the very least it is underutilized?" Grant asks.

"It either is underutilized or nonexistent. And I really don't give a shit if the lights are on in North Korea or not. Where is this heading? Weren't we talking about your mind meld advanced learning sessions with ET? Please turn on the lights for me there. Get on with it." Steve is getting uncomfortable, ready to leave his lawn chair.

"We're getting closer. Just be patient. At your house, the electricity enters via a junction box then distributed to an electrical outsource system: outlets, lighting, computers and such. Your home is at the end of a power grid."

"You're not telling me anything I don't already know. When did we leave North Korea?"

"Only using North Korea. I want you to envision the darkened peninsula assume it has, an established infrastructure. Not being used. Why not?" Grant waits.

Steve gives a descriptive reply. "It has to do with their tyrannical communist political system that doesn't give a rat's ass about the people, nor their freedom and life-sustaining elements."

Grant agrees, but pushes farther. "OK, for the sake of our discussion let's say there was a change made within the societal structure of the North Korean government. The change encompassed economic, political, and personal freedom. The changes mirrored the society of South Korea. There was no longer an impediment that precluded the use of their established infrastructure. The lights came on."

"Far-fetched idea." Steve is out of his lawn chair. "Again, what does this have to do with your advanced learning episodes with ET?"

"Bear with me. Would you agree that whatever the change that took place was at least a stimulant to the North Korean way of life? Something that expanded the scope of the entire culture in North Korea?"

"OK, sure." Steve ready to move on kicks the neatly rowed empty beer cans off the Oval; they immediately return lined up as if they were never disturbed.

"Thanks. Here are the final pieces that will clarify the scope, depth and meaning of my sessions with ET."

"Great, fire away. I can hardly wait." He is looking at his empty beer cans, neatly in line.

"I want you to imagine the initial dark features of North Korea is representative of an average human brain's electrical activity. The darkened features basically represent the lack of activity in the majority of the brain as indicated by the limited neural electric impulses. A brain MRI would show a different display of neural impulses, but for my purposes North Korea works. In effect, what you see in my 'North Korean brain' is what you see in an average moderately intelligent person. Now comes the fun part. In order to light up the brain activity within my North Korean noggin, there needs to be an awakening to turn on the lights and energize the cerebral neural electric grid."

"Well, I have to say, you seem a bit brighter after your ET lessons." Steve uses his hands and arms to imply an explosion above his head. Steve is actually enjoying this part. "Are we still talking about memory having a part in this episode of cosmic learning?"

Grant replies with an acquired unconscious memory response, "It is widely accepted that the synapse plays a role in the formation of memory. As neurotransmitters activate receptors across the synaptic cleft or gap, the connection between the two neurons is strengthened when both neurons are active at the same time, as a result of the receptor's signaling mechanisms. The strength of two connected neural pathways is thought to result in the storage of information, resulting in memory."

"Holy shit—you are clearly smarter." Steve shows another explosive hand gesture. "Brighter than the brother I know."

Grant continues, with a dismissive nod to Steve. "Memory is synapse neural pathways activated in a brain. With an increase of these neural pathways, IQ, the ability to learn, and memory storage increase significantly. The neurotropic aerosol type drug introduced by ET increases neurotransmitters and receptors across the synapse gap, which increase memory and learning potential." Grant brings the discussion down to earth. "Imagine it is my brain prior to any interaction or knowledge of ET," pointing to a North Korean image, a very dark landscape. "What are the components that would be required to fire up the neural infrastructure? Neuron synapse neurotransmitters assume the position of junction boxes in brain's electric grid."

"Lights on!" Steve gets it. Thanks to the North Korean symbolism; the lights came on in Steve. "Your brain's electric infrastructure, or whatever, is turned on, supercharged by the aerosol flux. It's nitro/ether in the intake manifold. Your brain, zero to 60 in two-tenths of a second. You just haul ass on those neural pathways. No guard rails. No speed limit. No stopping. No Shit." The alcohol is wearing off, Steve has eyes focused on the North Korean image.

"The introduction of the neuron synapse stimulation basically acts as an electronic jumper cable that opens access to dormant portions of the human brain and neural pathways. Neural circuitry is activated from an infrastructure of trillions of neurons and companion synapses. The effect is turning a brain that's like a barren North Korean night into a bright and pulsing nighttime image of light. The image, if seen via an MRI, would consist of a well-lit image—bright, active and pulsating with neural circuitry." Grant recites from his unconscious database of memories. "A neural circuit is a population of neurons interconnected by synapses to carry out a specific function when activated. Neural circuits in or connect to one another to form large-scale brain networks."

"The neural circuit quotation definition, I assume, came from your unconscious lock box database memory." Steve would really like to down a beer about now. "I assume it is correct because I'm not smart enough to decipher or challenge it."

"Unfortunately, the effect or knowledge is not permanent or long-lasting. I have an insight of what it may be. It isn't advanced learning. It is exposure to advanced brain function comprehension and mental acuity, an intellectual boost. An awakening, not solely learning.

"I have a database of implicit memory, which is unconscious memory that I can't access directly. It emerges due to a stimulus response initiation. It is memory that is the unconscious storage and recollection of information. An example of the process would be the unconscious learning or retrieval of information by way of procedural memory. In effect, it is the process of subliminally arousing specific responses from memory and shows that not all memory is consciously activated."

Steve is trying to wrap his brain around this technological memory maze conundrum his brother has presented. "So, if I broach a subject of advance technological significance, you may not answer or not know the answer?"

"Yes, that happens more often than not: the exposure to future event technology is difficult to comprehend and mentally straining. Most of these so-called advanced learning and time-compression sessions consist of observations of events and technology far into the future. With implicit memory, those observations are stored and will be accessible at some point in the future."

Steve is still groping for clarity. "But you are able to access that memory database on an impromptu unforeseen recollection? I have been here when you spout the technical expertise and seem stunned at what just came out of your mouth." Steve is puzzled, mixed with a bit of confused understanding.

"I agree, impromptu and unforeseen data recollection not in my control, I am caught off guard in a memory holding pattern releasing data beyond my complete understanding as to source or origination point. I wonder how I get there?"

Grant's newly encyclopedic mind absorbed a numbing number of facts, each connected like the links of a website to corresponding data. For the books he had read, he could remember practically every page, but something was eluding him in the shadowed corner of his mind. His implicit memory was that dark corner beyond the periphery of his consciousness. He couldn't bring these memories to the surface by command; they only seemed to emerge after random keystroke verbal inputs. The randomness of these keystrokes was as unpredictable as they were opportune.

Grant realizes that his training session and observation experiences are similar to what Nostradamus went through. Nostradamus knew even less than Grant 500 years prior. His exposure had to have been utterly earth-shattering in terms of comprehending 500-plus years into the future. Grant discovers that his inability to access total memory comprehension is most likely a benefit and allows for a soft landing intellectually and keeps him purposely underexposed to future cosmic technological vistas beyond his scope of understanding. An intellectual speed break metering him safely into the technological and cosmic future. Cosmic training wheels.

Michael Nostradamus
1503 - 1556

Nostradamus's gift of supposed mind-boggling prognostication was provided by alien encounters and meticulous mentoring of future events and technology. He understood the advances and his lack of comprehension of them. As a scientist and doctor, he had an inquisitive scientific nature, which made him search for understanding of the alien encounters and the knowledge they brought.

Nostradamus provided insight into future events. Because of religious bigotry, intolerance, and limited scientific knowledge of his time, he was cautious, wary and fearful of disclosing his actual experiences of future events and knowledge. He had to use coded verse to avoid a perceived heretical concept while offering insight into future events and technology. To do otherwise would be a death sentence.

Nostradamus lived during Renaissance Europe, along with da Vinci, Galileo, Michelangelo, Copernicus and Kepler, et.al. The Renaissance was a time of scientific discovery and expansion of the arts coupled with the Inquisition of the day. In essence, the Inquisition placed new thoughts, ideas, and philosophies in the crucible of religious dogma and thereby culled out any perceived heretic concepts. Such dogma challenges were met with religious condemnation and execution.

* * * *

The Complete Prophecies of Nostradamus, Introduction
By Henry Roberts, in 1946

November 1946, Words that the author claimed held no significance for him, took on for me a definite meeting, became clearly focused into patterns of events — past, present and future...The bulk of his work was based upon his awesome gift of prognostication.

Second Edition Introduction
By Henry Roberts, 1949

What to the contemporary critics of his day, for want of a better term they chose to call magic or occult, we today now recognize as the operation of certain tenuous and imponderable laws that permeate the entire Cosmos. These intangible but all-pervading forces we group today under the general title of 'Extra Sensory Perception.'

* * * *

Michael Nostradamus's prognostications are related to his introduction to ET-like aliens who guided him into future events—ones for which he was not prepared. In the 1500s, he held religious beliefs and doctrine as a way of life. He couldn't grasp or encompass the scope of his visual sensory scenes. They were not unlike early Man encountering fire for the first time—he could not comprehend its source, power, or use. Only time cures the learning curve. Nostradamus observed aircraft, cars, radio communications, and other electronic devices with his sixth-century science perspective. A perspective that was wholly inadequate in understanding future technology. He was left to judge these events as associated with an occult religion-based focus in his time and beliefs. It wasn't occult driven, but occult blamed.

If Nostradamus had no realm of scientific intellect to comprehend observed events, then they became something that could attribute to demonic occult reasoning. In those times, the Inquisitions were ongoing, and burning at the stake was practiced too often to answer incomprehensible events for scientific and religious societies. Simply put, he was a time traveler ill-equipped to completely comprehend his travels and his many observations of the future. His quatrains were wrapped in verse and not clearly defined in the time and place or people. They clearly missed the salient direction for what, where, and when. There is no simple answer to explain where Nostradamus found his "gift" or how it came to be.

The predictions are not easily assigned to any source, but he leaves the source dilemma to the individual reader or researcher. Henry Roberts' introduction to Nostradamus was written in 1946 and 1949, many years before computers, the Internet, moon landing, space travel, etc. Many things were unfamiliar to Roberts, much as those items were foreign concepts to Nostradamus hundreds of years ago. Nostradamus had less ability to reasonably understand any of those future concepts. Generally, today we know computers as a way of life, but as little as 100 years ago, not so. Five hundred years ago, Nostradamus would have had been dumbfounded by these and other inventions of the 21st century and beyond—ones he could only struggle to comprehend yet understand. His predictions summarized his experience in a 16th century thought pattern. He most likely had no idea of what and how such events came to be. His reasoning was based upon his day's knowledge to include scientific and religious dogma complete with bias, prejudice, and ignorance of a 500-plus-year future.

The first printing press, invented in 1440, was about 60 years old when Nostradamus was born. The lead pencil was invented in 1564. By the mid-1500s, there were many presses throughout Europe, and these were world-altering inventions. Consider placing in the hands of a scientifically trained individual in 1520 a portable radio, a cell phone, desktop computer, or a TV. None of those items would work if the scientist couldn't turn them on, assuming the batteries are recharged. Of course, radios, desktop computers, and flat-screen TVs require an infrastructure network that didn't exist then. No electricity at that time; a simple flashlight or laser pointer would completely perplex a scientist of that day, and could well be considered witchcraft. The scientists of the day hadn't any clue what a "hard drive" was. The term, at that time, would most likely relate to a difficult move of cattle or other livestock over a long-distance taking days. Maybe?

Nostradamus explained his observations in a format that met his day's religious dogma requirements as he didn't want condemnation as a heretic by Inquisition activists. He lived in a society where anything other than spiritual thoughts and beliefs, were under suspicion by church doctrine. Additionally, his scientific vocabulary didn't provide adequate supporting vehicles of explanation that could carry the observed concepts in the 16th century "modern perspective." He needed a new language with a new vocabulary that encompassed future events as he viewed them.

* * * *

Henry C. Roberts,
The Complete Prophecies of Nostradamus
November 1946
CENTURY II, Quatrain 21 Page 50:
The ambassador that was in the small ship, In the middle of the way, shall be repulsed by unknown men,
And from the salt, To his rescue shall come four great ships,
Ropes and chains shall be carried to the Black Bridge.
Theoretical meaning: Rudolf Hess, personal aid to the German Fuhrer, Hitler, flew solo to England to contact influential British leaders with his unofficial peace terms which were rejected in a closed session of Parliament.

CENTURY II, Quatrain 25 Page 51:
The Garrison of strangers shall betrayed the fort,
Under the game of hope of a higher union.
The garrison shall be deceived, and the fort taken quickly
Loire, Saone, Rhone, Gardone, outrage by death.

A . J . M E R I N O

Theoretical meaning: A garrison of extraterrestrials arrives, defects, and seeks the asylum in the "hope of a higher union." *Anticipates the arrival of a breed of extraterrestrials.*

MAN 17

* * * *

**A Brief History of Time
Stephen Hawking
Copyright 1988, 1996 by Stephen Hawking,
page 165-166**

There might be a good reason why it would be unwise to give us the secret of time travel at our present primitive state of development, but unless human nature changes radically, it is difficult to believe that some visitor from the future wouldn't spill the beans.

Grant and ET return from yet another accelerated-compressed training session after nearly three hours, which equates to most of three days 'time-traveling exposure. They both follow a routine. The sessions always start with an entry point or gateway into a holographic time image library. Once entered, ET orchestrates and implements the subject matter and concepts that Grant assimilates actively and subconsciously during the session. Grant receives a dose of aerosol as usual; his memory database opens to record.

Grant explained to Steve earlier that time travel was similar to a train moving through time visually. In contrast, during these sessions, Grant's exposure is aboard a cosmic bullet train, bounding forward through limitless time, without speed limits. A kaleidoscopic road-trip venture looking over the edge of time.

Grant and ET both re-enter and step onto the Oval. Grant slumps in a lawn chair and drinks fluids; he pushes the honey bucket aside with his foot. ET makes his way to the recharging Oval and enters a trance-like state for a couple of hours. Nothing is said or mind-tended.

Steve has spent most of the day sitting in his lawn chair sorting through data stacks, the holographic history stacks, reviewing and viewing his and Grant's life patterns. He doesn't understand why his brother's patterns have been altered by ET.

He has a feeling that Grant's life is somehow of specific interest to their alien host. "We need to talk," says Steve.

"Can it wait? I'm kind of worn out. These time compression training sessions are exhausting."

"No," Steve says. "I've been in the stacks all day, for several days now while you were gone on your training adventures. I've discovered some very interesting facts that directly affect you and your life pattern since you were a teenager."

"What facts are you talking about? What were you doing looking at my life patterns?" Grant is puzzled and tired; he doesn't even try to rise from his lawn chair; he drinks more fluid. "Our life patterns were the same except for a few years."

"I found that our life patterns—yours, in particular—are very different from what we remember. In fact, you have a great number of altered true-life patterns, and I'm trying to understand why." Steve turns toward Grant; both sit next to each other.

"I have no idea what you're talking about."

"I'm not sure if I know what I am talking about," Steve says, "but you have altered life patterns. Several altered life patterns."

Grant is now irritated. Stretching, "I still have no idea what you're talking about. What altered life patterns are you referring to?" Turns to look at Steve for answers.

"From what I can determine, you have led a charmed life. Several of them."

"What are you talking about?" Grant waves Steve off. "What?."

"All right, I'll get right to it. I was curious or maybe I was just nosy and was trying to find out how accurate the historic records contained within SAM's data management system were. I thought that going to some historic event would be interesting, but I wasn't completely sure about the accuracy of such events."

"All right, so you were accessing the database system to view events from years ago. You already did that with Nostradamus? da Vinci?" Grant focuses on a headache he's getting.

"Nostradamus and da Vinci were completely different," Steve says. "If you remember, they were selectively instructed at a subconscious level by alien mentors and project managers. They didn't remember sources of influence or ET-like encounters. They were chosen to become part of an alien intelligence-enhancing experiment. Both of them, as a result, had a significant impact on human development."

Grant says, "Okay, I know about both of them, so are you saying you had some questions about the accuracy of what you found about them or other events?"

"I realized that I didn't have a baseline upon which to determine the accuracy of any event. SAM provides the ability to look back and observe historic events; however, all we have done in the past is to assume everything in SAM's database is accurate. So, I began to question if we should continue to assume that.

"Okay, so do you think SAM provides us inaccurate information? To what purpose?" Grant looking for an answer.

"I was never able to answer that question. I needed to find a baseline to make a judgment regarding accuracy of the data and events we are observing," says Steve.

"A baseline? Why wouldn't you just ask SAM? He is an impartial, impersonal treasure trove of millions of years of data collected on Earth and all its inhabitants?"

"I couldn't be sure of SAM's impartiality. Remember SAM stands for 'Smart Ass Machine.'"

They initially gave SAM the name HAL, the interactive computer in the film "2001 A Space Odyssey" HAL, an acronym for Heuristically Programmed Algorithmic Computer 9000. SAM's naming came later after their experience conditioned a more endearing meaningful, accurate name. The perceived personality of HAL better suited the acronym SAM. All of which was meaningless to either HAL or SAM.

ET reprogramed the database system manager to accommodate Steve and Grant's lack of alien capacity and expertise. In essence, the computer database and operations system accurately interacted by voice recognition to provide Grant and Steve the necessary information they were seeking.

At the beginning of this relationship, an initial period required Steve and Grant to carry on conversations with SAM. This was for SAM to understand the inner workings and capability of the two human personalities it was attempting to engage on an intellectual level. After a time, the working relationship fostered what could almost be called a friendship. SAM was the lead dog, Steve and Grant were mutts in training.

SAM became a lead player in the Dragonfly scenarios. Grant and Steve struggled to learn and accept SAM as an ally in their mission to learn. SAM responds to voice recognition that ET authorized. However, there was a significant learning curve for the "three." Simple requests to find, travel, view an event in history required a new paradigm for all three.

Initially and early on, when asked to reference an event specifically by month, day and year, SAM had no concept of or understanding of "dates by years." SAM's system didn't register them. Instead, it referenced "data error" or "no source of data." The alien data system was based on a system beyond human standards.

"SAM, we have a problem," indicates Steve.

"What is the problem to which you refer, Steve?" SAM said with a seemingly somewhat superior in delivery. Confirms Smart Ass Machine moniker by Steve.

"It seems that we are not able to communicate my request for a specific date and time event. For some reason, your database doesn't recognize it."

"My database encompasses all dates and time for several million years," reports SAM.

"If I can't access those database records, it limits our ability to understand historic events and milestones." Steve feels that SAM is holding back data access.

"You simply need to ask for a specific event to access it." Steve replies, irritated, "Apparently, I don't know the appropriate terminology to access your database SAM."

"I sense stress in your voice," SAM replies.

"Well, son of a bitch." Steve is being frustrated in his search for specific data sets.

"Need more information to comply."

"I just want information regarding a specific date and time." Steve is up and leaning on the back of a lawn chair, thinking about tossing it over the Oval's edge.

"Is the specific date and time associated with a particular event?"

"Yes, The Vietnam War."

"The Vietnam conflict lasted for a significant period of time." They both agree on something.

Vietnam Rekindled

Steve was stationed at Camp Eagle in the northern portion of South Vietnam, about 20 miles south of the DMZ. He flew cobra gunships and provided close air support for the Army ground troops. Grant was an Air Force pilot and flew Jolly Green Giant helicopters out of Da Nang Airbase about 100 miles south of Camp Eagle.

The pilots had very different missions. Steve would fly combat patrols and expect to engage the enemy ground forces and be shot at while providing ground support. Grant was trained to provide combat search-and-rescue (SAR) operations to recover American pilots and crew members shot down in North and South Vietnam and Laos.

Both flew combat operations but with entirely different objectives and outcomes. Cobra gunship crews were typically aggressive and engaged with enemy forces with machine-gun, cannon fire, and rockets. Grant's missions and tactics were planned and formulated to save the lives of American crew members by trying like hell not to get shot down. Steve's cobra gunship would enter a combat environment looking for a fight. Typically, the Vietcong (VC) and North Vietnamese soldiers would avoid firing at cobra gunship because they knew they would return fire. The Jolly Greens were most vulnerable when they hovered above the jungle floor, typically 100 or more feet. While in a hover, a pararescueman, [PJ], on a jungle penetrator at the end of a 250-foot cable would be lowered to the jungle floor to assist the downed American crew member. In some cases, the crew member could climb onto the jungle penetrator's fold out seats unassisted. If the crew member was injured, the PJ would be required to assist him, and both would be extracted. And that is when the bad guys would open fire—during their best chance to inflict maximum damage and knock another aircraft and crew from the air. Both aircrews, Army and Air Force, did their jobs gladly, one attempting to protect lives, the other to save them from capture and execution.

Two very different rescue missions had a life altering impact on Grant. In both, he and his counterpart rescue crew members approached each mission with confidence of borderline combat tested arrogance. Willing to face hostile opponents determined to insure mission failure with deadly accurate anti-aircraft artillery rounds. He and his counterparts were facing deadly high odds of taking on those rounds. The Jolly Green mission was to fly toward those high-risk combat conditions; facing them head-on. They didn't enter those environments unprepared. Prior studied exercised scenarios of realistic practice kicked in.

There were coordinated meticulous preplanned strategies of all participating aircraft and crews. In essence a detailed orchestrated articulate battlefield ballet had already been created, planned and practiced. The only missing elements were where the stage and performance was going to take place. It didn't matter where, only when and how soon to initiate the definitive rescue plan. From practice to reality; in a hurry before someone dies.

CONSIDER MAN

The first mission required a rescue attempt of an F-4C pilot and navigator shot down in Laos near the Ho Chi Minh Trail. It became the largest combat aircrew rescue mission of the Vietnam War. December 5, 1969. The early morning mission went wrong almost from the start. Two U.S. Air Force F-4C Phantoms, call sign "Boxer 22," diverted from their primary target due to cloud cover. Their alternate target was north near the village of Ban Phanop, Laos, a chokepoint where the Ho Chi Minh Trail crossed the Nam Ngo River. In Boxer 2-2, the trailing aircraft, was pilot Capt. Benjamin Danielson and weapons systems officer 1st Lt. Woodrow J. "Woodie" Bergeron Jr. on their first flight sortie together. Just after dropping their ordnance, the Phantom suddenly pitched up, then down. Their flight leader called over the radio: "Boxer 2-2, you're hit! Eject! Eject! Eject!" Danielson, Boxer 2-2 Alpha, and Bergeron Boxer 2-2 Bravo came down on opposite sides of a dogleg bend in the river valley a mile across and a thousand feet deep, walled with karst limestone cliffs and caves. They were just 10 miles from the North Vietnam border, but only about 65 miles east of NKP—Nakhon Phnom Royal Thai Air Base, the main base for Air Force Special Operations Squadrons specializing in search and rescue. The crew of Boxer 2-2. immediately became hunted prey.

Lemon 2-1's runaway prop caused a night bailout over the South China Sea off the Da Nang coast was the second meaningful rescue attempt. It started June 6, 1970, six months after Boxer 2-2 was shot down over Laos.

Post Script
See Extract for Boxer 22
detailed mission sequence/narrative

The night after Boxer 22 Bravo's rescue, Grant and crew attended the most euphoric celebration they ever expected to experience in the Jolly Green hooch. They had flown two days in the largest search and rescue mission of the Vietnam War, Boxer 2-2.

On December 14, 2010, "Jolly Green 2-2," one of the HH-3Es that Grant flew on several Vietnam missions, was dedicated to the National Museum of the United States Air Force at Wright-Patterson AFB. The aircraft had been completely restored into combat configuration. Many of the Jolly Green crew members who participated in the "Boxer 2-2" SAR were in attendance, and all were celebrated as true war heroes.

In 2003 a Laotian fisherman discovered human remains, a partial survival vest, a survival knife, and Danielson's dog tags along the banks of the Nam Ngo. On June 15, 2007, Lt. Cmdr. Brian Danielson of US Navy Electronic Attack Squadron 129—18 months old when his father was shot down—laid his father to rest in his hometown, Kenyon, Minnesota. At the Vietnam Veterans Memorial in Washington, D.C., Danielson and Jolly Green7-6 tail gunner Dave Davison are remembered next to each other on panel 15W, lines 26 and 27. Technical Sergeant Clyde Alloway was never recovered, he is listed as MIA on panel 9W line 22.

The common ground for both were the lives lost; and how they died. Boxer 2-2's pilot, Captain Danielson was executed by enemy ground forces. Jolly 7-6 tail-gunner Airman 1st Class David Davison was struck in the head by ground fire. They died in the midst of an impeccably planned rescue and recovery operation saving the life of Boxer 2-2 Bravo. The Lemon 2-1 rescue operation highlighted the exact same executed planned process and saved the lives of nine of ten Lemon 2-1 crew members. All less than one mile off shore and the Jolly Green Squadron at Da Nang air base. The excruciating difference was an unplanned radio communications mis-steps and a over focused effort to locate the sole last survivor Tech Sargent Alloway. Speaking to a Man drowning while asking him his location, rather than use his knife to free himself from sinking parachute shrouding. The same process with a different outcome. One sowed the seeds of a haunted discontent for forty years.

On the Oval

Grant and Steve still sitting in a lawn chair on the edge of the Oval, Steve asks, "SAM, how does your database record history or items of interest? How do you record results of Earth operations? A better question, how do you record time?"

"Time is based upon the concept of the event sequences," SAM indicates.

"What are the sequences based upon? On Earth, time is based upon the relative movement of the Earth's rotation and orbit around the sun," said Steve.

"The database time sequence is based upon milestones of process outcomes and the positioning of the moving and expanding universe," SAM mind-tends.

"Are you saying that we need to distinguish the format between time on Earth and the associated time within the universe?" Steve senses an opening in logic.

"Yes, the format should be consistent."

Steve asks again. "Can you adjust the database format to be consistent with the concept of time as I have explained relative to the Earth's rotation and orbit around the sun?" The ET data management system operates on time element-based parameters, unlike those dependent on Earth's rotation and solar system orbit.

"Yes, it is done." SAM mind-tends.

"Well, hopefully, we will be on the same page moving forward." Steve says.

"To what document and page do you refer?" SAM without attitude.

"It was just a colloquialism we use from time to time. Forget I ever mentioned it."

"The database system does not forget data."

"Okay, let's move onto the next subject, shall we?"

Steve and Grant's early dragonfly operational, procedural training was hampered by Steve's stubborn resistance to an AI program voice. The perceived shortcomings of SAM moved Steve into thinking SAM was in some way limited in its capability. Nothing could be further from reality. SAM knew everything regarding the Earth, from its small beginnings to creating all living species over a vast history of billions of years.

SAM stored the nature of Man and his complete existence history in a data collection system. All of mankind was developed and manipulated via DNA sequencing, trigger switches, and time travel evolution models placed throughout the Earth's environment. The evolution models of primitive, archaic Man were controlled experiments over thousands of years to create the modern Man model now in existence. Current Example: Steven and Grant.

SAM was purposely leading Steve and Grant on an intense intellectual knowledge-gaining exercise that brought both of them to an acceptable level of alien understanding of Man. They were still cosmic worlds apart in terms of intellectual capacity. The use of the aerosol drug substance, as part of their intellectual enlightenment, enhanced their learning capacity and dramatically shortened the time frame to understand the many concepts they were exposed to. Steve's dose of the aerosol was significantly less than Grant's. His IQ and memory capacity spiked, but far less than his brother's. In the end, Grant and Steve understood their inadequacies and their shortcomings compared to SAM. They understood that SAM was the backbone of their learning experience and an integral part of their maneuvers with time travel, history, and Man's evolution. They discovered over the repetitive, accelerated learning process that SAM was something significantly beyond a computer system. Spoken commands, holographic images, and an immense database encompassed everything SAM. The database they learned included the history of Man and Earth in a holographic form. Steve and Grant referred to the individual accounts of Man as history stacks. It was a reference to library bookshelves arranged in "stacks" that they were familiar with from their college days.

SAM guided and mentored both while they attempted to navigate among the history stacks of holographic images related to Man's and Earth's evolution. At first, when at a history point, such as Gettysburg or Custers last battle, they were tethered to SAM, instructed, and guided on basic elementary observations of random events throughout history. ET was always in the background involved in other apparent Earth lab projects. He didn't disclose the extent or purpose of further Earth-related experimentation. ET and SAM were mind-tending at all times but their communications were blocked from Steve and Grant. Both ET and SAM were created as independent entities comprised of artificial intelligence, AI. ET, an advanced AI operating system with a physical structure incorporated with living tissue genetically related to human DNA and genome. SAM's system has no genetic material associated with its AI. Both AI structures communicate instantaneously, almost without exception. In essence, they share the exact same database management system. ET's genetic component is not considered a relevant factor. Both approach their existence without question of purpose. Yet, for ET, an unfamiliar genetic nuance is evolving.

MAN 18

ALTERNATE HISTORIES
* * * *

**A Brief History of Time
Copyright 1988, 1996 by Stephen Hawking,
Pages 71 and 167.**

There could be whole anti-worlds and anti-people made out of antiparticles. However, if you meet yourself, don't shake hands! You would both vanish in a great flash of light.

The other possible way to resolve the paradox of time travel might be called the alternative histories hypothesis. The idea here is that when time travelers go back to the past, they enter alternative histories which differ from recorded history.... rather like Richard Feynman's way of expressing quantum theory as a sum over histories,..the universe didn't just have a single history; it had every possible history, each with its own probability.

* * * *

**Alternate Universe Might Be Real After All, Scientists
Speculate
After Experiment
Hank Berrien
May 19, 2022 DailyWire.com**

Researchers working on an experiment with carbon atoms found evidence that could suggest an alternate reality actually exists. Victor Galitski and Alireza Parhizkar at the University of Maryland prompted speculation when they stacked two graphene layers together..."The scientists think that because the electrons can interact between two graphene layers, each just an atom-thick, they could exhibit other interactions from across space time."

* * * *

Over time, Steve begrudgingly learned by observing Grant, ET and SAM operating the Dragonfly, to develop the skill to access program records associated with time travel navigation. At first, it was difficult adjusting to the data management system.

But with a concentrated effort during hours left alone in the lab, Steve understood the Dragonfly operations and systems more thoroughly. While ET and Grant were involved in a continuous learning routine, Steve was learning on his own. Initially, Steve was schooled by ET on the rudimentary operations of the database system, which consisted of vast holographic records.

It took Steve some time to achieve a higher level of expertise in this driver training operations management environment; but, once there, Steve discovered that he could access the alternate history files or at least a limited number of them. The database system was based solely on verbal commands or requests from both Steve and Grant. Their access was modified, there was no keyboard, no mouse, only SAM, the data gatekeeper.

He found files by voice command. Request a specific time and place in Man's development, and the holographic record depiction appeared almost instantaneously. Thousands upon thousands of holographic records contained the historical records of mankind and Earth, going back literally millions of years.

Initially, Steve was wandering aimlessly through the data fields of mankind's history on a hit and miss basis. He found the database system allowed him to literally enter a specific time in Man's development or Earth's evolution. At first, he was an observer of various events that he had some interest in and just simple curiosity. It became a very serious incomprehensible jaw-dropping 101: "you got to be shitting me," life-changing event.

Calling out a name or date, in most cases, would bring up a holographic stack in the shape of a pyramid, a four-point base representing alternate histories or realities stacked one upon another. Older or original records formed the bottom, while the alternate histories were stacked on top, generally a much narrower upper level. It took Grant and Steve some time to figure out how to access the individual layers of these holographic levels and navigate within them. They found it interesting to travel back in time as an observer watching alternative histories with alternative outcomes. ET left them to explore without a great deal of concern and minimum monitoring as their "training wheels" became less necessary.

It took both of them some serious time, study, and experimentation before they could adequately navigate to appropriate periods and locations without SAM. Grant was the lead novice or pilot and was able, over time and experimentation, to adjust the Dragonfly operating system's voice command structure. It turns out, the more they screwed up in attempting time travel to a specific location and date, the more SAM would also learn from their inadequacy and modify future responses.

In essence, the operating system was "learning" to recognize Grant and Steve and their "capacities." It was much like a voice recognition system that learns to identify an individual's voice pattern's intricacies and add those to a known word and expression database. In SAM's case, it was an intelligence recognition pattern that adjusted and compensated for the various levels of operator intelligence or skill. Those recognition patterns were added to the Dragonfly's database, and within a short time frame, the communications and commands from Grant and Steve were clearly understood. They could move through those histories fore and aft, freeze frame, fast forward, and reverse with voice commands or hand motions. Grant and Steve found that they could travel anywhere on Earth at any time. If time sequence entry was required or desired, then the operation was a bit different: Pushback would be used as they had done during the cartel encounter on Corte Madera.

The holographic history display was typically visible through viewports that could expand the image to a life-size, accurate representation of the scene and people involved. Pushback could be engaged at any intermediate sizing stage; however, to enter a Pushback scene required a life-sized depiction. These were necessary parameters to prevent unintended consequences and perhaps damage to those entering the scene. Grant explained it to Steve as trying to put five pounds of oatmeal in a two-pound bag; some of the oats were gonna be spilled.

Once at the destination, Grant or Steve could maneuver in any direction as rapidly as desired. They could follow someone and observe them during their travels. During Pushback, which held people and objects in place, Steve and Grant could walk about quite freely without recognition. This technique came in handy when dealing with Mexican cartels and their money stash. It worked well when making anonymous donations with the drug money they'd seized. The only downside was for the cartel soldiers in charge of security for the cartel's money. They never had a plausible explanation for where and how millions of dollars disappeared. Even with time-stamped video monitors, no one could reasonably explain how the money was clearly visible, and the following second significant amounts were gone. The videos and security systems showed no one besides them had access, yet the money was gone. Heads did roll, literally.

Steve and Grant were authorized operators and provided semi-free access. They had to negotiate a labyrinth of complicated features, entry points, and procedural steps to access the database and the immense historical records volume. It was an unknown system utterly foreign to Steve's and Grant's all too human capabilities, accessed by an alien's mind. It was a stumble and error process until they made a note of and recorded all the sequence steps required to access the active holograph system. The database system and SAM recognized their marginal capability, and in essence, they were always in need of the "help tab."

Steve wants to take up again his discussion with Grant about SAM's database. "I don't know if it's accurate. SAM could provide us anything he chooses," Steve says. "He also doesn't allow us into future travel without restraints, can't go there for some reason. ET rules I suppose." Steve stands next to the lawn chair, looks over the Oval edge into space.

"Unbelievable," says Grant, waking up from another session with ET stressed, fatigued, and mildly constipated. "Okay, Steve, where are you taking me on this journey? I really don't see any light at the end of this tunnel."

"I didn't, either, until I understood or realized that the only factors that I knew for sure were the ones that I lived through. My life pattern, your life pattern were the baselines I was searching for. If our life patterns were accurate in the database, then I could assume the other database records were also accurate."

"So, can I assume that we're done with this discussion?" Grant asks.

"Accuracy was what I was looking for from your life pattern file, our life pattern file." Steve says.

"Steve, would you get to the end of this story, I'm weary of this. Were our files accurate?"

"They were accurate and very disturbing. Your files in particular."

"My files disturbing? In what way?" Grant is open-eyed awake, looks directly at Steve as he stands gazing off the Oval.

"Your life pattern, like mine started out simple, but yours is replete with detours and forks in the road. 'When you come to a fork in the road, take it. 'Yogi Berra said that."

"Yeah, yeah I know. Detours?" Grant asked inquisitively.

"Do you remember Blackie?" Steve intense "The boat you made, built with a couple neighbor friends, Jimmy and Mike."

"Sure, we built it in the backyard. About 10 feet long 3 feet wide, painted it black, hence the name Blackie. So, sounds like the database's accurate."

"After you guys built it, three of you took it out on the bay."

"I hope you're going somewhere with this. We did take it out on the bay. It was me, Jimmy and Mike. I think we had to carry it about a good quarter of mile to get it to the slough and access to the bay." Grant is up out of his lawn chair and stretches his fatigued limbs.

"The three of you took it out on the bay. Didn't Mike bring a single shot 22 rifle?" Steve stands with his back to Grant, still gazing off into space, arms crossed over chest.

"He did. Not sure why he brought it, maybe to shoot at a duck or two."

"Did he have any luck shooting at anything?

"The only thing shot was the seat I was sitting on. Mike was holding the gun in one hand while he was running a near useless four horsepower outboard motor. Somehow the gun went off and the seat was hit right next to me. That was a surprise on our initial voyage," Grant recalls, with a calm, warm sense of boating history.

Steve is deadly serious. "That trip on the Bay was the first detour in your life pattern."

Grant, replies irritated. "I don't remember any detour. We stayed out an hour or so 'til the wind came up. That's the way the trip went."

"Your file records the trip differently. There were three of you in the boat. Mike at the outboard controls holding the .22. It went off. Didn't hit the seat. It hit you in the chest, your heart. You died on that initial boat trip."

"Bullshit! That didn't happen. I remember it hit the seat right next to me." Grant shakes his head in disbelief.

"That's the way it happened after the detour, after the event-marker," Steve says, looking over his shoulder at Grant.

"What?" Grant lurches forward past his lawn chair, month open.

" Your life was detoured out on the bay that day." Steve is watching his brother closely

"I don't think so." Grant is stunned and exasperated; he needs to use the honey bucket more than ever. Can't move.

"It did happen," Steve says. "I can show you. It's all in the database stacks." He has SAM call up Grant's holographic life pattern, which Steve had paused.

"There has to be some error in the system." Grant is defiant. "I know what I remember. It hit the seat."

"Both database-recalled life patterns are accurate." SAM mind-tends. Grant grimaces at the comment.

From the data system pause, Steve manipulates the holographic pattern of Grant's life targeted to the very day he was on the bay. There are several views of the life patterns. On Grant's, there is an event-marker that indicates a change of direction. Examining the marker point closely, Steve manipulates side-by-side scenarios of the same scene. On the left the original video-like holographic replay of the three boys on the black homemade boat, Blackie.

Mike is at the rear, controlling the outboard throttle, loosely holding a 22 rifle in his left hand. Jim's on the right side, middle seat, and Grant is at the bow seat, facing the rear. On the right is the detoured holographic scene and a mirror image of the three boys and Blackie moving out into San Diego Bay. When Mike fumbles with the outboard throttle, he accidentally fires a 22-bullet striking Grant in the chest. A look of painful surprise overtakes Grant's face, and, within seconds, he slumps over, apparently near death.

At this point, the original holographic display pauses, and the accompanying detoured holographic display portrays a significantly different outcome: the bullet misses Grant and embeds in the wooden plank to his left. All three boys are stunned and, after an initial shock, manage to make light of the situation.

Mike puts the rifle down, and since it was a single-shot weapon, leaves it unloaded. Soon after, they return to their launch point and have a story to tell their friends. No one dies, no one's injured, but unbeknownst to them, they are on a detoured life path. Grant survives. From the event-marker of that day, Grant's life is going in an entirely different direction. It was detoured.

"Holy shit." Grant near speechless. He remembers the detoured life pattern scenario, not the original.

"Somehow, your life was manipulated that day on the bay. You apparently weren't supposed to die on those waters, in that boat, accidentally shot."

Grant is still in a state of disbelief. He knows SAM doesn't make mistakes or practical jokes. "This is, this is, what the...I don't understand. If you're not screwing around with me, I am fortunate to be alive."

"That's exactly what I thought the first time I saw it. I ran it about a dozen times. It is true. It happened. How fortunate someone is to have an opportunity to avoid a certain death scenario and move on with their lives. If you think about it, people just don't have those opportunities. What are the chances that would happen? Somebody given an opportunity to live beyond which would have been certain death otherwise," Steve asks, looking at Grant. "It is an incredible, once-in-a-lifetime happening, wouldn't you think?"

"Shit, Once-in-a-lifetime? I would think that it would almost never ever happen." Grant can't understand why he was given the opportunity to live beyond that day.

"Maybe some things are meant to be. Maybe event-markers and the detours associated with them are indicative of something significantly greater than we are capable of understanding. The event-markers and detours are the cairns stacked along life paths indicating a direction to follow. Life directions." Steve knows more about Grant's life patterns. He has discovered a puzzling maze of unanswered questions. More detours.

"Life directions?" Grant says. "I'm just fortunate to have had the opportunity to live past that day on the bay. I will forever be grateful."

"Actually, you are more than fortunate. You have more event-markers and detours on your life path. The episode on the bay was just the first. Let me show you."

Steve discovers his brother's proclivity for avoiding death. While researching historical patterns among the alternate history files and databases, Steve discovered event-marker detours at several stages of Grant's life. Steve had no such intervening events in his history; he wondered why. His brother, it seemed, was leading a charmed life, or at least a life redirected around several likely fatal events. Without those detours, Grant would've died as a teenager or several times since.

Steve was not a terribly religious Man, but he was familiar with biblical teachings and, in particular, the story of Moses. As the story goes, the Egyptian Pharaoh had ruled that all male newborns should be put to death to control the Jewish slave population. Moses' mother placed him into a basket made of reeds and set him adrift on the Nile River to avoid death at Pharaoh's hands. Steve saw this as a historical point that altered Moses's life path after being chosen by God. With that rudimentary religious biblical background, Steve began to believe that his brother was also chosen or at least selected.

Yes, what I discovered was alternate pathways for a number of events," Steve said.

"What do you mean alternate pathways'?" Grant is dazed, still in need of the honey-bucket, standing uncomfortably.

"Once I found the event-marker for the bay excursion on Blackie, I began to research your life pattern further. Even after that day, I found that you had more. Each resulted in an alternate pathway for your life pattern." Steve watches Grant closely. He wonders if Grant knows of the event-markers. Were they something that ET disclosed during extensive accelerated training and time travel episodes? Grant only offers a perplexed look of amazement. "You have event-markers, detours, associated with death events. Your death." Steve goes on.

"Wait, wait." Grant is engrossed by this new reality. He suddenly bends over, clutching at his stomach, grabs the honey-bucket, knocked the lawn chair nearly over the Oval edge, runs from the lab through the fluid doorway into the woods. "Well, hope he took the TP roll. Think he is going to need it.

Twenty minutes later, Grant returns without the bucket, takes a seat in the lawn chair. "Are you trying to tell me that I've been killed over the course of my lifetime several times, and have been resurrected, so to speak, to continue a new life pattern. An alternate path?"

"That's pretty much what I've found so far."

"Shit." Head in hands, bent over in the seat, "I don't believe it. What other death incidents have you found with these so-called event-markers?"

"In 1960, you and two of your friends were thrown from the back of a pickup truck, an off-road roll-over."

"I don't remember anything that has to do with the pickup accident."

"You were in the back of the pick up when it rolled out of control. You were thrown from the truck bed and landed in a dirt field with a broken neck."

"It never happened." Grant insists.

"Let me show it. I'll call it up." Steve maneuvers the database event-marker for July 7, 1960, at 9:30 at night, Bonita, California, with SAM's assistance.

Grant watches in disbelief as he can see the 1956 Ford two-door pickup racing down a hill of soft plowed soil with him and two friends in the bed of the truck. It was driven by his friend, Wayne, and two front seat passengers, Paul and Mike. Apparently, Wayne had been drinking and decided to do a little off-roading with passengers in tow. He crested the hill going faster than they should have for the conditions with the soft soil beneath. Wayne attempted to slow down, hit the brakes, and caused the truck to veer right and roll twice. He sees himself and his two friends tossed from the truck bed. Grant lands headfirst and lay motionless.

Two other truck bed passengers land less perilously in the soft soil, uninjured seriously

The holograph pauses and shifts to another version of the same event. The event-marker detour. The scene is the same: the '56 Ford pickup racing down the same hill, same conditions, and same passengers. But in the detoured version, Wayne maintains control of the truck. Instead of rolling over, the pickup plows straight into a 30-degree uphill grade, hitting the berm with the front bumper, giving passengers with a dirt shower. Injuries were not life-threatening, mostly bumps and bruises and Robbie ending up in a torso cast for six months.

Grant watches the scene with his mouth agape.

"I don't understand," he says.

"I didn't understand, either. It took some time after watching your event-markers."

Grant asks, "What do you mean? There's more?"

"There are."

"How many?

Steve takes a pause, looks at Grant. "You should see all the event-markers and detours. I'll call them up. SAM, if you please."

SAM mind-tends. "Compliance."

Steve recalls the holographic detours at event-markers that he is aware of. Grant still stands in disbelief next to him. Firearms were involved a couple times. The final event-marker/detour occurred in South Vietnam in 1970 while Grant was flying a Jolly Green Giant rescue helicopter near the Ho Chi Minh Trail. Just as his helicopter was in a position to directly cross over the trail, three rounds of 37mm anti-aircraft cannon fire struck the cockpit, killing the entire crew before the wreckage hit the ground. His death near the Trail took place 30 days before Lemon 2-1 took off from Da Nang on a night mission with a runaway prop and the night water rescue of nine downed air crewmen.

Grant is slow to respond. "I remember all those. I remember them so differently, and no one was killed in any of them. We joked about them all the time. Well, not the Ho Chi Minh trail crossing. That scared the shit out of my crew and me. We knew we just dodged a bullet, or we thought we had. I remember those 37mm tracer rounds were so loud and bright, just like lightning out the window."

"I remember the stories that you told, and we laughed about much of it. Do you remember talking about how lucky you were, that you had a charmed life?" Steve stands, walks around his lawn chair, and looks down off the Oval into open space.

"I still don't understand. Did you find a lot of event-markers for other people? The guys with me?" Grant wants to know.

"Only one of those guys is alive today."

"Didn't the event-markers, the detours, alter their lives as it did mine?"

"Not so much. The detours had a significant impact on your life, and those other guys, it seems, carried on without any significant impact on their futures," Steve says. "I followed the lives of those other guys, and the detours didn't seem to change their lives much."

"I still don't understand. Why me?"

"I don't completely understand it, either, but it seems you have some value our alien mentor sees, one that those other guys didn't have. I've been thinking of asking ET." Steve considers his strenuous previous and continued conversations with SAM and supposes an equal challenge approaching ET.

"I'm not special in any way." Grant approaches the Oval's edge next to Steve; both are looking for answers.

"You may not be special, but you certainly have been chosen for some reason. Our mentors must have a plan that includes you."

"There's no reason for it." Grant considers his random discovery of ET on Corte Madera. It was a purely chance encounter. There was never any significance to his life beyond a mundane pattern, like so many others.

"Hasn't ET given you some indication as to why he's putting you through this advanced intelligence training? There has to be something."

Grant is clearly confused. "He is providing advanced intelligence knowledge exercises so I can more clearly understand the concepts that encompass everything they have done and the purpose behind it." He sighs, then asks Steve. "Didn't you find something in your research of these alternate pathways or alternate histories that gives us some hint of where all this is heading?"

"The only thing I know for sure is that your life is different. You know, like Moses, sort of, chosen. If not that, then what? Your life has been extended at least three times. For what?" They both don't understand.

Then Steve asks, "Didn't they have a purpose for Nostradamus and da Vinci?"

"I'm sure they have a purpose for both of us." Grant picks up his backpack duffel and heads for the lab entry port and their bikes. He is eager to get on the road.

It has been a long exhausting day, three days' equivalent for Grant. "Let's take this up on the trip back home. I'm beat." he says. They take some time descending by mountain bike to the Four Corners parking area and don't have a chance to discuss anything on the way down. They loaded the bikes as usual, then headed back to Santee.

Steve speaks first, "Let's talk about Nostradamus. I found more data on him than da Vinci."

"No doubt while researching the effects of time travel sequence event-markers and detours in my life. Just great. Let's stop at the Starbucks in Alpine. I need a shot of caffeine." Grant says, not eager for the discussion that will follow.

Steve starts off. "It was a random search. I found Michael Nostradamus had an alternate history stored within the holographic history record stacks/library."

"Okay, I'll bite, what did you find out?" Grant is not sure what to expect.

"Nostradamus's history path alters in the 1540s for two to four years." Steve looks out the window as they head west on I-8; he's not concerned; he knows his research is accurate.

Were those altered life patterns, detours associated with Nostradamus losing his life a couple times?" Grant concentrates on his driving, not looking at Steve, watching for exit for Starbucks. He needs caffeine.

"To a limited extent Nostradamus was mentored by another· ET," Steve says. Introduced him to time travel exploration into the future, minus the aerosol."

"What do you mean minus the aerosol? "Grant starts to exit at Alpine.

"I don't believe Nostradamus ever was dosed with it, but he was influenced by his presence at future events. It was a semi-conscious display of events that clearly depicted items many years into the future. Not so sure Nostradamus had a clear recall of what he witnessed. No drugs." Steve confident of his research.

MAN 19

2010
Starbucks
Alpine, California

Grant pulls into the Alpine Starbucks lot; there are few other patrons at 3 p.m. Sunday. They find a table location away from the counter and the sweet rolls. Grant's having English breakfast tea, two egg sandwiches, and Steve some coffee latte combination. They continue their conversation about the significance of Nostradamus, his prophecies, and ET. They agree that Nostradamus lived in the 16th century and is well known for his predictions of future events.

It is from this point of agreement that their views of Nostradamus take divergent paths. From Steve's perspective, Nostradamus may have had some insights into the future; but, by and large, his prophecies are hard to reconcile adequately with the events that are attributed to them. Specifically, Steve feels that this 16th century physician managed to get a few things right; those who interpreted his quatrains read more into them than actually was there. They interpreted his prophecies and backed them into the actual events that occurred long after he died. His point is that Nostradamus, to prevent being labeled a magician or subjected to the Inquisition, used terms and descriptions wrapped up in four-line verses that took a stretch of the imagination to come to prophetic conclusions fitting future events.

Grant says, "He was a doctor and studied Hebrew. I agree with you that Nostradamus wrote his quatrains with obscure meaning and language." He inhales his sandwiches as if he hasn't eaten in days.

"Of course, he did, the things he forecast where unbelievable for his time," Steve says, swirling his latte.

"Yes, they were unbelievable and extremely incomprehensible for Nostradamus. He not only intentionally obscured the meaning of his quatrains, he had no choice."

For some reason, Steve in an intense reply. "That's what I've been telling you."

"I'm not sure you're following me."

"Not sure what you're referring to. It seems pretty straightforward to me. He did it to cover his ass." Steve replies.

"Yes, to cover his ass, but it's much more than that. It has to do with vocabulary and concepts that existed in the 16th century." Grant is insistent.

Steve is ready to leave. "Now I don't know what you're talking about." He spills part of his latte. "From what I know of Nostradamus, he was a learned Man, a scholar, medical doctor and had complete command of his language, regardless of the century." He soaks up latte with a napkin.

"He was all that, and yet he would've found it nearly impossible to describe what his prophecies foretold." Grant leans in and continues, "His 16th century vocabulary was nearly useless to describe the 21st century and beyond commonplace tools, mechanisms and technology."

"Again, I don't know where you're going with this." Steve leans in and raises his voice. Both brothers look around at customers and tone the volume down.

Grant speaks in a more subdued tone," Let me ask you a question: how would Nostradamus describe a 21st century hammer?"

"Really? A hammer?" Steve doesn't see where Grant is leading him.

"Go ahead. Describe a hammer from the 21st century"

"A hammer hasn't changed in a thousand years. It has a wooden handle and a forged metal hammer top. How's that?"

"That's not bad, considering the hammer has been around for thousands of years. And has changed only in form and types of design for the jobs it was going to do, basically a hammer is a hammer. The concept of the hammer hasn't changed dramatically."

"Okay, so what's your point?" Steve still wiping the table. Grant indicates they should finish their cleanup and continue their conversation outside Starbucks.

Grant stands and grabs a magazine left on a table; it has a Mac computer on the front cover. Pointing to it, he says, "Describe the computer." He heads for the door.

"Jesus, Grant, what now?" Steve asks as he follows Grant out the door.

They both are walking across the parking lot to their vehicle. "I want you to describe the Mac computer; it's that simple." He hands the magazine to Steve.

"Okay, it's a Apple IMac."

"Anything else you want to include?"

"And it has a power cord and Internet cable and connection." Steve is clearly frustrated now.

Grant points again. "And what are these?"

"The keyboard and mouse."

"How do they work? What are their functions?" Grant asks, still pointing.

"They're both connected to the Mac. Jesus, are we about done here?"

They walk near a metro bus stop and bench close to where they parked. There are no people near in any direction. Grant makes a gesture for Steve to take a seat; he shrugs then sits down. Grant sits as well, "Yes, I think we are about done with the 21st century description. Now I want you to describe the Mac, keyboard, monitor, and mouse with a 16th century vocabulary and related concepts."

Steve looks uninterested. He's not quite sure what he has been asked to do. "What are you talking about? I just described them!"

"You just described the Mac and associated equipment; however, your terminology and a description was based completely on your understanding of 21st century devices and technology." Grant asks again, "Now, I want you to describe those same items, but only in terms of a 16th century skill set and vocabulary. You should consider yourself wearing Nostradamus's shoes. I'll call you *doctor* if that helps."

Steve is completely baffled at this point and is not pleased with his brother. He doesn't have a clear concept of where Grant is trying to take him and is not looking forward to the trip. "Holy shit. This is amazing."

"Come on, Steve, give it a try. Or should I say, Doctor Steve?"

"What are you doing with all this? Just doesn't make any sense."

"It's simple. I want you to describe what you see on the front cover but only use terminology, words and phrases from the 16th century, Doc."

Steve clearly tries to conceptualize and find words and terminology that he could use to describe the iMac, but he can't. "This is BS."

"I'll give you BS. I think he could've used that term in the 16th century."

"What the fuck, Grant?"

Grant replies, "I think the term fuck is maybe from English origins, so you can't use that."

Steve is clearly not seeing where this conversation is going, "What? I'm not doing this."

"Do you mean you're not doing this or you can't do it?"

"I'm not playing this game anymore."

"Not a game. I think you're frustrated because you can't describe the Mac without using modern-day terms and related technology."

"This is bullshit." says Steve, tossing his latte at a waste bin. Misses.

"I already gave you that word, it's okay to use. It's all the other words that I'm interested to hear."

"I told you I'm not doing this." Ready to toss the PC Magazine after his latte.

Grant takes the magazine from Steve. "I think it's that you don't want to do this because, you can't do it. And that's okay. You are proving my point."

"And your point is?" Steve is clearly not into this game. Word game.

"What you just experienced by not being able to describe the Mac in 16th century terms is the same obstacle and frustration that Nostradamus would have felt in the 16th century. He would've been at a loss to find the words that would describe a monitor, keyboard and mouse to say nothing of how such devices operated."

"It's really a pretty simple concept to understand." Steve responds.

Grant is animated now. "Everything you see on that computer desk, on the magazine cover, that Nostradamus would see are completely foreign to him. Even if you were to set the good doctor down, how would you describe a keyboard? How would you describe all of the items in terms he could understand and comprehend?"

"There would have to be a way. He had to be a smart guy. The ETs must have a method to educate or bring him up to speed on the concept. How about the genius aerosol they used on you? They probably used something on Nostradamus." Steve knows that's not true by his research; he's grabbing at straws.

Grant says, "On the ride here, you said didn't think so. His explanations and quatrains leave so much to interpretation and no real specifics. I don't know that the aerosol would help to that level for someone from the 16th century. Again, how would you explain a keyboard?"

"The ETs would have handled that," says Steve, somewhat exasperated.

"Would you say that signals from this device, that have letters on them, and when you press the letter, a signal is sent to this device, the computer monitor and displayed there? You have to remember in the 16th century the printing press was only 60 years old when Nostradamus was born. Just as you couldn't describe the Mac in 16th century terms, Nostradamus had the same problem. Perhaps even more important: you have the advantage of understanding the technical, mechanical computer concepts. Nostradamus had none of that technical expertise. In addition, he had no related vocabulary to adequately describe a Mac in his observation. He would've had this obstacle in front of him for any of his observations, not just the Mac."

Grant searches for other ways of explaining Nostradamus's intellectual 16th century limits. "You could've had him observe open-heart surgery, and he would've been at a loss to describe that procedure adequately to people of his time without them thinking him crazy, possessed, describing that procedure that was hundreds of years into the future. How could he have explained that operation to physicians of his time when bloodletting was an accepted medical treatment? He would've been investigated by the Inquisition, perhaps as a heretic or some other evil godless manifestation. There could have been a stake with his name on it ready to be lit up."

Steve makes an attempt to counter Grant's arguments. "If his intellect was so fundamentally flawed and limited then why would he go through with it? He had to have been in awe of all he was shown by his alien mentors. How could one not want to explain it fully and open up for all to see the future?"

"That was his dilemma. I think he must've understood that there was a tremendous future for the world with incredible technology and inventions to be discovered. And yet he could not reveal much of any of it to 16th century Man. The men of his time were steeped in religious beliefs and suspicious of controversial theories that introduced new and unproven technologies. A hundred years ago the common Man in this country would have a difficult time visualizing much of what we take for granted today."

Steve stands up and responds, "A hundred years ago, someone would probably listen to you, but wouldn't want to burn you at the stake if they disagreed with your crazy ideas. I think he would have an easier time explaining a computer concept in 1916."

"Steve, Nostradamus had to write his quatrains in a vague fashion because some of the observations he had couldn't be explained in the language of the 1500s. And couldn't be understood with 16th-century knowledge. If he had tried to write about heart transplants, it would've been on his way to a barbecue where he was the main course. If in fact, a genius aerosol-like substance was used on him, it may have saved his life because he would've understood the limitations of those he would be trying to convince. It had the same effect on me. I am still amazed at all I learned from ET, much of it I still don't completely understand. If we went back to the 16th century today and spoke of the technology that we understand here in the 21st century, no one we encountered would understand anything we were saying. If you traveled back to that time and had a laser pointer and used it, you could very well be considered a magician, a practitioner of black magic, the black arts, and put to death."

Steve responds in a ninja stance. "If I went back, I would prefer having a light saber and kick some serious ass with it. That would really turn some freaking heads."

"Okay, Ninja Steve, here's an easy one. Explain in today's terminology the creation and extent of the boundaries of the universe?"

Silence. Still in his ninja stance, Steve looks at his menacing ninja hands, then puts them in his pants pockets and shrugs, "Okay."

After this Nostradamus Starbucks encounter with Grant, Steve wants answers to many questions. In researching the effects of time travel sequence and how it is used by ET, Steve Fredericks discovers Michael Nostradamus has an alternate history stored within the holographic history record stacks. He finds that Nostradamus's history path alters in the 1540s. For an approximate two- to four-year period,

Nostradamus was a "student" of ETs, which introduced him to time travel exploration into the future. Nostradamus, the student, was abducted in the year 1540. He was exposed to events hundreds of years in the future. He struggles with the futuristic society and the many advanced concepts and inventions that are routine. Nostradamus finds that he has no vocabulary to describe these everyday items. Today, the average individual understands the concepts, if not the intricate design of computers, coffee machines, telephones, radios, televisions, aircraft, and mundane items run by electricity. Nostradamus' intellectual realm of reference is 500 years out of date. He is perplexed yet can appreciate the nature of his excursion into the future and observe future events and inventions he clearly cannot comprehend. He struggles to relate on paper adequately describing his experience, those items, and events he struggles to understand in his notes.

His prophetic prognostications resulted from actual observations of future events and not an incredible gift of extrasensory perception. At best, he had an observation window into the future, and at worst, he was wholly unprepared intellectually to understand and comprehend his view. In his time, the lead pencil was a recent invention two years before his death. Nostradamus was ill-prepared scientifically, technologically, and intellectually to comprehend and absorb commonplace items hundreds of years into the future. Add to that a deficit in a vocabulary devoid of any terminology that could adequately explain or describe events or items unremarkable years into the future. He had to have felt a total sense of intellectual inadequacy. He had a wealth of knowledge without a technologically suitable vehicle to share it. He was captured and constrained in an intellectual dungeon with the door wide open, and he couldn't exit.

Grant knows from his training sessions with ET that, in the end, Nostradamus understood the gift he was given and how to use it wisely. He was once traveling in Italy and is said to have bowed before a passing young Franciscan monk, addressing him as "His Holiness." Onlookers were astounded and could not understand his behavior. Years later, that Franciscan monk, a swine herder named Felice Peretti, became Cardinal Peretti and was elected in 1585 to become Pope Sixtus V. Nostradamus had died 19 years earlier.

MAN 20

OBL

On the way home to Santee, Steve rekindles the Nostradamus debate. Grant is disinterested, yearns to be home. "We already had this conversation at Starbucks, remember?"

"We did," Steve says, "and you explained that Nostradamus could not speak of his experiences when he was gone for those two years because no one would believe him and he would probably be burned at the stake as a heretic or worse."

"We've already gone through this. He came back to an intellectual vacuum that was at least 450 years behind what he saw during the period of time he was with alien mentors. Remember, you were trying to explain the concept of a computer keyboard, screen and mouse in the terminology of 16th century Europe. You couldn't do it. There were literally no words that could've been used to explain 21st century technology. Remember the screen saver Flurry?" Grant is ready to end the conversation.

"Really, Flurry? Fuzzy star-colored tails. I have it on my computer so what? We were talking about Nostradamus, not screen savers." Steve wonders where his brother is off to.

"Try following along." Grant is tired and short-tempered." If Nostradamus would have been able to display a computer screen with just Flurry on it, he couldn't explain it to anyone of that period of time. More likely the result would've been hanging for Nostradamus. He wrote his quatrains in a code that allowed him to survive while offering insight into the future," Grant reminds Steve. "Ditto for da Vinci. Aliens did the same thing for him

248

during the period of time that he was gone. When he returned, he had a spike of intellectual capacity and creativity. And he was confined by the same restrictions. He had no peers with which to exchange the vast intellectual information that he was exposed to while with the alien mentors."

"So you're telling me they both were trained and educated with advanced scientific knowledge that they clearly couldn't use or apply in their day unless they wanted to tempt or challenge the church leadership and the ongoing Inquisition? It seems to me all that training and knowledge was wasted, like getting a degree in social psychology and working as a bartender, analyzing intoxicated patrons: *She doesn't understand me. I hate my job. My kids are screwed up. Hit me again, would ya. And by the way, she really doesn't understand me!* That was all worth it?"

"They became influencers of their day." Grant sees Steve doesn't buy it.

"Influencers?" questions Steve.

Grant struggling to make a point. "They were muzzled; on the feathered edge of going to an execution, theirs. They understood the risk and subtly maneuvered their contributions within the confines of the established moral and scientific standards of the day. They were as bright lights illuminated in a darkened age of dogma and ignorance. They did influence the future more so than their immediate impact in their time. Impressive graduate students, to say the least."

"Okay, influencers. I get that part. The Mona Lisa was a pretty good painting, I guess." Eager to change directions and boast a bit, Steve continues, "By the way, I took on a graduate project of sorts, while you were away with ET training for two days"

"Graduate project? What are you talking about?" Grant's brother is known for off-the-wall theatrics and outrageous behavior Grant can't guess what is coming.

"Travel management. My very first client is Osama bin Ladan, (OBL) arranged his air travel itinerary."

"ET said we couldn't touch him or take him out. He was off-limits untouchable. Tell me you didn't."

"No, I took him on as a client instead." Steve says with a slight smile of mischievous satisfaction. "You call, we haul—he needed travel arrangements. I managed it, my first client. No complaints."

"Holy shit, does ET know?" Grant considers his statement. Of course, he knows. "What did you do?" Grant is dumbfounded.

Steve and Grant realize that changing the past is not a simple exercise. Their experience provided evidence that they could not change their own life pattern. They found that they couldn't go back before 9/11 and kill Osama bin Laden without dramatically changing everything in their lives. The alternative was an event-marker that could change the life pattern of OBL.

bin Laden
The 9/11 Commission Report states:
In late 1995, when bin Laden was still in Sudan, the State Department and the Central Intelligence Agency (CIA) learned that Sudanese officials were discussing with the Saudi government the possibility of expelling bin Laden. The Saudis, however, did not want him since they revoked his citizenship. Sudan's minister of defense, Fatih Erwa, has claimed that Sudan offered to hand bin Laden over to the United States. The Clinton administration chose not to take the Sudanese offer.

The 1996 Sudanese officials began approaching officials from the United States and other governments, asking what actions of theirs might ease foreign pressure to be rid of bin Laden. In secret meetings with Saudi officials, Sudan offered to expel bin Laden to Saudi Arabia and asked the Saudis to pardon him. Saudi officials would not tolerate his presence in their country. Also, bin Laden may have no longer felt safe in Sudan, where he had already escaped at least one assassination attempt that he believed to have been the work of the Egyptian or Saudi regimes and paid for by the CIA.

Due to the increasing pressure on Sudan from Saudi Arabia, Egypt, and the United States, bin Laden was permitted to leave for a country of his choice. He chose to return to Jalalabad, Afghanistan, aboard a chartered flight of 2,764 miles on May 18, 1996; he forged a close relationship with Mullah Mohammed Omar. According to the 9/11 Commission, the expulsion from Sudan significantly weakened bin Laden and his organization. Some African intelligence sources have argued that the expulsion left bin Laden without an option other than becoming a full-time radical. Most of the 300 Afghan Arabs who went with him subsequently became terrorists.

Steve has time and opportunity on his hands when Grant and ET are on an accelerated learning session. He learns to absorb everything in his environment to include the database and holograph computer system. He determines the level of questions in queries asked of SAM to assess the level of response. It was apparent SAM knew the difference between operators and intellect. The system's "persona" wasn't condescending; SAM simply was using language and logic appropriate for the operators' "intellectual makeup." Steve was on a preschool level, Grant elementary school, and the aliens lightyears beyond any level on Earth. MIT, Harvard, Stanford, and Cal Tech were backwater dives.

After discovering the parallel patterns of his brother's life and his ability to travel back in time, Steve wants to kill Osama bin Laden to prevent the 9/11 tragedy.

The difficulty with this scenario is that Steve and Grant have found that they cannot effectively adjust the current life pattern that they are both on. In other words, they can't go back to the original 9/11 and prevent that from happening. They are contained within their current life pattern and are prevented from changing or revising the past without altering their present existence. ET has strict control over the Fredericks brothers' agenda.

OBL elimination: Charter flight 18 May, 1996
Khartoum Sudan to Jalalabad Afghanistan

The ensuing life pattern created with the elimination of OBL and the non-destruction of the World Trade Center would proceed in a parallel life pattern to Steve's and Grant's current life pattern. In creating this new parallel life pattern, they effectively save over 2,000 American lives on September 11, 2001. They also would have saved thousands of lives beyond the World Trade Center and halted the initiation of endless deadly war in the Middle East. The sorrow of 9/11 still remains with their current and historic life pattern, but there is some solace from what a new parallel life pattern has prevented.

The alternative is to create a parallel life pattern that incorporates the life of Osama bin Laden before he develops plans to bring down the World Trade Center: A Time-Loop. It is a segmented partition of time that continually repeats, similar to a video that plays over and over without end, such as that of a video replay of a home run. One is video, the Time-Loop is actual living life patterns, and participants are caught in a repeated sequence, unending. These were stumbled upon by Steve attempting to navigate and manipulate time. Regardless of his efforts to manipulate time, it is a constant, almost impervious to change without unforeseen consequences. While experimenting with a past event, intervening with a simple high school football game and one particular game-losing play, Steve sent the specific play into an endless circular repeating time-loop. The essence of that manipulation resulted in the "play" being run repeatedly without end or change but by the actual live players, who were caught in the Time-Loop. It would have lasted forever had not ET corrected and adjusted the results to fit Steve's original intent.

In the end, he learned that a sequence of manipulations could send a past event into a time repeated loop. The event could be a matter of minutes, hours, days, or some other length of an arbitrary time interval. Those so captured within the event would experience nothing out of the ordinary and repeat the sequence repeatedly forever or until further manipulation brought it to an end.

With this knowledge, Steve came up with a flight plan. Osama bin Laden scheduled a chartered flight in May 1996, leaving Khartoum for Jalalabad, Afghanistan, with a contingent of his terrorist followers. Steve initially anticipated placing an explosive device on that aircraft and killing them all, with the wreckage falling into the Red Sea; however, he realized that this scenario could embolden bin Laden's followers into reprisal scenarios.

Instead, Steve chose to send Osama's chartered flight on a Yogi, a detour to a time-loop and circular repeating life pattern. The flight departed Khartoum in May 1996 for a five-hour flight to Afghanistan. It never lands; the crew and passengers remained on an unending flight profile that takes off and remains airborne for an eternity. The aircraft never runs out of fuel. They are on a repeating time-loop from take-off to cruise altitude and never finish their in-flight meals. Before their actual descent to a landing in Afghanistan, the Yogi takes place, and they are "detoured," back on the runway in Khartoum, Sudan, for take-off on their unending chartered flight to nowhere. In this life pattern, bin Laden does not create the chaos and destruction of 9/11. He and his 300 co-conspirators are relegated to an eternity of accumulating thousands and thousands of air miles, subsisting on airline food. It could be a fate worse than death! But it was, on some level, a measure of payback, as Steve saw it.

MAN 21

Question:
Android - Cyborg

The Fredericks brothers are alone near the Corte Madera Lab, taking a nature's call. They have made this journey together several times. Since both are retired and avid mountain bikers, their time away biking is considered routine if not annoying by Becky. Steve, a bachelor, has no one to be accountable to. They're standing a few feet apart when Steve asks, "What is he, really? "

He's not from here." Grant had questions regarding the origin of ET before Steve was introduced. During his periods of time-compressed training, his intellect had advanced along with his curiosity regarding ET.

"I know he's not from here, but what is he, where is he from? Is he like us, human in some way? I'm beginning to think he can't be like us. We can't exist like he does. He doesn't eat, drink or sleep, other than time standing on that miniature oval recharging or whatever he is doing—hibernating, I guess."

Grant knows ET is beyond human. He doesn't survive or live as Man does. His sole requirements are his periods of recharging or replenishing his energy source. Grant early on inquired of SAM regarding ET's characteristics and genesis of existence. SAM provides only information regarding ET's responsibilities and duties. Nothing about his family: parents, brothers, sisters. SAM responds truthfully that ET is a combination of genetically enhanced artificial intelligence and biological material, in many ways similar in structure to that found in the human genome.

During one of the interactions, Grant asked SAM, "Is ET an artificially created being similar to an android or cyborg?"

"An android is a robot or other artificial being designed to resemble a human, and often made from a human-flesh-like material," SAM replies. "A cyborg is a combination of organic and mechanical parts. Both cyborgs and androids are often misportrayed in human visual displays and exhibit physical or mental abilities far exceeding a human counterpart; they are depicted as moving, thinking and speaking fluidly. In this category would be the fictional characters of Darth Vader, Bishop from Aliens, the Terminator, West-World, and Inspector Gadget. ET is a creation beyond those models."

Grant came to understand ET has modified and improved cellular biological systems consistent with human patterns but beyond any current systems and certainly far beyond that of Steve and Grant. They come to understand that ET is a hybrid combination of some sort. Perhaps android, cyborg, or most likely something far beyond their limited comprehension.

"He has a whole different biological structure than we do. His requirements for sustainability, survival are so different from ours," Grant says.

Steve is relieving himself in some sagebrush, "On the other hand, I think boredom wouldn't be a problem."

"Really?" says Grant.

Steve says, "Sure, think about the time you would save by not doing what we're doing right now on a daily basis."

"What?" says Grant, zipping up, "Pissing in the woods?"

Steve shakes a leg, doing the same, "Daily bathroom breaks got to be at least an hour or two per day. Eating, Jesus, that's got to take about three hours. Sleeping six to eight hours, and you get up still tired just to start it all over again, with another bathroom break."

"Okay, let's say you are able to live as ET does. How are you going to occupy your time and fit in with society?"

"Well, for sure you will save money." Steve is thinking out loud. "There'll be no need to buy food and drink. Time will become an asset."

"So how would you spend your time asset?"

They start to walk back to the lab entrance. "Any work-related project you can get done in half the time or less. Those extra eight or ten hours would come in handy."

"I think you would find you would be working alone. None of your contemporaries could keep up with you."

Steve gloats, "Well, that would take some adjusting to."

"What about your personal relationships?"

"What about them?"

Grant stops, turns toward Steve." Don't you think someone would think it rather strange that you are up and about all day and night? You don't eat, you don't drink, you don't sleep and you are a ball of kinetic energy."

"They would get used to it. Think how efficient I would be, getting things done."

Grant digs in," How many times have you been divorced? More than two?"

"Yeah, couple times."

"Didn't all your wives say you were a pain in the ass to be around at the end."

Steve turns away, looking down. "Well, they needed their space."

"Needed their space? You were always in their space. Now with your newfound energy you would be around 24-7."

"Well, I would have to make some adjustments."

"I would suggest a bullet-proof vest and a gun safe that only you have the combination to."

"Jeez."

"I've attempted to get personal information from ET—without much success," Grant says, "He is very different. Very different from us."

256

CONSIDER MAN

Numbers

"You say he's different?" Steve leads back toward the lab, taking a dirt path to the entrance. "Their number system is incredibly different."

Grant follows. "When I first saw the holographic number images floating above the Oval it reminded me of a *Sesame Street* lesson for preschoolers. I thought the images and shapes were a cosmic holographic screensaver, similar to Flurry. I only understood a portion of all the shapes, sizes, and objects that are their number system."

Steve looks over his shoulder to reply. "ET and SAM are so far advanced they can do those number symbol calculations in their head." Steve adds, "Well, at least in ET's head."

Grant says. "At first I thought they were just shapes of varied sizes, not numeric symbols of a highly advanced mathematic system." During his advanced accelerated training, Grant was exposed to the alien numeric system. "The system consists of shapes, colors, and textures, not Arabic numbers. It relies on internal cerebral images and holographs that relate to a numeric value. The image starts to change and evolve, and a third shape emerges. No computer, no notebook, no tablets. ETs see the answer as mental imagery."

"I have difficulty getting my head around it," Steve says with a clear measure of frustration. They arrive at the entry portal; Steve stops.

Grant goes on. "Even with the assistance of the aerosol neurotropic-like drug and repeated exposure during accelerated training, I doubt that I could have completely comprehended the relevance of the shapes, sizes, and colors. Their system is visually based beyond any numerics we understand from a digit-based expression. Math is math regardless of the visual presentation." Grant needed a mega drug dose to grasp ET's basic numerics.

"Holy shit, I forgot about colors," Steve says. "Colors in a mathematical calculation are components in the ET numeric system?"

Grant attempts to clarify, "In their system of math, shapes and different-sized objects interact with colors; and they all change and mutate to different shapes and colors to indicate a summation or calculation."

"Beyond numbered toy blocks in pre-school. Have to be a genius to figure it all." Steve had a hard time with this "new math" model.

ET had to adjust the lab's computer system management, SAM, to incorporate Arabic numbers and symbols for Grant and Steve. With training, they could incrementally attain an understanding and recognition of the holographically displayed alien numeric characters. Yet, accepting and adapting to the total foreign and alien "new math" was exceedingly challenging. There were no timetables to memorize, no pencil and paper calculations, and the numeric system couldn't be written. It was total mental imagery or holographs displayed by SAM.

In particular, Steve held SAM suspect in displaying a measure of egotistical computer versus human beat down. Steve and Grant learned portions of numeric images, yet they weren't completely assured working with SAM. They could remember frequent numeric shapes, sizes, and colors, but not enough to master the visual calculations. The numeric system was one of many significantly humbling experiences for the Fredericks brothers. SAM freely provided meaningful, although irritating, corrections.

"In the *Aliens vs. Predators* movie," Steve explains to Grant, "that's where I saw the numeric shape image system the Predators used; it was shapes and symbols. I wonder if ET influenced one of the writers on that film?"

"Don't think so. Both their math and ours remain, to a great extent, the same."

"OK. Show me?" Steve asks with a measure of skepticism.

"The only real and significant difference between Arabic and their visual math calculations is the visual portion of it. If you notice when SAM displays their visual representation of a numeric result along with the Arabic numbers, essentially the computations are identical. I believe their math system and ours are tied to a universal math constant. For example, the Fibonacci number sequence. They use it, we use it. It has been used for hundreds of years."

"Okay, you got me: who or what is Fibonacci?" Steve says.

Grant knows that the Fibonacci number sequence would most certainly be present in any numerics system universe-wide; once he started to train with ET, it became clear. "ET-type aliens provided the sequence's existence with the abduction of Medieval mathematician and businessman, Leonardo Fibonacci, near the year 1200," Grant says. "Later in the early 13th century, the scientific community discovered the sequence was a constant principle in the evolutionary process in the natural world."

"Okay, got the who, not the what?" says Steve, looking in the chair-side cooler for a drink.

"The Fibonacci Sequence. In 1202, Fibonacci posed the following problem in his treatise 'Liber Abaci': How many pairs of rabbits will be produced in a year, beginning with a single pair, if in every month each pair bears a new pair, which becomes productive from the second month on?" Grant recalls from his Wikipedia-like training and memory.

"That's the what: rabbits?" Steve opens a cold beer and waits.

"It is much more," Grant replies. "The Fibonacci sequence or numbers is the sum of two numbers that go before; a simple pattern that goes on forever." SAM pulls up the Fibonacci sequence numbers for one year.

SAM complies without thought: *0, 1, 1, 2, 3, 5, 8, 13, 21, 34, 55, 89 ,144...*is displayed holographically in companion with a series of numeric, color-tinged images.

"Okay, so we have 144 rabbits in twelve months. Where is the significance that you alluded to?" Steve asks, taking a long pull on his beer.

SAM answers, "While the Fibonacci sequence doesn't account for every structure or pattern in the universe, it is a major factor."

"It is just rabbits multiplying. How complicated can it be?" Steve asks.

"It is not complicated; it is essential as a numeric system for the entire cosmos." Mind-tending SAM.

"Everything about Man and his environment reflects the Fibonacci Sequence influence." Grant recalls this from his accelerated training sessions. Grant supposes and Steve still tries to embrace the kaleidoscopic array of numeric symbols, shapes, colors, and images.

"Sesame Street." Steve's hands are up, palms facing out, "I accept it is beyond my ability to understand, just give me the digits I know."

"Digits are examples of the Fibonacci sequence numbers, as are any images with a numeric value." SAM mind-tends.

"I'll need to see it."

Grant joins in. "It is a simple, recursive sequence known to mathematicians for hundreds of years. It has been found as a binding principle from ancient Greek aesthetics to growth patterns of plants and animals; to include rabbits. It is seen from the micro-scale to the macro-scale, and right through to biological systems and inanimate objects."

"Still need to see it." Steve needs to see to understand.

Grant continues, points to an image of a flower blooming. "Follow along. See this: The number of petals in a flower consistently follows the Fibonacci sequence. Allowing for the best possible exposure to sunlight, and others: pine cones, tree branches, shells, spiral galaxies thought the cosmos, to include the microscopic realm of DNA. A DNA molecule measures 34 angstroms long by 21 angstroms wide for each full cycle of its double helix spiral. These numbers, 34 and 21, are numbers in the Fibonacci series."

"I'm still in a bit of a numeric fog." Steve tries to focus on the scope of the numeric system and its impact on everything he has ever known.

"Closer to home. Your hand, my hand, has 8 fingers in total, 5 digits on each hand, 3 bones in each finger, 2 bones in 1 thumb, and 1 thumb on each hand."

"OK, OK, I get it," Steve is resigned to a small measure of understanding and a vacancy of knowledge.

White Cap Mural

CONSIDER MAN

Dream

Grant sits on the second row of scaffolding in painting shorts, shirt and shoes He is painting a surfing mural on the side of a commercial building. Another figure joins the scene below Grant; his name is Jim, "I didn't know you were this good of an artist. Jackie told me that I had to see for myself."

Jim says louder, "Hey, Grant!" Grant stirs, his head jerks side to side. Doesn't wake.

Grant, expects Jackie. "Jackie! What are you, aah, it's not Jackie' "It's Jim. I thought you were somebody else."

"Jackie said you really got into your painting."

"You know Jackie?" How could he? Jackie died long before Grant ever met Jim.

"Yeah, your friend from junior high. Drinking buddy? High school? Fighter? Lover? Untimely end?"

"How do you know so much about Jackie?"

"It is easy to find out things about anybody over here. Remember the clarity?" Jim says while adjusting his police-style sunglasses. He is wearing a tan civilian style flight suited boots. They both are standing on the scaffolding while Grant paints the mural's surfer's long wet hair.

Grant mumbles, "Clarity" in his sleep; turning uneasily in bed near the mattress edge; he may fall on the floor again. Becky stirs. "Clarity. I mean, geez. You guys have some celestial social network. Twitter for the souls?" Grant mumbles more, doesn't wake.

"No, nothing like that," Jim says. "Not needed there, just clarity."

"Well clarify this: How is this going to end for me?"

"I don't know," Jim says, unconcerned.

"So, clarity doesn't work on this side?" Grant is puzzled.

"It does, but not how you would think."

"You're not going to help me out here, are you?" Grant now paints the orange sunset skyline at the fourth level of the scaffold.

Jim has turned west, watching the surf breaking on an abandoned sailboat. His reply,

"The best answer I can give is you're going to have to find it on your own, Grant."

"Kinda like you have to do it yourself for it to have meaning?"

"Yeah, kind of like that." Jim touches the mural; it's fluid and wet.

Grant rolls again, closer to the mattress edge.

"Jim, do you remember what you said when your doctor told you that you had terminal liver cancer?"

"Fuck! Said it a couple times."

"You remember what I said when you told me?"

"Yeah, I do. Fuck."

"Those moments were the closest I came to understanding the concept of clarity, at least on this side." Grant stops painting.

"It's not completely different over here, but it is so much more." Jim focused on the breaking surf.

"You know you are still on the answer machine at your home. When I call Wendy, it's you for a brief moment. It's a good feeling but hurts at the same time." Grant turns back to paint on a wave break.

"Memories make it that way."

"So why are you here?" He should be waking up; it seems like another dream. Again.

"It could be any number of things." Jim says, now sits next to Grant.

"Shit, Jim. Things, what things?"

"There will be a point when it all becomes clear. I can't tell you when, only that you'll know. Wait for it."

"Wait for it? I've heard that before. Great."

"You should get back to your mural. It's late. Thanks for keeping track of Wendy and the girls."

"Didn't do much. Wendy has her hands full. You are missed." Grant laments.

"She and the girls are going to be OK. That's something I have to wait for." Jim and Grant watch a brilliant green flash sunset as the sun dips below the horizon.

"Wait for it? Guess that goes both ways."

"Get back to your mural. It needs your touch, personal touch. A lot needs your touch, Grant, don't lose sight of that."

"My touch, waiting for it and now losing light, great. Thanks, Jim."

Grant wakes.

Becky is again up from a sound sleep, "You need to sleep with a muzzle. Go to sleep; it's 2 a.m." Becky fluffs her pillows with a couple punches and rolls over away from Grant.

MAN 22

The Card Game

After returning from their June 6, 1970, visit to Da Nang and witnessing the circumstance of Lemon 2-1's demise, Grant and Steve realize they might have a slim chance to change Sergeant Alloway's destiny. Nine other crew members survived; Alloway drowned with a death grip on his radio, not the critical survival tool. It was a fatal error. He and all air force crews trained to clear their parachute lines and canopy after a water landing, he didn't. His knife was what he needed first. Cut yourself free and only then make use of the radio. He could have spent the night floating without that radio and be found that night or the next day. He had strobe lights and smoke flares. Grant needed to adjust Alloway's focus to his knife, not his radio; his second chance to live depended on it.

Following ET's admonishments to observe and record made it incredibly difficult to interfere on a positive level without an out-of-kilter far-reaching outcome. Don't go there; unintended consequences turn into a turbulent future resultant.

Grant and Steve, with Dragonfly, followed Sergeant Alloway for several days, looking for a trigger to push him into remembering his parachute procedures training; they found nothing. There wasn't anything. He repeatedly followed strict airborne operation procedures to near flawless perfection, but not a critical open water survival routine he had never practiced.

His strict adherence to "his duty routine" was going to kill him...and it did every night. Each night he flew his last flight...spoke his last words to Jolly 2-7's copilot. Same result is

264

repeated each time. Using Pushback, moving his flight gear, hiding personal items didn't change the outcome. He always drowns and dies that night in the South China Sea. By ET's direction, they couldn't interfere with his health or that of others. Alloway always persevered to fly the fatal mission. Steve and Grant followed along in Dragonfly, four nights; same snake bit outcome. Couldn't influence Sergeant Alloway's in-water decision-making, now two nights away from his fatal flight. They needed a paradigm shift for the non-swimming Cherokee Man.

ET observed all of the Pushback and scene manipulation attempts by Grant and Steve. They didn't categorize it all as bush-league applications of Pushback. ET, however, realized it was. In ET's alien mind, Grant's and Steve's repeated Pushback manipulation attempts were clearly fault ridden...his alien category of such events didn't include "bush-league." It is added at a later date.

ET communicates with the desperate for guidance, brothers Fredericks. "Typical solution to difficult issues can be solved by direct encounters."

Steve responds with a question. "How many encounters have you had with humans beside Grant and me?" Steve thinks ET is off-base.

"None, observation records data information." ET's study of the human race over hundreds of years indicates a possible blend of time travel and personal interaction with the subject of their Pushback dilemma.

"I thought you didn't want us to interfere with individuals on a personal level, contact them. Alter decisions?" Grant is wondering if a shift of policy is afoot.

"The altered decision is not yours; it is his, Sergeant Alloway's." ET mind-tending. "You can alter his thinking, not alter his actions in Pushback mode."

Steve counters for clarification, "So we can't give a push, a touch, an attention-grabbing kick in the butt," Steve slaps his head as an example, "to force a change of outcomes?

"Correct, physical outcome fails alternative shift of direct encounter." ET replies in not clear terms.

"By direct encounter are you referring to a hands-on approach such as conversations with other humans inside of Pushback and outside freeze frame?" Grant has his interest perking up. "A paradigm shift?"

"Correct. Mankind has historically solved various issues by communications component." ET mind-tends.

"Well, no shit, Sherlock...mankind has also destroyed others by false and faulty communications for thousands s of years." Steve gets back in the ring. "Look, trust is the issue."

"Not all communication is accurate, you are correct. Trust is not always deserved." ET replies. "Validation component of time travel is available."

"I think you have a point. An interaction with Alloway may be the most direct access to changing his actions by suggestion. Get him to trust in someone and himself." Grant is focused. "That could work. What do we know of his routine? Need to interact by direct contact...how hard could that be?"

Grant, Steve and ET decide a hands-on approach could be more meaningful. There was a one-time opportunity and a risk to gamble it all; play the cards they were dealt. The last opportunity was, in fact, a card game at the NCO club. A regularly played game of penny-ante poker with the same four supposed card sharks, including Alloway. On the night two days before the final flight, one of the regular players had a case of diarrhea. The Fredericks brothers had no involvement, courtesy of a plate full of mess hall liver and onions. They knew a chair was empty at the table. They watched the card game players for several nights and confirmed an empty chair on the target night. It turned out some of Grant's accelerated advanced learning was finally kicking in. He made use of the sharpest tools available in the ET toolbox. He orchestrated a one-person stage performance deserving of a Tony award consideration.

Both brothers determined that Grant needed to speak with Alloway a day or two before his fatal flight. Dragonfly delivered Grant unseen to the Da Nang NCO club, and the least intrusive entry port, the men's restroom. The brothers had extensive experience with drunken participants using the "john" and not paying much attention to who was coming and going—eyes always toward the urinal. Even a miscalculated entry, an accidental encounter, would most likely be attributed to alcohol. No one's going to tell the story, "You're not going to believe this, but I just saw a guy walking out of the wall in the head." And no one's going to believe that story from a drunken buddy. That's just the kind of story that would incur him responsibility for buying another round. Silence is golden and cheaper.

Grant was gambling everything on sitting in a card game with an opportunity to change the outcome two nights hence. It was a gamble, the results of which would determine whether or not Alloway lives or dies. Grant was the key if he could pull it off; he needed to be compelling, subtle, and convincing. He knew intimate details of Alloway's life that could be a significant life-saving asset or could derail his purpose into a side-rail-yard of failure at the bottom of the South China Sea. His character performance needed to be convincing and sell just one item so meaningful that it would save a life, Alloway's. Capture his interest with an intriguing challenge of forecasted events that were to take place in two nights. He needed to convince Alloway to consider how he would respond if an aircraft emergency scenario related by the card game stranger actually happened in two nights. Alloway lives or dies with his response.

Steve stayed with Dragonfly and was prepared to make an emergency extraction of Grant, who hoped to make Alloway comfortable with him during the card game. There was so much at stake; Grant needed to tell Alloway in a convincing way, alter his decisions in the water in two nights and live.

One of the more complex and somewhat mundane issues was clothing that fit 1970. It wouldn't do to dress in Tommy Bahama shirts, shorts, and Jordan Nikes. To overcome this, they searched through a Santee Goodwill store to find the appropriate dress attire he wore while in Vietnam, primarily neutral and bland. Grant's cover story was to say he was a Sikorsky helicopter technical representative, just arriving to assist the Jolly Green Squadron at the base. Grant had enough technical background regarding Sikorsky helicopters because he flew them and was somewhat confident about being passed off as a tech-rep.

Grant wasn't an expert card player, but he knew Alloway was generally a winner, based upon his background research and observing his gameplay on previous nights before this evening. Grant's two dilemmas influence Alloway to take different actions and make other decisions on his upcoming fatal flight. The other dilemma: the money he was going to lose could not be from 40 years beyond that in circulation in 1970. Steve took care of that via a time travel withdrawal from a Las Vegas loan shark and gambling establishment of questionable repute. They couldn't report the loss. The procedure came in handy circa 1970 Las Vegas.

That night, in the smoke-filled NCO club card room, Grant wore an ugly Hawaiian shirt, khakis, and loafers. Surprisingly, he doesn't look much out of place at 66, other than being a stranger to the NCO crowd. He approaches Sergeant Alloway's table asks if the empty chair is open. It is. He introduces himself as Luke Rio and sells the Sikorsky tech-rep line. The group is playing Texas Hold 'em, quarter-ante. So far, so good. Grant holds his charade through the first few hands, loses three, wins one. After winning, he bought a couple of rounds for the table and held his own in the card game, which ended up being a bit more than penny-ante poker. After two hours of drinking, gambling, and losing, he had his anticipated opening with Alloway after the other players took off, ending their losing streak. Leaving Grant to work his pre-planned script. He started by talking about his boring background and suggested he was pretty good at guessing others' backgrounds. Grant asks Alloway where he was born.

"Indian Reservation," Alloway responds. He has revealed that to very few people.

Grant answers back, "Oklahoma Territory?"

Alloway is surprised by the response. Most people wouldn't have gone that far. "Good guess. Cherokee Indian reservation. My father was a full-blooded Cherokee."

Grant knows his father's name but says nothing. "Your Mom Cherokee also?"

"My father met my mother there; she wasn't Indian. Regular white woman." Alloway never spoke of this to anyone before. Why he was telling this Tech-rep?

"You're half Cherokee." Again, Grant knows his mother's name is Millie and says nothing.

"I am, I was. I guess I still am." Rolling his vodka tonic glass in his hand and staring at it.

"Half breed. Like me." Grant wants a closer opening with Alloway.

"You? Half of what?"

"Mexican. Dad married a white woman, like your dad." Opening worked.

Alloway asks, "Do you speak Spanish?"

"No, not well. Dad didn't teach us. He wanted us to speak English, I guess."

"That happens." Alloway still holds his drink in both hands, watching the soggy limes shift around the bottom third of liquid.

"Do you know Cherokee? Speak it, I mean?" Grant knows Cherokees speak Iroquois.

"Iroquois. The Cherokee speak Iroquois."

"You spoke it, then?" Takes a swig of his beer.

"Some when we were in Oklahoma. As a boy."

"You ever take any crap about being half Cherokee Indian?"

"Not really. Didn't talk about it much." Rarely, actually.

"Me either, I guess. My friends didn't care one way or another. Although one girlfriend broke up with me because my father's first name was Carlos."

"That must've hurt." Sergeant Alloway watches Grant react.

"More puzzling than anything else, I guess. Didn't think a lot about it at the time. I moved on. She became an antiwar Democrat, I think."

Alloway follows up, "You never know about people and where they end up."

Grant knows where Alloway ends up. "So, you grew up on an Indian Reservation?"

"Until I was eleven. Then we moved to California."

"What took you to California?" Grant knows of his father's death and Millie's sister, Pearl. He has to keep Sergeant Alloway opening up.

"My father died. Mom moved me and my two brothers. Drove West to California."

"Didn't you have family there in Oklahoma?" Grant knows he did.

"We did. My father's family. That was the problem."

"What problem?" He knows Millie wasn't Cherokee and had no rights on the reservation. Grant takes a drink from his beer, watches Alloway react.

"I guess it was more than one problem. My father died of a heart attack. He was only thirty-three. In the Cherokee culture, it was considered a white Man's disease. Almost a disgrace to die from a heart attack."

Grant knows this story. "He was a young Man."

"He was. The other problem back then was that the children of the Cherokee Man belong to the Cherokee Tribe. Property of the tribe. After my father died, members of the tribe took me and my two brothers away from my mom."

"Jesus, Clyde, how'd they get away with that? What about your mom? She had no say in it?" Millie wasn't done by any stretch. She was pissed.

"She had no standing as far as the tribe was concerned. She wasn't Cherokee. We three boys belong to the tribe."

"How'd she get you to California?" Grant already knows.

"When the tribe took us away, my mom went to the sheriff and told him there was going to be a bloody mess if he didn't help her get her boys back." Mom had a 12-gauge and a Winchester 30-30. She was a good shot from deer and duck hunting. She was scary good, and the sheriff knew it.

"He helped?"

"He did. Before he left to go pick us up, he told my mom, 'Pack everything you have in your car, and when I get back with the boys, you have to leave Oklahoma. I can't protect the boys after today.' So, we left Oklahoma that night."

"Where in California did you go?"

"Fresno. We moved in with mom's sister. She got mom a job at Castle Air Force Base, working with her in the NCO club snack bar."

"So that is where you grew up?" Grant keeps Sergeant Alloway at a comfort level with him.

"Until I joined the Air Force."

"When was that?" Grant acts curiously.

"1953."

"1953. You must've been only sixteen."

"Actually I was seventeen."

"The Air Force took you at seventeen?"

"I lied about my age. It was fairly easy back then."

"Why so eager to join?" Grant has some of the details, not all.

"Got pissed at my mom. She remarried and got pregnant in 1953. It just pissed me off, I wanted out of the house and that situation. Went to Phoenix and joined the Air Force." Alloway adds more family detail. "My older brother got pissed a couple years later on. Mom got pregnant a second time with another step-sister. After that, he left for the military too."

"She had two more kids with your step-father then?" Grant asks. He finished a glass of stale warm beer.

"She ended up having a total of three more kids. Didn't want any part of that." Alloway shrugs.

Grant asks, "What was your career field?" He already knows.

"Aircraft mechanic. First assignment was to Pease Air Force Base."

"Long way from California or Oklahoma."

Alloway confirms, "It was."

"How long was the assignment?" asks Grant.

"I was there until they sent me back here for the second time."

"You're on your second tour now?" Grant knows.

Alloway responds, "Yeah, first tour I was crew chief working on A-1's for 602nd Air Commando Squadron, Nha Trang."

"Isn't it unusual to get more than one tour?" Grant fishing for Sergeant Alloway's story.

"I think so, but things seem to work out that way."

"What about family?" Grant keeps going.

"My wife wasn't happy either time. I guess she wasn't happy most the time."

"When did you get married?" "

"1960, Portsmouth, New Hampshire."

"Where did you meet your bride? Local girl?" Grant is legitimately interested.

"Yeah, met Marge where she worked at a restaurant. She was 18. On her own."

"She didn't have to leave town on your tours over here?" Grant is familiar with the situation with Marge.

"No, she stayed there each time while I have been in Vietnam."

Grant is finding it hard to keep up the charade. This Man may be dead in two days unless he can change his destiny. "Kids? Boys? Girls?"

"One each."

"Are they young kids?" Grant knows their ages.

"Yeah, nine and seven. Want to spend more time with them when I get back. All three of them. I told her I had a bad feeling about this last tour. Not sure I was going to be coming back. She really didn't like to hear that."

"How's she taking it this time?" Grant knows how she took his death forty years ago.

"She was angry for me going back to Vietnam, but she wasn't a happy person in general. She never really trusted anyone. Felt like she got the short end of the stick in life."

Grant knows; she was raised in a foster home system and learned distrust of life in general. "I suppose it is hard to deal with for some." Grant says.

"Tried to channel her anger while loading bombs on A-1s— I'd write a two word chalk note '*From Marge*' on the 500 pounders. A Marge message delivered to the VC or NVA to ruin their day. She is not a happy person, but she's handling it."

"I told her before I left if anything happens to me she should pick up and move back to California to be near my mom and stepdad, close to Vacaville and Travis Air Force Base." Grant knows that's precisely what she did.

After a new round of alcohol, beer for Grant and vodka for Alloway, and banal banter regarding Grant's family background, work history, he pushes the envelope to get Alloway near water. At least thinking about it. He knows that Alloway's squadron did make some overwater flights and hence the chance they may put down in it. Aircrews were supposed to know how to swim and survive in that environment. But Grant knew Alloway didn't know how to swim. Grant got him to admit it while talking about waterhole swimming on a reservation in Oklahoma. There weren't any water holes. He asked Alloway if he ended up in the water what the most important tool he had to assist his survival would be.

"Your radio," replied Alloway.

Wrong answer. Grant pushes further, "Why do you think that?"

"You need to be able to contact help."

"You're right. You need to talk to people. But what if you're tangled in your parachute or your life vest is not inflated? How will the radio help you then? What if your parachute is pulling you under? How will the radio help?" If Grant doesn't change Alloway's thinking, the sergeant will find out in two days.

Alloway is puzzled. "Well, you're going to need the radio at some point."

"How long will it take a rescue team to find you if you're a mile or two offshore at night?" Grant is very deliberate. He takes a drink of his cold beer, asking the right questions.

"It could take a while I guess." Alloway's confused a bit. Alcohol talking. Including the latest round of vodka tonic and lime. They are the only two sitting at the card table, two decks of cards stacked neatly along with about twenty dollars' worth of chips that they don't seem to know whose they are. Grant assumes they're his, part of his planned losses. Their chairs are close, and the alcohol is not helping either balance glasses of beer and vodka.

Grant needs to gain control of the conversation and questions. Grant presses on, "It could take a lifetime to find you in the ocean at night. Why didn't you ever learn how to swim? You're good at cards but a lousy swimmer." They laugh and drink some more. "Geez, back off a notch. I can handle surviving in the water." Not really, Grant knows.

"I'll tell you one thing, Clyde, if you focus solely on your radio, your chances of survival are diminished in that ocean out there. The item that you take out after you hit the water is not your radio, it's your survival knife. Use that knife to cut the parachute cords and free yourself to float safely and await pick up. Once you're floating free, use the radio. Not before."

"I got to use the head." Alloway needs a break from this brand of reality.

"Before you go, one last question to think about, okay?"

"Sure, why not,." Alloway agrees. He stands with both hands leaning on the table, attempting to remain upright after all the vodka and tonics. "Fire away."

"What if you had to tell someone the most important thing in the world for them to know and you knew they would never believe you? Would you tell them?"

Thinking for a hazy moment, Alloway says, "I guess I'd try. Could be life or death, I suppose." He pushes off the table and leaves for the head.

Grant raises his hand to catch the waitress's attention to bring the check. Her name is Mai, meaning apricot blossom. She is trilingual, French, English, and her native tongue. She is also biracial, an outcome due to her father, a French civilian employee during the French Colonial Administration before the 1954 losing battle of Dien Bien Phu. She is a favorite of NCO club clientele, not so much by her native counterparts. She arrives at the table.

"You want another drink, sir?" He doesn't.

"No, Mai just the check. I'm going to leave a note for Sergeant Alloway. Would you please see that he gets it when he returns? It is very important." He places the note just adjacent and slightly under Alloway's partially finished vodka tonic.

"Yes, of course." She places the check on the table. He picks it up and hands it back with a stack of bills to Mai. It is an amount far above the total bill. She is not sure of Grant's intention. Change or a huge tip?

"Keep the change, Mai. Thank you for your assistance." Grant stands and smiles with a slight head bow and a light hand touch to Mai's forearm. He turns and leaves the card room down the hall, past the men's head to a strange entry portal back to Dragonfly.

When Sergeant Alloway returns, Grant is gone. Only a new vodka tonic and an envelope on the cleaned-off table. He is bewildered. Mai paid for the new vodka tonic from Grant's more than generous tip. Mai has made a point of watching for Alloway's return to the card room. She approaches. "Your friend is gone and left a note for you.

Clyde opens the envelope, removes and reads the note:

> Clyde,
>
> There is something I had to tell you. I know things only you know and no one else. Don't dwell on how I know these things because you would never believe it. Just trust that I do know.
>
> Members of the Cherokee tribe took white men's names after they marched to the Oklahoma Territory in the 1830s from their Georgia Territory. The forced march was called the Trail of Tears because so many died. I know you are now at the same age as your father when he died in 1948. Your father's name is Christopher Columbus Alloway. Your mother's name is Millie, and when she drove you and your brothers from Oklahoma, it was the first time she ever drove a car. You moved in with Aunt Pearl in California. The chalk note you wrote on the 500-pound bombs you loaded on the A-1's, on your first tour was three words, not two: "From Mad Marge." She was an unhappy foster home system kid. That is why she is so angry and distrustful. I hope I got your attention now?

You must remember the following three items you need to live up to your Cherokee blood as a warrior. Clyde, on your next night mission, you need to be prepared for three things: first, a runaway prop when your aircraft reaches 10,000 feet; second, wait for your AC's final command to jettison the flare package; and, finally, use your knife to cut away your parachute first after you hit the water. I will be talking to you soon. Thanks for the card game.

An old acquaintance.

Clyde was taken aback by the fact that the note and envelope were typewritten. He was completely thrown off guard by that. How could this Luke Rio have prepared it while he was in the men's room for no more than five minutes? The envelope and note were written on NCO club stationary, the only typewriter was in the NCO club manager's office, and it was closed.

Clyde realized the note had to have been written before their card game. That was impossible. The note contained detailed family background information and names that he had never told anyone. Their conversation earlier that evening didn't include his parents' names, Aunt Pearl, and his mother's driving inexperience, items that Clyde never disclosed.

He caught Mai's attention. She took a drink order from another table then came over to his. "Did the Sikorsky tech-rep, the civilian sitting here, go anywhere while I was out of the room? Did he leave the table?"

She answers with a big smile, with thoughts of her best tip ever. "No, he sat at table until just before you returned."

Not even for a minute? You saw him sit here the whole time I was gone?"

Her smile is not so bright with the flood of questions. "Yes, he sat until just before your came back."

Alloway is searching for something. "Did he speak to anyone?"

"No. He left that envelope." She gestures toward it. "And spoke to no one."

Alloway can't figure how he could have missed him. She smiles slightly now. "He ordered another vodka tonic for you." Not true. She did. "He paid the check, left a tip, walked out down the hall. She hopes he comes back. "Oh," She remembers. "He didn't walk out the front doors; he went into the bathroom."
At that Alloway is drop-jawed, puzzled. "Shit. No way, No way."

Grant and Steve used the Pushback feature available with Dragonfly to freeze time during the five minutes Clyde was in the men's room. During Pushback, Grant had access to the NCO club manager's office, typewriter, and stationery. Owing to his lack of experience with typewriters in the past 20 years, Grant spent nearly 20 minutes to complete the final note. It took him three attempts at typing the message and carried out three botched sheets of stationery with him.

Once completed, he returned to his table and terminated the Pushback. The timing was seamless. Grant never left the table or spoke to any other customer or staff from the waitress's perspective. He left Mai with money for the check, tip and then left the room.

Clyde left the NCO club with the note. The rest of his night was restless and sleepless. What just happened? The encounter with Grant stayed on his mind for the two days before his last flight. There will be two Grant Fredericks aboard the Jolly 2-7 flight in two nights. The first one will sit in the copilot seat of Jolly 2-7 on a rescue mission for ten members of Lemon 2-1 in 1970 off the coast of Da Nang. The second one will be riding shotgun aboard Dragonfly, hoping to see positive results from his card game manipulated intrigue of Sergeant Alloway. It will be a three-person replay, two Grants and one Clyde, from April 6, 1970, that offers a second chance to save a life; change the score. Ten for ten crew members picked-up from Lemon 21.

Déjà vu all over again

Jolly 2-7 night rescue underway, April 6, 1970, off the coast of Da Nang, South Vietnam. 2100 hours. Captain Hoilman pilot, Captain Fredericks copilot. Grant and Steve are flying formation

277

with Jolly 2-7 in Dragonfly. They are monitoring the radio traffic closely to hear if and when Sergeant Alloway changes his fate. Does anything forecast in the note left at the table two nights prior at the NCO Club, affect his actions before or after the bailout, and he hits the water? There was a positive sign after Lemon 2-1 reaches 10,000 feet and experienced the runaway prop. When the pilot directed the "stand-by" command to jettison the flare package, Sergeant Alloway waited, rather than sending it early as he did the first time around. All the radio chatter has been exactly as it was on the original flight. Both Steve and Grant are tied to each transmission, waiting for a change, any change in terminology, or reply.

Off the China Beach coast again. Jolly 2-7 repeated picking up Lemon 0-7 for the fifth time. On Jolly 2-7, the Flight engineer reports on the intercom, "Captain. Hoilman, we have the PJ and survivor onboard and secure. The survivor is okay, cold, and wet."

"They are flying just as they did the other four times," Grant says. The rescue scenario is playing out just the same as the previous nights.

"We are early yet," Steve replies. "That's Lemon 0-7, not Alloway."

Jolly 2-7 copilot is the younger Captain Fredericks, "Feet-Wet" survivors, we're having a good night. Let's go see if we can find Lemon 1-0."

"You seem to have had an attitude when you were that age." Steve pokes at Grant. Grant is focused; ignores him.

"Roger that. Have you heard any other transmissions?" The Jolly 2-7 pilot replies to copilot Fredericks.

"I'm getting broken transmissions from Lemon 1-0. Sounds like he is struggling to stay above the surface." Copilot Fredericks reports limited contact with Lemon 1-0.

"You have his location?" Captain Hoilman asks.

"No can't figure it. With all the radio traffic, it's hard for an accurate fix. Lemon 1-0, Lemon 1-0. Jolly 2-7. What is your location from Monkey Mountain?"

Lemon 1-0, exhausted voice, "I am...not sure."

"He wasn't near there, found nothing that night," Grant interjects." He is tired, you can hear it in his voice. Shit. Come on, Clyde, hang on."

"Lemon 1-0, Jolly 2-7 can you see the lights on Monkey Mountain or Da Nang Harbor? Can you see our aircraft lights?" Copilot Grant calling.

Lemon 1-0 very weak, "No...not sure."

"That's Lemon 1-0; he is fading again," Steve says from his position in Dragonfly, flying a parallel time travel course with Lemon 2-1 and crew.

"We're at the two-hour mark. Alloway's struggle is getting worse." Grant is second-guessing his reaction from 40 years ago.

Jolly 2-7 Copilot to Pilot, "Bill I can't get any visual reference from this guy. I can tell he is in trouble. Exhausted, caught in his chute."

"Come on, Clyde; get your knife out and cut free, the radio is going to kill you if you don't." Grant from Dragonfly, imploring Sergeant Alloway to recall the notes' forecast.

"Keep trying," orders the pilot.

"Lemon 1-0, Jolly 2-7 can you pop a flare? Do you have your strobe on?"

Extremely weak halting reply, "No...I think...I'm drowning...can't get out of my chute. It's pulling...me...under." He is exhausted.

"Turn on your fucking light." Steve yells out, "Jesus Clyde. He's going to do it again. He didn't read the note. This is the fifth time he's done this. Shit."

Jolly 6-4 breaks in intermittently talking to another crew member in the water. "Lemon 0-3 Jolly 6-4 we have you in sight."

Copilot Fredericks implores, "Lemon 1-0, pop a flare, and we'll find you. Can you see our searchlights? Can you see the parachute flares?"

Increasing weakness, a sense of futility, an acceptance. "No...I'm caught...It's...can't get out."

"Son of a bitch; he's doing it again." Grant in Dragonfly is pissed and frustrated after all their work to save his sorry ass.

"Lemon 1-0, Jolly 2-7 do you read? "Pop a flare," Jolly 2-7 Copilot Grant.

"Damn, shit, fuck." Steve ranting. "He's done"

After what seemed to be forever. "Jolly 2-7 I'm here." An exhausted Alloway.

"Holy shit." Grant, then Steve.

"That you Lemon 1-0?" Copilot Jolly 2-7 asks with a sense of relief. "Jolly 2-7."

"Jolly 2-7 yeah, Lemon 1-0. Almost a goner. Thought it was over, then remembered."

"Remembered, remembered what? Say again Lemon 1-0?" Jolly 2-7 Copilot Grant.

"The note. He remembered the note I left." Grant says.

"I can't swim." Talking is difficult and exhausting. "Cut away the chute lines so I could float." Lemon 1-0 breathlessly. "Almost forgot."

"The note. It was the note he remembered. Shit-hot." Dragonfly Grant yells.

"Lemon 1-0, great time to figure it out. Now turn on your strobe and pop a flare so we can find you floating out there somewhere." Jolly 2-7 pilot says. Then speaks to his crew. "You got to be shitting me: remembered he can't swim?" Shaking his head back and forth. "One lucky SOB, Sierra Hotel." (Shit-Hot)

"With just a little help from old friends." Grant is pleased and relieved on Dragonfly.

Steve and Grant knew their adjustments to Osama bin Laden's life pattern would not fit Sergeant Alloway's. There was no time-loop initiated. The surreal NCO Club card game conversation and a note from an odd Tech-rep were all they had. Sergeant Alloway searched for tech-rep Luke Rio in the days after his rescue. He couldn't be found anywhere. The card-playing, future describing, sixty-plus-year-old tech-rep from Sikorsky was long gone and only there for one night, for a solo, one-time important performance. He didn't exist. Sergeant Alloway found there was no record of a Sikorsky representative at the Jolly Green squadron for three months. He found that the last tech-rep was much younger, taller, and spoke with a distinct south-in-the-mouth Southern drawl. Alloway was looking for someone he'd never find.

Grant wonders: did anything forecast in the note left at the NCO Club card table affect Alloway's actions before or after the bailout, and once he hits the water? Coincidentally, the day after the night rescue, Sergeant Alloway thanked, in person, the Jolly 2-7 crew that pulled him out of the water. Later at an aircrew celebration barbecue north of the officers' quarters, reviewing the night before, Sergeant Alloway asked the young Grant, "You were the copilot on Jolly 2-7?"

"I was. Glad we were able to pull you out last night. It was touch and go on your location. Thought we lost you a couple of times." The Jolly 2-7 copilot says.

"I was losing it in the water for the last hour or so. Caught in the chute lines, overpowering the LPU, pulling me under." Alloway looks closely at the copilot, trying to put pieces of the night before together. He asks, puzzled, "Have we ever met before? You look and sound so familiar." He was sure he knew the young Jolly 2-7 copilot from somewhere.

The copilot replies, he had never seen Sergeant Alloway before. "No, I don't think so."

"Your voice last night was so familiar. You sounded like a fellow at the NCO club two nights ago, A Sikorsky Tech-rep, Luke Rio. You even look like him, but much younger, he had to be in his 60s. A relative maybe?" Sergeant Alloway asks, the alcohol-influenced, younger Captain Fredericks.

"No. I just fly 'em, don't know any Tech-reps that work on 'em." Grant offers with a heavy tongue.

He did see this copilot somewhere before. They played cards a couple of nights back, 40 years ago, at the NCO club in Grant's Dragonfly world. The copilot's name was Grant Fredericks, age 27; he had been in Vietnam since August 1969. This young captain was the one person that Sergeant Alloway thanks for the radio contact and conversation they had the night before. His voice and reassurance were a pivotal element in saving his life.

"It was your voice on the radio, back and forth, that got me to remember. Woke me up." Alloway is pensive and grateful sounding.

"Yeah, what the hell was that? Never expected to hear 'I remembered something; I can't swim. 'Where did that come from? We thought you were gone." Grant, the younger can't figure this guy out.

"The Sikorsky guy from the NCO club. I heard him talking to me, as strange as that sounds. Reminded me to cut the chute lines; it worked. I was going to drown talking on the radio until then."

"Holy shit, Sergeant. Don't understand it, but apparently it worked." The much younger version of Grant takes a long draw from his Budweiser.

Sergeant Alloway survived his second night in the water; he didn't drown. He returned to his family and had grandchildren in a parallel life, a Yogi. Tragically, however, the life pattern that included Grant as a young copilot on the initial failed rescue attempt ended for Sergeant Alloway on that night in the water off the coast of Da Nang in June, 1970...forty years ago.

Fall 2010
Moon Lite Night
Dream
Elfin Forest

The Elfin Forest 784-acre Recreational Reserve and Olivenhain Dam near Escondido, California, includes approximately fourteen miles of remote hiking, mountain biking, and equestrian trails. An ocean view from the topmost point and clear views of the distant Laguna Mountains. Switchback trails surrounded by vegetation, including oak riparian, oak woodland, coastal sage scrub, all chaparral. Olivenhain Dam is a gravity dam constructed between 1998 and 2003 as part of San Diego's Emergency Storage Project. Water is pumped in to fill it.

It is just at sunrise. Grant in Levi's, short sleeve red shirt, and loafers walks on the dam overlooking a drop of fifty feet above water that is seventy feet deep. He takes out his revolver and leaves his backpack on a small table at a viewpoint with a panoramic view out to the reservoir. He walks out and sits on a guard rail facing the water, in deep thought. Unnoticed by Grant, Sergeant Alloway approaches from the direction of the table.

Alloway asks, "You planning some redneck fishing with that gun?"

Grant removes his headset for an iPod. "I'm sorry, I didn't hear what you said."

"Redneck fishing with that?" Alloway awkwardly looks at the revolver resting on Grant's lap.

Grant recognizes him, "No. Eh, Sergeant Alloway?

"Clyde, first name's Clyde." He is in an Air Force flight suit.

"Okay, I'm Grant. Wasn't sure I was going to see you again."

"I think I knew after our first meeting. It felt like we had some unfinished business,

something to talk about."

"We have a lot to talk about." Grant is leaning on the guard rail over the dam.

"Where do we start?" Alloway is tossing stones at the water below them.

"I think where we left off 40 some years ago." Grant thinking about the unfinished conversation. Memories.

"We talked about those at Starbucks. Not much there."

"That was the beginning." Grant is sitting on the guard rail.

"From my perspective, it was an end and a beginning. Memories I missed started after I died." Alloway sits at the table with a deck of cards, red and white chips stacked twelve high. "Marge moved in August, 1970 about two months after I went missing. Vacaville, near Travis Air Force Base. Had a memorial service there, my daughter named her oldest son, Travis, I think because of that connection."

"That's cool. What became of your brothers and mom?"

"Both brothers joined the Air Force, a few years after me and mom raised her new kids. All of them are gone, now on this side." He shuffles the cards of four decks, two decks in each hand.

"Wow. All of them?" Grant seemed surprised.

"Yeah, they lasted a lot longer than I did."

"I lost three brothers all to cancer. Two older, one younger" Grant is sitting at the card table with a Texas Hold 'em hand and a stack of blue chips.

"We could open a cancer club on this side if we had clubs." Alloway dealing solitaire

"That some celestial humor, Clyde?" Grant has a look of disinterest while studying his Hold 'em hand.

"We do a lot of stand up, up here."

"You're killing me, Clyde." Grant shakes his head at the bad joke.

"Not my department. I could introduce you around, though." Clyde, the celestial comic.

"No, thanks."

"You seem to have come through okay." Alloway states.

"Yeah, I guess. Drinking didn't help much." There is a pint of Old Turkey on the table and several glasses. Bucket of ice dripping with moisture.

"Do you play cards?" Alloway is asking and deals again.

"Some, from time to time. Not real good at it." Last card game 40 years ago at a Da Nang NCO club. Grant remembers that game.

"I was pretty good at it. Poker used to supplement my income. Mad Marge hated it. Thought I lost mostly, but I won more often than not."

"You were good at cards. But a lousy swimmer." Grant thinking the card game Yogi saved Clyde's life once upon a time.

"Not many swimming holes on the reservation and not a lot to do there, played some cards. Played more once I left home and joined the Air Force. I had a poker face that always smiled, drove the other guys nuts."

Grant remembers the smile from forty years ago. "Clyde, you really enjoyed life, didn't you?"

"I did, but things were out of my control. Don't know if it was fate or what. My father and I both died in our thirties."

"You were warriors. The good tend to die young."

"I wasn't a warrior. I was scared most the time when we flew over there."

"Clyde, we were all scared. Combat tends to do that, but we all did our jobs. Warriors don't turn away from danger. They face it. Being scared, shit, it showed you were human. You were a warrior."

"Couldn't swim. I drowned with my parachute?"

"Yeah, you couldn't swim. Didn't keep you from flying over water."

"No, didn't have much choice."

"Bullshit." Grant spouts with dismay. "You could have been taken off flight status. You could have self-initiated it. One trip to the flight surgeon; he'd have taken you off. You didn't do that."

"I couldn't." Alloway looks down, focused on his cards.

Grant faces the water below the dam. "No, warriors don't do that. Brave scared men don't do that. They push through, suit up and face it. We all did it. Weren't you the guy who hung out the back of the gunship calling out ground fire?"

"Not just me. There were others guys." Still shuffling.

"Not just you, your whole crew did. Flew with a band of warriors. All of 'em professionals, dedicated, Clyde, just like you. Everyone on Lemon 2-1."

"They were good."

"Not just good. You could depend on them. No second thoughts, trust 'em, your life in their hands. Theirs in yours. Weren't you last to bail out?" Grant stacks more red and white chips.

"I was Jump Master. Everyone went before me except the AC."

"You made sure everyone got out first before you were ordered to jump, right?"

"That was my job."

"Exactly. A warrior's job. Jesus, Clyde, you have Cherokee blood. You lived and died a warrior."

"I was still scared."

"We all were. There's no courage unless you're scared, and you did what you were afraid of. You faced it head on. You were not alone. "

"I'm not scared anymore!" Clyde admits.

"You scared, Grant?"

"Of you? This?"

"No. Of everything else."

Grant caught on. "Yeah, I guess I am."

"You're scared, but you're going to face it, right?"

"Yeah, sure." Grant hesitates and looks at the gun now in his hand.

"Let's face it together."

"We have the Air Force in common and one night a long time ago."

"What else? Tell me what it was like living on a Cherokee reservation?"

"How about I show you?"

Surprised, Grant asks, "What do you mean, show me?"

"The Cherokee reservation. Road trip to Oklahoma! I'll drive. We have people to meet, lots of people."

"How can you...we do that? I mean, you drive? what?" Grant caught off guard and tongue-tied.

"Not what you think. But I'll get us there. Think of it as a travel pass on the spiritual bullet train. You can bring your gun. There's no security."

Standing next to the now wooden guard rail, Grant looks from his revolver toward the open water. After a moment, he tosses it into the deep water. Grant, still very flustered, "How? Sorry, I don't understand."

"You ready?" Now they both are standing on a wooden rail station platform with a set of rail tracks extending off into the distance across a wide summer grass-filled prairie.

Grant says, "Hold on, Red Rider." Trying to get a mental grip on the bullet train scenario." You got to be shitting me!" A train whistle blows. They are long gone from the dam and reservoir. "

Oh that's a 1-0-1." Alloway quotes the Falcon Code.

Grant, confused, "What? 1-0-1?"

"Actually I think it's a 1-0-9." Alloway again refers to the Falcon Code.

"1-0-9? What are you talking about?" Grant is not getting it. Not yet.

"You said' you got to be shitting me. 'That's a 1-0-1. Falcon Code, 1-0-1."

"Holy shit!" Grant says with frustration. It is a fast-moving scene; he needs to keep up.

"That's not in the code."

"Jesus, Clyde!"

"Whoa! Careful, different code." Alloway reprimands Grant. Don't take the Lord's name in vain, even in a dream.

"What the fuck?" Grant is still lost. Still on the train platform. A train is approaching.

"That's a 1-0-4."

Grant resigned, "Okay, you win. I get it."

"Great. You ready now?" Alloway asks.

Yeah, I guess, "I'm not asking any more questions!" But, asks a question despite himself, "Ah, what now?"

"It is a 1-0-9, beautiful just fucking beautiful. This way Kemosabe. Hold onto your scalp, try to keep up and watch your step getting aboard." Clyde leads the way, starting down the rail platform to a waiting spiritual bullet train. Grant tries to catch up. The train is floating, with no tracks, bright silver, blue Air Force stripes. Once aboard, the train travels in a blur across the grassland prairie toward Oklahoma and the Cherokee reservation. Grant and Clyde sit at a card table; the Old Turkey pint is there with decks of cards and poker chips. A smiling Mia, the waitress from the Da Nang NCO club, is there waiting to take their order.

Grant recovering to the current and present spiritual reality, "Sooo, tell me? As a kid did you run around in a loin cloth, hunt buffalo?"

"No, white Man—and no swimming holes."

"Bows and arrows?"

Alloway shaking his head. "This is going to be a long day." Grant has recovered and is on board. Looking at each other after a pause, they both break out in heavy laughter.

Becky was startled from her sound sleep at 5 a.m. "Grant, wake up. You're dreaming again."

"I know," Grant laughing out loud, "I know."

Cherokee Lament

By Paul Revere and the Raiders
...They took the whole Indian nation.
Locked us on this reservation
Though I wear a shirt and tie
I'm still part red man deep inside.
Cherokee people, Cherokee tribe
So proud to live, so proud to die
But maybe someday when they learn.
Cherokee Nation will return, will return,...

MAN 23

The
Guardian

Grant, from the time spent with ET on time-compressed learning and intelligence modification, he knows he is something beyond human, and seeks answers and understanding about everything alien. SAM is the repository source of background data regarding ET.

Before Steve's entered the picture, Grant accepted ET as a creation of a far superior source of intelligence nonexistent on Earth. Grant yearns to learn more about the existence of ET and others like him. Where do they come from? How long have they been here? What is their purpose on Earth? The search begins.

SAM indicated that the data system and source of information requested would be meaningless to Grant. The language was "alien." The concepts and reference materials were beyond current human understanding and development. Grant wasn't deterred and kept asking questions related to ET and his background. "Is ET's biological or genetic makeup similar to mine or the human genome?"

ET is in his charging Oval in a hibernation state. Grant is in his lawn chair. "They have a similar pattern," SAM replies by voice.

"How genetically related are they?" Grant asks for more.

"That is difficult to determine." SAM seems reluctant to provide the data requested. Grant is getting increasingly frustrated; SAM doesn't typically speculate. "How old is ET? Please answer in years, as on Earth."

"As in revolutions around your sun." A statement, not a question.

"Yes, from birth." Grant had never thought of ET as having been birthed.

"Do you mean, from activation forward?"

"Okay, whatever, just some idea of how long he has been around." Grant is standing and pacing near the Oval platform edge, gazing at the galaxies shown.

SAM asks, "Around in years?"

Yeah, in years" He turns and looks over at ET, still charging.

"305"

Grant, somewhat stunned, belts out, "ET is 305 years old?"

"Around 305." Smart Ass Machine says.

"Then he has no parents, brothers, sisters, family?"

"No data available."

Grant walks to the cooler, takes a can of beer, pops it open, and nearly drains it. Grant pushes on, "He is an only child?" Expecting some information for clarification.

"He's not a child." SAM relates by voice.

"SAM, an only child is just an expression." Grant pacing more with a nearly empty can of beer.

"Noted." Mind-tending SAM.

"Shit. I need to speak with ET. Your database contains information about the human genome and genetic research conducted by ET and Others, is that correct?"

"There is a database containing the information. Correct."

"Can that information be translated into a form and language that I can understand?" Grant asks.

SAM displays reluctance at this request. "What is the purpose of your request?

"Research. Background research."

"To what end?" SAM waits.

"I want to find out answers to the nature of my existence." Going a bit beyond Grant's knowledge base.

"Your existence is patterned on a genetic model specific to your kind, Humankind."

Grant feels he's getting a computer-generated runaround. "I want to find out where humankind started." Apparently, SAM is stalling.

"That is an indeterminate request. Unable to provide an adequate answer."

Grant asks, "Are you indicating that the information is not in the database? Or is the information unavailable to my request?"

"In your terms and understanding the information you request. Unavailable." SAM could very well be a lawyer, a defense lawyer.

"Help me to understand. The information I seek is in the database, however unavailable for my access at the present time."

"Correct."

"Could access be granted or attained?" Grant pacing, takes a last drink of beer, drops can over the edge of the Oval; can returns near cooler.

"Possible," SAM answers.

The pacing and questioning continued. "Is there a process that would facilitate the release of the data I seek? Is there an access code?" Grant is tired of SAM's dodging.

"No."

"There's no process or no access code?

"No access code." SAM could keep this up for an eternity.

"I'm wasting my time with you, SAM."

"Acknowledged. Time not well spent."

An idea pops in Grant's mind, "I think ET could."

"The Guardian."

"ET is the Guardian?" The definition of the word *guardian* floods his mind: a person who guards, protects, or preserves. "Is he protecting us. Standing guard?" Grant has not been exposed to the term as it relates to ET. A new vista opened without clarity.

"Affirmative," SAM replies.

"All of us? From what?"

"Human condition." SAM mind-tending

"ET is guarding us from our nature? Human nature?" Grant is puzzled. Sits down.

"Mankind tends to achieve when emotions are controlled." SAM replies.

Grant no longer responds to SAM but talks to himself. "Not sure this is a good or positive development, but I think I agree. At least somewhat. Emotions are powerful catalysts both positive and negative. Control is vital to achieve meaningful outcomes."

Grant is thinking about his and Steve's journey with ET and the emotional strain that the encounter has placed before them. They have questions about their very existence and the beginning of mankind. And where they are headed, what is the future within this new dynamic science fiction reality? Why them?

The relationship between ET and SAM is based upon their alien data platform and operating system. Their AI calculations are mirrored and nearly identical with one exception. ET's data platform and operating system includes a human genetic DNA aspect, SAM has none. ET carries within his biological materials a human sourced DNA genetic component. It is subject to mutations and genetic human-like alterations, He is evolving.

SAM operates and performs tasks associated with lab operations as ET's surrogate. They communicate on a telepathic "mind-tending" level of cerebral consciousness. ET and SAM also share any database input, including their research observations, evaluations, and project manipulations. Any observations and interactions with Grant and Steve are instantaneously available to ET and SAM, recorded by the database management system.

To a great extent, they mimic one another in the decision operations process, but ET is the focused center of their operations. The term "Guardian" as used by SAM was an adaptation adopted for the Fredericks brothers' benefit. Relationships within ET's alien realm are far beyond the personal emotional characteristics of their human subjects. The "personal touch" is typically a nonexistent factor within the context of the alien or extraterrestrial construct.

CONSIDER MAN

ET - Lab

Grant sits in his lawn chair while ET, no longer charging, stands. He always stands. ET is the Guardian, aware of Grant's exchange with SAM. Doesn't miss much, ever.

Grant pushes further regarding genetics and, more specifically, the similarities between genomes. "Are they, we, genetically related?"

ET knows the conversation, knew it as it was taking place. ET mind-tending, "Within your understanding of the genetic process, we are not exactly related." ET responds truthfully as always, explaining that he is a combination of genetically enhanced biological material and artificial intelligence that, in many ways, is similar in structure to that found in the human genome. He has modified and improved cellular biological systems consistent with human patterns, but beyond any current systems and far beyond Grant. ET is a hybrid combination, but neither android nor cyborg-like.

Grant is somewhat dumbfounded, not expecting ET's answer. Grant is up out of his lawn chair at the edge of the Oval, looking out to the galactic view. "What is your genetic makeup?"

ET stands nearby expressionless and faces Grant. He doesn't gesture with hands or arms, other than adjusting holographic images. There isn't much that requires physical movement. His dark blue-eyes can be penetrating, associated with subtle head movement. "Similar to yours in many ways. It has evolved and been refined over thousands of years. I have no need for nourishment in your context requirements. My biological systems structures have developed and purposely created to end need for sustenance."

"You've also eliminated the need for biological waste. That is something that we were curious about." Grant watches ET. There is no physical recognition or interaction during these conversations, other than Grant's. Minor head movement is the most that ET offers.

ET responds, "The biological system creates no by-product. Function eliminated, conserves energy and efficiency."

"Steve thinks eliminating the need to eat, drink, and elimination is something he could get used to, with the exception of beer."

"We have no internal structure to process such items."

Grant continues on, "SAM indicated reluctantly, that you are 305 years of age, in Earth years. Is that correct?"

ET replies, "That is an accurate representation of current operational existence." He gazes into the emptiness surrounding the Oval platform.

Grant is somewhat perplexed by that answer, "Current operational existence? I am not sure I understand the concept. What does that mean?"

"In the context of current configuration biological material has been developed on a continuum for thousands of your Earth years."

"Are you saying that your biological composition is that old? Thousands of years?"

"The source materials could be categorized in that timeframe and older," ET conveys.

Grant, not sure where this is going, responds, "I am staggered by the biological advancements you represent. What your biological materials alone represent. Your appearance is not consistent with an individual 305 years old."

Of course, Grant has no frame of reference. No one on Earth has ever lived to 300 years or more. Although he recalls Bible references indicating that Methuselah and his grandson Noah lived over 900 years. He has no idea what such an aged individual would look like. Moses lived for 140 years or so, but Grant never saw him either.

"Not an individual, a genetically modified adaptation, coupled with an artificial intelligence database management system. In the vernacular of your time, a hybrid being." ET, still gazing.

"For clarification, as you stand before me now, SAM indicated you were activated 305 years ago. Is that accurate?"

"Activation completes the process of integrating the artificial intelligence database management system with the biomechanics structure."

"What is the nature of your biomechanics structure?" Grant is intrigued. "It appears to be somewhat similar to human in design."

"The biomechanics structure consists of a cellular matrix that is genetically similar to human bone tissue in a genetically altered form." ET turns his head and eyes slightly toward Grant.

"So you have an internal structure as we humans have a skeletal structure?"

"Humans developed their internal and external structure simultaneously." Without emotion, ET continues, "I was developed in a similar mode without the accompanying consciousness experienced by humans."

"Would you say you are the end result of a genetically modified cellular growth management system or model?"

"Physical structure was created independently."

"Your physical structure contains genetic material. Is your knowledge, intelligence characteristics contained within genetic material? Is it inherited?" Grant wants to understand what ET is.

"Inherited in the sense that a genetic linkage is apparent?" It is unusual for ET to ask a question because he knows all the answers.

"I know we share a portion of genetic relationship, unless SAM was misleading me."

"SAM, as you call the database management system, is without error."

Grant has wondered whether ET is more closely aligned to a cyborg/robot than a human, with artificial intelligence implanted with associated hardware? He is beginning to think that ET is something more. "Your reference to intelligence leads me to ask..."

Before Grant can finish the question, ET answers. He mind-tended Grant's forthcoming question. ET rarely answers with a personal pronoun. "My intelligence system, as you would call it, is similar to artificial intelligence, however, the source is not artificial or bio-mechanical. It is the result of DNA and genetic manipulation for a considerable length of time. Methodology and specific processes are far beyond any genetic research and development studies associated with the scientific community on Earth at the present time. My physical structure, as designed, exists without supplementation, and has been coupled with an equally genetically altered intelligence system at the cellular level. Gene editing existing for many hundreds of millennia, your compressed learning and training is only a small example intervention by artificial means."

"The compressed training altered me genetically?" Grant is stunned. "I've not advanced to a level anywhere consistent with your's or SAM's level of comprehension. I understand more, and am surprised by it. I am not you, though. Nowhere near it."

"Your training sequence provided a limited advancement, initiated artificially." ET mind-tended

"You mean the aerosol?" The aerosol substance ET administered before each compression learning session was a catalyst that initiated Grant's ability to absorb information and expand his understanding of the concepts involved. It was necessary because the concepts were new and advanced, and time was essential to accomplish the task.

"Yes, as you discovered, Nostradamus's deficits were associated with his place in history. You have a knowledge deficit as well. There are concepts beyond your scope of understanding, as was Nostradamus 450 years ago," ET explains.

Grant fights back a losing battle. "I could learn. I have learned a great deal in a foreshortened time span. I know I can learn more."

"Not enough time." ET has insight as to what is in store for his Grad Project human associates. There will be an accounting affecting the human condition. The oncoming sixth extinction. He indicates its strengthened by political influence, a record of disjointed policies and low polls trolling the US president. Limited success evidenced at local or national level governance.

Social structure chaos is persistent. "Time is of the essence to adjust the human condition." ET's reply is concerning.

"What has changed? Grant asks, "Is there something we don't know?"

"More to accomplish in limited time remaining."

"What is primary, what first?" Grant is searching for answers.

"Time. Time to adjust human conditions. Need to accelerate active intervention. Adverse impact on subject Monitors." ET leaves a question of monitors. More of his kind?

Grant taken aback by reference to *Monitors*, who are they? "Monitors...so we are getting Monitors?" Grant puts forward. "Steve, ET is thinking we may run out of steam, gas or energy. Need Monitors."

MAN 24

ET'S
Grad Project

When ET was pinned under a 300-pound granite slab, he immediately knew his rescuer. ET had encountered Grant on several occasions: he was the subject of an experiment to redirect and change a life path by altering life patterns through Pushback applications. It happened more than once.

ET was the experiment project monitor and recorder, though their encounter on Corte Madera was random. Grant Fredericks's discovery of the trapped ET was purely a cosmic chance; even ET was astounded in his hybrid alien way of thinking. ET's purpose was to observe and record outcomes, within a human subject life pattern lab setting on Earth.

ET had been managing and altering, his subject, Grant's life path since he was a boy. There was no way of knowing that their unscripted encounter would happen; they were never supposed to meet and were undoubtedly never to interact—nothing close to an interpersonal relationship. Clinical not personal.

Something random happened, and the granite slab changed ET's concept of his existence. It caught him and a rescuer's eye, Grant's. The earthquake shook the Earth; with it, a crack developed in ET's perception of a particular human. His genetic being, even as a hybrid, was seemingly trying to connect. ET, for the first time, experienced puzzlement. He had never before been at a loss of understanding. His puzzlement was somewhat a human-like reaction. ET had the answers for literally all circumstances, yet Grant's chance encounter opened a range of responses he hadn't experienced nor completely understood. He never expected to react or interact with a human at other than a "observe and record" level, never a physical interaction. Never a direct exchange of mind-tending communications. ET's puzzlement was problematic and associated with his Earth assignment, Project Grant. After their meeting, ET saw what seemed to be program errors related to his artificial intelligence system. He ran self-diagnostics to identify the seemingly unusual error pattern, to no avail. ET was experiencing unknown aspects of his programming that seemed to impact his logic pattern. In essence, it was an unknown and affected his observations and recordings of his human subjects. He had experienced a transient affective state. ET was experiencing feelings and emotions for the first time, from his human linked DNA and genetic background. ET was suffering from stress—an utterly unknown component within his operational construct. An un-programmed genetically human DNA-sourced mutation had access to his biological artificial intelligence system's architecture, not by a hack, but evolution. A shared Human genetic trait.

They weren't program errors. They were the beginnings of human emotions associated with ET's shared DNA. His genetic composition was evolving. ET, since activation, had no concept of human emotions, but now he had an insight into them. For decades at a slow pace, he had begun unknowingly relating to them somewhere within his bio-intelligence component. ET is experiencing an unknown input for the first time. ET, years ago, chose a challenge to moderate his very human feelings and emotions: Grant. His untimely death at an early age aboard his homemade boat opened the door for ET to start his graduate project on Earth.

Alien intervention
Round One

Grant and Steve stumble upon another alien intervention: the War of 1812 had more than one outcome. In the brothers' new discovery, the British prevail.

In the alternate parallel version of this history point, the British march on Washington in August 1814, route the

American forces, burn the capital, and go on to win the war. The Battle of New Orleans never happened. And Francis Scott Key doesn't write the Star-Spangled Banner, as the garrison at Fort McHenry surrendered without much of a fight after Washington's burning.

The primary effect of the American loss in the southern campaign was the limitation on the American ability to move west into the Louisiana Purchase territories. A British/Native American state, combined with an alliance with Spain, blocked westward expansion and forced an abandonment of New Orleans. This blocked western expansion, in turn, allowed Mexico to relax its northern border policies. Texas never invited American immigrants to Texas. In turn, there was no Mexican-American War, which meant there was no previous battle experience for such Civil War leaders as Robert E. Lee and Ulysses S. Grant.

Moreover, the Civil War was mainly a result of the debate about whether slavery should expand to the West. But in the alternate version of events, there is no Western Territory. Hence, there is no Civil War. However, slavery existed far longer; even though Britain outlawed it in 1843, it remained in the U.S., mostly unmodified until almost the 1900s. The Industrial Revolution had an impact as a result of the requirement for a mass labor supply. Slavery became untenable, and yet the condition of the African-American labor force improved little. There was no secession of the Southern states before a Civil War and no 500,000 casualties. There were major conflicts in the 20th-century among unlikely adversaries and incredible losses into the millions.

Completely reincorporating the US into the British Empire was never a British war aim. And based on the British inability to defeat the thirteen colonies during the Revolution, the US's continued existence was never at stake. Contrary to the persistent focus on American sovereignty on the high seas and international trade, the war was about territory in the West. The British victory involved successful campaigns in the Great Lakes region and New Orleans, ultimately forcing Americans to cede Louisiana territory. United States territory extended only to the Mississippi river. Later in the 19th century, an industrialized US waged another war against Britain focused on the western territories to complete the "Manifest Destiny" doctrine that the U.S.'s expansion throughout the American continent was both justified and inevitable.

The only real significant difference between the two 1812 war versions was the unexplained tornadoes ripping through the British forces that turned the tide for the Americans. There were torrential rains, hurricane-force winds, and tornados that put out the fires and slowed the British advance. The storm winds were so fierce they tore buildings off their foundations, uprooted trees, and knocked men to the ground. Buildings collapsed, killing British soldiers seeking shelter within them. Historians have stated that there is no doubt that the storm that struck Washington on August 25 did more to save the U.S. capital than the American forces ever did. In the end, the battered British soldiers retreated to their ships that weren't washed ashore during the cyclic storm. The storm played a prominent role in the decision to cut short the Washington occupation. The alien redo-version of the War of 1812 is the one with the altered outcome that is a historical event-marker that is a reality today. Taught in American history classes, the British and the United States signed the Treaty of Ghent on December 24, 1814. Two weeks later, Andrew Jackson and his ragtag army defeated the British in the Battle of New Orleans. Grant and Steve discovered other alterations. In 1776, the British were ready to destroy Washington's army on Long Island when an unexplained heavy fog delayed their plans and allowed the American colonists to escape across the East River to Manhattan.

The Mongols' attempted sea invasion of Japan was prevented by what was called Divine Winds that destroyed the Mongol fleet twice, in 1274 and 1281. Without the windstorms, Japan became a colony of the Mongol nation and has a very different future. Some alien theorists and researchers think all those events were altered to change the outcome of those conflicts—results extraterrestrials preferred not to happen, so they were rearranged via time-phased Pushback. All these American and Mongol conflicts are very significant battles that change the structure of world events. Perhaps the original outcome was viewed as not acceptable to an overall evolutionary model for the development of both Japan and the American colonialists.

Steve later refers to these as alternate histories after discovering that the "viewing ports" were stacked upon one another and depicted parallel realities. He finds that there are competing parallel lives, people with different outcomes for those in each. It is various populations living in parallel, each with different outcomes and futures; flora and fauna over millions of years.

Grant hasn't had the time to view and study a significant number of the holographic library records. They are a visual depiction of evolution during specific periods and locations. He does not entirely understand how the ports can capture, store, and, more importantly, preserve the experiments contained within each. In other words, they are worlds unto themselves, kept for observation and manipulation.

It is not apparent to Grant, but ET and SAM are operating outside the scope of their alien mandate and Earth project. Their operations process has strayed from those precepts. The inadvertent involvement with Grant and his rescue efforts changed a subtle dynamic ET had never encountered in their many years of operational experience with humans.

For the first time, he experienced interpersonal relationships with a human subject. The earthquake and entrapment of ET led to a force-feeding of human compassion and curiosity. It wasn't in his playbook. ET saw a legitimate application of concern for his wellbeing by Grant. He was pinned under a massive boulder and couldn't effect a time freeze or Pushback. There was a new paradigm with one human subject that has a life pattern quilted in altered outcomes.

Lab Work

Grant and ET are standing near the Oval platform edge; their dialogue and mind-tending go on. Grant moves on. "So, you came into existence 305 years ago? Your birthday?"

"No, the artificial intelligence system existed many years prior to that period of activation."

Grant is perplexed by ET's youthful appearance: he has smooth skin, much like a newborn. No flaws, no signs or indication of age. ET could pass for a short, bald child in a skin-toned onesie. "Okay, your AI predates your biological structure, I still don't understand the lack of an aging component in your skin, hybrid skin." Grant wonders how was that accomplished? "So your skin was genetically modified?"

"Through genetic manipulation, gene editing, telomere modification." ET continues, "A portion of your compressed learning was specifically directed toward an understanding of your human genome."

"There was an emphasis on human genetics, I assumed it was in anticipation of understanding Man and interaction with your kind." Grant had absorbed the genetic subject matter to a graduate-level extent, far beyond any prior interest.

"You understand the purpose of telomeres in relation to chromosome deterioration?" ET asks.

Grant is stunned when he gives, by rote, a partial definition of *telomere*. "A telomere is a region of repetitive nucleotide sequences at each end of a chromosome, which protects the end of the chromosome from deterioration or from fusion with neighboring chromosomes." Grant's mouth opens in self-surprise. "Holy shit."

ET continues, "In humans, average telomere length declines from about 11 kilo-bases at birth to less than four kilo-bases at old cellular age, with the average rate of decline being greater in men than in women."

"I know sections of the telomere are lost during each cycle of cellular replication." Grant states with authority.

"In humans, telomeres are self-sacrificing components that shorten because the DNA replication of chromosomes does not begin at either end of the DNA strand, it starts at the center." ET mind-tends to Grant, who speaks in return.

Grant understands: during chromosome replication, the enzymes that duplicate DNA cannot continue their duplication to the end of a chromosome, resulting in a shortened chromosome. The telomeres are disposable buffers at the ends of chromosomes, which shorten during cell division. Their presence protects the chromosomal genes from being truncated. The telomeres are protected by a complex of sheltering proteins and the RNA that telomeric DNA encodes. "Okay, over time, due to each cell division, the telomere ends become shorter. I got that part," he says.

Grant's mind is flooded with a comprehensive knowledge of DNA replication. He can't turn it off. The knowledge stream flows steadily and uncontrolled. It continues, Grant's mouthing the words, not speaking, semi-mind-tending: "The shortening of telomeres with each replication in biological cells have a role in biological aging, and can induce replicative aging which block cell division. This is because the telomeres act as a sort of time-delay fuse, eventually running out after a certain number of cell divisions and resulting in the eventual loss of vital genetic information from the cell's chromosome with future divisions." Grant finally speaks out loud, nearly uncontrolled, "Telomere shortening in humans can induce replicative cell aging, which blocks cell division. This mechanism appears to limit the number of cell divisions."

"What is the end outcome of the shortening process?" ET asks.

Grant apparently can't stop his recitation of the DNA replication process. He is surrounded by a knowledge bubble that forces him to continue, "If telomeres become too short, they have the potential to unfold from their presumed closed structure. The cell may detect this as DNA damage and then either stop growing, enter cellular old age, or begin programmed cell self-destruction depending on the cell's genetic background. Many aging-related diseases are linked to shortened telomeres. Organs deteriorate as more and more of their cells die off or enter cellular old age or senescence. It has also been demonstrated that telomere extension has successfully reversed some signs of aging in laboratory mice and the nematode worm species."

ET presses, "In your learning process and knowledge absorption, what is your conclusion regarding telomeres and aging?" ET is in control of where Grant will eventually arrive. A milestone in their relationship.

Contained within his knowledge bubble, Grant recognizes that reversing telomeres shortening may be a potent means to slow aging. This alone would theoretically extend human life because it would slow cell division. "Three routes have been proposed to reverse telomere shortening: drugs; gene therapy, or metabolic suppression; and hibernation. So far, these ideas are not proven in humans. Telomere shortening reverses in hibernation, and aging is slowed." Grant finishes his acquired technical dialogue chain.

"Your information regarding human applications is accurate. What is your conclusion regarding my genetic construct?" ET asks.

Grant tries to put into words his concept of ET. Without compressed learning enhanced knowledge, he wouldn't have had an answer. "You are the living embodiment of what was, prior to our meeting, only possible as a fictional tale. You are a genetic biological wonder coupled with superior intelligence." Grant also realizes that ET is an end product of genetic manipulation, and enhancement of his cellular system to near immortality. He now especially must know who created ET.

"We share a portion of the same genetic background," ET mind-tends. "The intelligence component is artificial."

MAN 25

2018

* * * *

November 26, 2018

San Diego Union-Tribune
China Researcher Claims First Gene-Edited Babies
By Marilynn Marchione AP News
In recent years scientists have discovered a relatively easy way to edit genes, the strands of DNA that govern the body. The tool called CRISPR-cas9 makes it possible to operate on DNA to supply a needed gene or disable one that's causing problems. It has only recently been tried on adults to treat deadly diseases, and the changes are confined to that person. Editing sperm, eggs, or embryos is different; the changes can be inherited...

* * * *

November 27, 2018
San Diego Union-Tribune
GENE-EDITED BABY CLAIM MET WITH CRITICISM
Associated Press
summary edit
A researcher of the southern university of science and technology of China altered the DNA of twin girls born earlier this month to try to help them resist possible infection with the Aids virus...a dubious goal, ethically and scientifically.

CONSIDER MAN

* * * *

November 29, 2018
San Diego Union-Tribune Thursday,
Chinese scientist Gene-edited babies have opened
Pandora's box. Brace yourselves.
By Chris Reed

...A bombshell reports by MIT Technology Review and the Associated press—that renowned Chinese scientist He Jiankui said he had used the CRISPR-cas9 gene-editing tool to create the world's first two genetically modified human babies — led to headlines around the world...

* * * *

December 3, 2018
San Diego Union-Tribune
Embryonic Gene Editing Has Arrived; Now What
By Bradley J. Fikes

Morally acceptable or not, germ line editing arrived faster than expected. CRISPR uses an enzyme that cuts DNA, and a genetic template to direct the enzyme to a spot containing the proper DNA sequence.

* * * *

December 16, 2018
San Diego Union-Tribune Sunday Opinion
By Ali Toakmani

Germline editing will initially benefit only those privileged enough to access it early, but will eventually benefit all...Today anyone can order their human genome online for less than $1000...Consider the possibility of humans engineered...to resist radiation and bone loss due to space travel.

* * * *

February 12, 2019.
San Diego Union-Tribune
UC Granted Gene-Editing Patent.
By Bradley J. Fikes

A powerful technology that has been compared in its powers to the invention of the word processor. It is a tremendously powerful technology that allows faster and more precise editing of genetics sequences than has been possible before.

* * * *

2013
S. Matthew Liao
Human Engineering
Edited Summary

Liao is well-known for pioneering the idea of human engineering as a potential solution to accelerating climate change...This line of thought has been the subject of significant discussion and, in 2013, Liao gave a TED Talk on it in New York City.

* * * *

Mongols

ET's counterpart alien monitors effectively influenced and created a unique Mongol prototype soldier. Genghis Khan's warriors survived on little food and water for long periods. A Mongol army could camp without starting a single cooking fire. The Mongols were much healthier and more robust than any of their combat counterparts. Their diet was one of meat, milk, yogurt, and other dairy products. The men they fought lived on meals made from various grains. It left them weak, prone to disease, and required steady, consistent replenishment.

In contrast, even the poorest Mongol soldier ate mostly protein, thereby giving him strong teeth and bones. Unlike soldiers dependent on a heavy carbohydrate diet, the Mongols could more easily go a day or two without food. Germline editing and alien genetic manipulation created a formidable Mongol soldier that influenced the world that followed. The Mongols were the subject of gene manipulation by ETs, the Others. Specifically, the AMY 1 enzyme gene allowed Mongols to digest, break down and sublimate starches of a high-protein dairy diet. Their opponents could not.

Grant continues his questions of ET. "In actuality," Grant says, "the intelligence aspect of your being is easier to accept than the biological genetic DNA component." He then asks two questions that will affect their future relationship. "What is the source of your existence? How did you come to be?" He stands unsure if ET will answer.

ET begins, "You know of the shared genetic component. Your's acquired through cell replication from an unmodified source, inherited. We share genetic components created by separate and distinct applications in comparable DNA and genetic modifications resulting in an artificially-created biologic life-form."

Grant responds, "I am the result of a human reproductive process, born with distinct characteristics. You are the result of a controlled reproductive process that can be combined, assembled. You are unique as a creation." Grant has come to understand that ET's creation involves a biologically-based AI creative process. "I am unique as solely one." Grant, for some reason, doesn't entirely accept the premise and totality of ET. There are *Others,* ET's creators.

ET recognizes that he and Grant are similar in questioning their very existence. The artificial intelligence component of ET's creation and existence results from genetic manipulation and editing of cells. However, they are genetically modified to replicate a data-seeking intelligence platform, not unlike their human counterparts, coupled with a main-frame like information storage management and logic application system.

If ET is a synthetic or hybrid creation, Grant wonders, where are his creators, his mentors? How long have they been involved with Man? "I assume that your existence comprises patterns that have been replicated," he says. "Are you one of many duplicates that exist as you do and contain the same biologic mechanical intelligence pattern?"

"There are others that are consistent with the pattern." ET mind-tending.

So, there are more of him out there. "Do you communicate with your counterparts, your identical selves?"

"Communication is accomplished by database management system."

There is a consciousness that is the essence of how they communicate: think it, send it, receive it, understand it, know it. There's no chitchat, gossip, meandering conversations, or idle talk; however, there seems to be a developing dent in the genetic armor. Genetics, DNA, and evolution can, over time, make adjustments on their own.

"Okay, so you have no interpersonal relations with your look-alike counterparts? There isn't one of your selves that you have a closer relationship with than the others? A favorite among the many? Someone, one of yourselves you would hang out with. Anyone? Grant is looking for something: a human trait, an emotional connective tissue. What of curiosity, concern, compassion, stress?"

ET, doesn't have an answer. Apparently, there is no one.

There are no such favorable elements to ET's existence. At least there weren't any before the earthquake encounter with Grant on Corte Madera. He was trapped and, at some point, knew he could not escape. He wasn't scared or fearful, yet he was intrigued by his confinement. ET was, for the first time in his existence, face-to-face with circumstances beyond his control. There was no exit point, no strategy to remove the rock confining him. Superior intelligence offered no solution. He couldn't communicate with his database management system, SAM, with his arm trapped under the granite.

Then along came Grant, a Man ensconced within the lab experiment Earth, a bit player in the petri dish of evolution. Grant was one of those who had an alternate life pattern adjusted by the circumstance of his life. Statistically, Grant should have been dead several times over.

When he was 14, Grant's death by gunshot aboard a homemade boat activated a Pushback response and his first event-marker; a young male specimen with no existing health issues and no other project research interaction fits the alien/ET project requirements. It was a straightforward prerequisite to fulfill, random and unscripted. It is the same action that Steve uncovers in the alternate history database for Grant. It was the first event-marker of many that reflected the curious and troubling death-laden background associated with his brother's apparent propensity for dying at the hands of others. It wasn't dying and not staying dead, but reemerging at an event-marker sending his life in an alternate life pattern. There seemed to be many of these event-markers reflecting Grant's death alternative life directions, narrow escapes. From Steve's perspective, he lived a high-risk life pattern. Grant avoided death while involved with some life-challenging events and consistently event-markered to prevent it. The ET rescue had no association with Grant's life-altering events and subsequent Pushback, time-freeze, event-markers, and redirected life pattern. It was also incredibly random, with odds of the encounter somewhere near winning a $587 million Power Ball jackpot twice. It just didn't happen that way. ET's human-DNA-like evolving genetic curiosity was the sole source of the graduate project. A reflex impulse pushed to the forefront of his human shared evolving genetics. An outlier and unique alien script; the study of alternate life patterns after death was avoided by Pushback and redirected to another life pattern. Grant's pattern was found to be unusual, even by ET. For some reason, Grant had a remarkable propensity for stumbling into situations that would have resulted in his death without ET's intervention. Steve thought of his brother as the *Evel Knievel of Corte Madera*. Some would say, though not ET, that it was karma or cosmic destiny. The two were supposed to meet.

Lab Talk

Grant presses on again, "Okay I know you are not going to tell me where your kind came from, and I don't think I would understand if you told me. In your relations and communications with your kind, do you have names for each other? Call signs, identifiers so you know who you're communicating with?"

"There are no identifiers. No names. You and Steve refer to us as SAM and ET." ET mind-tends without movement or expression.

"Yes, we do. We did that since there was no formal introduction. You and SAM didn't fit our paradigm. We humans name everything: dogs, cats, children, body parts, cars, boats, motorcycles and extraterrestrials and their sidekick computer." Grant laughs, pleased with himself. Looks over at ET for a reaction. Comic relief, there is none. Grant returns to his lawn chair and takes a water bottle from the cooler.

"Recognition doesn't exist by the use of names. It exists without them," ET mind- tends.

"ET, do you know what *humor me* means?" Grant is going to push his point to make perhaps an impact on his no-name extraterrestrial guest.

"Going along with something that seems stupid or pointless for the sake of another person. Perhaps agreeing with someone to keep them happy." ET quotes an urban dictionary he accessed.

Grant thinks they are making progress. "Yes *humor me* can mean something like *tell me anyway*. It means don't argue with me, just do it or just listen. So, *humor me* now.

"I can listen to your logic."

"When communicating, do you recognize a pattern or a logic stream that would indicate the source of the communication?" Grant asks.

"Yes."

"You can distinguish between sources?" Grant is attempting to make a logic point himself. "So you can accurately determine between several sources. They are distinct and separate."

"That is correct." ET confirms.

Grant presents his counterpoint, "The distinct and separate recognition characteristics of your communication sources could just as well be their names. A name accomplishes the same thing. A rose by another name would smell as sweet, Shakespeare."

ET instantly accesses another database. "William Shakespeare, 26 April, 1564 to 23 April, 1616, was an English poet, playwright and actor, widely regarded as the greatest writer in the English language and the world's greatest dramatist."

"Yeah, 'Romeo and Juliet.'" Grant says without almost any conscious effort. "The reference is often used to imply that the names of things do not affect what they really are."

ET is strangely silent, yet he knows this formulation is a paraphrase of Shakespeare's actual language. Juliet compares Romeo to a rose, saying that he would still be Juliet's love if he were not named Romeo Montague.

Grant asks ET a question that will set in motion a set of circumstances that he hasn't dealt with during his lab experiments on Earth. "When I came upon you trapped under the granite rock, what were your expectations of the encounter?" Grant is curious himself, particularly since learning of his life-altering relationship with ET. He changed the future while entirely unaware of any of it.

"Puzzling concern," ET responds.

"A puzzling concern? That doesn't sound like a reaction I would have expected from an extraterrestrial Earth caretaker." Grant goes on, "Did you recognize me as one of your subject humans?" Still wanting more answers.

"You were a known factor." ET's Grad project subject. ET is aware of something. Grant came into ET's view as a young teenager, not by direction or planning but by unexpected circumstances. The circumstance drove by budding uniquely human traits, feelings, boredom, curiosity, interest, self, stress, all new to an alien counterpart. ET was nevertheless following research protocols and establishing a hypothesis reflecting the human life patterns altered by death or nearly so.

"You didn't stop time or Pushback. Why?" Grant, still seated in his lawn chair, takes another couple of swallows of water; ET is standing as he always does. There have been no recent trips either forward or back in time. One could say they were jaw-boning or killing time, perhaps for the first time between two somewhat related species sharing some of the same genetic material.

ET is thinking, not mind-tending. Grant can't hear him. He has seldom used this technique in front of Grant or Steve;

typically, he has nothing to hide. "The wrist mounted Gateway was under the obstacle inaccessible," he finally says.

Grant doesn't buy it. "Bullshit, you could have done a time freeze like you did with the Mexican cartel gunman. You didn't use gateway then. The only difference was you couldn't move physically."

Grant's compressed advanced training seems to be paying off; he knows ET had other options. There had to be something in that unexpected encounter on Corte Madera that altered ET's perception and reaction. Grant knows it.

And ET knows it. "Unexplained and unfamiliar recognition response, not experienced prior."

"It was a surprise then. For both of us. You knew me as a subject of some sort of life pattern manipulation, and I wondered what you were," Grant confirms.

"Correct. Surprise. New concept. Not experienced at any time."

"How did you deal with it? Or better yet, why?" Grant is genuinely curious.

"Your life pattern and direction different from others. A unique sense, in your terms, curiosity. Seeking further understanding."

The door was open for Grant. "That's it—you recognized me from your ongoing study of life pattern event-markers and were curious to see how I would respond! I was one of your lab rats! You need to be careful; curiosity killed the cat."

"Curiosity killed the cat is a proverb used to warn of the dangers of unnecessary investigation or experimentation." That recitation from Wikipedia goes through ET's and Grant's minds. "You are the cat?" ET asks and is somewhat perplexed for the first time by Grant's answer.

"No, you are."

"Do not recognize that conclusion." ET doesn't follow Grant's logic.

"When I encountered you on Corte Madera, you recognized me and were apparently curious. I have an idea where the curiosity came from, but in any case, you made a metered attempt to alter my approach to assist you. The head pain while I approached. You could have stopped me cold. From my logical demonstrated action plan, you recognized I was legitimately concerned about your welfare. You may have gained some insight into my reaction from our prior indifferent association, experimentation on your part. I acted and responded only knowing someone needed assistance and help. Fulfilling that part of who I am, opened a new avenue inside you, one not traveled before."

ET is mostly silent, almost without mind-tending words. "Not sure of your direction."

"You are part of the new paradigm. When you stopped the Mexican cartel from killing us, that was either out of concern or curiosity."

"It could be both." ET is discovering his human genetic side. He struggles to be a bit more human, a concern for Man, and his lab experiments become real. The experiment goes off track when affected by human compassion rather than by an alien template. A factor not programed but diverted by emotion and the feature of right or wrong, a human component. ET is at the outer edge of his human DNA/genetic evolution. Perhaps, he is the first of his kind to discover his ancestry and is moving beyond his control into a new frontier. He is at the edge of acquiring a human inherited emotional self-concept—an alien *Outlier* on the edge of an initial sunrise of human experience.

"Have you ever interacted with humans as you have with Steve and I?"

"No."

Chaos Theory
Butterfly Effect

Chaos Theory: Small differences in initial conditions, such as rounding errors in computation and timing, yield widely diverging outcomes for rendering long-term prediction of behavior or results. The Butterfly Effect describes how a slight change in one state of a deterministic nonlinear system can result in significant differences in a later state, e.g., a butterfly flapping its wings in Brazil can ultimately cause a hurricane in the Gulf of Mexico.

"So, we were the first." Grant is searching for something. "Were you breaking any rules regarding our interaction?"

"Perhaps."

"Do others of your kind know of our interactions? Do you jeopardize your position? Is there a chain of command?" Grant asks.

"Earth is an outpost location in your terms. No others will arrive for a significant time. No jeopardy of position."

Reflecting on his military background and remote assignments, Grant asks, "Is this location, Earth, your choice or were you sent here?"

"Sent."

I assume that you came here from a location very far from the Earth and our solar system by Wormhole, Stargate, Gateway, or some other pathway?"

"It is a gateway from a distant system, unknown to Man at this time."

"Is the gateway travel associated with the time travel elements we have learned to use here? Can we access it?" Grant asks, curious, and searches for enlightenment.

"You have used the gateway here. Only limited excursions related to time travel."

Letter to Family of deceased Friend

The distinction between past, present and future is only a stubbornly persistent illusion.
Albert Einstein.

"We could have traveled to your world." Grant is intrigued by the thoughts of finding a door to ET's source of existence. Where he started from; his Earth-like platform or planet. What kind of intelligence source created, designed, planned, and brought ET and others of his kind to a hybrid consciousness? Who designed the exceeding intelligence of fabricated intellect associated with a shared human traceable DNA component? Who are the engineers, creators of AI, design managers? Who and what are they? What DNA do we share with them? These thoughts raced through Grant's mind.

ET read Grant's mind, "I hear your thoughts." ET has never encountered a reason to explore the source of his existence. His database indicates a creation and activation sequence, yet he has never questioned any reasoning why.

He was designed and created to monitor and manage the laboratory Earth. Observation and recording were the hallmarks of his responsibilities. ET had the latitude for experimentation and his "Grad Project" exploration regarding the effect on his human subjects.

"Okay, I was going to ask you this before, knowing you probably wouldn't tell me, but here goes: where do you come from?" Grant has a curiosity reflected in the source of ET's creation and the significance of shared DNA among the three of them.

"Existence a function of creation process. Location holds no significance. Created at time sequence interval appropriate for AI initiation and consciousness acquisition. Question has no meaning. No place to come from. Irrelevant data request." And abrupt ET response consistent with his alien being and a touch of attitude evolving human DNA genetics. Yet there is something changing within their relationship. They seem to be connecting on a deeper level. ET was evolving due to his highly selective genetic profile, including a pinch of free-wheeling genetic material. A genetic abnormality opening to an unexpected and unanticipated genetic alteration before Grant.

A butterfly flapped its wings somewhere along ET's alien genetic flyway, causing the beginning of a genetic disturbance. From that chrysalis, a new consciousness emerged slowly, yet profoundly. ET has been affected by genetic change, evolving beyond alien control. The nature of this evolution was not planned, forecast, or foreseen. Unintended evolutionary DNA consequences led to self-awareness, the concept of self-awakening. A selfless embodiment.

MAN 26

Petri Dish Evolution
Tell the story…Change the world
Paradigm Shift

* * * *

A Brief History of Time
Stephen Hawking
A Bantam Book
Copyright 1988, 1996 by Stephen Hawking
Conclusion: We find ourselves in a bewildering world. We want to make sense of what we see around us and ask: what is the nature of the universe? What is our place in it, and where did it and we come from? Why is it the way it is?...If we find the answer to that, it would be the ultimate triumph of human reason–for then we would know the mind of God.

* * * *

May 25, 2022
Ancient footprints provide new evidence of humans in NOVA's "Ice Age Footprints"
NEW DOCUMENTARY *"ICE AGE FOOTPRINTS"* UNCOVERS REMARKABLE ANCIENT HUMAN FOOTPRINTS THAT COULD BE THE EARLIEST EVIDENCE OF HUMANS EVER FOUND IN NORTH AMERICA
One-hour film follows a team of scientists as they date footprints found in White Sands, New Mexico to more than 21,000 years ago...But when were the footprints made?...mainstream archaeology community held that

humans first arrived in North America about 13,000 years ago....radiocarbon dating on ancient seeds found buried between the footprints and find that the footprints were made between 21,000 and 23,000 years ago...it puts humans deep in North America at the very height of the Ice Age.

* * * *

Since her 2014, White Sand National Monument parking lot job interview, Samantha French has become an integral staff partner and research colleague. The "Ice Age Footprints" discovery came after nearly eight years of intense, dedicated efforts to collect, study and categorize age-related evidence for the thousands of fossilized animal footprints collected. Samantha remained a bit of a Gothic outfitted outlier research staff member. Once the Ice Age prints were carbon dated to nearly 10,000 years pre-Clovis, she took an immediate one-year research sabbatical and left in a newly outfitted and equipped state-of-the-art off-road Mercedes travel van. It was a Mobil-wired research lab; her itinerary was road trips to several pre-Clovis sites from North to South America on her bucket list. She continued to follow the evidence of the petri dish alien managed human evolution, a life's calling.

ET's study of humankind relied on his database system to provide subjects fitting within experimental parameters of various research projects on Earth. Over the years, there were no interpersonal relations or feelings regarding subject materials, i.e., humans. Alien managers would fill their project requirements without any consideration other than the required numbers. The select species parameters included: sex, age, DNA/genetics, and location. ET fulfilled his requirements typically without regard to any atypical outside influences. He did that consistently for decades, but things tend to change in DNA genetic evolutionary sequencing dynamics. Evolution made adjustments on its own, reflecting inside influences where both ET, Grant, and humankind share a portion of the same DNA formulation. They are related genetically by design for ET. For Grant and humanity by heredity. All are evolution-driven and sourced by the *Others* and created. The Others are the Genesis-like creators and start point of all that encompasses life forms on Earth. Their existence is without measurable defined boundaries; have always been. They are the monitor-managers of the Earth laboratory since its existence. ET is one chain link of many prior lab monitors and is the Others' anchorage on Earth.

When Grant was a young teen and shot aboard his homemade boat on San Diego Bay, the event fit ET's Earth lab parameters. What didn't work was how often Grant faced seemingly disconnected life-ending ventures.

The evolution simmering genetically within ET altered the projected course of Grant's event-marker, death-poxed life. Grant was traveling on a Yogi railway alternate, an unknown parallel life course. ET was the conductor and engineer without a destination clearly defined. Butterfly Effect.

Grant, as a passenger on his life-altered-express, had questions. He didn't initially ask ET because he couldn't engage intellectually, nor comprehend fully, as an equal; he still doesn't. Yet, during each session of his time-compressed training over several months, his IQ grew quantitatively. He gained and developed a significant measure of intellectual confidence to engage ET. The result is an accelerated IQ capacity and expansion of his implicit memory. A side effect due to the growth of his temporal cortex by physical volume is the associated post accelerated training headache; a painful move to first class on the ET conducted life-altered express train.

* * * *

February 5, 2019
Human Intelligence: What single neurons can tell us
Elaine N. Miller
Chet C. Sherwood
elifescience.org
The George Washington University

The architecture of individual neurons in the human cortex is connected to IQ scores.... Higher IQ scores are associated with a thicker temporal cortex, which features pyramidal neurons with more elaborate dendritic networks and faster electrical impulses. A lower IQ score is associated with a thinner temporal cortex containing pyramidal neurons with less complex dendritic networks and slower electrical impulses.

* * * *

Grant is never to be equal with ET, but conversant at a high level of understanding and stoic patience from his accelerated expanded knowledge base. He could engage in a logic pattern unavailable to him before ET put Grant through repeated accelerated mentor sessions.

Grant plunges in again, asks ET another creation source question he has avoided before. "Where do your creators come from?" Sitting in his lawn chair, he holds a new can of beer. Steve is sitting in a lawn chair next to Grant, following the dialog.

"Another existence, dimensions far from here." ET mind-tending.

Grant has limited knowledge regarding the concept of dimension existence beyond his. How, where, and travel there are beyond him and his implicit memory and accelerated knowledge exposure. He is far short of concept reality and its understanding. Grant figures that. "Are they of the same physical construct as you?"

"They are not."

Grant asks. "Do we share a portion of the same DNA with them?"

ET answers, "Affirmative."

"What of their physical appearance?" Grant asks, "Are we and they of the same make-up and physical features?"

"Different." mind-tending ET." Closer to human in appearance."

Grant looks up from his beer with a frown-driven look of curiosity. "In what way?"

"Taller, without follicles." Factual report by ET.

Almost laughing, "Come on? So, they are like me, but taller and hairless? Can you bring up an image?".

"I second that request," Steve interjects. "Hairless, no beard and no shaving? Like you, ET."

ET indicates he cannot. "There are no requirements, parameters, or function of images as you request. You share similar features. Man possesses less functional adaptations, biological, physical, and cerebral. Comparison not valid."

Grant still wants more. "Not valid? What does that mean? We look something alike; Man is shorter?"

"Are we talking about some cosmic cousins we're related to?" Steve is affected by alcohol.

"Your term: Apples to oranges by comparison similar." ET replies with a human-like retort. "Functionally widely different. Not the same."

Grant still searches for a foothold. "I then assume that you are closer functionally by way of your AI construct."

"We're talking artificial intelligence, right? AI?" Steve was trying to follow.

"Correct. AI component design replicates significant portions of innate biological counterpart."

"They inherited it?" Grant asks.

"Cousins," Steve chimes in. "Hard to believe. Do they drink?" His irrelevancies are ignored.

"Unknown attribution source. No database reference." ET doesn't know the answer to Grant's question. Another human trait.

"Then creators arrived or came with a biological model that is the foundation of yours?" Grant, still sitting, opens his cooler for another beverage. Steve takes another.

ET answers to infer a conclusion based upon a mixture of artificial intelligence and human-like logic. "That is a reasonable conclusion. Source was founded or created elsewhere. I have no supporting data."

Grant asks, "Are they constructed of artificial intelligence and biological manipulative materials, human-like?"

ET indicates they are not that. "No database evidence of artificial intelligence. Composed of natural occurring biological process," ET speculates, human-like again. "Possible genetic manipulation well within scope of recorded capabilities."

Grant assumed that possibility, asks, "How do you know that? Did you learn by communicating with them?"

"In your terms, 'overheard' communications. Applied logic to assume genetic manipulation conclusion far removed from current period. Genetic expertise established in distant past."

"The term is 'eavesdropped,' Grant replies "If you were not supposed to have been included in a communication. You heard or mind-tended a communication of others. Don't SAM and you share all communications without effort? Automatically?"

"That is correct."

"Damn right that's correct." Steve has some heartburn regarding SAM.

"And the Others?" Grant refers to ET's creators.

"The Others also."

"With that being true, *overheard* or *eavesdropped* does not apply within your communication network." Previously ET has bypassed Steve and Grant with mind-tending communication with SAM. "You can't be a non-participant in your communications system as I understand it," Grant says, getting up from his lawn chair. ET and SAM hear or mind-tend everything, nothing missed.

"Logic interesting." ET has stepped into a human perspective from an alien one. Touching a near-human reaction: curiosity.

Grant takes what he can get. "What are they called? Do they have a name?"

ET answers, "They have existence without name."

"How long have they, the *Others*, existed?" Grant takes a drink after asking, not sure he will get a meaningful answer. "And where?" He asks again.

"Their operational existence is indeterminate. From other dimension."

"How long have they been involved in the evolution on Earth?" Grant asks.

"Since the beginning." ET answers.

"What does that mean? How many years or decades?"

ET doesn't answer. A first. ET is slipping slightly to his human side.

Grant asks another question. "Have they ever been involved with a human to the extent of you and I?"

"And Steve. Don't forget Steve." Steve interjects.

"No." ET goes on, "For many thousand years, involved with other human counterparts, observe and record the development of human species."

Grant chokes on his beer. He is taken aback. "How did it turn out, the studies?"

"Not always successful, learning curve based upon evolution and genetic manipulation of Man." ET with emotionless confidence.

Grant stares open mouth over the Oval edge into surrounding space, considering the extent of petri dish evolution on Earth. He hadn't considered the totality of aliens' impact until now. What is next? "What of abduction?" Grant changes direction. "Was the introduction of advance knowledge and future events introduced to my abducted predecessors?"

"Abduction was carried out for research experimentation, biological, genetic and DNA sampling, no interactive dialogue." ET replies.

"What of: Fibonacci, da Vinci, Einstein, Nostradamus?" Grant mentions his knowledge acquired in training sessions. He drinks more beer.

"Those guided by suspended states of consciousness allowed minor recalled interaction. Not interactive with counterparts as you and Steve. Their journey was intelligence expansion, seeding implicit memory, recall by visualization future concept subject matter. Logic pattern enhanced, expanded. Limited innate reference data source precluded more extensive exposure."

"I get it, with the exception of Einstein, their exposure to a 20th century environment, such as simple electricity, was beyond their comprehension capacity," Grant says. "They would have had been bewildered and intellectually lost."

ET moves on. "The cultural dogma of religious practice and ignorance precluded full disclosure of discovered material. Their lives in jeopardy, varying degrees."

"Einstein. One of your project subjects then? His life falls within your existence?" Grant asks.

ET responds with a hint of regret, "He, perhaps most intelligent subject guided in last 150 years. Lived in comparatively enlightened times, technically advanced subject. Not likely candidate, needed little guidance. Contribution and influence would change the direction of mankind's future existence."

"He was instrumental in initial development of nuclear weapons. People died as a result," Grant says, looking over the Oval edge toward the constellation Sagittarius.

"Without Einstein's event-marker, Germany developed first nuclear weapons." ET turns to face Grant, an unusual gesture for him. "World War II outcome changed. The continued structure of Man's survival would have been altered."

Grant knows there is more to this. "Okay, you say Germany gets the A-bomb. Do they use it?"

"Affirmative. Twice, London and Moscow, 3.6 million casualties." ET still faces Grant, with Sagittarius in the background.

"Holy shit...twice? Fuck me!" ET's statement has sobered up Steve amazingly fast.

Grant is equally astonished. "Where was Einstein before his event-marker? When?" Grant knows he had to have at least one event-marker.

"Without event-marker, his life pattern kept him in German empire. Arrested 1937, sent to Buchenwald, died there 1939."

"Damn, a death camp victim." Grant walks around, returns to his lawn chair, sits, head in hands. "When did he leave Germany?" Grant knows Einstein left Germany before World War II began and long before Germany could have developed nuclear weapons without him.

"1932 event-marker and your term, *Yogi,* placed him and family on known altered life pattern. Once in your country, his history follows as you know it." ET turns back to open space.

Grant looks over at ET, asks. "You mentioned the continued structure of Man's survival would have been altered had Germany attained the nuclear weapon. What was your underlying alternative outcome?" Grant is concerned with ET's answer.

ET gives a short, direct clinical response. "In your terms, mankind came to edge of extinction event."

"Was the extinction event going to be Man-made or imposed by your kind? Grant asks.

"Circumstance dictated the end decision."

"Saved by an event-marker and Yogi." Grant replies, "Man had to be saved by an intervention it was one Man who brought us there: Hitler," Grant mumbles. "His contagion was lethal for many."

"It was one who brought mankind back." ET follows with a human trait, "Einstein. With a bit of help."

Grant overlooks ET's quip. "Was there thought of a sixth great extinction event?"

"Considered. Another of your terms: too invested, point of no return." ET continued.

"Explain further." Grant is puzzled.

Paradigm Shift

Before ET's creation, his mentors considered a paradigm change to alter the direction of Earth and the human species. They experimented with spiritual sects and Man, Moses for one, and others to take the mantle of leadership for the human race. Mohammed, Hinduism, Buddhism all failed to a certain extent. Likewise, historic ancient empires: Persian, Byzantine, Arab, Spanish, Arab/Ottoman, and British, six Chinese dynasties, 300 years of Romans. None united the human race and species. The Third Reich took Man to the edge of a belligerent nuclear age, controlled by one incoherent nation. The use of such weapons destroys the environment and mankind. One event-marker and

Yogi altered one Man's life pattern and saved the world for a time.

"Not all of mankind...extinct?" Grant is up again facing down ET. "You stopped it. The Others?"

ET clarifies the solution. "Not initiated by numbers, yet solely by a single voice. A unifying catalyst change...one human." ET responds mind-tending: "Earth worth saving."

"Who are we speaking of?" Grant is nearly pleading with ET. "One human leaves a lot of room for a selection committee. Einstein needed a boost and event-marker. He was not alone in his venture." Grant knows ET and Others had a hand-in this.

Who is ET thinking of now? Mind-tending Grant.

"Change agent. Your term." Mind-tended ET.

Grant rejoins, "Change agent? Do you have someone in mind, another Yogi?"

"In progress, set to take place." ET.

"Holy shit! Why are we having this conversation? You, the Others, have made a choice, a selection?" Grant is not sure he's ready for the answer.

"Uncertainty in outcome." ET sounds almost hesitant. There must be a risk of some sort.

After a period of silence and self-realization, Grant asks, "You know the outcome, choice of outcomes. Your uncertainty is which one to choose?" Grant is trying to read ET's expressionless face.... nothing. "What are you telling me...us?"

"Outcome to be determined. More than one." ET responds to Grant's thoughts. He is experiencing a touch of uncertainty, a human-like response.

"You mean more than one choice?

"More than one to implement."

Grant is wondering. "There's more than one event-marker to take?"

"Correct, impact significant for mankind." His human DNA introduces a touch of uncertainty. New experience. "First event, climate impact starts in ten years."

"It's a worldwide condition: you're talking global effect?" Grant thinks "What's new?"

"Involved in clear-sighted policy implementation, results in not seen events." ET mind-tends. The convoluted statement unlike him.

Grant rephrases ET's words. "You are saying the policy on the climate is *far-sighted* and contains or results in *unintended consequences*. We or mankind have a habit of implementing those choices that tend to routinely effect an opposite detrimental outcome not foreseen."

* * * *

May 11, 2021
San Diego Union-Tribune Tuesday
The challenge of charging EV's
struggling to find a business model that works.
By David R. Baker

President Joe Biden's plan to wean US drivers off of fossil fuels requires massive investment in public charging stations to power the electric car revolution. So far, none of the companies that deploy the equipment has figured out how to make a profit.... The US Department of Energy estimates that 80% of EV charging happens at home...takes hours for a full charge.

* * * *

June 8, 2021
San Diego Union-Tribune Tuesday,
Automakers face a threat to EV sales: Slow charging times
By Tom Krisher

DETROIT (AP) — If the auto industry is to succeed in its bet that electric vehicles will soon dominate the roads, it will need to overcome a big reason why many people are still avoiding them: fear of running out of juice between Point A and Point B.

CONSIDER MAN

July 9, 2021
San Diego Union-Tribune
Stellantis: Most models to be EV by 2025
Combined Fiat Chrysler and Peugeot company catching up with rivals

By Tom Krisher

DETROIT — Stellantis is a little late to the global electric vehicle party, but on July 8 it pledged to catch up and pass its competitors...by 2025, 98% of its models in Europe and North America will have fully electric or plug-in gas-electric hybrid versions…no fewer than 80% will run on batteries alone, Tavares said.

* * * *

ET starts to clarify. "Industrial countries implement fossil fuel restrictions through 2030. Direction toward electrical dependency for transportation, powered vehicles and electrical supply generation. Industrial population country moves to control and implement dependency upon electric battery-powered transportation. Fossil fuel dependency lessened 75 percent through your country and what is termed Western world."

"That is a popular outcome that has been spoken of for years without results," Grant says. "What country and what is the issue you are aware of?"

"China and Russia false intentions to deplete dependency on fossil fuel."

"Does that mean they are not going to move toward an electrical energy policy to combat climate change?" Grant is perplexed; he doesn't see a problem.

"Your term, *false flag,* pursues projects that would otherwise remain unrealized."

"So, they are not legitimately moving toward an electrical energy policy and climate change. You have seen the results of these policies in time forward, is that correct?" Grant's attention is focused.

"The future policy of both nations is electrical dependency of your country and Western European nations while calling for diminished use of fossil fuel." ET is reporting, as a matter of fact. "They will invest in electrical vehicle transportation manufacturing. China took ownership of Volvo, a Swedish vehicle manufacturer. End process is production dependency upon electrical generation and transportation systems. Minor fossil fuel supplies remain available."

"When did China buy Volvo?" Steve is unaware of the ownership change.

"Volvo acquisition this year, 2010." ET answers.

* * * *

Jan 27, 2020
Wikipedia
How much of Volvo does China own? 20%. Nowadays, Volvo says that China is the largest market for the brand...The success of Volvo in China wasn't an accident, either.

* * * *

Steve doesn't hide his contempt for China's ownership of Volvo. "Okay, how are the commie-pinkos going to bring the world to submission? We have a lot of energy resources and backup systems."

ET relates the future as he knows it is to play out in the following decades without event-markers and Yogis. "Your governments will declare climate change recovery priority. Fault petroleum, carbon emissions."

"What do you mean governments...more than one. Ours...when?" Grant questions ET's source. Not in his data vault.

"Your government and others in 2020-22," ET replies.

"But our carbon emissions are getting smaller each year. What about China and India, they produce more than us?" Steve surprises himself with actual facts.

"Confirm, China's forecast to peak carbon emissions by 2030.... doubtful. Current largest carbon climate source."

"I knew it...get them to shut it down," Steve is pleased with his data reference.

"False premise, assigns fossil fuels, carbon emissions to be cut 800 million tons largest reduction since history of energy. Ongoing." ET relates factual data of next twenty years. "European proposal to reduce emissions 40 percent by 2030. Last of fossil fuel vehicles sold by 2035."

"Is the concept to replace all fossil fuel vehicle uses to electrical ones?" Grant asks.

"Correct." Stone faced ET.

* * * *

July 15, 2021
San Diego Union-Tribune
EU unveils plan to do shift from fossil fuels
New York Times

Paris. The proposals also include eliminating the sale of gas-and diesel-powered cars in just 14 years, and raising the price of fossil fuels...China, currently the world's largest emitter of carbon, has said only that it aims for emissions to peak by 2030.

* * * *

January 25, 2021
Biden wants to replace government fleet with electric vehicles
As of 2019, there were 645,000 vehicles in the federal government's fleet
theverge.com
By Andrew J. Hawkins@Andrewjayhawk

President Joe Biden will start the process of phasing out the federal government's use of gas-powered vehicles and replacing them with ones that run on electricity.... Those vehicles traveled 4.5 billion miles in 2019...And he pledged to spend billions of dollars to add 550,000 EV charging stations in the US.

* * * *

"When is all this electrical shit going to happen?" Steve not holding back.

"By 2040 your government to operate only electrical vehicles. Exchange 650,000 fuel vehicles with electric, civilian, military and your mail service."

"How's that going to happen?" Grant scoffs. "No manufactures will buy into an all-electric system of transportation, it does not make marketing or common sense." He can't believe any of this is heading their way in the next two of decades.

"Seventy percent of General Motors, Ford, Volkswagen, BMW, Honda, Chrysler, Volvo products, electric battery powered 2035. Near 100% at 2040." ET has an accurate data-chain source, the future, without event-markers or Yogis.

* * * *

March 17, 2021
BMW raises target for EV sales, plans new electric-focused platform
Automotivenews.com
Bloomberg and Reuters contributed to this report
MUNICH -- BMW...targeted a steep rise in electric-vehicle sales. The automaker plans for about half of total sales to be fully electric by the end of the decade...

* * * *

April 23, 2021
Honda will phase out gas-powered cars by 2040
theverge.com
By Andrew J. Hawkins@Andrewjayhawk
Honda said it will stop selling gas-powered vehicles by 2040....Honda is the latest car company to commit to an all-electric future, with General Motors, Ford, Volkswagen, Volvo, and others making similar promises in recent months...

* * * *

July 23, 2021

CONSIDER MAN

San Diego Union-

GM issues 2nd Bolt recall; faulty batteries can cause fires
General Motors is recalling some older Chevrolet Bolts for a second time to fix persistent battery problems that can set the electric cars ablaze

By Tom Krisher AP Auto Writer

DETROIT -- General Motors is recalling some older Chevrolet Bolts for a second time to fix persistent battery problems that can set the electric cars ablaze.

Until repairs are done, GM says owners should park the cars outdoors, limit charging to 90% of battery capacity, and not deplete batteries below 70 miles of range...Ford, BMW and Hyundai all have recalled batteries recently...

* * * *

September 29, 2021
Rolls Royce Will Stop Making Gas-Powered Cars by 2030
So long, V12.

By Hannah Elliott Bloomberg News

"By then, Rolls-Royce will no longer be in the business of producing or selling any internal combustion engine products."

* * * *

September 29,2022
Toyota Comes Out AGAINST Electric Cars: "Not the solution"

AAN Staff - Climate change

The company that made hybrid cars no longer an act of science fiction and brought them to households for affordable prices is now dialing back efforts for EV cars.

* * * *

"That is one hell of a forecast and a lot of batteries requiring charging stations here and Europe-wide," Steve says. He, too, is skeptical of the electric vehicle concept at the scale depicted by ET.

"There are anticipated near one million charging stations, 550,000 in your country by 2030," ET replies.

"Good luck with that...especially if governments are the contractors." Grant doesn't buy it. "What about the military inventory of vehicles, aircraft, armor, ships?"

* * * *

September 13, 2019
Union of Concerned Scientists.
By Union of Concerned Scientists

For 2017 alone, the U.S. military bought 269,230 barrels of oil a day and spent more than $8.6 billion on fuel for the Air Force, the Army, the Navy, and the Marines, and the military remains the single largest consumer of fossil fuels on the planet, according to the Union of Concerned Scientists.

* * * *

2021
Wikipedia
Defense Logistics Agency

The Department of Defense uses 4,600,000,000 US gallons of fuel annually, an average of 12,600,000 US gallons of fuel per day. A large Army division may use about 6,000 US gallons per day.

* * * *

"All combat vehicles rely and operate on fossil fuels. Land, naval and air forces all use petroleum fuel sources." ET responds.

"Well, no shit, Sherlock. How does a military combat force operate within the confines of varied battle environments by electrical means?" Steve knows the answer. "They don't."

"There would be limitations to consider. Battery life, recharging limits/time, environment, scope of engagement." ET mind-tends without judgment.

CONSIDER MAN

* * * *
June 17, 2021
Defensenews.com
Commentary
Replace fossil fuels for the military? Not so fast.
By: Matthew Kambrod

The Army is not alone in owning vehicles...each of the other services needs one form of ground transportation or another to function. The issue is exacerbated when you include aircraft and ships...While incredibly varied as combat vehicles are, they do have one absolute thing in common: They all operate with fossil fuels.

In reality, the scenario is unlikely, as such a program totally defies logic. But we're in a time where much defies logic in America...our Green New Deal, if advanced in the direction discussed, does little but severely threaten U.S. national security.

* * * *

Grant says, "There would have to be a rewrite of the rules of engagement. Time out for recharging batteries. There are no electrical resupply or fuel transport vehicles...can't put spare electricity in a five-gallon Jerry Can. No air power involved since there are no electric powered aircraft. Naval battle operations would require self-sustained electrical sources on board every vessel. No need for aircraft carriers, since there are EV no aircraft of any kind. Whoever thought up this scenario didn't think. A bureaucratic brain trust, most likely. There is a complete lack of operational knowledge somewhere beyond the limits of reality."

"Correct, assumption regarding complete dependance upon renewal energy sources. Electric dependance is linchpin for China/Russian strategy to control economic and political structure of your and Western governments." ET continues to mind-tend. "Strategy complete upon reliance of electricity source and abandonment of abundant petroleum-centered dependent infrastructure."

"No longer an alternative of fuel sources, no backup systems." Steve replies with distain. "How do they take over...by force?"

* * * *

December 29, 2020
Biden's Assault on Fossil Fuels Jeopardizes America's
Military Strength
realclearenergy.org
By James Marks Realclearenergy.org

...Over the past decade, the U.S. oil and gas industry transformed our country's energy outlook—from dependence on foreign suppliers to becoming a supplier ourselves. In fact, last year the U.S. became a net-energy exporter for the first time in nearly 70 years.

That independence is not only good for American consumers, who benefit from access to affordable and reliable fuels...it is also critical to our national security interests. U.S. warplanes and battleships run on petroleum. Supply chains at home and abroad are carbon-powered. Modern defense technologies, like carbon-fiber vehicles, Kevlar body armor, even sophisticated computer chips, are made with products derived from fossil fuels. Carbon neutrality is aspirational but unattainable...Over the past ten years carbon emissions have been cut by 800 million tons—the largest reduction "in the history of energy."...To walk back the hard-won progress of the past decade would undermine our interests, at home and abroad, and leave our nation vulnerable.

* * * *

ET goes on, "Electrical grids damaged and off-line for periods of time, destruction not necessary. Interior supportive opposition climate activists in each country will implement effective stoppages, shortages. Energy supply reduction causes transportation, delivery, electrical infrastructure to fail."

"They are going to stop all those systems with a reduced supply of electrical energy. Grant opens up. "I don't see how that can be accomplished."

"Once electrical shortage implemented, recharging of electric dependent transportation system will stop society functioning." ET asks Grant, "Do you see how that can be done, possibilities?" Grant fires back with his implicit memory data knowledge base. "All those electric vehicle dependent systems will deplete their charge within hours. If available, the charging station lines could exceed miles since each recharging requires significantly longer time for a full capacity charge. Level 1 recharging replenishes two to five miles of range during one hour of charging." For EVs, MPH refers not to speed but to miles in distance or range that can be driven for a time charging. "Level 2, 240V 22-26 miles or MPH at a complete one hour charge, Level 3 fast charge at a roadside charging station, up to 300 mph. A 300-mile range. With a partial electric grid failure all categories are effectively without a fuel source. Time, as you're saying, is the Achille's heel. Time to refuel is the linchpin weak link. Man finds EVs are a liability with power grid rationing and recharging that takes, not hours, but days. Electrical over-dependency of those nations' functional recovery. Fossil fuel refilling take minutes, not hours or days. No source of portable electricity to battery powered vehicles, as you could with petroleum fuel, gas- or diesel-powered ones. As you say, no Jerry Can."

"Shit sounds like a mega goat-rope," Steve adds his sentiment. "Fossil fuel V-8 sounds pretty reasonable in that environment. Goat-rope."

"Goat-rope?" ET doesn't recognize the slang expression.

Steve just shakes his head. "Later, dude."

Grant taken off track, responds to Steve and ET, "More novel references or the movies?"

Data information chain links for ET, "Goat rope, slang, a confusing, disorganized situation often attributed to or marked by human error. A convoluted issue that is contested by many parties."

Steve goes on. "Time is the critical component, now Man would need it...there won't be any or enough. Waiting in line kills in a failed electrical dependent system."

"In actuality, it is a strategically subtle way to incapacitate an adversary without firing a shot conventional or otherwise. How do we stop, prevent it?" Grant is looking to ET for answers. "Can I, we assist in some way?" Grant, volunteers Steve who doesn't know what his brother is ranting about, "Whatever it takes." Grant has stepped into a void. He is eager yet unprepared for the task at hand. Conceptually, it is beyond his comprehension and capability. Unarmed and unprepared, knowledge-deficient, and dimension travel- training-wheeled non-proficient. What could go asunder, the entire Earth and humanity with it?

ET replies that Steve and Grant could be monitors after event-markers are initiated. However, "change agents would have other skill sets critical to successful implementation of Yogis."

"Okay, we are monitors .Who, then, are the change agents?" Grant thinks he has a unique qualification based upon his accelerated time compress knowledge and intelligence enhancement. His implicit memory is far beyond his human contemporaries. He can attain those items he doesn't have mastered with ET's mentoring. He is nearly panicked in his response, agitated to a near-hysterical state.

ET knows Grant is not prepared for the task, like Michael Nostradamus. Grant can't operate 500 years beyond his expertise. Quantum mechanics, quantum entanglement, mastery of dimensional travel are beyond his grasp.

ET responds. "You are in same position Nostradamus occupied." Proving a point, he asks Grant, "Define quantum foam?"

Grant has no clear answer, yet his Wikipedia implicit memory erupts with a knowledgeable definition that he doesn't totally comprehend: "Quantum foam or spacetime foam is the quantum fluctuation of spacetime on very small scales due to quantum mechanics. The idea was devised by John Wheeler in 1955. This fluctuation is the temporary random change in the amount of energy in a point in space." He says it but is functionally lost as to meaning. He is in Nostradamus's shoes. They don't fit.

Steve jumps in with a bit of background from his fiction reading list. "Would you say that in a form that I can understand? Michael Crichton wrote about that in one of his novels, "Timeline," I think. Time and dimension travel, worm holes."

Grant, still off track, responds with implicit memory cranking, "Crichton's research found: For billions of years after the Big Bang, the universe expanded as a sphere that contained galaxies clumped and clustered irregularly in the universe. The expanding sphere had incredibly small imperfections at sub atomic dimensions. These very small dimensions of spacetime have ripples. They are a roiling collection of virtual particles, collectively called quantum foam. According to quantum physicists, virtual particles exist briefly as fleeting fluctuations in the fabric of spacetime, like bubbles in beer foam. Quantum Entanglement or Interference."

ET mind-tending. "Correct depiction of concept in human definition. Not factually correct."

"Crichton's story is fiction, straight-out fiction." Steve pushes back, still seated in his lawn chair. On to another beer. "It is an account of time travel to the medieval 1300s.

A quantum computer system would use the quantum characteristics of individual electrons to compress a three-dimensional living object into an electron stream—direct transmission to another universe.

"Quantum mechanics," Grant begins, "is a fundamental theory in physics that provides a description of the physical properties of nature at the scale of atoms and subatomic particles. The photon is a type of elementary particle. It is the tiniest possible element of electromagnetic radiation. It is a unit of light that cannot break into smaller particles. They are massless, always move at the speed of light. Quantum entanglements exist when two particles act and react to one another across a span of light years. It is a system in multiple quantum states at the same time. A communication system at work that cannot be viewed by the naked eye that allows them to mirror each other regardless of their distance of separation. Quantum computing makes use of superposition and quantum entanglement to perform computations at a much higher speed far beyond contemporary computers. They cut years to a matter of seconds in solving complicated computational problems."

"Your Quantum computer concepts somewhat accurate, beyond human current knowledge." ET dampens Grant's knowledge data parade.

"I didn't get it when Creighton wrote it, still don't," Steve adds.

"Dimensional travel, arrive at another Wormhole-accessed universe...billions of miles away?" Grant reflects confidence, yet he knows only of dimensional travel.

Steve opens up. "You are not yet a qualified conductor. You have nowhere to go, lack knowledge of how to go, and don't know the operating language...you're dimensionally travel-blind." Steve is out of his element as well. "ET, help us out here. Clear up this fictional tale."

"Steve's correct." ET is referring to Grant's semi-conscious hint as to something more than monitors. "You have knowledge access beyond Nostradamus, functionally, to current environment."

"That's what I said." Steve jumps in. "Taking cartel money is simple; no explanation needed. Changing someone's direction of research is beyond unexplained cash withdrawals. Out of our element. Just like *Dirty Harry,* "*A* man's gotta know his limitations.'"

"Another movie reference, I assume?" Grant holds his hands up in surrender to his movie buff brother. "You need to get out more. Movies?"

"Clint Eastwood, Dirty Harry, 1973, *Magnum Force.* My kind of law enforcement guy." Steve takes a swig of his brew.

Grant can't provide the change agent incentive nor influence. Essentially his is, as ET is, an observer and recorder. Grant does have the vocabulary and understanding, not the connections.

ET brings the mystery to a close, a surprising one. "Eloit Maxwell is one."

Eloit Maxwell, the multi-billionaire? He is the one event-marked? He could buy a country with his money." A bit of unbelief for Grant. "Why him?"

ET responds with his awkward style from a data file, "Eloit Maxwell invested research heavily alternate energy generation sources in conjunction with private organization's planned exploration of Mars. Principle hold back, fuel and power source to support extended journey and settlement facility."

"Okay, so what?" Grant has a bit of a database reply of his own. "The success of his ME-Space vehicle venture are beyond cost-effective compared to NASA. He is known as an outlier maverick entrepreneur industrialist and far-sighted visionary. He does not fit the mold of those who came before. Some say he is a complete SOB with an incredible focus on task where others fail and fear to tread. Success and failure are not unknown to him and his ventures." In the end, Grant is aware of his record of real success.

"He is selected to discover process of cold-fusion an alternate fuel source beyond electrical generated currently in use."

"How and when is that going to happen?"

"Within days." ET is focused.

"He is the change agent? What criteria was used to select this guy?" Steve has an opinion of Eloit Maxwell that is less than flattering. "He's no Einstein."

"As you would say he does not *fit the mold.* He has a pattern that will be adjusted to achieve designed results." ET mind-tending to both. "Just as Einstein didn't fit the mold."

"Fit the mold?" Steve says. "From what I can recall he appears to be one arrogant son of a bitch. His business deals, his negotiating skills and personality, to say the least, are irritating."

Grant says, "Steve when you were in Vietnam flying combat what was the personality type of those who flew with you?"

"What the shit does that have anything to do with Maxwell?" Steve asks, thrown off by the question but answers anyway. "They had better be skilled, prepared, aggressive and determined to not fail."

"How about *flower-child like,* any of those flew with you?"

"Not many and not for long. They didn't last."

"Why not? Didn't you depend upon them for backup, got your back? That's what saved your ass from time to time...right?"

"It was right until they didn't, then they were never trusted again. Had to watch your own six. They didn't last." Steve remembers his combat narrow escapes. "Were we on the ground, they may have been fragged. You never know."

"So, those who you trusted your life with, were they top-notch category guys?"

"Quite a few of those top-notchers were sons of bitches in the extreme. They could be real assholes." Steve smiles at the recollection.

"Those were the SOB's you *didn't* want to fly with then, yes?"

"No, shit no. Those were the only SOB's I *would* fly with. We were a beer-drinking collection of MF'er SOBs. They, and I'm one of them, were who you could trust if your life depended on it, and it did more than once. Wouldn't have it any other way." Steve takes a swig from his beer in respect of all the SOB MF'ers he served with.

Grant seems to relate. "Worst time I had was working with a group of assholes, all fighter pilots. Couldn't get them to agree on most anything except how shit-hot they were. Arrogance beyond belief, presidents of their own fan club." Grant pauses to let his comments sink in with Steve.

"Beyond that, however, they are exactly the SOBs that I want flying those single-seat fighter aircraft into a dogfight fur-ball or triple-A, SAM-protected target-rich environment. Armed and unafraid, and kick-ass ready."

"Sounds familiar, different branch of the military." Steve takes another drink of beer.

Eloit Maxwell is an SOB right up your alley, then. He doesn't BS and does accomplish the mission. And he is incredibly loyal to his charges, employees; doesn't put up with weak decision-making. Takes the risk, personal risk. He's a leader and faces opposition from 'Point.' Does he seem to be your kind of guy?

Steve mulls it over. "Well, shit, he may be the right one, then."

"I'll drink to that. Cobra pilots, fighter pilots, Einstein, Maxwell, SOB's all." Grant takes a swig.

ET has been observing the banter. He is in wonder of the Fredericks brothers. Perhaps it's understanding and a touch of shared DNA.

"So, ET, how is the new change agent, Eloit Maxwell, going to Yogi the electric-generating landscape from a Chinese-Russian cabal in twenty-five years or sooner and build a settlement on Mars?" Grant asks.

"I would like to hear that as well." Steve chips in, looks in the cooler for another beer. "And while you're at it, climate change too? All ears."

ET responds, "Eloit Maxwell, Fibonacci, Da Vinci, Einstein, Nostradamus interaction was guided through suspended states of consciousness. Objective, intelligence expansion, seeding implicit memory, recall by visualization future concept subject matter. Logic pattern enhances and expanded—implanted conceptual solution for scalable alternate cold fusion energy generation and space operational energy. Concepts implemented gradually will change focus of electrical generated power to abundant level with reduced cost factor encountered and reduce by 57 percent carbon dioxide emissions. Scalable infrastructure suitable to majority of environments. Fully established earthwide by 2040."

* * * *

September, 26, 2021
San Diego Union-Tribune,
A blast into a clean energy future? Scientists tout nuclear fusion breakthrough Experiment using 192 lasers throws off more than 10 quadrillion watts of power.
by Rob Nikolewski

...The burst of energy threw off more than 10 quadrillion watts of fusion power — about 700 times the generating capacity of the country's electrical grid at a given moment. Fusion emits no greenhouse gases... "And you would assume if these power plants were then available around the globe, you would not have an energy crisis in any way. And development in poorer regions would then be possible..." Mike Farrell, vice president for Inertial Fusion Technology at General Atomics.

* * * *

January 19, 2022
San Diego Union-Tribune
Nuclear Fusion Device Updated
General Atomics 'powerful magnet part of research on
making commercial fusion power plants a reality
By Rob Nikolewski

After a shut down of nearly six months for upgrades, a powerful magnetic chamber on the campus of San Diego's General Atomics that is instrumental in the search to someday make nuclear fusion a practical source of energy is posed to restart operations.

* * * *

"What of the Chinese and Russian deception?" Steve asks.

"Abandoned with the advent of cold fusion technology. Climate enhancement a contributing factor."

"Mars, does that happen?" Grant is looking to the future.

"Initial success, followed by some loss."

"What loss?" From Steve.

"Mars failed landing configuration. Technical system error. Members lost to pressure exposure. Established living component successful. Twenty-three remain established. Conditions improving, greenhouse established, water source marginal." ET mind-tended.

"What's the future hold for them on Mars?" Grant is not confident. "After 2035?"

"Marginal, not viable to sustain life systems."

"Shit, I guess I was hoping for a better outcome," Grant says.

"How does Maxwell take it all in? He has fulfilled a dream to go there. Maybe start colonization for Man away from Earth.

"He is there. Will be." No expression from ET.

"On Mars? He goes there? When?" Grant waits.

"In 2035. His was the third arrival, after mishap."

"When does he return? To Earth?" Steve is still sitting, beer in hand. Maxwell just got his attention.

"He does not." ET knows it's by choice.

Steve ponders for a moment, "Got his wish. Here's to you," Steve hoists his beer in tribute, "You SOB, beautiful just fucking beautiful, that's a 1-0-9. Just made the code. He chose to stay. Bought his way to Mars."

"There were more than one event-markers you spoke of?" Grant is referring to ET.

"The Others are returning."

"So you say the Others are returning?" Steve in a moment of clarity. "From what I can determine the Others have never really left?"

ET answers, "There has been a presence on Earth for thousands of years."

"Yeah, a bunch of years. I suspect that your tenure here is short compared to those that preceded you—305 years is long enough to get your feet wet," Steve says.

ET caught without understanding "Your term, feet wet?" ET is asking for a human-like clarification, uncommon for him ever to ask.

Grant follows with a data chain, "A slow and simple way in order to become more familiar with a task. A gradual understanding of a concept, issue or problem."

"You are correct—there were different monitors prior. Feet became wet." Mind-tends to both, with an awkward human-like attempt to fit in.

"Holy crap. You can ruin a saying without trying." Steve is shaking his head and taking his seat. "What about the UFO's here, are they part of your operational system...they report to you or Others?"

"Observations you refer are not associated with monitor role. They are separate function."

"What is their function?" Grant asking.

"Scouts." ET refers to a term they can relate to in a broad sense.

"Scouts, you mean like military scouts or Indian scouts?" Steve is locked on now. He knows of army scouts in Vietnam, a vital resource in combat. "Little Big Horn-like scouts?"

"Purpose?" Grant asking.

"Evaluate interval capabilities of humankind." ET responds.

"Like observing war games, we both had them in the Army and Air Force. The Others are testing and observing our readiness at various intervals in time." Grant elaborates, "The Others determine our progress toward an expected potential outcome. We are the game pieces in a real-life evolutionary process. Play on."

"Yeah, are they setting us up, evaluating our weaknesses?" Steve doesn't like being spied upon. In Vietnam, it was critical to conceal information and operational capabilities. Steve and Grant saw the bloody results of being unprepared or surprised. They will see it again in the near future.

"With the Others, there is no place to hide." Grant says with acceptance. "By time travel they have control with event-markers and Yogis. They can end-run Man to several end events, including extinction."

"Are they, the UFOs, armed? Bring Man to a sixth extinction, that seems hostile?" Steve wonders aloud.

ET mind-tending. "There is no hostile intent."

"Who are the pilots, AI, ETs or Others?" Grant asks.

"In your terms, 'lab monitors,' AI levels near SAM. Compare, record data of other-dimensional locations."

* * *

December 8, 2020
Former head of Israeli Space Security Program says extraterrestrial aliens have made contact with mankind but will remain hidden until humanity is ready
Tim Sticking for Mailonline

An Israeli space official has claimed that aliens are real and secretly in contact with America and Israel - but are keeping their existence quiet because humanity 'isn't ready.' Haim Eshed, who was head of Israel's space security programme for nearly 30 years and is a retired general said aliens are real and secretly in contact with America and Israel. He claimed the aliens will not come into the open until humanity 'evolves'...

* * * *

May 30, 2021
Skeptics: UFO Videos May Have Mundane Origins,
Andrew Dyer

SAN DIEGO —An exposé on 60 Minutes. A 12,000-word treatise in the New Yorker.... The coverage of Navy videos purporting to show evidence of strange, unknown aircraft has featured the voices of so-called ufologists — UFO researchers...The UAP Task Force's examination of unidentified phenomenon is ongoing...

* * * *

June 4, 2021
San Diego Union-Tribune
U.S. Finds No Evidence of Alien Technology in Flying Objects,
but Can't Rule It Out, Either
Julian E. Barnes
Helene Cooper

A new report concedes that much about the observed phenomena remains difficult to explain, including their acceleration, as well as ability to change direction and submerge.

WASHINGTON — American intelligence officials have found no evidence that support alien spacecraft.

* * * *

"In our war games," Grant says, "we always received a critique of positive and negative features to continue, or those to change. Both Steve and I saw people fired as a result of marginal results. What are the results of the UFO scouts, what did they report?"

"Man is not the apex life form," ET replies. "Not at the apex of existence."

"What, meaning...we are expendable? I know we are at a significant lower level of development than you and the Others. We do have some worth to consider. To saving, keeping around?" Grant is at a low point with his interaction with ET.

"Mankind is a paradox of contradiction. High level of potential, sustained with self-inflicted shortcomings," ET continues, "Man can be and is influenced to diverted illogical reasoning patterns. Power and strengths are paramount without regard to outcome. Man can and does deceive...to eager acceptance of flawed results."

"You are the guardian of mankind? You used an event-marker to continue the structure of Man's survival with Einstein." Grant is pressing. "Without it, Man's survival would have been perhaps altered. Another marker long before 2035, Eloit Maxwell is guided to cold fusion and electrical subsistence worldwide."

ET replies, "Decisions improved climate, survival for a time. Unintended consequences from byproduct of Manhattan Project research. Einstein involved in clear-sighted policy implementation, results detrimental in future events."

Grant saw ET's mind-tended words, clearly repeated, a word-for-word statement, from an earlier knowledge session referring to climate on Earth. Why? He can't read ET's mind; Grant wonders where ET is taking him. With his implicit data-accessed memory, he repeats his earlier answer. "You are saying the project of nuclear development was *far-sighted,* yet resulted in *unintended consequences.* Mankind has a habit of implementing those choices that tend to routinely effect an opposite detrimental outcome."

"Correct, Einstein's involvement in the Manhattan Project. Detrimental outcome."

"I don't know of what you speak. The Manhattan project researched, developed and produced the first nuclear weapons, the A-bomb. Einstein's involvement was instrumental in that success and contributed to the end of World War II, saved upwards of a million lives by no invasion of the Japanese islands."

ET mind-tends Grant to search further his implicit memory. "Correct, access data C8 to complete scenario."

Grant is dumbstruck by his Wikipedia data findings. "Perfluorooctanoic acid PFOA, also known colloquially as C8, is a product used worldwide as an industrial surfactant in chemical processes and as a material feedstock. It is a product of health concern, subject to regulatory action and voluntary industrial phase-outs." The C8 data has no context for Grant, and it is not clear what it has to do with Einstein's research.

"Access data to include DuPont Teflon," ET suggests.

Grant's implicit memory data spills out. "C8 was first produced in conjunction with the 1940s nuclear weapon Manhattan Project for use in gaseous diffusion barriers in uranium enrichment. The chemical was later used in DuPont's production of Teflon and other household products. Teflon is used in waterproof clothing, stain resistant carpets, nonstick pans, fast food wrappers, and a large menu of other products. DuPont's internal corporate research found in the 1960s that C8 was toxic to animals and discovered in the 1970s a high concentration in the blood of its factory workers. A corporate study in 2007 found that C8 was in the blood of 99.7 percent of all humans. It is known as a "forever chemical" because it never fully degrades. Later research determined C8 can be found in the blood of nearly every living creature on Earth. C8 is linked to six or more possible conditions: testicular cancer, kidney cancer, thyroid disease, ulcerative colitis, pregnancy-induced hypertension, birth defects and high cholesterol. DuPont exposed the Earth's environment extensively to C8 by disposal and manufacturing methods: burning exhaust, landfill leaching, and tributary disposal water systems for 70 years."

Steve cannot hide his anger with his fellow Man; he kicks his lawn chair off the Oval toward Sagittarius. As usual, it returns at his feet. "It was an operational necessity to defoliate the jungle foliage with a cancer inducing chemical substance. That was the BS they fed all of us." Steve and Grant were exposed to Agent

Orange in Vietnam. Steve flew and lived in a targeted area near the DMZ. His exposure was much higher than Grant's. He had prostate cancer surgery several years ago. He also had bone cancer near stage three when he was first introduced to ET. The ET lab environment systems automatically screened and detected genetic abnormalities and substances including cancers. Steve's prostate cancer was suppressed in conjunction with the aerosol drug used for advanced learning. Steve was and is still unaware of the alien system's curative features. He had suspicions and far fewer symptoms.

Both Steve and Grant blame humanity's hidden factors, the inhumanity of Man, and his boundless brutality.

Grant finishes his data input. "Einstein brought both good and evil to Man's attention. Atomic weapon development spun off a supporting production agent of C8. Saved lives one way and unknowingly opened an avenue for corporate profit incentive to take others with a toxic agenda. Bhopal, Chernobyl, Love Canal, Seveso are just a few of the names that have entered the lexicon of devastation wrought by the foolishness of mankind. Ecological travesties afflict the seas: the dead zone at the foot of the Mississippi River, the Exxon Valdez or the North Pacific Gyre. Other disasters we have engineered intentionally: Hiroshima and Nagasaki. Land mines. No one can change history, but how have we learned from the past? Are the laws named after these disasters effective? And is there a lesson here that can change our path into the future?" Grant generates an accompanied holographic depiction listing manufactured environmental and war's carnal damage brought on by mankind in the past 100 years:

Gulf oil spill: 2010
Picher, Oklahoma, lead contamination: 1967-2009
Exxon Valdez oil spill: 1989
Tennessee coal ash spill: 2008
Libby asbestos contamination: 1919-1990
 Pacific garbage patch 100 million tons: 2010
Love Canal: 1920-1978

CONSIDER MAN

Dust bowl: 1930-1940
Tuskegee experiment on Black Americans: 1932-1972
Three-mile Island: 1979
Gulf dead zone...current
Poison Minamata Bay Japan: 1923-1968
Ecocide in Vietnam, Agent Orange: 1961-1971
Dying oceans...krill depletion: Ongoing
Amazon logging, farming, cattle, roads. ongoing

Last 100 years
35 Wars
500+ million dead
"I know not with what weapons World War III will be fought, but World War IV will be fought with sticks and stones."
—Attributed to Albert Einstein

1891-1937: Boxer Rebellion, Russo-Japanese, War, Mexican Revolution, World War I, Armenian Genocide, Russian Revolution, Chinese Civil War, Holocaust.

1933-1962: Holocaust, World War II, Cold War, French Indochina War, Korean War, French-Algerian War, Cuban Revolution,

1963-2021: Vietnam War, Six-Day War, Soviet-Afghan War, Iran-Iraq War, Persian Gulf War, Rwandan Civil War-genocide, Third Balkan War, Kosovo conflict, Afghanistan War, Iraq War.

* * * *

The holographic display depicts each event in vivid reality for Steve and Grant, sitting in their lawn chairs, beers in hand, stunned by the statical nightmare ET has conjured by Grant's implicit memory. "Is that why the Others are returning?" Grant is searching for reasons and answers.

"Man has no unified identity, competing species variation of power, control, disunity." ET mind-tends as if providing evidence. "Current and future factors evaluation."

351

"Are you saying that they come as an inspection team to give Man an evaluation?" Grant attempts to find context to understand.

"It's an Inspector General (IG) inspection, a readiness evaluation...we both had them in the military." Steve is familiar with them. "Make or break a career. The Army had some real assholes on their teams. Some desk jockeys all saying, 'We're here to help.' That is a 1-0-8."

"Chill, Steve. Had my share of them: some good, some not; fired a commander I had in Michigan. Booted him because of aircraft maintenance issues."

"Are they concerned about the climate changes threatening the Earth?" Grant wonders in light of the plans for cold fusion discovery.

"Will evaluate climate of the human condition. Extinction event ongoing for the past 11,000 years. End event." Factual reporting from ET.

"That is some hell of an IG inspection." Steve steps in. "We are being evaluated and don't know it's been ongoing for thousands of years. That is BS, ET. How are we expected to survive an extinction event if we don't know it's ongoing?" Steve pauses. "Although, maybe we should have known."

"The future of our climate is going to be altered with a positive cold fusion outcome," Grant says, "just in 20 or so years. CO_2 reduction is significant; it has to have an impact for our climate."

ET clarifies. "What you say is true regarding Earth's climate, cold fusion."

"I am really confused. If cold fusion is a turning point for Earth what is the need for an extinction event?" Steve asks, though Grant may know why.

"They are not concerned with Earth's climate; they seek change to the climate of the human condition. Man is on the chopping block, not CO_2 generation." Grant sees a pothole-filled avenue of future change events.

Steve is silent as he looks beyond the Oval. "Why?" he says, looking at ET.

"Man is not essential. Earth's climate will survive without Man, may be damaged by him. Cannot take place." ET mind-tending both. "Fractured human existence leading to climate destruction, Man is not required. Human condition in climate structure, flawed premise. Long-term result impacts climate and all species survival. Failure, extinction event follows to conclusion, 40 years."

Grant, recognizes a reasonable conclusions within ET's logic. It makes no sense to him. Yet, he knows the story as it replays in his mind.

Grant points to ET. "You are saying that this nation or other nations on Earth are proceeding to a condition of a totalitarian state?" He takes a breath and continues, "You have evidence of that? I don't see it."

"The evidence to come, next ten years. By 2020, visible shift to violations of freedom of expression, totalitarian leadership, population surveillance, ethnic confinement, termination. Nuclear armament enhanced, poised for use by 2025, many nations with unstable leadership. ET goes on, Hitler was one, now more followed, many nuclear arsenals. Government leaders reflect, non-rational logic prevails. Use cannot be allowed, destruction substantially consequential for Earth's environment."

"Evidence, ET, show and tell?" Steve pipes in; he sees a future he doesn't want to be part of.

ET knows and mind-tends to Steve and Grant a database-generated forecast and description of events to follow. "Nations increased nuclear capabilities and military presence structure. Institutes internment of religious minority, bans religious practice and language. Your term: practice of racism and ethnic cleansing. North Korea, Iran confident in nuclear development with intent to initiate provocation and influence-driven threat negotiations."

* * * *

January 4, 2021
Iran ramps up uranium enrichment and seized tanker as tensions rise with US.
By Rob Picheta, Ramin Mostaghim and Mostafa Salem, CNN

Tehran (CNN) Iran announced Monday that it had resumed enriching uranium to 20% purity, far beyond the limits laid out in the 2015 nuclear deal, in a move likely to further escalate tensions with the United States...

* * * *

April 16, 2021
San Diego Union-Tribune
Iran starts enriching uranium to 60%, its highest level ever
Nation-World
By Jon Gambrell AP

DUBAI, United Arab Emirates — Iran began enriching uranium Friday to its highest-ever purity, edging close to weapons-grade levels...

* * * *

November. 4, 2021
San Diego Union-Tribune
China Military Power Report Highlights
Concern over 'Taiwan Contingency'
By Abraham Mahshie

The Pentagon's new report on Chinese military power released Nov. 3 highlights a 2027 military modernization milestone that positions China for "credible military operations" against Taiwan...

* * * *

May 24, 2021
San Diego Union-Tribune
Official: Iran Nuke Inspector Deal Ended
Associated press

TEHRAN, Iran (AP) — Iran's hard-line parliament speaker said Sunday a temporary deal between Tehran and international inspectors to preserve surveillance images taken at nuclear sites had ended, escalating tensions amid diplomatic efforts to save the Islamic Republic's atomic accord with world powers...

CONSIDER MAN

* * * *

December 3, 2021
Russia planning massive military offensive against Ukraine
involving 175,000 troops, U.S. intelligence warns
An unclassified U.S. intelligence document on Russian
military movement.
(Obtained by The Washington Post) By Shane Harris and Paul
Sonne
As tensions mount...U.S. intelligence has found the Kremlin is
planning a multi-front offensive as soon as early next year
involving up to 175,000 troops,.."The Russian plans call for a
military offensive against Ukraine as soon as early 2022...

* * * *

January 15, 2022
North Korea is testing hypersonic weapons.
Should the West be worried?
Scott Neuman, NPR, Twitter
Korean Central News Agency/AP
The U.S., Russia, and China all have them. And now, North
Korea claims to as well: hypersonic weapons...If fully realized,
the new capability could present a significant challenge to U.S.
and South Korean-based missile defense systems.

* * * *

"What of China? If North Korea and Iran are acting up, China
surely has to be involved in some capacity," Steve, who does not
trust the Chinese, chimes in to get ET's attention. "They were
principal backers of the North Vietnamese during the Vietnam
war."

ET responds. "The Chinese have interest in denigrating your
nation's electrical grid dependency. Intent to disrupt functioning
of Western nations. Reduce fossil fuel dependency."

Grant steps in. "We know that Russia and the Chinese are
colluding to affect the economic structure of the Western world
via dependency of electrical infrastructure and its failure—
resulting in greater power and influence for both of those

355

nations. Dramatically increasing their strategic goals to control both by economic and military power into the foreseeable future." ET and the Fredericks boys know establishing a worldwide Sino-Soviet totalitarian state could be catastrophic to the West. Any recovery from such circumstances would be nearly impossible with the surrender and acceptance of the Western world to electrical dependence vulnerability. Marxist–Leninist-Maoism reign supreme.

"You stopped that scheme with Eloit Maxwell and cold fusion, right?" Steve looks for reassurance from ET.

"Correct, that portion of strategy dominance is forestalled. Replaced by another from the Chinese," ET mind-tends.

"Shit, what replacement strategy?" Grant and Steve are thinking the same thing.

MAN 27

Autumn 2003
Setting The Stage
* * * *
2004
**THE SARS EPIDEMIC AND ITS AFTERMATH IN
CHINA:
A POLITICAL PERSPECTIVE**
Yanzhong Huang
Affiliations
John C. Whitehead School of Diplomacy and International
Relations, Seton Hall
University. Adapted from The Politics of China's SARS Crisis.
Harvard Asia Quarterly
In November 2002, a form of a typical pneumonia called severe
acute respiratory syndrome (SARS) began spreading rapidly
around the world, prompting the World Health Organization
(WHO) to declare the ailment "a worldwide health threat." At the
epicenter of the outbreak was China.... the epidemic caught
China, at first, unprepared to defeat the disease...it caused the
most severe socio-political crisis for the Chinese leadership since
the 1989 Tiananmen crackdown...Soon after, the illness
developed into an epidemic in Hong Kong, which proved to be a
major international transit route for SARS.

* * * *

The results of SARS experienced by the Chinese government resulted in chaos for its economic and social structure. Entrenched bureaucrats 'glacial response forestalled any meaningful counter measure to SARS. However, the Chinese learned from that epidemic in the next 15 years of research and gene editing, how to export it to others. To the U.S. and Western world, to crash and weaken those systems, by a SARS outbreak. Affectively, the Chinese embraced the Chaos Theory and exported or proposed to export a virulent virus as a weaponized assault on Western nations.

* * * *

May 9, 2021
(ANI) updated report. 18:23:59 hours
Chinese scientists discussed weaponizing SARS coronaviruses,
5 years before pandemic: Report
https://www.aninews.in/news/world/asia

A document written by Chinese scientists and health officials in 2015 states that SARS coronaviruses were a "new era of genetic weapons" that could be "artificially manipulated" into an emerging human disease virus, then weaponized and unleashed, reported Weekend Australian.

...World War Three would be fought with biological weapons. The document revealed that Chinese military scientists were discussing the weaponization of SARS coronaviruses five years before the Covid-19 pandemic. The report by Weekend Australian was published in news.com.au.

* * * *

June 4, 2021
Wuhan Biolab Leak Theory Revives Concern
about CCP China's Biowarfare Program
americandefensenews.com| Paul Crespo

The theory that the COVID-19 pandemic began as an accidental leak from a BSL-4 biolab at the Wuhan Institute of Virology (WIV) in China has gained new found traction…The release of

Dr. Anthony Fauci's emails has only fueled controversy about why the leak theory was so aggressively suppressed...

While this current COVID-19 novel corona virus may not have been an engineered bioweapon, it should still focus attention on China's very real, clandestine, offensive biowarfare research program...

The U.S. Air Force Air University (AU) just published a study this month that acknowledged China's offensive biowarfare capabilities... "that China likely possesses a covert biological weapons program, but the extent of that program remains unknown to the public."...Today, it is likely that China's current dual-use infrastructure acts as the basis for its offensive biological capability." The Chinese military have at least 50 laboratories and hospitals being used as biological weapons research facilities.

* * * *

To the brothers' question about a "replacement strategy" for China's conquest of the West, ET replies: "Strategy introduction of coronavirus to your population and Western nations."

"Bastards," Grant fumes. "When is it going to happen?"

"In 2019."

"How many die, how effective is it?" Both brothers are wondering about family.

"Over three million die. Your country one million. Disrupts economic structure worldwide 24 of your months." ET reports without emotion.

"How was it delivered? Was it by military methods, an act of war?" Serious shit now.

* * * *

May 9, 2021
Faucian Bargain
The most powerful and dangerous bureaucrat in American history p50-51
Posthillpress.com
by Steve Deace and Todd Erzen

"In this important book the authors do the job our un-inquisitive media has failed to do throughout this ordeal. Confirming with cited and sourced details the enemy of both liberty and logic the lockdowns have proven to be. Which also proves too much power in the hands of an unelected bureaucrat, regardless of his intentions, can no longer be our new normal." —U.S. Senator Rand Paul (R-KY)

* * * *

June 15, 2021
More evidence suggests COVID-19
was in US by Christmas 2019
Study: Seven people infected before first U.S. case identified
By Mike Stobbe AP

A new analysis of blood samples from 24,000 Americans taken early last year is the latest and largest study to suggest that the corona virus popped up in the U.S. in December 2019 — weeks before cases were first recognized by health officials.... A CDC-led study published in December 2020 that analyzed 7,000 samples from American Red Cross blood donations suggested the virus infected some Americans as early as the middle of December 2019.

* * * *

COVID-19, ET explains, came to the U.S. "By your transportation system, commercial aircraft, by infected carriers. Students traveling within countries of shared education systems."

"Passengers from China?" Steve asks.

"Positive carriers arrive throughout your world. Spread virus."

"Shit, the Chinese Communist Party weaponized their own people, young people. Sent the virus worldwide? Intentional?" Not hard for Steve to believe. "Son of a bitch, they read Clancy's novel."

"What are you talking about?" Grant is not happy about another novel reference from Steve's reading list. "Really, a novel reference now? Jesus. Stow it."

Pushing back confidently, Steve says, "I read, *Executive Orders*, 1996, Tom Clancy. It's the same story line. The Iranians and Iraqis form a United Islamic Republic after years of war and join together to develop a weaponized airborne Ebola variant highly contagious and deadly. An aerosol weapon disguised as a shaving cream dispenser. Victims bleed to death from the inside out in about ten days; very painful and ugly death. Their agents, posing as airlines passengers, fly undetected worldwide to dispense the Ebola pathogen. Some real shitty stuff." Steve is concerned about the China intentions with Covid variant in ten years, in 2020, and how to stop it.

"Well how does Clancy stop the spread? What's the cure for Ebola?" Grant says, pressing the novelist researcher.

"There is no cure for Ebola, then or now." ET mind-tends.

"You read the Clancy novel?" Grant glares at ET.

"Referred to Clancy Ebola data fiction." ET replies. "Significant research by Clancy. Ebola was and is an infectious disease, started from a single source. There is a first victim, called Patient Zero, viral material then spread to and by others."

ET quotes from Clancy. "Bio war...at the strategic level means starting a chain reaction within your target population. You try to infect as many people as possible...And that's not very many; we're not talking nuclear war here. The idea is for the people, the victims, to spread it for you. That's the elegance of bio-warfare. Your victims actually do most of the killing. Any epidemic starts slow and ramps up, slowly at first, like a tangential curve, and then it rockets up geometrically. So, if using bio in the offensive role, you try to jump-start it by infecting as large a number of people as you can, and you opt for people who travel."

"You actually read the book, ET?" Steve is impressed with ET's reading list, adding, "It was a nun working in Sudan as a nurse. She caught it and was used as a guinea pig host to propagate a large supply of infectious material for aerosol canisters before she died. It's a very ugly painful death."

"So, how did Clancy stop the spread?" Grant asks.

"Getting there." Steve makes a bow to ET, his newfound reading list buddy. "ET, you want to fill in the method here?"

ET complies: "Clancy in his novel used convention sites with the convention attendees infected and then traveling by air to all corners of the United States and other parts of the world."

Steve takes over. "In the novel, knowing the convention connection, President Ryan and staff figured the only way to contain the epidemic is to shut down all places of assembly: theaters, shopping malls, sports stadiums, business office, everything. He also stops interstate travel." Steve takes a breath and goes on. "The Chinese intent is not to use overt warfare and weapons, it is rather to bring the United States to collapse from its own doing and restrictions regarding business, travel, interstate commerce, etc, etc. Their intent is to disable the United States from within, using our Constitution and laws to prevent an unconstitutional restriction on travel and commerce. It's right out of the Clancy playbook. Son of a bitch, those clever bustards."

ET offers a conclusion. "The Chinese purpose weakening American interests and reshaping world into their own design. China directly develops COVID and spread to the world by air passengers. They would retain their trade and respect as a super power and influence over American policy—If they weren't found out."

"What other gifts should we be wary of from China?" Grant poses.

"Virus sent to cripple economy structure and social discourse. Loss of confidence in Western nations 'stability." ET mind-tends.

"So are the Chinese planning or working toward specific goals—world domination, for instance?" Grant asks.

"Their intention clear for past years."

"What does that mean?" Steve blurts. "Are they planning a military operation?"

ET replies, "Expanded economic structure to detriment of competing nation-states. Material resources controlled to accelerated industrial output. Limited competition pressure. Environmental impact detrimental worldwide. Challenged to restrain future outcome. Focus on economic and military strength as measuring metric. Flawed conclusion. Detrimental consequences for humanity's existence approaches with haste."

CONSIDER MAN

* * * *

May 6, 2021
By Rhodium Group Report

Based on our newly updated estimates for 2019,..China alone contributed 27% of total global emissions, and the US—the 2nd highest emitter—contributed 11%.

The report was so damning that even far-left climate activist Greta Thunberg slammed China on Twitter, essentially saying that China will ruin the world unless they cut emissions.

"Yes, China is still categorized as a developing nation by WTO, they manufacture a lot of our products and so on. But that's of course no excuse for ruining future and present living conditions. We can't solve the climate crisis unless China drastically changes course," Thunberg tweeted.

* * * *

May 9, 2021
China's Emissions Exceeded Those Of All Other Developed Nations Combined: Report
By Ryan Saavedra • DailyWire.com

A new report released late week found that communist China's greenhouse gas emissions in 2019 were higher than the rest of the developed world combined. The report was published by the Rhodium Group, a leading independent research provider that specializes in matters involving China, energy & climate, India, and economics....the report said. "China's emissions were less than a quarter of developed country emissions in 1990, but over the past three decades have more than tripled, reaching over 14 gigatons of CO2-equivalent in 2019."

* * * *

October 18, 2021
China Power Struggle – But Not The One You Think!
Self-Reliancecentral.com
By Kelly

China may have to set aside its ambitious plans to cut carbon emissions — at least in the short term — in order to tide over its worsening power crisis, said analysts, says CNBC. Boosting coal supply cannot be a permanent solution to address the power shortages, given the need to reduce carbon emissions over the long term, said Morgan Stanley. *(Yeah, right!)*....CNBC has fallen for the BS from the CCP over China's emission-cutting plans. It doesn't have any.... Instead some towns are seeing as much as 80% reduction in power availability. Cue the coal industry!

* * * *

November 4, 2021
Global Carbon Dioxide Emissions Near 2019 Levels
World has seen a dip during lockdowns from pandemic
By Seth Borenstrein, AP
Glasgow Scotland

The dramatic drop in carbon dioxide emissions from the pandemic lockdown has pretty much disappeared in a puff of coal fired smoke, much of it from China, a new scientific study found...China's jump was mostly from burning coal and natural gas...In addition...China's lockdown ended far earlier than the rest of the world, so the Country had longer to recover economically and put more carbon into the air.

* * * *

Another Shoe to Drop
ET adds somewhat solemnly, "Earth numerous threat jeopardy, environmental damage, nuclear weapon, and social divergence with no clear direction of resolution. Sixth Extinction remains active possible alternative, solution by *Others*."

Grant and Steve look on in stunned silence.

ET continues, "Nation-sponsored terrorism, military force, nuclear and bio weapons, carbon pollution. Terror groups, religious and cultural driven conflicts, racial discord, and distrust. Genetic-driven gene manipulation and editing alter humankind to the detriment of some and advantage to others." ET ends. attribution list of concern for Man's continued existence. "Change required."

* * * *

"Well, that about covers the end-of-the-world scenario: the Sixth Extinction by possible nuclear device." Steve is somewhat at a loss. He is up and pacing, searching the cosmic heavens beyond the Oval, hoping to find answers.

Grant waits for more. "Religion, culture, terrorism, bio-weapons and climate with an unknown apparent capstone of gene editing of which we know nothing. Super elite humans on the way. Terrific; where can I get off this train wreck?" Grant leaves his lawn chair, focusing somewhere beyond the Oval edge.

"Isn't there any good news, positive events produced by Man? Is it all that bad?" Steve looks for a redeeming feature, get credit for something.

"Vaccine developed 2020 to protect against Corona viral effects accomplished in rapid time. Many lives saved." ET adds. He knows the vaccine is moderately successful. However, people will still contract the virus and die.

"How did that happen? Viral research takes years to perfect?" Grant asks.

"Your leader instituted a concentrated response structure. Less than year to usable vaccine." ET Mind-tended. "67-75% effective."

"Was that leader you speak of the president of our nation?" Steve knows who that would be or thinks he does.

"Correct."

"I know who it was or will be."

"ET, don't tell him, let's see how accurate his guessing is." Grant knows they haven't taken Dragonfly into that future point in time; mostly, they've traveled back years into Mexico for cash fundings. He has a bit of an attitude and data overdose at present. No games.

Steve is eager to foretell. "Grant, you should know it too. Remember this politician has always wanted to be president to set a precedent for others. A senator, secretary of state, wealthy, a very popular Democrat. She has run before. My money is on, rather I know it's Clinton—Hillary Clinton finally makes it. Correct, ET?"

"Well, you're sure of that prediction then?" Grant says. "It will be the 2016 election. She won, rather, if she wins, I know Billy-boy Clinton is a happy camper back at intern heaven. Wonder how that's gonna work. More BJs at the White House?" Grant shakes his head, turning for a lawn chair ringside.

ET confirms an accurate portion of Steve's choice, "Candidate Clinton received more than three million votes than opponent." Factually correct. Steve doesn't ask about Electoral College results. Minor details. ET knows there is a factual error and waits to see how the issue unfolds. His human DNA's curiosity steps in.

"Shit, yeah, it was her time." Steve wasn't a real fan but a realist when it came to politics and politicians. "Don't know how effective she's gonna be, but sounds like she nailed the Corona virus vaccine research. She must have kicked some butt to get it done early. Now she'll get some respect maybe."

Grant asks ET, who is standing watching the Fredericks brother interact regarding political actions. "Who was Clinton's opponent it the election. I'll guess it was another of the Bush's, the Florida guy: Jim, James, Judd, something?"

"Donald Trump." ET relays straightforwardly.

"Wow, that's a shocker. I never would have guessed that." Grant ponders.

"Wait a minute," Steve says, "are we talking about the Donald Trump, *The Apprentice* show Trump, New York real estate rich guy, likes to fire people on the air—that Donald Trump? He is a complete SOB ass hole...runs for president. I bet Hillary kicked his butt. Beat him in a landslide. Democrats love the Clintons. Forgave Bill for all his shit in office. Interns love the guy. Though he is an asshole as well, more than likely well qualified as a dirty old Man." Steve drifts off in thought, swigs some beer.

"We were just talking about assholes the other day," Grant notes. "You flew with a few and so did I. Remember the guys 'got your six'—those MF'ers,"

"Yeah, I do, so what's your point?"

"I think 'the Donald 'is in the category with fighter and cobra pilots. He is unafraid: arrogant, confident, takes charge, and kicks ass along the way. Wouldn't hang out with the guy most likely, but I'd want him at my six. I'd buy a round of drinks with him, like fighter pilots MF'ers. He would cover your six."

Steve responds, not quite yet out of his political stupor. "If he ran for president, must have appealed to some MF'ers? Got the nomination over other assholes."

Grant recalls, "I think Oprah asked him if he would run for president someday. So, I guess he will."

" Gonna lose though. It's a tough business." Steve remarks, "It'll be interesting to watch in six years. Could lay on some bets, make some money."

"Yeah, it will be interesting."

ET knows the future as it is supposed to play out. Steve and Grant learn from a condensed version of data-related material. Nation-states are strengthened and further institutionalized throughout the bureaucracy and the military. There is a focus upon the destruction of institutional features of existing societal foundations, freedom of speech, the individual, law and order, family. A redefining of gender to a menu of ever-evolving choices. There is a coming social structural war on women, regulated to label definitions, leading to women being obsolete as a gender.

* * * *

March 31, 2021
CNN

"It's not possible to know a person's gender identity at birth, and there is no consensus criteria for assigning sex at birth."

* * * *

Imprimis
June/July 2021 Vol 50, Number 6/7
Gender Ideology Run Amok
Abigail Shrier

Author, *Irreversible Damage: The Transgender Craze Seducing Our Daughters*
The following is adapted from a speech delivered on April 27, 2021, in Franklin, Tennessee, at a Hillsdale College National Leadership Seminar.

The Assault on Women's Sports and Safe Spaces

No discussion of gender ideology can ignore the ongoing movement to eradicate girls 'and women's sports and protective spaces...This movement promotes dangerous bills like the Equality Act, which would make it illegal ever to distinguish between biological men and women—and thus to exclude a biological male from a girls 'sports team or a women's protective space, whether it be a restroom, locker room, or prison.

* * * *

September 11, 2021
UN chief: World is at `pivotal moment 'and must avert crises

By Edith M. Lederer
Associated Press/apnews.com

The U.N. chief said the world's nations and people must reverse today's dangerous trends and choose "the breakthrough scenario...immediate action is needed to protect the planet's "most precious" assets from oceans to outer space, to ensure it is livable...including measures to reduce strategic risks from nuclear weapons, cyber warfare and lethal autonomous weapons, which Guterres called one of humanity's most destabilizing invention..."We must make lying wrong again," Guterres said.

* * * *

October 22, 2021
Putin Warns Wokeness Is Destroying The West: It Happened In Russia, It's Evil, It Destroys Values

By Ryan Saavedra Daily Wire.com

Russian President Vladimir Putin slammed during a speech on Thursday the far-left woke ideology that he said is causing societal ills throughout the Western world, saying that it is no different than what happened in Russia during the 1917 revolution...the Bolsheviks followed the dogmas of Marx and Engels....

The proponents of new approaches go so far as they want to eliminate the whole notions of men and women, and those who dare say that men and women exist and this is a biological fact, they are all but banished...instead of breast milk, you say human milk.

* * * *

October 26, 2021
Bad News: How Woke Media Is Undermining Democracy
By Batya Ungar-Sargon
Encounter Books, 2021
A Review
Something is wrong with American journalism...That's because the majority of our mainstream news is no longer just liberal; it's woke...*Bad News* explains how this happened, why it happened, and the dangers posed by this development if it continues unchecked.

* * * *

November 10, 2021
The Abolition of Sex: How the "Transgender" Agenda Harms Women and Girls
Amazon.com By Kara Dansky
The so-called "transgender" agenda is a misogynistic assault on the rights, privacy, and safety of women and girls—and is being fueled by a massive, vicious, and well-funded industry...This book shines a light on the truth about "gender identity," the "transgender" agenda, the very real threats that they pose to all of society—specifically to the rights, privacy, and safety of women and girls—and what the global Women's Human Rights Campaign is doing to fight back.

* * * *

December 7, 2021
Biological Man Claims to be transgender Beats Entire Team of Females During College Women's Swim Meet

By Jerry Anderson - Own work, Matthew Williams - Politics - americanactionnews.com, AAN

As The Daily Wire reports:

Over the weekend, a swimmer from the University of Pennsylvania who swam competitively for the men's team for three years before switching to the women's team, destroyed the biological women in the competition, winning the 1650 free by a gargantuan 38 seconds ahead of the young woman finishing second,...Her results in all three races set new Penn records along with meet and pool records," Outkick reported.

* * * *

March 19, 2022
DailyWire.com
Marked By Simmering Resentment Over Biologically Male Trans Swimmer, NCAA Women's Swimming Championships Conclude
By Mary Margaret Olohhan

"I try to ignore it as much as I can," said Lia Thomas. "I try to focus on my swimming, what I need to do to get ready for my races."

ATLANTA — The NCAA Women's Swimming Championship wrapped up Saturday evening, accentuated by rumblings in the deep over fairness in women's sports and the inclusion of a biologically male swimmer in female races...the athlete also is broad shouldered and clearly has a male anatomy...it is "a sad day for the sport."

* * * *

March 21, 2022
Nation & World News
Babylon Bee names Dr. Rachel Levine 'Man of the Year, ' gets Twitter suspension
By Claudia Dimuro - cdmureo@pennlive.com

The article reads as if Levine—who is a trans woman—is the actual recipient of the Bee's "first annual Man of the Year" title.

CONSIDER MAN

December 21, 2021
Elon Musk
Sits Down With The Babylon Bee CEO
(partial transcript)

RED ALERT: this is not a joke. Elon Musk sat down with Babylon Bee CEO Seth Dillon, EIC Kyle Mann, and Creative Director Ethan Nicolle for an in-depth interview on wokeness, Elizabeth Warren, taxing the rich, the Metaverse, which superhero Elon would be, and how the left is killing comedy.

Musk pointed to what he called "arguably one of the biggest threats to modern civilization." That is, wokeness. You've mentioned that wokeness, like a mind virus and is destructive. Then why do you think wokeness is so destructive? Musk, "You know, generally I think we should be aiming for like a positive society and a you know it should be ok to be humorous.

Wokeness basically wants to make comedy illegal," he stated, "Trying to shut down Chappelle, come on man, that's crazy. So do we want a humorless society that is simply rife with condemnation and hate basically. At its heart, wokeness is divisive, exclusionary, and hateful. Basically, it gives mean people a reason...it gives them a shield...to be mean and cruel. Armored in false virtue."

* * * *

September 7, 2022
Memo: Biden State Dept. to enforce tenets of gender ideology as
U.S. foreign policy
by Staff, WorldTribune

Team Biden is set to begin putting pressure on other nations to push vulnerable children into gender transition hormones and surgeries, an analyst wrote, citing a leaked State Department internal memo...

* * * *

"I know we are in the later stage of your Sixth Extinction event and the Others are or may be returning to turn off the last light switch on Man. But don't the Others take into account positive action by Man to counteract the *Human condition?*" Steve has found his tongue inside of his abundant alcohol presence.

"Correct, other events take place in 2021 to weaken position of Man." ET relates.

"Life circumstance isn't all pleasant times and roses, shit happens and we, Man, move on to the next challenge." Steve vocal angry, not making friends.

ET relates from his data base. "Your term, 'shit happens' is a common vulgar slang phrase that is used as a simple existential observation that life is full of unpredictable events. The phrase is acknowledgment that bad things happen seemingly for no particular reason."

"Correct, so what is the Earth moving event that has you and the Others all bound-up and ready to shit?" Steve clear as mud.

"Strange wording." ET goes on. "The twenty-year conflict hostilities held within the borders of Afghanistan enters a new decisive stage."

Grant pipes in. "Well, that is good news, but twenty years doesn't that seem a bit extreme? It's been ten years now, could last longer."

Steve joins in. "Twenty years is about right, Vietnam started in '55 ended in '75. We, the U.S., were out in 73." Steve feels the years since then.

"The conflict with indigenous people culminates withdrawal of all western presences," reports ET. "Twenty-year presence terminates 2021."

"Same as the Vietnam evac. Shit happens, all over again," Steve says. "Then there must have been a final peace settlement with the Taliban and Afghan government."

Steve interjects. "I have it now, President Clinton was re-elected in 2020 and sought a peace agreement with the Taliban. She had a track record of pushing to develop a vaccine for the China-introduced Corona virus."

"Peace terms attained with Afghanistan and Taliban forces in 2020 before your presidential election." ET mind-tending both brothers.

"I knew Clinton was smart, capable; and just enough corrupt to ensure a winning hand in the Afghan-Taliban high-stakes poker game. She had practice going back to Arkansas White Water dealings, cattle futures, Billy's sex escapades and timely deaths for a few staffers. Like the Teflon Don, nothing stuck." Steve is a real fan for some reason. She's in the MF'er category it seems.

"Your president established withdrawal plan stipulating specific milestones to be met by Taliban insurgence. Adherence was principal element enforced by hostile response if not attained or met. Deviations from determined events would delay final milestone. All foreign military personnel and associated equipment assets to be removed in conjunction with, and prior to final stages to conflict end. Progression moved appropriately until 2021. "ET finished his conclusive recap of Afghanistan.

Grant, not a fan, says, "I agree she is an MF'er...not so sure she would cover your six, though." He seems to be toasting the comments with his beer. "ET who was the Republican candidate in the 2020 election?"

"Donald Trump." ET has decided to let the brothers banter a bit from his human DNA side and withholds who the Democrat candidate will be, not Clinton.

Steve choking on his beer. "You got to be shitting me: Trump runs again?" Coughing. "Did he lose by more or fewer votes the second time she kicked his tail? Steve is almost glowing.

ET mind-tending, "By nearly seven million votes." ET continues to withhold accurate Presidential election results. Trump loses to a democrat candidate, a former Vice-President.

"Wow she picked up near four million more votes from the first election. Don't know if that has been done before." Grant is surprised and wonders how it happened.

"Yeah, Trump must have stepped on his dick big time to lose in a landslide." Steve replies, somewhat pleased.

ET nearly asks the meaning of Steve's comment on dick-stepping. He doesn't and categorizes it to comments like "shit happens." In fact, shit does happen regarding Afghanistan in

2021, including dick-stepping by the American evacuation plan and accompanied disaster.

ET determines it is an appropriate and a first time to bring Grant and Steve into a complete knowledge condition of events in the 2021 future. He uses a drug-like aerosol nearly identical to Grant's training formulated dosage for both brothers. Bringing a semiconscious state of rapid absorption of a data-chain dump of future events leading to the Afghanistan withdrawal condition eleven years into the future, 2021.

Primary factors and impressions of data dump impact by both brothers: 2021 media coverage was included, and fault line milestone events missed, changed, or ignored.

Steve and Grant were informed that Clinton lost to Trump in 2016 in the Electoral College. That nearly brought Steve to a conscious state from the hours of compressed data archives and implicit memory. Steve's and Grant's cut-to-the-chase interpretation of ET's supplied data was tempered by their years of military operations experience. Their unfiltered conclusion: It wasn't Clinton's plan; it was Trump's. Steve nearly awakened again. Trump's graduated hard-milestone draw-down evacuation withdrawal plan was severely altered early in 2021 by a combined effort of the newly elected insistent Democrat president, the state department, and Joint Chiefs of staff. They countered with a politically laced and driven incoherent tactical/strategic change of operations plans. Replete with leadership failure of epic proportions worse than the Vietnam evacuation. Thirteen American service members died at the blood-stained hands of incompetent and distant leadership: Malarky bullshit. According to Oxford Dictionaries, malarkey is "meaningless talk; nonsense." Desperate and ham-fisted at best, yet thought to be politically opportune. It wasn't. It was a fluctuating target-controlled, directed, and pragmatically managed by the Taliban terrorists with kowtowed compliance by U.S. forces due to their feckless politically driven leadership both within the military and White House. By comparison, General Custer fought outnumbered and surrounded at the Little Bighorn. He and his Calvary died fighting to the last Man. General Robert

E. Lee lost the battle at Gettysburg, many Americans died in both battles. Custer and Lee fought outnumbered and in seemingly lost causes; however, they both stuck to their developed operation plans. Neither sought favor from a longtime opponent nor asked for clearance to defend or establish their positions. They fought for an objective regardless of how difficult to obtain.

In 2021 Kabul, there was a milestone of geo-political-military failure to show strength and commitment to a cause worth fighting. Failed leadership costing thirteen U.S. military lives, $85 billion in front line equipment/weapons, and a soiled bloodstain legacy ranking with The Little Big Horn and Gettysburg without the fight. Most significant leadership rollover in U.S. history with more to come.

* * * *

August 26, 2021
State Department Cable Shows Team Biden Knew Afghan Collapse Was Imminent

Americandefensenews.com Pentagon Watch US Military, Paul Crespo

Even as U.S. intelligence estimates warned of a pending collapse after Biden's hasty and reckless Afghan withdrawal, an urgent July State Department memo shows that administration officials were cautioned about the Taliban's lightning advance....

The Biden deception, or cluelessness, about the rapid Taliban advance being unexpected extends to his Defense Department and Joint Chiefs of Staff (JCS). Gen. Mark Milley, chairman of the JCS at the Pentagon, has said that rapid collapse of the U.S.-supported Afghan government and army was never anticipated.

"There was nothing that I or anyone else saw that indicated a collapse of this army and this government in 11 days," Milley stated on Wednesday. **ADN**

* * * *

August 26, 2021
U.S. officials provided Taliban with names of Americans, Afghan allies to evacuate

realcleardefense.co
By Lara Seligman, Alexander Ward and Andrew Desiderio
08/26/2021 Updated: 08/26/2021

The White House contends that limited information sharing with the Taliban is saving lives; critics argue it's putting Afghan allies in harm's way.

The decision to provide specific names to the Taliban, which has a history of brutally murdering Afghans who collaborated with the U.S. and other coalition forces during the conflict, has angered lawmakers and military officials.

U.S. officials in Kabul gave the Taliban a list of names of American citizens, green card holders and Afghan allies to grant entry into the militant-controlled outer perimeter of the city's airport,...It also came as the Biden administration has been relying on the Taliban for security outside the airport...

"Basically, they just put all those Afghans on a kill list," said one defense official, who like others spoke on condition of anonymity to discuss a sensitive topic. "It's just appalling and shocking and makes you feel unclean."...

* * * *

August 30, 2021

American University of Afghanistan students were told we have given your names to the Taliban and there is no evacuation coming

Robert Jonathan, Bizpacreview.com

About 600 American University of Afghanistan students, their families, and staff members are reportedly stranded on the ground in or near Kabul, and to make matters far worse and more dangerous, the Taliban knows who they are.... "They told us: we have given your names to the Taliban. We are all terrified, there is no evacuation, there is no getting out," one student told The New York Times. Information shared with the Taliban by U.S. military also reportedly included passport information. In what must be the very last thing on the minds of students currently in harm's way, the university (President) was committed to ensuring all enrolled students would finish their degrees remotely."

CONSIDER MAN

* * * *

September 23, 2021
Taliban official: Strict punishment, executions will return
By Kathy Gannon AP

KABUL, Afghanistan (AP) — One of the founders of the Taliban and the chief enforcer of its harsh interpretation of Islamic law when they last ruled Afghanistan said the hard-line movement will once again carry out executions and amputations of hands, though perhaps not in public.

* * * *

October 10, 2021
The Taliban say they won't work with the U.S. to contain the Islamic State
Abdullah Sahil/AP

ISLAMABAD (AP) — The Taliban on Saturday ruled out cooperation with the United States to contain extremist groups in Afghanistan...Taliban political spokesman Suhail Shaheen told The Associated Press there would be no cooperation with Washington on containing the increasingly active Islamic State group in Afghanistan....

* * * *

AFTER THE FALL
"Holy shit, the pullout of Afghanistan sounds and looks like Vietnam—Saigon all over again, but worse." Grant is puzzled

Steve is puzzled that Trump's plan would have had a better chance to succeed in leaving Afghanistan. He is further blown away that Clinton isn't nor ever was President. "Holy shit" is all he can say for a while. The Afghanistan debacle is hard to accept after his Vietnam experience. "Shit, it happened again, but worse."

Grant is frustrated with the idiocy of humanity. He understands why ET and the Others may not wish to re-consider Man. Mankind heads in a direction beyond reasonable expectations. The historical pattern of the past hundred years shows "Man" as innately capable of unrestrained violence and

377

disordered waste of their kind. One hundred years of conflict could culminate in destroying the Earth as a life-sustaining environment for humanity and other life forms, combined with a social legacy that encompasses a kaleidoscopic view of mankind. The consideration of Man may be beyond recognition as a fractured life form to sustain in its current formulation. The petri dish of Earth's evolution may need cleansing.

MAN 28

Going Forward

ET and Grant, do they move forward at some altered pace? What is there to accomplish? Aliens move Man's chess pieces to avoid a nuclear holocaust. Grant knows extinction could be an option, for a sixth time, if Man doesn't alter course. Not on his watch, he thinks, if he can influence another altered outcome for mankind. What would that look like? ET left the road open for Grant and Steve to accomplish a change of sorts. As monitors.

What to consider of ET's Lab project? The nature of human existence floats precariously toward an approaching slack tide. Idle water. There is little unity of purpose and direction, multiple self-serving disjointed aggressive policy applications. This contagion grows worldwide, leading to the dysfunctional chaos, distrust and deterioration of the human condition. The future of mankind is in the midst of an ongoing Sixth Extinction. Can it be stopped? Can Man be considered worth preserving? The Others, have to re-consider Man. Others face Earth policies examined for the future totality of a human species and mankind. Mankind cannot survive without a robust, vibrant and sustainable environment.

The Others have not left...they were always here as represented by ET, as they are at other Earth-like locations, dimensions far and away from Earth's solar system and galaxy.

"What now, ET? Is this the legacy of mankind ending with a sixth extinction?" Grant has few words left. "Are we to simply monitor what's left of the Earth legacy for us?" He taps his chest.

"Correct," ET replies. His response is puzzling for the Fredericks 'brothers.

"What? That's it: correct? No response for all your work with us and 305 years gone." Steve says with a bit of disbelief and anger. "This is BS. 'Correct,' my ass. We can do something to change the direction of the human condition, as you call it."

"Is this how you want all of this to end?" Grant asks with a desperate concern. Both Steve and Grant are standing, staring, facing ET.

ET is unaffected, offers a confident, erect posture. He has at his command an extensive vocabulary of worldwide proportions, all languages encountered on Earth, yet he is not a wordsmith; his word usage or meaning is not always clear, or inference met. Language is not an ET verbal component; it is relayed via mind-tending without tone-associated subtleties. A native speaker, on the other hand, would comprehend and associate with specific comments, word choice, and tone. These subtle tone liturgies are often lost in mind-tending translation. The brothers are struggling to understand their own language nuances as to usage of *correct*. ET expands his mind-tending to convey further detailed word choice and meaning. "In the context of your language, *correct* is at times used as a verb incorporating significant derivation of meaning."

"You're questioning our understanding of *correct*. Its meaning. You gotta be shitting me." Steve's tone is almost hostile.

"Grant, give us your derivation of *correct's* meaning?" ET directs Grant subtlety to access his implicit memory.

Grant responds, "*Correct*: To set or make right; remove the errors or faults from." He goes on, "a change to alter, repair, redirect, solve a problem. Conforming to accepted standards: correct social behavior."

"*Correct*." ET, mind-tending and stepping out of his alien comfort zone into theirs, adds, "Right-on," rather stiffly.

Both Steve and Grant are startled by ET's command of the linguistic situation and truly awkward mind-tending use of American slang. "Dude," Steve attempts to clarify, "when you describe something as right-on, you mean it is good. You say right-on to encourage someone or to emphasize that you agree with them. Is that what you mean? Don't use right-on again, please, dude."

Grant jumps in, "Are you saying using *Correct* as an action to repair what it is wrong, mend, rectify, remedy. Right?" Grant understands ET's butchered attempt at jargon.

ET almost is gloating, "*Correct*, in context as you would repair an aircraft or diesel engine." Not a confirmation of an affirmative response to Grant's question regarding monitoring what's left of the Earth's legacy.

"Holy shit." Steve is not on board. "Would one of you linguistic sages answer me this: is there going to be a Sixth extinction or not? And correct is not an answer."

ET responds, "Together we will make whole Man's future by joining together a system of differentiated parts."

"Well, that's clear as mud. I feel like I am in a hole. Send help." Steve not quite there yet in his concept comprehension...it's coming.

"SAM enters the dialogue, "Steve, consider the monitoring tasking as a practice of disassembling a diesel engine by components and rebuilding it into a more powerful end product. Therefore, the term *correct* as used reflects these factors."

"ET, you got to be clearer in the future, dude," says Steve hoping for no more.

"Correct...will respond appropriately." ET with a human-tinged reply.

Grant is glad to be off the *correct* linguistic battle. Asks, "What are the systems of differentiated parts that is going to make Man whole?

"It will initiate 2017: A mandate for your Defense Advanced Research Projects Agency. DARPA to develop a vaccine that will prevent/cure a corona virus pandemic in the future. It is an event-marker opportunity orchestrated by another human entity, a president of your nation." ET standing still as always.

"That entity would have to be a President Trump, not a President Clinton?" Steve has an awkward view of the new found reality of presidential politics.

"Correct." ET gives an affirmation of future political conditions. Decides not to use right-on.

"I have no clue what DARPA is or does," Grant says. "I thought it was a CIA offshoot, working on classified security system advancements."

ET provides an alien push. "Access your implicit data base for clarification."

Grant recalls DARPA from his data base access. "The genesis of that mission and of DARPA itself dates to the launch of Sputnik in 1957, and a commitment by the United States that, from that time forward, it would be the initiator and not the victim of strategic technological surprises. For sixty years, DARPA has held to a singular and enduring mission: to make pivotal investments in breakthrough technologies for national security. The ultimate results have included not only game-changing military capabilities such as precision weapons and stealth technology, but also icons of modern civilian society such as the Internet, automated voice recognition, language translation, and GPS. It works within an innovation ecosystem that includes academic, corporate and governmental partners, with a constant focus on the nation's military services. The life-saving vaccine developed in record time owes a debt to these programs."

* * * *

September 5, 2021
Military programs aiming to end pandemics forever
60 Minutes
Bill Whitaker
www.DARPA.mil
...DARPA explicitly reaches for transformational change instead of incremental advances...The DARPA director was very clear. "Your mission is to take pandemics off the table."...technology he hopes will ensure COVID-19 is the last pandemic.

* * * *

After Grant is done explaining DARPA, Steve goes off. "Holy crap, ET, enough database research. We got it. Trump pushed this DARPA outfit to attack the Covid virus full force in 2017 and they did it. So how does that help our scenario for shortcutting the Sixth extinction?"

"Event-markers start at DARPA. Subtle assistance by subconscious means." Mind-tending ET.

Grant asks, "So we as monitors track the viral research milestones to ensure they achieve outcomes that stops the pandemic in 2019?"

"The achieved outcome starts January 2020." ET adds. "Conforms to Chinese effort to import viral contagion across nation boundaries worldwide. Initial viral infection rate expands rapidly. DARPA vaccine is introduced as experimental factor. Medical research intervention alters severity of viral effects to slow the loss of life."

"Does it work?" Both Steve and Grant.

"Affirmative." ET moves away from *correct*.

"You mean length of time. Short cuts." Steve, the linguist, remarks, trying to understand his role as a monitor. "We stir the data, accelerate the discovery process?" He adds yet another novel reading reference. "Geez, this is just like the Rainbow Six intervention rescue team, without guns, prima-cord, and entry tools.

"What are you talking about this time. Not another movie reference?" Grant is not pleased again.

ET replies. "Not a film. A 1998 novel by Tom Clancy. *Rainbow Six* is a secret, international task force dedicated to combating terrorism worldwide. There are two teams of approximately ten individuals, each highly trained. The teams are composed of former military members from the U.S., United Kingdom, Germany, Israel, and France. They operate worldwide with accurate deadly surgical-like precision."

"Yeah, that about covers it. Just like what we are going to be used for...without the need for firearms and explosives. We have Pushback." Steve goes on. "We are the messengers behind the scene, like drill instructors or flight examiners. We handle corrective action and steer this research vessel to a port to off load the vaccine in record time. Our action is unnoticed and undetected; it's just lifesaving viral vaccine management. The fix is in; we know it, they don't."

"So, we start Pushbacks as early as 2017 with a Trump directed DARPA vaccine mandate. No one has a clue that a pandemic is approaching on the Chinese horizon. This is the event-marker? Trump's?" Grant asks. "You said that we fix Man's future by joining together a system of differentiated parts. Where are the other parts? Looks like we monitor Man four years until 2021. What comes next? You said Trump loses the 2020 election, said his Afghanistan plan is shit canned and the US suffers a horrific military and political loss. The only good coming out of those two different events is forestalling a pandemic sent by China, while getting our butts kicked out of Afghanistan. What are you not telling us?"

ET mind-tending, "You are correct in your combined assessment of future events. There are other factors that play a part in the year 2020. As you are aware, your lives have been affected by numerous event-markers. That led to alternate life patterns or parallel life patterns."

" Yogis, we know about how they work and have impacted Grant's life in particular." Again, Steve has taken the lead. "Are we going to Yogi something or someone?"

"The concept is a method to alter Man's condition," Grant says. "To save him from extinction."

Then he adds, "What is the choice we face?"

"Only one. Initiated by 2017 event-marker."

"The Trump marker...DARPA?" Grant wonders where ET is headed, "How is that going to work, he loses the 2020 election in a landslide?"

"Incorrect. He wins election."

"You have set him up to Yogi the 2020 election." Steve sees where ET is going.

Grant doesn't. "What are you talking about? He loses the election to the former Vice President."

"Correct." ET referring to Steve.

"Holy shit, ET," Grant says. "What the hell is happening here? He either wins the election or not."

"They both win elections," Steve sees where it is all heading. "Remember a Yogi is a detour to another life pattern, a parallel life pattern. Isn't that right or correct, ET?" Hands Grant a fresh beer

"Right-on." Not quite as awkward this time around. ET knows where it's all headed.

Shit, shit, fucking shit," Grant losing the concept. "Right-on, you're shitting me?

"ET, let me explain it to my brother, You might want to sit for this," Steve says, directing Grant to a lawn chair.

Grant takes a seat. "Fire when ready Gridley,"

Steve takes the helm confidently. "It starts in 2017, the initial and only event-marker Yogi. That's nearly four years before the 2020 election." Steve's apparent new found understanding baffles his brother. "It was the set up. It required time to place elements in place." Steve goes on. "President Trump instructed DARPA to research a solution and cure for the corona virus and any future virus. Avoid a pandemic."

"No shit, I now know the dates, don't know the why." Grant takes a drink.

"The card game. You remember the card game with Alloway." Steve points at Grant.

"Yeah, so what?" Grant has an attitude.

"It was a setup to get Sergeant Alloway thinking about his next and fatal flight, right?" Steve is up and walking, talking, thinking, and drinking.

"That was different, we knew what happened to him 40 years ago. Had to change his thinking to save his life. And it worked," Grant says.

"Correct. We knew he died on a specific date, had to change his routine." Steve grabs another beer from the cooler. "Needed to set him up, get him beyond his routine, thinking out of the box in only one night, right? How'd we do that? How'd you do that?"

"The card game?" Grant, more lights on. Thinking, recall.

"Welcome aboard, Sherlock." Steve says. "It was a set up. We knew what had happened when and how he drowned, had to impact his thinking. Swim, Sergeant, swim. We knew the alternative."

Grant has some clarity, "We don't know what we don't know about the workings of DARPA. They are approaching a research problem by direction of the president." Grant pauses, thinking, pacing. "They don't yet know the answer or if or when they could provide a Covid viral vaccine, let alone a cure. If they don't know, we sure as hell can't help direct the research process without input from ET and SAM. We are not Covid tech-reps; hence, DARPA needs time to research and develop the vaccine on their own."

Steve goes on filling in details. "Four years is very timely in that field of science problem solving. We can assist as needed by ET's guidance. We use Dragonfly and Pushback as necessary and stay out of the way. This is a different sort of combat than we are now experienced in. Our team, ET and SAM, like Rainbow Six, changed the outcome as the card game did."

The card game setup changed everything for Alloway. He was given insight to respond in a way he hadn't before. It ended up saving his life in a parallel life pattern. He essentially had two life options. He used one 40 years ago and died. In the second one, he used his knife, and was rescued by the crew of Jolly 2-7. So, he lives his life in a parallel life pattern, same as Grant.

The DARPA Yogi detoured a four-year research study that developed the Covid vaccine and on to a cure by late 2019. The Covid treatment is ready by March of 2020 and implemented, staving off a social and economic shut down. It proceeds and exists in a parallel life pattern from then on. Two alternate parallel histories.

"Two 2020 Histories play out," Steve says, "just like there were two Blackies on the bay. One carried you to your death by an accidental .22-caliber bullet to the heart. The other one had a 22 shot into the seat next to you. One Yogi, two boats, two parallel lifes and lives, and two history patterns. Simple really."

Grant sees a glimmer of light in the Yogi logic tunnel. He understands his place in an alternate history pattern following a Yogi, more than one Yogi. The original history of 2020 and newly elected Democrat president survives as a parallel history in a similar time-loop as Osama bin Laden's. A significant event-marker affects a possible Sixth Extinction for humankind. Set aside by the 2017 Yogi is a parallel history pattern encompassing Grant and Steve as ET Monitors.

Steve even has ET listening. "Here is what I think happens on the Yogi side of 2017-2021. Covid virus cured and controlled, thousands of lives saved, Pandemic shortened, minimal economic/society impact, fall football, controlled withdrawal from Afghanistan and 13 American service members survive August 30, 2021; get to go home. That's what I think happens on one side of history 2020. The other side is the shit ball we saw in the future before the 2017 DARPA Yogi.

"There is shit load of detail you've left out. How do all those details, whatever they are, get sorted into a cogent joining together system of differentiated parts. Not sure what those parts are at this point." Grant, says, facing Steve, then turning to ET. "ET, you need to point us in a direction. Sounds like we have four years of Dragonfly travel to right this goat-rope adventure?"

ET, "Correct, you will monitor the human condition and make adjustments. A great deal of your monitoring task will influence alter direction as indicated by end results."

"How do we oversee such an enormous undertaking; there are only the two of us?" Grant asks.

ET makes an awkward hand gesture toward his chest. "We will observe all actions." He and SAM will oversee all event decisions, tempered by a mix of human intuitive body language interpretation and human guesswork from the Fredericks brothers. "You and Steve are vital to a desired human condition outcome."

Steve questions ET's assumption that he and his brother are needed at all. "Why do you need Grant and me? We are part of the human condition you wish to fix, change, redirect. You and the Others can do it all without us—as you have for millions or thousands of years. You have capabilities far beyond our capacities; what do we offer that is essential to your mission?"

"Well stated, Steve. I'd like to hear the answer, ET." Grant adds.

ET is ready. "Steve, when you repair a diesel engine, what is the time required to complete the adjustments?"

"Depends on the problem; could be any number of issues, some unknown until the engine is disassembled."

"Grant, when you were flight testing a repaired helicopter, was there a routine to ensure the aircraft airworthy?

"There were guidelines and procedures to complete a test of systems performance in accordance with expected standards."

"Were those systems accurate to ensure air-worthiness?" ET nears a junction point for the brothers.

"Yes, they indicated air-worthiness." Grant replies.

ET relates a test flight that Grant flew in the Air Force. "In 1972, you were involved with engine failure near 1,500 feet above ground level. What system indicated the engine was going to fail, gave a warning of failure?"

"There wasn't one. The engine just quit." Grant recalls.

"How can that be: you had engine performance systems to provide approaching failure? What failed?"

"It wasn't a mechanical failure."

"The single engine failed in flight?" ET presses.

Grant recalls. "There wasn't a system to indicate failure was approaching. It was human failure."

ET knows the answer why "No warning system for human failure?"

"Metal locknuts were left in the engine air intake."

"Their purpose in that location?" ET asks.

"No purpose, left by mistake, an error." Grant says, frustrated. "Engine airflow intake took one locknut into the turbine, causing major damage, lost all engine power."

"Unexpected condition, no insight or logic of result. Prevention possible?" ET is asking for a logic-based result or solution.

"ET, a mechanic over looked them there, no telling how or why. Shit happens sometimes." Grant's solution.

Steve relates to helicopter mechanical issues; he had some in the Army. He adds, "There's always Murphy's Law; you can't get past that ever."

ET immediately quotes from his expansive data base: "A supposed law of nature, expressed in various humorous popular sayings, to the effect that anything that can go wrong will go wrong. Random events that impact outcome, not planned and detract from anticipated reality."

"Correct," Grant says. "Events beyond ET's alien control, freeborn events."

ET mind-tending. "Prevention not possible. Shit happens, according to the Laws of Murphy."

Steve shakes his head in disbelief. "ET, you screwed that up: it's Murphy's Law not the Laws of Murphy. Please."

ET ignores the correction. "You have experience with unintended consequences of the human condition. Understanding faults is valuable asset recognizing the jeopardy in human condition. Metal locknuts out of place with no apparent logic or reason." ET makes another awkward hand gesture, referring to himself and SAM. "Need human view to recognize fault condition not sensed by our experience. Notice before shit happens by Murphy's Law."

Grant struggles to understand ET's need for a human view for humanity to move forward. "You have been involved with the evolution of mankind for over 305 years, and the *Others* longer. Your lengthy experience only reflects, observes and records—human evolutionary records, correct?"

"Correct." ET acknowledges.

"You don't make decisions based upon human-to-human interaction?"

"Correct."

"Your reporting criteria is sterile of human emotion. There is no reporting category for the human touch or contributing emotional psychological impact, feelings." Grant rolls on, "No human impact noted in your observation reporting. That portion of your reporting criteria is a blank page—nothing noted, observed or recorded. There is no understanding of the subtle interaction of the human condition; mankind is a chess piece without impact beyond movement on the chess board by others."

Steve takes over, "You need a human view to recognize fault conditions not sensed by your and SAM's experience. Notice before shit happens. Correct?"

"Fault condition not sensed accurately. Experience limited." ET mind-tends.

"This so much bullshit." Steve huffs. "You and SAM are light years ahead of us intellectually. We can't compete with you on an intelligence scale, but we know the human condition dictionary beyond you both. You and SAM can't see the forest for the trees, or better put, see mankind for what he is." Steve's experience with reading men is where he's headed.

Grant has a realization. "You don't know how to read the nonverbal cues Man offers? Body language, you two don't know how to read it, interpret, or respond to it?" He is in a discovery mode. "You observe and report without an interpretation of Man's condition, attitude, emotional state. Static observation without touching or approaching the essence of your subject? More to Man than you understand."

Steve jumps in. "For 305 years, you manage evolution without a symbiosis connection to your evolutionary DNA related subjects. Not until, somehow, you connected to Grant on the Bay event-marker Yogi." Steve goes on, "What does symbiosis mean to you and SAM? It is simple."

SAM replies, "Symbiosis, interaction between two different organisms living in close physical association, typically to the advantage of both."

"ESP?" Steve throws in.

"ESP: extrasensory perception, called sixth sense, reception of information not gained through the recognized physical senses, sensed with the mind alone," ET replies.

"How about instinct?"

"The ability to understand something immediately, without the need for conscious reasoning."

"Intuitive?" The brothers have opened an opportunity and reasoning exercise.

"Intuitive: Using or based on what one feels to be true even without conscious reasoning." ET and SAM respond in unison.

Grant asks, "So, what exactly is intuition?"

Mind-tending together, ET and SAM, "It is the ability to know something without analytic reasoning, filling the gap between the conscious and non-conscious parts of one's mind.

"The boys are making progress," Grant continues," Without the conscious reasoning part down. Now do you get it?" Asking ET and SAM.

"Correct," both state.

"Can't see the forest for the trees?" Grant repeats Steve's earlier observation for ET.

"To not understand, appreciate a situation, problem, because considering only a few parts of larger whole. ET and SAM reply. AI programing offers no access to evaluate the body language aspect that encompasses those terms. No ability to know something without analytic reasoning, filling the gap between conscious and non-conscious parts of one's mind. Our AI has no measuring metric feature, a deficient vacant application."

"ET, it isn't a programing flaw in AI," Steve says. "For you, it is an untapped portion of the DNA we share. Ours lets us access those innate subconscious attributes that are unavailable to you. We are genetically related. Grant and I take all those terms and focus on reading the body language of Man. You may never achieve a fluency in body language; however, you have insight as to how it works, how we use it as an intuitive tool."

Grant finishes, "I think we see a clearer picture of where we fit in with attempting to adjust the human condition as you do. You need our assistance to determine an appropriate translation of body language, as your psychic gurus and our genes, not yours."

"Correct." SAM and ET in unison.

Steve and Grant will be looking for the out of place "locknuts" of the human condition, elements of the game. They lament the future they see that encompasses unsubstantiated random concepts not based on the scientific biological, and genetic reality of the human genome construct, a troubling state of the human condition focus and direction.

Nuclear war and insane reality acid Trippin nonsense are two principal threats. That is the society that Grant and Steve find in the future, where life exists in an accepted fictional reality of dream-like consciousness. There they choose not to wake up to the approaching nuclear sunrise and life beyond the existence of background noise and static of thoughts and ideas existing only in their imagination. A society cultivated without substance and boundaries. Faulty reasoning, yet implemented across human society at the apex of supposed reasoned existence. Driven, interpreted, and implemented as a free ranged mind-expanding journey without guard rails. A fool's paradise of absurd terminal existence and extinction event justified. Earth is cleansed by genetic manipulation; replace the human model with a Sixth Extinction. Steve and Grant, as monitors, attempt to redirect the climate of the human condition before the equal time point of the Sixth Extinction.

As change agent monitors, they'll work with the human experience of past events. Judgment with outcomes will be based on what is known and expected. Locknuts: all the unexpected events are the card playing—it is unknown what some players will play. However, over time it is learned what to expect. There's no cure for shit that happens. Just need to expect it. Plan on it as a feature of the human condition. The difference between the card game message and monitoring actions of the human condition is a moving target-rich environment. Steve and Grant face an Earth-wide, free-fire zone without counter opposition or hostile intent. Neither ever had such conditions in all their combat experience; someone always took a shot.

"Okay, Lone Ranger and Tonto," Steve addresses ET and sidekick, SAM, "if what you propose is the no shit F-ing truth, then we're going to need some leverage to access the minds of those troublesome humans we will be approaching, reading and influencing. We understand Pushback and Dragonfly gets us there. Once there, what tools are in our tool kit to manipulate these fellow unknowing species of the human race?" Steve pauses. "Will it be the same tools or processes used with Nostradamus, de Vinci, and Einstein?"

SAM deadpans his ironic reply, "Nostradamus, da Vinci, Einstein were highly intelligent."

"Thanks for the words of confidence." Grant gets it. They were smart indeed.

Steve chimes in with a bit of apprehension regarding 'tools.' "I have had some experiences with acid trips, bad acid trips. An LSD trip becomes a destination not just a journey. Murphy's Law of abandoned reason."

"Murphy's Law of abandoned reason? That's a new one for me." Grant is curious to hear a definition from either ET or Steve.

ET mind-tending, "Human condition, faulty reasoning, yet implemented across the future human society at the apex of supposed reasoned existence."

Steve adds, "As near as I can tell it will be an acid-like free ranged mind-expanding journey that became the destination."

Not sure what either meant, Grant asks, "Not clear enough?"

"An acid trip acceptance of any whim of an overdosed reality of free-flow nonsense and insegredious bullshit. Kool-Aid drinkers drunk minds without guard rails of reality. I have more memories."

"Insegredious isn't a word." Grant laments without another question.

"Used it all the time to define worthless or meaningless bull shit concepts...like this one." Steve is done.

ET adds nothing more.

"Your point?" Grant asks.

"My point is the human condition resembles acid trippers that woke up and found their journey became a way-station destination along the tracks of a harebrained acid-driven mind-bending touchstone of acid reality. Think it, live it,...acid experience. Driven by kaleidoscopic-like-acid-trips inspired, interpreted, and implemented as reality-based concepts."

"Your ability to access the human mind will be enhanced to level consistent with sufficient skill." ET adds tool clarification. "You will be exposed to application that expands your level of consciousness, quality of self-awareness, abstract thinking, and higher reasoning."

"As well as higher level of intelligence," SAM adds, an almost showman response.

"Are we going to be able to accurately decipher the thoughts of the subject individuals without tying them to a chair?" Grant asks, not sure of how such mind access is going to happen.

"Correct." ET needs the boys because they can read 'Man 'as he and SAM can't. What Grant and Steve are supposed to accomplish encompasses vast numbers of people who need influencing, understanding the minds of others, seeing people or aliens' thoughts, and asserting their quiet, subtle powers. That power closely aligned with what the *Others* are capable of, not ET, from a more human perspective. However, his genetics led him to the human side of his shared genetics with Man.

"We could use mind probes." Steve interjects. "Like Obi-Wan Kenobi. He did it, got out of trouble using it. Good information source."

ET has no answer.

"Are you really referring to Star Wars, Ben Kenobi?" Grant says, displeased.

"Star Wars, a fiction film from long past date." SAM replies.

"Exactly, however they had some interesting concepts introduced." Steve is on a Star Wars jaunt. "We could use something like their mind probes—an ability that allows us to sense or even sift through the thoughts, emotions, and memories of someone, seeking useful information."

"Are you done?" Grant knows his brother's obsession.

"No," Steve says, still speaking to ET. "Does the application you provide us include telepathy to read the state of minds or mind-tending communication? We could interact with the minds of others."

"Not a necessity." Mind-tended ET. Steve and Grant currently lack the capacity for telepathy.

"Millennium Falcon replaces Dragonfly with Han Solo as pilot?" Grant is over the Star Wars suggestions. Steve needs to stop citing movies as a source of meaningful data. "What do we offer that is essential to your mission?" Grant asks.

"You find the misplaced *locknuts* left by Man in the inlet of the human condition." ET's insight on his and SAM's shortcomings in reading the human condition. "Avoid engine failures."

Grant and Steve, in essence, provide an interpretation of human conditioning messages. Interpreters/monitors of the language of Man, not always spoken, but sent and displayed.

Grant and Steve will develop the operations strategy necessary to impact the human condition consistent with Pushback and the effective use of Dragonfly. They'll observe and measure subtleties of interpretation of Man's conscious and subconscious mind, an all-too-human *feel* of intuitive interpretation. From those human body language observations, ET will determine the direction of future impact, alter appropriate response action and impose preventive measures as necessary:

- Control impact on the climate of the human condition.
- Direct appropriate response in conjunction with the Fredericks brothers' input.
- Formulate a solution, note impact on the evolutionary development of Man.

It will mark extraterrestrials' first-time milestone collaboration with mankind, Grant, and Steve.

As designated ET Monitors and armed with SAM's instantaneous language conversation to English, Steve and Grant could eavesdrop on any conversation anywhere on Earth. They could observe, record, and add or interject change to outcome reflecting a divergent future direction shift where possible. With event-markers, Yogis or interference, they may alter results to world preservation and avoid nuclear conflict implementation. Change agents: Steve and Grant, subtle manipulation, drive-by observation on trial and error, implementation, validation, and successful verification. Volunteer Earth contract monitors. As part of Earth's history, they have become powerful elements, shepherded by an extraterrestrial sidekick and SAM. They're not unlike the CIA station chief, the head of a team for the entire Earth. They make decisions with prejudice and influence the favorable outcome to avoid nuclear holocaust and extinction of mankind.

Decisions by Grant, Steve, and ET will involve advanced time travel forward, examining near and long-term results, making vetted database decisions, avoiding losses, and ensuring a favorable global human climate. It might just work! We got through the cold war once, and now it is heating up again, with more bad acting by bad actors.

Prep Work

Grant and Steve went through enhanced and accelerated training; mentored to access the human mind of targeted individuals. They record within their implicit memory critical factors that affect the decision processes of their human counterparts. As a result both brothers attained, as SAM suggested, a higher level of intelligence. Grant, Steve, SAM, and ET were the first and only board of directors-like team of extraterrestrials and humans.

All future human influence adjustments affected by the team were time travel sorted by quantum computer algorithms with instantaneous solutions. Grant and Steve became analytical, precise observers of the human targets they were to influence. There were trial and error design decisions made that were reversed by pushback. ET was always available to counter errors in an erroneous conclusion.

Field Trip

Grant returns to the lab after spending two days at home coordinating the repair of a water leak and replacing their third water heater in eight years. As he entered, Steve and ET returned from an accelerated three-day observation and recording session. Steve is animated, wearing a John Rich concert t-shirt from a Deadwood, South Dakota, event at Outlaw Square.

Grant asks, "Why all the hype, did you find a secret to the universe?"

"No, I went to a couple old and future concerts this trip."
Steve was clearly impressed with himself. Pointing to his concert
t-shirt dated 4 August 2022.

Grant stunned, not believing his brother's boast or t-shirt.
"You didn't."

"Yep, went to three concerts. Great dragonfly seats, used
Pushback for this t-shirt transaction."

No, you didn't," knowing he did, "why?" Grant waiting for
an answer. "ET, you went with him to these concerts?"

"Logic proved to be accurate."

"What logic includes a John Rich concert…in twelve years,
2022 in South Dakota?"

"The logic pattern Steve provided was a relevant insight to
the status of the human condition at various time periods." SAM
mind-tends.

* * * *

July 13, 2022
Washington Examiner
Starbucks's wokeness comes back to haunt them as coffee chain closes 16 stores

by Christopher Tremoglie, Commentary Fellow

Starbucks is closing 16 stores because of a dramatic increase in
crime and drug use throughout the country. The illicit activities
have allegedly endangered many of the company's employees.
The disruptions have coincided with the country's soaring crime
rates, which are largely the result of radical left-wing criminal
justice policies.

Starbucks's decision was made after employees disclosed to
the company's management that they felt threatened because of
customer drug use, violent crimes, and theft, the *Wall Street
Journal* reported….

Ironically, Starbucks was the company that closed all of its
locations for one day in 2018 so it could implement "woke" racial
sensitivity training…Four years later, it's obvious the "training"
failed miserably. The company's executives thought they were
more enlightened than everyone else and could brainwash their
employees with woke training to cure what they perceived as

society's ills...However, the refusal to remove any loiterers because the company did not want to come across as "racially insensitive" ultimately led to an environment that endangered employees.

It's worth noting that all of these locations are in cities with large, bureaucratic, and ineffective Democratic city administrations...Starbucks is now seeing the fruits of its awful decision-making...Unfortunately, the employees in these 16 Starbucks locations learned this lesson too late.

* * * *

"Most people and fans of music, and in particular country music, know it for the most part reflects the condition of the society in which it is played." Steve is confident. "I queried the data base with SAM's assistance and determined the context of the assumption to be true and reasonably accurate."

"His data related assumptions were accurate." SAM.

"Three concerts, old and new, for what purpose?" Grant unconvinced.

"Grant, listen, Country music is a truth and bull shit detector for society. For the most part it knows and shows the lies and the truth of what's happening in real world terms."

"I don't get why three concerts." Grant is still in the dark.

ET adds, "1984, Lee Greenwood, God Bless the USA, Country Music Association awards song of the year. 2002, Toby Keith, Courtesy of the Red White and Blue.

"Meaning?"

"1984 mostly positive conditions, 2002 turmoil throughout societies, war." SAM.

"And 2022, twelve years from now, what's the forecast?" Grant waits.

ET mind-tending, "A simple outward, yet subtle, indicator of success for the human condition reclamation task. It was or will be a new song released in July 2022 by Country music star John Rich entitled "Progress." The lyrics then directs that societies' progressiveness be placed anatomically where the sun doesn't reach."

"Shit ET, you do screwup a great county song's message. Rich sings, stick your progress where the sun don't shine. In other words, put progressive's progress there."

Grant pipes in, "That is in the song...stick it up your ass?"

* * * *

July 24, 2022
Washington Examiner
Woke Culture
LISTEN: Country star John Rich tops iTunes with anti-liberal song 'Progress'

By Heather Hamilton, Social Media Reporter, 1 July 24, 2022
Country music starJohn Rich hit the top of the charts with a song slamming liberal "progress" and bypassing what he called the music industry "machine." Rich released his song "Progress" Friday on Truth Social and Rumble. Within hours, it soared to No. 1 on the Apple iTunes song chart.

"Felt good to beat the machine today:) Thanks to all of you for the massive support! We are making good #Progress #NumberOne #Worldwide," tweeted Rich, who is half of the country music duo Big & Rich....

The song's lyrics include several direct messages challenging the views of liberals.

"They say building back better will make America great," Rich sings. "If that's the wave of the future, all I've got to say is, stick your progress where the sun don't shine. Keep your big mess away from me and mine. If you leave us alone, well, we'd all be just fine."

"Progress" beat out new releases from Billie Eilish and Lizzo, as well as "Running Up That Hill" by Kate Bush.

"Here I am with no record label, no publisher, no marketing deal," Rich *Just the News*. "It is bypassing this machine that they've built, going right around the machine, going right to the people."

* * * *

"Yeah that about says it." But, unfortunately, Steve says, "Society is waking up from one of those acid-like bad trips that formed a faulty destination of insegredious BS."

"Insegredious isn't a word." Grant again.

"For some of us, it is." Steve pointed to his John Rich t-shirt.

"How did you get in and pay for that?' Grant means the t-shirt.

"A Pushback gateway door at a county music concert isn't hard to hide from drinking cowboys and girls."

"Confirm access undetected." ET.

Grant asks, "How'd you pay?"

"No problem, paid cash for the John Rich shirt. Used cash which was old in 2022, still current though."

"Keith and Greenwood too?"

"Yeah, Left over cash from our 1970 Da Nang night flight." ET gave the Ok; apparently, the transactions affected no life-altering life patterns, only a few minor ripples.

"Correct." ET and SAM.

Grant laments, "You should have been a cowboy just like Keith sings about."

"That's right," Steve attempts to sing the lyrics. "I should've learned to rope and ride, Wearin' my six-shooter, ridin' drag on a cattle drive...Stealin' the young girls' hearts
Just like Gene and Roy..."

"I don't think ridin' drag on a cattle drive is part of what Toby Keith sings about. "Drag is a dusty dirt-eating job. You wouldn't get any girls either." Grant corrects Steve.

"Steve's sing-song reply, "I could be 'Ridin' shotgun for the Texas Rangers. "

"Yeah, you could have done that cowboy." Grant replies, ready to move on.

"Seems to me we're doing both, riding drag in the dirt and dust of the Sixth Extinction of the human condition and riding shotgun for the outlaw elements we're chasing. Same as a cattle drive minus the cattle."

"How do you mean same as a cattle drive?" Grant wonders aloud.

Steve goes on, "We're keeping the strays from losing their direction, getting lost at event-markers, and drifting away from the herd and going off trail, off a cliff, endangering the herd of the human condition's well-being and reason. Survival of Earth's environment to include Man's existence...rather continued existence. A modern cattle-like drive. You and I are riding drag behind a human condition drive to avoid extinction.

Instead of ropes, we use yogis off trail to direct and focus on change. Change we need to shepherd mankind toward a viable and successful existence of both environments, Earth's and Man's. So be it

EPILOGUE

Buckle Up

This journey started with two chance encounters, the first forty years ago, off the coast of South Vietnam. First, a failed 1970 night water rescue ended in a life lost, and the second in, 2010, culminated in saving an alien life on a remote mountain mesa. While mountain biking on that remote trail in the East San Diego County Mountains, Grant Fredericks found his world thrust into a life-altering journey of discovery. He stumbled across an earthquake-caused avalanche, injured and trapped alien, an outlier extraterrestrial alien with whom he finds shared a portion of DNA. Once rescued, the ET, for profoundly unclear reasons yet human-like, introduces Grant into his world of highly advanced technology, evolutionary management, and time travel. Grant's learning, comprehension, and knowledge capacity were expanded artificially by a neurotropic aerosol drug that allows him to absorb, retain, and utilize complex concepts untold years into the future. In addition, Grant is inundated and infused with an extraordinary amount of highly advanced technological knowledge via time travel compression learning, repetition, and brain capacity enhancement.

Grant's brother, Steve, is brought into the process and incorporated into the ET's world, yet not at his brother's skill level. Steve's unannounced introduction into an ET's alien world was, in fact, a mind-shattering, brutal life-altering encounter with aliens, indeed...Mexican cartel aliens.

It began as they approached the meeting on Corte Madera. However, the meeting agenda went off-road in a hurry. On that day, riding mountain bikes, the brothers discovered the wreckage of an ultra-light aircraft, a dead pilot, and two canvas duffles containing $6 million in cartel cash. Within minutes, they were chased by gun-carrying, motorcycle-riding soldiers of a Mexican drug cartel. The soldiers fired their automatic weapons at the brothers, stopped by a dead-end 40-foot granite wall. Steve was mortally wounded, yet both brothers survived. However, at home, the ultralight pilot's wife, was mistakenly suspected as involved, tortured, and murdered by cartel gunmen. Neither brother, at this point, knows of history points and event-markers. They will; this is a brutal initiation event for both. That senseless death encounter led to a series of alternate history points specifically targeted to create chaos within Mexican cartels, costing millions of drug dollars.

Steve discovers Grant's life pattern is replete with several history points and event-markers, each of which takes his life. He further learned how to manipulate the time travel device and developed a basic understanding of the laboratory file systems. The troubled brothers never envisioned a partnership with an Alien, ET, and his AI partner, SAM, nor commonly shared DNA traits. Instead, the distant cosmic cousin's trio were bound together in a focused journey to avoid a Sixth Major Extinction on Earth.

They learn from the ET that they can go back in time and accomplish meaningful results that engendered a look back at changing past life experiences; one particular night in June 1970 and one incident in September 2001. They could alter outcomes with a couple of life-altering changes. Grant wanted to save a life, and Steve wanted to take one. The cosmic trio is to directly influence and protect the Earth from a human extinction event that started 12,000 years ago by changing the climate of humanity. They, in the end, discover and follow a path to redirect the future of humanity and alter the ongoing Sixth Extinction of mankind. Earth can survive without Man. Humankind can't survive without a change in the fragile environment of the human condition. A fool's errand, perhaps, but certainly a risk worth taking.

Extract

The following are the source materials and documented edited/shortened extracts referenced within the manuscript body. Sources: Publicly available information, academic, Internet, print news articles, unclassified military mission reports, and other public outlets. Source articles edited for length and clarity in Extract.

Boxer 22
December 5, 1969

The early morning mission went wrong almost from the start. Two U.S. Air Force F-4C Phantoms of the 558th Tactical Fighter Squadron, call sign "Boxer," found their primary target cloud covered. They diverted north to the village of Ban Phanop, Laos, near a chokepoint where the Ho Chi Minh Trail crossed the Nam Ngo River on a target run. In the trailing aircraft, Boxer 2-2, pilot Capt. Benjamin Danielson and weapons systems officer 1st Lt. Woodrow J. "Woodie" Bergeron Jr. were on their first flight or *sortie* together. Just after dropping their ordnance, MK-36 antipersonnel mines, the Phantom suddenly pitched up, then down. Their flight leader called over the radio: "Boxer 2-2, you're hit! Eject! Eject! Eject!"

Boxer 2-2 was about to become the objective of the biggest rescue mission of the Vietnam War. Ejecting, Danielson became Boxer 2-2 Alpha and Bergeron Boxer 2-2 Bravo—came down on opposite sides of a dogleg bend in the river, in a valley a mile across and a thousand feet deep, walled with karst limestone cliffs, caves, and sinkholes formed by underground drainage systems. Boxer 2-2 Alpha landed in a work area on the west side of the Nam Ngo River, between it and Route 23. Telephone poles lying on the ground, an outhouse, and well-worn paths leading to the river. Boxer 2-2 Bravo was at the river's edge on the east side, and behind him was a twenty-foot-high embankment that shielded him from the ground above. Three hundred meters behind him rose a 1,200-foot karst formation extending to the north. The river was fifty feet wide, and the two airmen were about seventy feet apart. Small arms firing was on the west side – the east bank was quiet.

They were just ten miles from the North Vietnam border but only about 65 miles east of NKP—Nakhon Phnom Royal Thai Air Base, the main base for Air Force Special Operations Squadrons specializing in search and rescue. The crew of Boxer 2-2. immediately became hunted prey.

By 11:20 a.m., a flight of A-1s carrying antipersonnel ordnance arrived, supplemented by F-100s, F-105s, and forward air controller spotter aircraft to direct the attack on specific targets. The standard procedure was to find and extract downed airmen before enemy forces concentrated on their position. But unfortunately, the enemy was already concentrated around Ban Phanop. Two Jolly Greens, which had arrived just as this operation began, held in orbit southeast of the downed airmen's position. Both survivors were talking with Sandy and giving him information on the location and intensity of the ground fire.

"Sandy 1, this is Boxer 2-2 Alpha," Danielson radioed the first Skyraiders to arrive. "I need help now! I've got bad guys only 15 yards away, and they are going to get me soon."

If ground forces found the Boxer 2-2 crew were in immediate jeopardy of being executed. The Pathet Lao insurgents didn't take prisoners.

Sandy 1, 1st Lt. James G. George, the Skyraider leader of a flight of four A-1s, answered the call: "Boxer 2-2 Alpha, this is Sandy 1; keep your head down. We're in hot with 20 Mic Mic."

They began the first step of the rescue operation— suppression of the ground fire.

The four Skyraiders raked the enemy troops with 20mm cannon fire; they would thread the needle with cannon rounds, dangerously close to both Boxer 2-2's for the next two and a half days. This action continued while Air Force jets struck against the larger guns to the north. This went on for an hour and twenty minutes. Finally, two Jolly Greens orbited southeast of the downed airmen's position, avoiding direct gunfire. The ground force didn't sit without responding; it was as if the entire valley answered back. The enemy opened up with 23, 37, and 57mm anti-aircraft artillery and heavy machine-gun fire from positions in the karst paralleling the river. Aircraft flying down the valley were being caught in a crossfire. Particularly troublesome was a 37mm gun located in a cave at the foot of the karst 300 meters directly behind the navigator, Bergeron.

Sandy 1 informed King 1, the HC-130 Hercules airborne command post orbiting 24,000 feet above Laos, "We are going to need everything you can get a hold of."

American airpower converged on Ban Phanop: F-100 Super Sabres, F-105 Thunderchiefs, Navy A-6 Intruders, Phantoms, and more Skyraiders—guns from all over Indochina and bombs, rockets, and napalm. The ordinance was dropped precisely near the two crewmembers, including teargas, napalm, and Paveway, a first-generation laser-guided 2,000-pound bomb. Lieutenant Bergeron reported later that the two-day ordinance display was incredible and literally lifted him off the ground several times.

Sandy1 assured Bergeron and Danielson, "We are going to bring in the Jollys to scarf you up, and we'll all go home for a beer. Let's get this done. I don't think we can waste any time."

By 1240 p.m., after the A-1's suppressed hostile ground fire, Jolly 3-7 attempted a pickup. The plan was to pick up the pilot first. He was nearest to the most significant activity of bad guys. Jolly 3-7's pilot, Captain Bill Hoilman, rapidly descended into the valley from the southwest. Ground fire followed them as they approached the pickup point. As they slowed to a hover over Danielson's position, Jolly 3-7 became a stationary target. Nearly every enemy gun took aim and fired relentlessly. Suddenly, the horizon turned red from muzzle flashes, surrounded by ground fire; Jolly 3-7 took hits on all sides. Finally, Hoilman climbed out of the valley with the turbine engines overheating. Jolly 3-7 limped back, unescorted, to NKP for repairs, a narrow escape from a shooting arcade. The rescue scenario was repeated another five times that day. Skyraiders saturated the cliffs with napalm, other ordinance, and the valley with tear gas. However, when Jolly 0-9 arrived, small arms and two 23mm cannons from the karst caves drove them off with a transmission leak, high engine temps, and malfunctioning flight controls. In less than two hours, both Jollys were shot at by hundreds of small arms weapons and high caliber anti-aircraft artillery; they took several hits and were driven off with nearly fatal damage. Neither helicopter flew again for several weeks.

The third attempted rescue was Jolly 7-6, with pilot Holly Bell. Jolly 7-6's, crew experienced ground fire hits sounding like they were caught in a popcorn machine. As they swung in over Daniclson, tail-gunner Airman 1st Class Davison opened up on half the valley with a 4,000 rounds-per-minute mini-gun, but he was outgunned. They took multiple gunfire hits to the fuselage and rotor blades, which began severe airframe vibrations. Jolly 7-6 is forced to leave the valley without Danielson, Boxer 2-2 Alpha.

After the helicopters' first three attempted rescues, the bad guys learned quickly from their battlefield losses to the A-1 Skyraiders trolling for ground fire. If they shoot at the A-1s, they'll shoot back with devastatingly accurate 20mm cannon fire. They waited. Don't fire at the A-1 Skyraiders trolling. Instead, wait for a bullseye target Jolly sitting above the tree's topmost branches, then start the gunfire. It worked on the fourth attempt. A burst of fire cut a hydraulic line in Jolly 6-9, the spraying fluid caught a spark, and the helicopter climbed away, gushing flames. Major Hubert Berthold remembered seeing the entire area lit up with a shower of tracers on both sides from the karst and the valley floor. The Jolly 6-9 crew was lucky to survive. The last rescue that first day was attempted just before dark. Jolly 7-2 got to within 30 feet of Boxer 2-2, Alpha, pilot Danielson before being driven off. Same script, same result! Five of seven Jolly Green helicopters had taken serious hits and were unlikely to be repaired by morning, and it was unclear if the remaining two would ever fly again due to battle damage.

All told, ninety aircraft had dropped almost 350 bombs and rockets on the Nam Ngo valley, but as night fell, the enemy was still there, and tracer rounds streamed up at the orbiting aircraft. Finally, at 1750 p.m., Sandy 1 radioed the Boxer crew that it was becoming too dark to continue the rescue operation; they would resume with first light the following morning. "Be back tomorrow."

"Good night, see you in the morning," Bergeron replied. He stayed where he was in a grove of bamboo and dug deeper into the foliage and debris. The bad guys continued to search for the pilot through the bushes on the east bank. Danielson didn't reply to Sandy 1 due to the danger-close proximity of enemy personnel.

DAY 2

Boxer 2-2 Alpha and Bravo didn't sleep. Danielson and Bergeron had front-row night seat views of the enemy supply convoys. The people night searching for the Boxer 2-2 crew were without flashlights. Consequently, many were killed or severely injured when they activated antipersonnel mines dropped by Air Force aircraft during the night. The North Vietnamese knew Danielson was still there, nearby. They would go to a clump of trees or brush and fire off a few AK-47 rounds. During the night, Bergeron kept intermittent radio communications with the King aircraft high overhead. He reported enemy activity searching for Danielson on the east side of the river; it stopped at some point later that night. They were instructed to remain radio silent, concealed, and hidden unless there was a significant event to report. Both would be contacted at first light by King and Sandy1. Neither was in a position during the night to receive air support if needed.

At first light, Bergeron reported to King that the North Vietnamese had just killed Danielson. They found him hiding in a bush bramble near the river bank and shot a long burst from an AK-47. Bergeron said he heard Ben scream. He took cover for the next few hours. There was no time to mourn. Enemy troops were already wading the river toward his position. He called in Skyraiders and Phantoms to strafe the river with 20mm fire. They did so, and the soldiers "physically disappeared in a red mist."

The valley was cluster-bombed, napalmed, rocketed, and shot up for five hours, with ordnance hitting dangerously near Bergeron's position. The closest they came to him with 20mm cannon rounds was about one foot. A tear gas bomblet bounced off his chest just before it went off. During this time, the enemy moved men and equipment into the area, preparing for the slow-moving exposed helicopter that would follow. Bergeron reported that all aircraft were subject to small arms and automatic weapons fire as they made low-level passes through the valley.

The A-1's used white phosphorus to mask the location of the current rescue attempt. Down in the acrid haze, visibility dropped to near zero. Jolly Greens made six rescue attempts, but whenever the air over the Nam Ngo valley wasn't thick with smoke, it was full of bullets and cannon rounds. As soon as the Jollys came to a hover over Bergeron—one so low that its rotors clipped the trees—their rotor wash swept everything clear, and the enemy gunners found them.

In Jolly 2-7, Capt. Grant Fredericks was waiting his turn with four other Jolly Greens standing by five miles to the southeast, prepared to make a pickup attempt. Those Jollys were in the air since 12 p.m. with a ringside view of the air operation below them. Most of the Jollys aerial refueled with an HC-130 tanker three times that day.

At 6 p.m., the second day's last rescue attempt failed. Night fell, the American planes drew back, and the North Vietnamese closed in. Immediately after the previous rescue attempt, Bergeron told Sandy 1 and King he was moving to a better-concealed position for the night. "This hide is compromised after all the focus of the Jolly's to converge here. So I am moving about 20 yards to the north and staying in the river and thicker vegetation along the bank. Signing off for a few hours."

"Roger that Boxer 2-2 bravo. We'll be back." Sandy 1 responds.

"You bet your sweet ass we will." King sends a good night.

His timing was prophetic. About 15 minutes after dark, three enemy soldiers emerged from cover, tossed a tear gas bomblet into his vacant bamboo thicket, and sprayed it with AK-47 rifle fire. All they found was some discarded survival gear. Boxer 2-2 Bravo had dragged himself to a bush overhanging the bank with only his eyes and nose above the water; he got under it. Bergeron had moved 40 feet to the north and was hiding under exposed tree roots. Lying in the darkness, half-covered with water, exhausted and hungry, the bush-root tangle remained his hiding place until morning. If those bad guys had a flashlight, they would have found him. Killed him.

DAY 3

Both sides were well organized for the three-hour gun suppression operation that got underway at first light. Air Force aircraft took out the remaining heavy gun. Enemy soldiers came within 25 feet of Lieutenant Bergeron. He directed the A-1s, and they fine-tuned their 20mm canon-stitching skills to eliminate the threat. After nearly 48 hours in enemy territory, Bergeron was on his last legs, drinking water out of the river and surviving on a bit of food. At 5:15 a.m., the lead, Sandy, picked him up on the radio and asked him to authenticate. "What's your best friend's name?" He replied, "Weisdorfer."

The Sandy 1 pilot had to laugh. "I don't even have time to check it, but it's gotta be you."

By 6:30 a.m., the valley was under a renewed attack. After one rescue attempt in which the Jolly Green received heavy ground fire, the area was sanitized for another three hours with smoke, tear gas, and ordinance. By noon the Armada was formed for another attempt. Fresh smoke allowed Jolly 7-7 in for the pickup and was immediately submerged in it. On the river, they could see absolutely nothing. But the enemy could see them. The helicopter took fire from a camouflaged truck, and an estimated 500 to 1,000 troops were seen. The truck's gun was quickly silenced by one of the Sandys. Sandy leader Major Tom Dayton had flown four helicopter escort missions during the past two days, only to see all rescue attempts fail.

The Sandys formed two rotating "daisy chain" formations on either side of Bergeron's position, named 10 West and 12 East, circling like a pair of gears to grind the enemy with smoke, gas, and cannon fire. The valley was sanitized and saturated with smoke. Jolly 7-7 was aerial refueled and ready for another try. Dayton gave the go-ahead at 11:40 a.m. Coming from the east, Jolly 7-7's crew couldn't spot Bergeron. Dayton, flying overhead, talked them in. They flew over Bergeron and lowered the jungle penetrator with spring-loaded flip-out seats. He bolted from his hole, waving the Final Escape chart and map's white side. The penetrator landed about four feet away from him,

Meanwhile, Jolly 7-7's tail gunner fired his mini-gun at 20 to 30 enemy soldiers; the left-side gunner sprayed troops across the river. The crew dragged Bergeron aboard, and the Jolly Green powered upward.

"We've got him," pilot Lt. Col Shipman announced, "and we're coming out!"

Every radio over Ban Phanop promptly jammed with cheers. Dayton ordered everybody home. Over Nakhon Phanom, the Jolly Greens streamed red smoke from their tail ramps in victory. Every ground crewman, aircrewman, and command staff crowded around Shipman's aircraft, and Bergeron emerged to roaring applause. Bergeron was awarded the Silver Star for his professional excellence, survival skill, and decision-making during an extremely high-risk operation at the Nam Ngo Valley. After returning home and pilot training, he flew A-10 Thunderbolt IIs, retiring in 1987 as a lieutenant colonel.

Over three days, a total of 336 sorties were flown by aircraft that expended 1,463 smart bombs, high-explosive bombs, cluster bombs, smoke bombs, napalm bombs, and rocket pods. Skyraiders alone flew 242 sorties; the HH-3 and HH-53 Jolly Green helicopters, over 40. Five Skyraiders were damaged, but the Jolly Greens got the worst of it. Five of the ten involved never flew again.

Post Script

That night, Grant and Bill Hoilman attended the most euphoric celebration they ever expected to experience in the Jolly Green hooch. They had both flown two days in the largest search and rescue mission of the Vietnam War, Boxer 2-2.

During Major Holly Bell's Jolly7-6 egress from the Boxer 2-2 river valley rescue operation, tail gunner Davison was struck in the head by ground fire. He received, posthumously, the Silver Star. Two months later, on a rescue operation, Bell's Jolly was shot down by a North Vietnamese Mig-21. Six lost.

On December 14, 2010, "Jolly Green 2-2," one of the HH-3Es that Grant flew on several Vietnam missions, was dedicated to the National Museum of the United States Air Force at Wright-Patterson AFB. The aircraft had been completely restored into combat configuration. Many of the Jolly Green crew members who participated in the "Boxer 2-2" SAR were in attendance and celebrated as true war heroes.

In 2003 a Laotian fisherman discovered human remains, a partial survival vest, a survival knife, and Danielson's dog tags along the banks of the Nam Ngo. On June 15, 2007, Lt. Cmdr. Brian Danielson of U.S. Navy Electronic Attack Squadron 129—18 months old when his father was shot down—laid his father to rest in his hometown, Kenyon, Minnesota. At the Vietnam Veterans Memorial in Washington, D.C., Danielson and Jolly Green7-6 tail gunner Dave Davison are remembered next to each other on panel 15W, lines 26 and 27.

Bibliographic Sources

There are several research elements that were vital to the completion of this work to include human sources of a wide variety. I am thankful for them all. Published public forum articles have been edited for length and clarity. For original versions refer to publications source as provided and online.

Ancient Aliens Series, A&E Television Network, History channel

donhollway.com/boxer22, August, 2018

22 surprising Facts About The Early Humans, Anna Burke, tworeddots.com June 7, 2016

Executive Orders, 1996, Tom Clancy

Rainbow Six, 1998, Tom Clancy

Arthur C. Clarke's 1968 film 2001: A Space Odyssey

Timeline, 1999, Michael Crichton

March 31, 2021, CNN report from this week that initially claimed a person's "gender identity "Tim Sticking for Mailonline, Daily Mail.co.uk

Protein helps Genghis Khan conquer the world, by Michael Eades, MD

Clint Eastwood, Magnum Force - A Man's Got to Know His Limitations (1973)

Alex Epstein, The Moral Case For Fossil Fuels, 2014

Time Bandits is a 1981 British fantasy film co-written, produced, and directed by Terry Gilliam, starring Sean Connery and John Cleese

A Brief History of Time, Stephen Hawking, A Bantam Book,
  Copyright 1988, 1996
Henderson, Bruce (1998). Trace Evidence: The Hunt for an
  Elusive Serial Killer.
New York, NY: Scribner.
C William Hoilman, War Stories-NKP-Boxer22-Marine.doc
David M. Jacobs, is an American historian and recently retired
  Associate Professor of History at Temple University
  specializing in 20th-century American history. Jacobs is
  particularly well known in the field of ufology for his
  research and authoring of books on the subject of alleged
  Alien abductions.
Rudyard Kipling, Macdonough's Song, Poemhunter.com
LivingCosmos.com dinosaur extinction no asteroid 10/ 23/15
LivingCosmos.com/evolution.htm, 1999
The Falcon Code
The Gemini Contenders, 1976, Robert Ludlum , P276
The Janson Directive, Robert Ludlum, 2002
Human Intelligence: What single neurons can tell us Elaine N.
  Miller, Chet C. Sherwood The George Washington
  University, Feb 5, 2019
Mono U2, 2010
Indian Reservation, by Paul Revere and the Raiders. Source:
  LyricFind Songwriters: John Loudermilk / John D
  Loudermilk
Henry Roberts in 1946 and 1949 wrote: The Complete
  Prophecies of Nostradamus
www.thoughtco.com
War of 1812, Bob Teisher, Dr. Pat brown
Genghis Khan and the Making of the Modern World Paperback
  – March 22, 2005, by Jack Weatherford

* * * *

News media: Articles edited for length and clarity.
June 21, 1969, CycleAct Crack Him Up, The San Diego-Union,
  Saturday, Handsome, limping and hurting Robert Craig
  Knievel is a Man of steel. By Johnny McDonald

2004, THE SARS EPIDEMIC AND ITS AFTERMATH IN CHINA: A POLITICAL PERSPECTIVE, Yanzhong Huang, Affiliations: John C. Whitehead School of Diplomacy and International Relations, Seton Hall University. Adapted from The Politics of China's SARS Crisis. *Harvard Asia Quarterly*

AGU.org How much radiation does it take to kill you? 1 September 2009, Posted by Dan Satterfield

June 8, 2016, San Diego Union-Tribune-New Fossil Strength For 'Hobbit' Species By Carl Zimmer

June 9, 2016, San Diego Union-Tribune, Liang Bua cave Flores Island Indonesia   2003. University of Wollongong Australia

November 18, 2018, San Diego Union-Tribune Sunday, Farm animals may soon get new features through gene editing. AP

November 18, 2018, San Diego Union-Tribune Sunday, Next – Gen biotech foods heading for stores. AP

November 26, 2018, San Diego Union-Tribune Monday, China researcher claims first Gene – edited babies. By Marilynn Marchione AP

November 27, 2018,   San Diego Union-Tribune -Tuesday, Gene – edited baby claim met with criticism, Hong Kong. AP

November 29 2018, San Diego Union-Tribune–there is significant data/research that addresses Genetic-Editing today. How Long Until Parents Demand It. By Chris Reed

November 29, 2018 San Diego Union-Tribune – commentary: Chinese Scientist Gene eEdited Babies Have Opened Pandora's Box, Brace Yourselves, By Chris Reed

December 3, 2018 San Diego Union-Tribune –Embryonic Gene Editing Has Arrive; Now What? By Bradley J Fikes

December 16, 2018, San Diego Union-Tribune-Opinion. Frenetic Engineering – Flawed Launch For a Promising Tool, Germline editing will initially benefit only those privileged enough to access it…By Ali Toakmani

February 5, 2019, Human Intelligence: What single neurons can tell us, Elaine N. Miller Chet C. Sherwood, The George Washington University, elifescience.org

February 12, 2019. San Diego Union-Tribune –UC Granted Gene-Editing Patent. By Bradley Fikes

April 11, 2019, San Diego Union-Tribune-A new human species discovered, AP reporting, article.

May 6, 2019, San Diego Union-Tribune Monday, Take UFOs Seriously. There is a well-known dilemma known as the Fermi Paradox

June 21, 2019, San Diego Union-Tribune-1969 Evel Knievel Jumpd at the Carlsbad raceway. , By Merrie Monteagudo

September 13, 2019, Union of Concerned Scientists. By Union of Concerned Scientist

December 8, 2020, Former head of Israeli Space Security Program says extraterrestrial aliens have made contact with mankind but will remain hidden until humanity is ready. Tim Sticking for MailOnline

December 29, 2020, Biden's Assault on Fossil Fuels Jeopardizes America's Military Strength, realclearenergy.org By James Marks Realclearenergy.org

January 4, 2021, Iran ramps up uranium enrichment and seized tanker as tensions rise with US. By Rob Picheta, Ramin Mostaghim and Mostafa Salem, CNN

January 25, 2021, Biden wants to replace government fleet with electric vehicles. As of 2019, there were 645,000 vehicles in the federal government's fleet, theverge.com By Andrew J. Hawkins@Andrewjayhawk

March 17, 2021 Automotivenews.com BMW raises target for EV sales, plans new electric-focused platform

March 31, 2021, CNN report from this week that initially claimed a person's "gender identity"

April 16, 2021, Iran starts enriching uranium to 60%, its highest level ever, Nation-World, By Jon Gambrell AP

April 16, 2021, PLAYING GOD: Human-Animal Hybrid Embryos, Created in California Lab, The ethical concerns here are rather obvious, By Andrew West, Flag and Cross.com

April 23, 2021, Honda will phase out gas-powered cars by 2040 theverge.com. By Andrew J. Hawkins@Andrewjayhawk

May 6, 2021, Rhodium Group, Based on our newly updated estimates for 2019, global emissions reached

May 9, 2021, China's Emissions Exceeded Those Of All Other Developed Nations Combined: Report, By Ryan Saavedra • DailyWire.com

May 9, 2021, (ANI) updated report. 18:23:59 hours, Chinese scientists discussed weaponizing SARS coronaviruses 5 years before pandemic: Report https://www.aninews.in/news/world/asia/

May 9, 2021, Faucian Bargain, The most powerful and dangerous bureaucrat in American history. p50-51, Post Hill Press, 2021 by Steve Deace and Todd Erzen

May 11, 2021, San Diego Union-Tribune -The challenge of charging EV's struggling to find a business model that works. By David R. Baker

May 24, 2021, Official: Iran Nuke Inspector Deal Ended, Associated press

May 30, 2021, San Diego Union-Tribune-Skeptics: UFO Videos May Have Mundane Origins, Andrew Dyer

June 4, 2021, San Diego Union-Tribune-U.S. Finds No Evidence of Alien Technology in Flying Objects, but Can't Rule It Out, Either, Julian E. Barnes, Helene Cooper

June 4, 2021, Wuhan Biolab Leak Theory Revives Concern about CCP China's Biowarfare Program,China Threat, americandefensenews.com, Paul Crespo

June 8, 2021, San Diego Union-Tribune Tuesday, Automakers face a threat to EV sales: Slow charging times, By Tom Krisher

June 15, 2021 More evidence suggests COVID-19 was in US by Christmas 2019, AP News.com, By Mike Stobbe

June 17, 2021, Study: Seven people infected before first U.S. case identified, AP News.com By Mike Stobbe AP Commentary

June 17, 2021, Replace fossil fuels for the military? Not so fast. Defensenews.com By: Matthew Kambrod

June 25, 2021, washingtonexaminer.com- Researchers say 'dragon Man' skull found in China could be new human species, By Kaelan Deese, Breaking News Reporter

Imprimis June/July 2021 Vol 50, Number 6/7 Gender Ideology Run Amok, Abigail Shrier, Author, Irreversible Damage: The Transgender Craze Seducing Our Daughters. Adapted from a speech delivered on April 27, 2021, in Franklin,Tennessee, at a Hillsdale College National Leadership Seminar.

July 9, 2021, San Diego Union-Tribune, Stellantis: Most models to be EV by 2025 Combined Fiat Chrysler and Peugeot company catching up with rivals, By Tom Krisher

July 15, 2021, EU unveils plan to do shift from fossil fuels, Paris, New York Times

July 15, 2021 Jon Voight, Fox News 8.62 subscribers,Tucker hosts explosive interview with actor Jon Voight on faith, 984,878 views (partial transcript)

July 16, 2021, Just 7% of our DNA is unique to modern humans, study shows, Washington associated press, Christina Larsen.

July 23, 2021, San Diego Union-Tribune, GM issues 2nd Bolt recall; faulty batteries can cause fires.General Motors is recalling some older Chevrolet Bolts for a second time to fix persistent battery problems that can set the electric cars ablaze.

August 20, 2021 State department cable shows team Biden new Afghan collapse was Imminent, Americandefensenews.com Pentago Watch US Military Paul Crespo

August 26, 2021 U.S. officials provided Taliban with names of Americans, Afghan allies to evacuate, realcleardefense.com. By Lara Seligman, Alexander Ward and Andrew Desiderio

August 30, 2021 American University of Afghanistan students were told 'we have given your names to the Taliban 'and there is 'no evacuation' coming Robert Jonathan, Bizpacreview.com

September 5, 2021 Military programs aiming to end pandemics forever 60 Minutes Bill Whitaker www.DARPA.mil

September 11, 2021 UN chief: World is at `pivotal moment ' and must avert crises, By Edith M. Lederer, Associated Press/apnews.com

September 23, 2021 Taliban official: Strict punishment, executions will return By Kathy Gannon apneas.com

September 26, 2021, San Diego Union-Tribune-A blast into a clean energy future?

Scientists tout nuclear fusion breakthrough Experiment using 192 lasers throws off more than 10 quadrillion watts of power, by Rob Nikolewski

September 29, 2021 ROLLS-ROYCE: FULLY ELECTRIC BY 2030, So long, V12. By Hannah Elliott Bloomberg News

October 10, 2021, The Taliban say they won't work with the U.S. to contain the Islamic State, Abdullah Sahil/AP, npr.org

October 18, 2021, China Power Struggle – But Not The One You Think!, Self-Reliancecentral.com, By Kelly

October 22, 2021, Putin Warns Wokeness Is Destroying The West: It Happened In Russia, It's Evil, It Destroys Values By Ryan Saavedra Daily Wire.com

October 26, 2021, Bad News: How Woke Media Is Undermining Democracy, By Batya Ungar-Sargon, Encounter Books, 2021, A Review

November. 4, 2021, San Diego Union-Tribune-China Military Power Report Highlights Concern over 'Taiwan Contingency' By Abraham Mahshie

November 4, 2021, Global Carbon Dioxide Emissions Near 2019 Levels, World has seen a dip during lockdowns from pandemic, phys.org, By Seth Borenstrein, AP

November 10, 2021, Amazon.com-The Abolition of Sex: How the "Transgender" Agenda Harms Women and Girls, By Kara Dansky

December 3, 2021, Russia planning massive military offensive against Ukraine involving175,000 troops, U.S. intelligence warns, An unclassified U.S. intelligence document on Russian military movement. (Obtained by The Washington Post) By Shane Harris and Paul Sonne

December 7, 2021, Biological Man Claims to be transgender Beats Entire Team of Females During College Women's Swim Meet, By Jerry Anderson - Own work, Matthew Williams - Politics - americanactionnews.com, AAN

December 21, 2021, Elon Musk Sits Down With The Babylon Bee CEO (partial transcript)

January 15, 2022, North Korea is testing hypersonic weapons. Should the West be worried? Scott Neuman, NPR, Twitter, Korean Central News Agency/AP

January 19, 2022, San Diego Union-Tribune, Nuclear Fusion Device Updated, General Atomics 'powerful magnet part of research on making commercial fusion power plants a reality, By Rob Nikolewski

Thursday, March 17, 2022, Swimmer Lia Thomas becomes NCAA's first transgender D-I champion in any sport, By Jason Owens

March 18, 2022, Twitter explodes over trans swimmer Lia Thomas winning national title: 'A slap in the face to women and girls' Thomas lived as a male until transitioning to female in 2019, By Brandon Gillespie - Fox News, Beyond Words

March 18, 2022, DailyWire.com, Emma Weyant Praised As 'Real Winner 'After Trans Swimmer Lia Thomas Takes First "Second is the new first." By Amanda Prestigiacomo

March 19, 2022, DailyWire.com, Marked By Simmering Resentment Over Biologically Male Trans Swimmer, NCAA Women's Swimming Championships Conclude, By Mary Margaret Olohhan

March 21, 2022, Nation & World News-Babylon Bee names Dr. Rachel Levine 'Man of the Year, 'gets Twitter suspension, By Claudia Dimuro - cdmureo@pennlive.com

July 13, 2022, Starbucks's woeness come back to haunt them as coffee chain closes 16 stores, Christopher Tremoglie, Commentary Fellow

July 23, 2022, "Finding unity in the pain': country superstar's anti- woke anthem hits number one on iTunes, Ashley Hill, www.bizpacreview.com

July 24, 2022, Woke Culture LISTEN: Country star John Rich tops iTunes with anti-liberal song 'Progress' By Heather Hamilton, Social Media Reporter

* * * *

Smithsonian Natural Museum of History: Genetic Evidence Smithsonian, February 2013. by Guy Gugliotta The archaeology course book: an introduction to themes, sites, methods and skills, Early Man.

* * * *

Wikipedia.org:
Alien Prototypes, 1992, David M. Jacobs recently retired Associate Professor of History, Temple University.
Cherokees
Defense Logistics Agency
Human evolutionary genetics Origins
Human evolutionary genetics Divergence times
Extinction events
Evidence of human habitation pre-Clovis
The 9/11 Commission Report
The Fibonacci Sequence
2013 S. Matthew Liao Human Engineering
Omo I, Omo River, Ethiopia 1967 team led by Richard Leakey, Age: About 195,000 years old, Species: Homo sapiens
Cyborg
Cyborg. – Manfred E. Clynes and Nathan S. Kline
Da Vinci, Nostradamas, Einstein
Chaos Theory Butterfly Effect
Jurassic Park is a 1990 science fiction novel written by Michael Crichton
DUF1220 protein
German/Mexican heritage
Drug trafficking organizations, DTO's
Human evolutionary genetics Origin of apes
Genetic bottleneck
Mitochondrial Eve
How much of Volvo does China own? 20%. Nowadays,

Made in the USA
Monee, IL
24 January 2023

8d130138-d090-4414-96c9-4b46a332cb53R01